CAPTURED!

They tied Alytha to a fallen log and left her alone while they cooked and ate the game. They did not offer to feed her nor did they come near her.

Why had they captured her? They wanted Tal dead—but if him, why not her too? And then the realization came to her. They were going to kill her too, there was no doubt of that.

But first. . . . The thought of death she did not fear so much, but the other—Alytha shrank within herself at the thought of the ordeal she was about to face.

We will send you a free catalog on request. Any titles not in your local book store can be purchased by mail. Send the price of the book plus 50¢ shipping charge to Tower Books, P.O. Box 511, Murray Hill Station, New York, N.Y. 10156.

Titles currently in print are available for industrial and sales promotion at reduced rates. Address inquiries to Tower Publications, Inc., Two Park Avenue, New York, New York 10016, Attention: Premium Sales Department.

THE ETERNITY STONE

Aden Foster Romine

and

Mary Cox Romine

TOWER BOOKS   NEW YORK CITY

A TOWER BOOK

Published by

Tower Publications, Inc.
Two Park Avenue
New York, N.Y. 10016

Copyright © 1981 by Tower Publications, Inc.

All rights reserved
Printed in the United States

ONE

The night was young.

The silver arch across the blue-black heavens marked the span of the inner rings, tilted forty degrees off the planet's equatorial axis. The reflected sunlight off the moving band that had once been a single satellite cast weirdly flickering shadows among the tangle of ironwood trees near the ravine where the figure waited.

The boy—or man—was not over eighteen, nineteen winters at the most. He was obviously waiting for someone—and desiring that his waiting should be unobserved.

His homespun breeks were tucked into his rough-tanned leather boots and his sleeveless leather tunic was almost sueded from long wear. His black hair, held back by a beaded headband, fell nearly to his shoulders and was rudely bobbed just above his wide blue eyes. Only his sword and dagger and the six-foot lance he carried revealed the hours of care and work and practice he had put in to become the youngest lance warrior in Thongor. He was Tal Mikar—and of him was much expected.

At his birth, a peregrine falcon flew from the wild to perch on the ridgepole of Sar Lon's hunting tent and, when the lance lord of Thongor had made to cast at the bird—totem of the Thongors since their founder left Breakwater—the falcon had flown from the net and circled twice over the newborn babe ere it disappeared into the distant Wild.

Tal had grown straight and tall and strong. At ten, he could best the lads of thirteen or fourteen winters and by fifteen, he could cast a lance with the men, albeit a lighter lance, of less than war heft.

True, much was expected of Tal Mikar—but what glory lay in his future lay *there* and not in his present. In his present he was only the youngest and newest of Sar Lon's lance warriors, as yet unproved in battle and with no deeds—save deeds of omen—to be sung by bards over flagons of red wine and in the depths of a winter evening.

Like other fledgling lance warriors, Tal should have been listening to Sol Makor sing the deeds of mighty warriors, or else been lying in his sleeping furs praying to Shandor to hasten the day he would win limitless glory, wealth, and women by the strength of his sword arm and the sureness of his lance.

Instead, like a thief or a tribeless Outcast, he crouched among the rocks of the ravine and watched the moving shadows of the ironwood trees.

And then, moving wraithlike among the other moving shadows, Alytha came.

Her soft brown hair fell in clouds across her back and shoulders and the coarse drabness of her homespun robe could not for a moment conceal the softly supple lines of her newly matured body. She had seen seventeen, perhaps eighteen winters and her father, Man Tavis, boasted that among all the Thongor women there was none more beautiful than his brown haired, gray-eyed daughter, whose fair skin and slim lissomeness spoke of her mother's lowland blood.

Alytha paused once in the ringlight and Tal gave the cry of a distant wind owl. For just a moment Alytha listened, then she came quickly to the ravine and into Tal's waiting arms.

They kissed and embraced with a passion that only first love can kindle in the very young. Then, as they drew apart, Tal saw the depths of unhappiness layering Alytha's gray eyes.

"What is it, my love?" he asked, fear clutching at his heart as his mind guessed the reason for her pain.

"My father—" Alytha could hardly speak. "My father—" And then: "Oh, Tal! Tal! I love you so much!" She clung to him and wept.

"Oh, my love, my love, what has he done? What has he done to you?" And Tal cradled her soft, warm, trembling body close against the lean hardness of his own flesh.

"It's what he has done to us," whispered Alytha, through her tears. "He has betrothed me to Jad Thor."

The words lay like a shield between them. Tal stepped clear of her and looked, with disbelief and shock, into the depths of her eyes. Alytha did not turn away from this scrutiny.

"But Man Tavis knew I loved you," said Tal, still not believing. "He knew I would ask for you within the next summer season—or winter, at the latest. Why would he do this?"

But Tal did not have to ask. He well knew the answer. Jad Thor was one of the mightiest of Sar Lon's lance warriors. A giant in height and built much like a cave bear, Jad Thor could snap a war lance (or a neck) between his hands as if it were a dry twig. In battle, Jad Thor was second only to Sar Lon and in the hunt, second to no one. He had three wives and half a dozen sons and daughters by each, but Alytha would be a choice prize for any man. Her betrothal could make Man Tavis wealthy—and Jad Thor could easily afford the price.

"How much did he pay?" Tal's voice was bitter and his mouth twisted angrily.

"I do not know," said Alytha, "but it was much. Very much. My father said that no one in the tribe had ever had a more valuable daughter. He was greatly pleased."

"I cannot permit you to marry Jad Thor!" said Tal fiercely. He seized Alytha and crushed her to him. "You are to be mine and, by Shandor, I will have you!"

"But—what can you do, Tal? My father has betrothed me to Jad Thor this very evening."

"Your father betrothed you to *me* last planting season! I will go to him and remind him of that. A warrior's promise is binding."

Tal took Alytha's hand in his and led her out of the ravine. They passed through the grove of ironwood trees, which momentarily blocked out the ringlight, then they emerged in the cleared fields where the women of Thongor planted and harvested the potatoes, squash, okra, zagrots, picciors, tomatoes, peas, guavarinos, and other edibles to supplement the fresh meat the warriors brought in from the hunt.

The sentry at the gate recognized them and waved them through. He made no comment at their appearance, but Alytha was known as the most beautiful maid in Thongor and Tal Mikar was as handsome as he was strong. What he may have thought, only the sentry knew, but he smiled as they walked past.

Outside the lodge of Man Tavis, Tal bade Alytha wait while he entered and spoke with her father. He gave her his war lance to hold. The girl nodded miserably, but it was plain she held little hope for the meeting's success.

Tal tapped on the tightly stretched drumskin by the lodge flap and waited. After a moment, a voice from within called out: "The lodge of Man Tavis welcomes all who come in peace!"

Tal lifted the flap and stepped within.

Like all the lodges, this one was divided into three chambers by curtains hanging from the ridgepole. The few simple furnishings in this chamber—the working, eating, and visiting quarters—were covered with thick rugs made from the skins of animals Man Tavis had slain in the hunt. The Thongors were not too far removed from their nomadic heritage.

Man Tavis sat to one side of the crackling hearthfire, a flagon of red wine held in a gnarled fist. His hard, flat eyes peered at Tal Mikar, but without hostility. This night Man Tavis was mightily pleased with himself.

"Welcome to my lodge and to my fire, Tal Mikar. Have wine." He made a sharp gesture and a slim girl, Alytha's half-sister, handed Tal a flagon of red wine.

"I thank you for the hospitality of your fire," replied Tal, giving the formula answer. He took a ritualistic sip of the wine, disguising his distaste for the acrid liquid, then he carefully placed the flagon to one side.

"I am here to speak of your daughter Alytha," he said, coming straight to the point. "Last planting season I spoke to you of my affections for your daughter and told you that I would ask for her as soon as I had offering to make fit for her betrothal. At that time you indicated that this would not find disfavor in your eyes."

"Nor would it," agreed the old man. "Much is said of Tal Mikar and his omens of promise. But omens do not feed an empty belly nor warm one when the dark winds of winter blow down from the mountains. Where are your offerings? Where are your bearskins? Where are your buffalo and pronghorn and reindeer carcasses to feed on? Where are the gifts to make glad my heart at parting from my daughter's presence?"

Tal burned hot at each question, but he could make no reply. Since becoming a lance warrior, Sar Lon had kept him as sentry rather than huntsman and there had been, as yet, no battle in which he could win plunder. He kept his face still, but his blue eyes smoldered.

"Jad Thor comes to me with many gifts: bearskins, buffalo robes, carved flagons to drink from, a knife like none other in the tribe, and more—much more. Am I to cast this wealth aside and wait for the promises of a *boy* who has killed nothing fiercer than a sparrow and is unbloodied in battle? Much is expected of you, Tal Mikar, but much is *done* by Jad Thor. He will provide well for Alytha, and for me when I am too old to hunt. I have sworn before Shandor. It is done!"

"But Alytha loves *me*!" said Tal, fiercely, striking his chest with a clenched fist. "And I love her. Does love count for nothing?"

"Love is like the scent of the flowers in the spring," responded Man Tavis. "It counts for much when all other needs are met. But like the scent of the flowers, love counts for naught toward filling the belly or warming the lodge hearth of a night nor preparing an old man's food. When all these things have been done, whatever is left can be used for love— or for smelling the scent of the flowers in the spring." He looked not unkindly at the tall youth before him. "You are young, Tal Mikar. To the young, both love and the scent of the flowers are important. At my age, a full stomach and a warm bed are more important. You will learn what life is about if you grow older."

"I know only that I love Alytha," said Tal, in a hoarse whisper. "I love her now and I will love her till the day I die!"

"Enough!" said Man Tavis, with a sharp gesture. "The question will be discussed no further. It is settled. Alytha will become Jad Thor's bride before the end of harvest season!"

"Then I will be dead before the end of harvest season!"

Both men sprang erect at the sound of Alytha's voice from the entranceway. The girl stood there, framed against the darkness outside, and a fire blazed in her gray eyes that made Tal's heart leap within his chest.

"I have pledged my word, Father," she said, her voice filling the silence like the dark winds of midnight fill the empty village streets. "I love Tal Mikar. I will die before I will submit to being Jad Thor's bride."

Before Tal could move, Man Tavis took two quick steps forward and struck his daughter a sudden, sharp blow across the face.

"Be silent!" he thundered, even as he held up a warning hand to stop Tal's advance. "You will do what I say, when I say. As for you"—he turned to face Tal squarely—"you are a guest in my lodge, hence I will not raise my hand against you. But I say this to you by the blood of Shandor and lay the saying of it to your heart: come not again to my lodge or to my fire. Speak not to my daughter nor to me. Take naught from here save that which you brought. And know that you are no longer welcome at the hearth of Man Tavis."

For a long moment Tal hesitated, then he literally hurled himself out of the entranceway. Seizing his war lance in one hand, he strode into the darkness, wrapping his fury about him like a cloak to ward off the chill of what was about to happen to his beloved.

Tal ignored the sentry at the gate as he passed once more beyond the village. By the oddly flickering ringlight, he made his way back to the grove of ironwood trees where he had waited for Alytha. Once there, he drew himself back into the deepest shadows and squatted, his back against an ironwood bole, a heavy embankment to his left, an impenetrable tangle of ironwood roots to his right, his war lance thrust out before him, and gave himself over to meditation on his plight.

It was about the second resting before dawnlight when the idea came to him. All night he had wrestled with the question. He had considered it from every possible angle—

had even invoked Shandor's aid—but he could see no other option open to him.

The idea was a poor alternative, a bleak and lonely choice, but none other gave any hope at all. Anything less than what he planned would mean that Alytha would become Jad Thor's bride. And Tal knew that he could not live each day in Thongor seeing Alytha with Jad Thor, seeing her bear his children, seeing her age and wither in his lodge. Better they both should die!

So it was that as dawnlight broke over the Wild and turned the rings to bands of gleaming gold and mauve arching across the clear blue morning sky, Tal Mikar reentered the village of Thongor and went to his quarters—the lodge of the unmarried lance warriors—and broke his fast with dried meat, black bread, goat's milk, and a fresh dew melon.

He squatted outside the lodge and honed his sword carefully on a whetstone, but his blue eyes kept a furtive watch on the village life as it bustled about him.

Soon he saw that for which he was waiting.

Alytha emerged from the lodge of Man Tavis and carried two water bottles on a shoulder yoke toward the village well.

Quickly, Tal sheathed his sword, dropped the whetstone in his belt pouch, and sauntered casually toward the well. If his judgment of Man Tavis were anything like accurate, the old warrior was soundly sleeping off too much wine drunk the night before and would not be up peering out of his lodge at this early hour.

Alytha did not acknowledge Tal's presence as she filled the water pots and he drank from a brimming gourd, but he saw that her eyes were red and puffy and her cheek was bruised where Man Tavis had struck her.

"Tonight," he said, without looking in her direction. "At the ironwood trees. Bring a change of garments and food if you can. We will be"—he hesitated before he said the word—"Outcasts."

There was a sharp intake of breath. Alytha knew what being Outcast entailed. Outcasts were the lowest of the low, people without a tribe—fair game for any warrior who chanced upon them. It was the loneliest, harshest, bleakest possible existence. There would be no shelter, no friendship, no protection. All men's hands were against the Outcast. Being Outcast was the hardest punishment, short of death, visited upon a lawbreaker by the tribe, and many warriors preferred death to being an Outcast.

Yet Alytha did not hesitate, even for so long as Tal had done when he said the word. "I will be there," she murmured, then, with the shoulder yoke in place, the water jars full, she walked back toward her father's lodge and no one, watching, would have known the terrible future to which she had just committed herself out of love.

Back in his lodge, Tal assembled a pack. He put in his other headband, a spare dagger, all the dried meat and black bread he could lay hands on. He included a small axe, flint and tinder for fire, some braided rope, and some rolled up sleeping furs.

He filled one bladder with goat's milk and one bladder with water from the well. He considered the possibility of taking a goat or a chicken with them, but he discarded it quickly. Outcasts would be pursued a distance, then forgotten. Thieves would be tracked down and punished.

Tal loaded the pack on his back, slung a filled bladder from each shoulder, and walked out of the village of Thongor without looking back.

It was not an easy thing to do. Thongor was his home. It was his family, his village, his nation. But in it, Alytha could never be his—and he loved Alytha more than life itself.

All day he waited in the grove of ironwood trees. He stretched out on the leaf-strewn ground and dozed, the sunlight dappling his recumbent figure in molten gold.

In the evening, when the rings were buttermilk bands across the darkling heavens, Alytha came.

"Tal?" she called softly, moving quietly among the trees. "Tal? Are you there?" And then she was in his arms and her lips were sweet and warm and soft against his.

"I love you, Alytha," he said. "I can give you no more than that. If you come with me, it is only for love."

"It is enough," she said simply, dropping her eyes.

And they passed, hand in hand, into the darkness and vastness of the Wild.

TWO

Half a galaxy away, the skies rained hell on Aryor.

A hundred spaceships whirled and dipped and darted through the upper atmosphere. On their battle-scarred armor plating was splashed the giant bloody handprint that marked them as Ilriks—the barbarian invaders of Aryor's civilized solar systems.

The Aryorian civilization had spanned three solar systems, all within a few parsecs of each other, and, despite the manner of their leaving Earth, they referred to themselves as Earth colonies.

The Ilriks had appeared at the outer system two centuries before. In a matter of three years, both habitable planets had been reduced to Ilrik satrapies—virtual slave states.

Fifty years ago—Ilrik spaceships could not exceed light speed—they had reached the second system, which had four habitable planets. In a single year all four had fallen before the fire and death which had poured down from the sky.

Now, less than a year before, the Ilriks had reached the Aryorian system. Only Aryor, of the twelve planets circling the middle class star that had been invisible from Earth, was capable of sustaining life. But Aryor was an incredibly fertile planet.

The Aryorians had fought desperately. Their neuron guns had slashed against the barbarians' shielding and many a bloody handed spaceship had landed its last screaming horde of battle maddened savages.

But in the end the Ilriks were winning.

More of them came. The Aryorians slaughtered them, but more came. And more.

Now, on this day of death and despair, all of Aryor lay captive and helpless before the Ilrik barbarians, excepting only Aryor City, the capital, and its defenses were crumbling fast before the wave after wave of attacking spaceships that bombarded it.

Dr. Fel Palmerin was acutely aware of this as he supervised the loading of the specially shielded shuttlecraft in the hangars atop the Central Palace.

Dr. Palmerin was the one hope Aryor had left and he was acutely aware of this fact, as he worked.

High above the atmosphere, anchored in a stationary orbit that held her directly above the Central Palace at all times, shielded—so far, at least—from discovery by the molecular-warping nature of her deflector screens, waited the means whereby Dr. Palmerin hoped to save as much of Aryor as he could.

It was the starship X-97. The starship that had brought the original Aryorians from Earth to their new home a millenia and more ago.

The starship had orbited there—a shrine, a sacred relic—for all those centuries. Preserved by the total vacuum of space, her internal parts carefully maintained out of a semireligious sense of ritual, she should, theoretically, be a functional starship.

Theoretically.

And that was the catch—as Dr. Palmerin had had pointed out to him repeatedly. Theoretically she should be functional, but everything aboard her was untested for several thousand years and could not now be tested without alerting the Ilriks to her presence.

"That's true," Dr. Palmerin would reply, when these arguments were offered. "But can anyone suggest a better solution?"

No one could and so the preparations had gone on at full pace. Overhead, coordinating the activities aboard the X-97, was Dr. Palmerin's associate and immediate subordinate at the Aryorian Cultural Museum, Dr. Tishir Sequa.

Dr. Sequa was in charge of packing and storing the

equipment and supplies that were ferried up by the specially shielded shuttlecraft. He and Dr. Palmerin had already done everything technically to the ship that could be done without actually firing her rockets. Now it was a matter of getting the supplies and personnel aboard her before the Ilriks overran Aryor City.

A distant explosion shook the Central Palace.

Dr. Palmerin realized that was a bad sign. If the special shielding had been breached badly enough for an Ilrik disrupter to blast the palace, then their defenses were weakening faster than he'd thought.

He took the last of the old star maps and ancient data spools from their case and carefully placed them in the shielded container. All that was left was the Chalice of Time. Once that was aboard, the balance of the personnel could be ferried up. Dr. Palmerin hoped that within the next twenty hours, planet time, they could warp the *X-97* out of orbit and head for Earth—the planet their ancestors had left so long ago.

Dr. Palmerin hastened down the hall. He was a tall, spare, gray-haired man, whose blue eyes had gone watery and white with advancing years. His black uniform with the scarlet triangle and golden sunburst made him look almost cadaverous.

Carefully, he fitted the electronic key to the magnetic lock and the always-sealed doors slid soundlessly open.

Inside, resting on its private nul-grav field, was the softly glowing force field that protected the Chalice of Time.

Instinctively, Dr. Palmerin halted when he entered this holy of holies, this sacred shrine to the most revered relic on Aryor.

The Chalice of Time was a circular metal dish, perhaps three millimeters thick, and absolutely without ornamentation. On the inside lip, all around the inner edge, were tiny recesses, where jewels might once have been, but which were now empty. The outer surface of the Chalice was a soft golden color, the inner surface a reflective, nontarnishing silver.

Dr. Palmerin released the force field and reverently touched the Chalice. He had lifted it before and was always surprised at its heaviness and by the slight tingle he felt when he touched it.

Another rumbling explosion shook the palace and dust sifted down. Hastily, Dr. Palmerin reactivated the force field and lifted the nul-grav unit which supported the Chalice and its protective devices.

At the end of the marble hallway was the carefully shielded jetboat hangar where the one shuttlecraft fitted to run the gauntlet of Ilrik spaceships was being loaded.

Feverish activity was going on here. A dozen or more men and women were hastily loading the automated conveyors that were moving the equipment aboard the jetboat. Onboard, four brawny men and one woman were seeing to its careful and proper stowage.

The one woman was black-haired, blue-eyed Lanawe Palmerin. On all Aryor, she alone knew how much uncertainty had gone into her father's desperate escape plan.

"No more this trip!" Lanawe called, signaling for a reversal of the conveyor belts. "This is all we can safely handle at lift off."

"We've got enough for one more load," one of the men said, indicating the food stuff, clothing, and weaponry still to be moved. "We may need all this."

Lanawe saw her father approaching with a bulky, black-wrapped object held in his arms and a shielded container dangling from his right wrist.

"Dad!" she called, waving to get his attention. "We're going to have one more trip with supplies. What do you think?"

Dr. Palmerin consulted his chronometer.

"If we have time." He handed the bulky object up to his daughter in the jetboat's companionway. "I want you to get the personnel ready and up here. I'm going up with this load and see that the Chalice is properly stored"—everyone involuntarily took a step back when they realized what the bulky object was—"and then I'll be back down on the next shuttle. It'll take at least three trips to get all two hundred and fifty people up to the *X-97*."

He had joined his daughter inside the jetboat as he had been talking. Together they had carried the Chalice of Time to the one enclosed cabin just aft of the bridge.

"I know," said Lanawe, her lovely brow creasing into a frown. "I'll load some supplies and some people each trip. In four more shuttles we should have everything aboard."

"All right," agreed her father, "but remember, in a pinch, the personnel are more important. I believe we have enough supplies now."

"Right!" Lanawe gave him a quick kiss and darted back toward the companionway. She still had a very great deal to do and very little time in which to do it.

She was not even there for the liftoff. At the moment that the functionally invisible shuttlecraft rocketed up into the sky filled with death-dealing Ilrik cruisers, Lanawe Palmerin was in a chamber deep in the heart of the Central Palace arguing earnestly with a blond, bronzed young man named Alun Akobar.

"I want you to go aboard the *X-97* this trip," Akobar was saying. "I want you safely out of this."

"My place is here," Lanawe replied. "Until Aryor City falls, my job is to handle the loading and upshipping of supplies and personnel. I'll go up on the last shuttlecraft run."

"And what if the Ilriks overrun the palace between flights—while the jetboat is at the *X-97* and you can't liftoff?"

"Then I die, or become a slave, like so many other Aryorians."

"I won't have that, Lanawe!" Akobar seized her by the shoulders. "I love you. I love you and I want you to be safe."

Lanawe frowned slightly and gently pulled away from Akobar's grip.

"I appreciate your feelings, Alun, I really do. But this is my job. Each of us must do our part if Aryor is to be saved."

"Aryor can't be saved!" Akobar's face twisted in anger. "Only those of us who get away in time on the *X-97 may* be saved. Aryor itself is already lost."

"But there *is* a chance!" Lanawe insisted. "*If* we can reach Earth and *if* we can find the Eternity Stone—"

"The Eternity Stone is a legend, a myth. It does not exist. The Chalice of Time is just a pretty cup, nothing more than that. It's all superstition, Lanawe. You're a scientist. You ought to know better."

Lanawe looked exasperated.

"If you feel that way," she demanded, tartly, "why are you coming with us? You know the whole plan is to reach Earth, locate the Eternity Stone, and place it in the Chalice of Time to release the power that's locked within it, and then use that power to defeat the Ilriks back here on Aryor. If you don't believe in any of this, why are you coming with us?"

"Because there's no hope on Aryor," the young man replied, running his fingers through his short, blond hair. "All your talk of secret powers and mysterious forces is superstition, all right, but the Ilriks are on Aryor and the X-97 is leaving Aryor—*that's* why I'm with you!"

Lanawe Palmerin looked at him and her blue eyes narrowed in anger.

"Your support is appreciated," she snapped, then she spun on her heel and stalked away.

High overhead, the shielded jetboat lifted upward through the last layers of the planet's atmosphere and made contact with the sensors aboard the orbiting starship.

An Ilrik battlecruiser slashed past less than a thousand meters away but the relatively small shuttlecraft passed safely by its scanners without detection.

Within minutes, Dr. Palmerin was emerging into the hangar deck. Dr. Tishir Sequa was waiting for him.

"We're ready, Fel," said the small, almond-eyed descendant of a Terran Oriental. "Do you have the programming tapes?"

"Yes." Dr. Palmerin handed the shielded container to his assistant. "And I have the Chalice, too."

"Good! I'll take these on to the bridge."

After Dr. Sequa left, Dr. Palmerin carried the black-wrapped, bulky object over to the transporter shaft. He rode the nul-grav lift to the proper level and stepped off on the main slidewalk that carried him to the branching corridor that housed his quarters. There, he carefully sealed the protected Chalice in its specially prepared force-field-reinforced receptacle and locked the magnetic lock with an electronic key, of which only he and Tishir Sequa had replicates.

In five more minutes he was with Dr. Sequa on the *X-97*'s bridge.

"We need time for four more runs," he said, as the doors contracted behind him. "What's the surface situation?"

"Bad," replied the scan operator, a slim girl whose golden hair and fair skin looked radiant against her black uniform. All personnel wore the black uniform of the Aryor Science Institute, on the double-breasted tunics of which were the scarlet triangle, representing the three solar systems in Aryor's domain, and, in the center of the red triangle, the golden sunburst that symbolized the light of knowledge gained through science.

"How bad?" Dr. Palmerin crossed to the scanners.

"The Central Palace is all that's defended now," said the girl, her head bent to the hooded receiver. "The north wall is badly damaged. A breach is possible. Ilrik foot soldiers are advancing with hand disrupters."

"Time estimate?" The fear was plain on Dr. Palmerin's face.

The girl considered and ran a quick computer verification.

"Perhaps one hour—if we're lucky," she finally said. "Certainly no more. Probably less."

"It's not enough!" cried Dr. Palmerin. "It's not enough time!"

Back in the Central Palace, Lanawe Palmerin had gathered the first contingent of personnel into the jetboat hangar. As they waited, they divided the remaining supplies into four equal divisions. Alun Akobar ran a series of figures down his mini-computer and determined that they could not transport everything even in four trips, plus bringing up the two hundred and fifty specialists who were selected for this mad— and possibly doomed—adventure.

Steady blasts were shaking the Central Palace now. The Ilrik disrupters were doing tremendous damage. The banks of neuron guns still flamed their deadly destruction, but the barbarians had pinpointed most of their locations and were maneuvering around them.

Suddenly, on the secondary readout panel, a whole row of tattletales flashed red.

"North wall is breached," someone said, unnecessarily.

"The Ilriks are inside the palace now."

"How long does that give us?" someone else asked.

"Only a few minutes," the first speaker replied, a note of hysteria in his voice. "The guards can never hold them in hand to hand fighting."

"Wait a minute!" Lanawe's voice was a whiplash cracking in the highly charged atmosphere. "We still have a chance!" She leaped atop a bale of clothing ready for shipment. "The shuttlecraft will return in less than five minutes. Those of us here now can make it *if we don't panic!*"

She looked around quickly. "We've got to barricade all entrances to the hangar, place armed guards at the two north doors, and be ready to load and lift off as soon as the jetboat docks."

"What about the others, the ones still below?" asked Akobar.

"We're all there's going to be," Lanawe replied. "The others . . . won't make it." And she did not add the thought that was uppermost in her mind: *they* might not make it, either.

On the bridge of the X-97, the golden-haired scan operator looked up from her hooded receiver and said, "North wall is breached. The Ilriks are inside the palace." Her face was grim.

Dr. Palmerin froze, the refresher cup forgotten in his hand.

"The jetboat?" His question was a bare whisper.

"It's down there now. It docked at the Central Palace"—the girl checked her chronometer—"two minutes ago."

"Then we've lost the shuttlecraft!" Dr. Palmerin flung the foamex cup away angrily. "Lanawe and all of our crew and the jetboat. . . ." He sank onto one of the padded contour couches. "There are what?—ten, twelve of us aboard? Even if we could fly the X-97 with that small a crew, without the shuttlecraft we couldn't get planetside once we got there. It's over. It's all over; and it's all been for nothing!"

"Wait!" The scan operator's voice was a knife thrust into the heavy silence. "The shuttlecraft's lifting off. She's getting away! She's coming back!"

There was a crackle of static from the main beam

communicator and suddenly Lanawe Palmerin's voice filled the bridge: "Shuttlecraft safe. Forty-three crewmembers and two hundred kilos of supplies aboard. ETA in four minutes. Palmerin out."

"Activate the auxiliary rockets!" snapped Lanawe's father, his former briskness returning in a rush. "Begin countdown procedure. We'll warp out of orbit in six minutes and twelve seconds."

And even as the hangar door dilated to accept the last shuttlecraft up from Aryor, the gigantic nacelles of the starship *X-97* were trailing streamers of activated ions for a thousand kilometers behind her as her tremendous nucleonic engines warmed up.

At their first triggering, instruments on half a hundred Ilrik space cruisers had registered her presence. Like sharks on the scent of blood, the barbarian spacecraft had zeroed in on the *X-97's* position.

But they were too late.

Slowly, ponderously, heavy as time, the starship swung away from Aryor and broke free of the orbit she had held for more than a millenium of Terran time. Like some great, living creature of the deep, the *X-97* moved away from Aryor and out into the void. At last, after so many long and lonely centuries, after so many generations were dead and dust, at last, she was going home.

THREE

Alytha was beautiful.

Tal Mikar, holding her naked body against his own, felt certain that Shandor had never created another half so beautiful as she.

They lay, wrapped in sleeping furs, in a cave high above a wooded canyon far from Thongor in the vastness of the Mountains of Mordon. Here they had come, after days of wandering the Wild, frightened as only tribeless Outcasts can be, and here, in this remote mountain valley, hidden from all their world, they had found their place and had made their camp.

Tal bent his head and kissed Alytha on the lips. She smiled and murmured in her sleep and moved against him and his desire rose hot and hard yet again.

And so he took her once more, with the soft dawnlight just lightening the haze beneath the conifers and not yet piercing the shadows over the silver ribbon of waterfall at the head of the valley. In the blue-purple vault of the heavens, the rings were twin bands of iridescent light, reflecting the morning sun.

Alytha awoke with Tal making love to her and her response was warm and wet. She moved to meet his driving thrusts with a hunger and a desire that matched his own.

The release came simultaneously for both of them and Alytha cried aloud in her pleasure. Tal crushed her so tightly against him that he feared her bones might snap.

Then it was over and they lay together, relaxed and happy,

and watched morning come, step by step, into their tiny kingdom.

The valley was a good place for their camp. It was far enough from the nearest tribal hunting ground that there was little danger of their being discovered. It had fresh running water, plenty of game—and game that had never been hunted—a plentiful supply of wild nuts, berries, and vegetables; soil suitable for Alytha to have a small garden and, best of all, the cave itself; located well above the valley floor on a practically inaccessible ledge. All in all, it was as if Shandor had devised this valley especially for them.

They had camped the first night among the conifers in the valley by the stream before Tal had seen the cave. Actually, he had only seen the ledge; the cave itself was invisible from the floor of the valley, and he had wondered if there *might* be a cave of some sort up there that would provide them shelter.

He knew that it was now late summer, but when winter came—and it would come early here in the high country—the snow would heap up in the valley, the river would freeze, and the waterfall itself would be transformed into a glittering sheet of ice shimmering down the cliffside. When winter came, they would need shelter from the storm wind, plentiful wood and it ready at hand to keep back the chill, and much meat dried and as many vegetables and nuts stored as could be kept.

This first winter would be the hardest, Tal knew. If they could survive it, by the next winter his hard work and Alytha's hard work could transform the valley and the cave into a permanent, defensible, settled homesite—*their* homesite.

"I am going to hunt today," said Tal, throwing back the sleeping fur and stepping out to meet the still chilly morning. "I may set out those traps I made." His lean, hard muscled body rippled with power as he pulled on his breeks and boots and leather tunic. He tied his beaded headband around his head to hold his long, black hair out of his eyes, and picked up the belt supporting his sword and dagger.

"I will fish while you hunt," Alytha said, smiling up at him from the still warm bed. "And I will smoke the fish I catch with the meat of the pronghorn you killed yesterday."

Tal looked back at her from the entrance to the cave. "I love you, Alytha." He said it once and then he was gone.

That day Tal hunted and the hunting was good. The next day he hunted and the next. Shandor smiled on him. There was meat, plentiful and fat. No day passed but that he returned to the cave with the carcass of a deer or a mountain goat or a wild pig slung across his shoulders. Once, near the mouth of the valley, he brought down a buffalo calf with a well thrown lance, then dispatched the angered mother with his sword. He regretted having to do it, because there was no way he could get the full grown buffalo cow back to the cave and he hated to see so much good meat go to waste.

Alytha, meanwhile, caught fish every day and smoked them over slow burning hardwood logs. She also harvested nuts and berries, wild tomatoes and wild potatoes and wild onions and the still native corn. She cleaned the cave inside, made their pallet with fresh pine boughs, which scented the air with a cool, sweet fragrance. She piled up heaps of firewood inside the cave itself and on the ledge just outside. She also carried up rocks to be used to block the cave entrance in case of attack.

Both Tal and Alytha were very happy. In the evenings, they bathed and swam in the pool below the waterfall—their naked bronzed bodies flashing through the water like golden otters—and afterward they lay, enfolded in each other's arms, beneath the arching rings, and their love was like a lullaby to soothe them to sleep each night.

Each of them thought often of Thongor, but each carefully avoided speaking of it to the other. Alytha missed her half sisters and the closeness and warmth of her family hearth, for Man Tavis had not been a cruel father. Tal missed the laughter and camaraderie of the other lance warriors and, he admitted in his heart before Shandor, he missed being pointed out as one of whom omens foretold. Each of them, before the other, carefully maintained the pretense that Thongor never crossed their thoughts at all.

But they were happy. They made love each day and with their lovemaking, the bonds between them grew. It sometimes seemed to Tal that he had more happiness than Shandor intended men to have. It seemed to him that such happiness must bear a price, must be paid for with an equal amount of sorrow.

And when he thought of this, he shivered as if the chill winds of winter midnight had touched his heart and he held Alytha to him with a fierceness the girl did not understand, but to which she responded with a gentle kindness that helped, for a time, to alleviate the fear that gnawed at the roots of his happiness.

It was two days after he killed the buffalo cow and calf that Tal found the tracks.

He was coming back from a successful hunt, with the fat carcass of a pronghorn slung across his wide shoulders, and was entering the valley from the narrow ribbon of trail along the rim opposite the cave wall. Suddenly, there in the dust before him, was the clear impression of a moccasin print.

Tal saw it and instinctively crouched, his lance coming up, the pronghorn carcass flung aside. His keen blue eyes washed the rocks and scattered clumps of conifers with a penetrating look that missed nothing.

The area was as completely deserted as ever. Yet that moccasin track had not been there when Tal had emerged from the valley that morning, Without moving, knowing that simple immobility was an excellent camouflage in itself, Tal carefully examined every inch of exposed terrain.

Whoever the unknown visitor was, he was a big man. Tal's boot would scarcely cover the inside of the moccasin print. The warrior had come upon the valley from one side—had obviously chanced upon it during a hunt—and had walked along the trail to investigate.

The tracks turned away from the valley after a bit. Apparently the warrior saw nothing of interest. That relieved Tal immensely. He offered a short prayer of thanks to Shandor that Alytha had not been at the stream fishing when the visitor came by. He realized he would have to warn her and they would both have to be much more wary than they had been.

Tal shouldered the carcass of the pronghorn again and moved slowly along the trail. He kept a watchful eye in the direction where the disappearing moccasin tracks had been heading. Going in that direction, who could it be?

Arcobanes.

The answer was simple. The Arcobanes were the Thongors' hereditary enemies. Sar Lon had led many raids against them and twice in Tal's lifetime they had attacked Thongor. Tal's own father had died with an Arcobane lance twisted in his guts.

An instinctive, tribal hatred caused Tal's upper lip to draw back in a snarl as he considered Arcobanes invading his and Alytha's private little world.

He was already so far down the trail that he was below the lip of the canyon and so could not see where the Arcobane had emerged and disappeared, but he looked back anyway—as if to be sure there was no one behind him.

The thrown club struck him at just the moment his head turned.

Tal twisted half around and the pronghorn carcass fell, going skittering and bouncing down the canyon wall in a rattling shower of loose dirt and small rocks. The second club caught Tal across the shoulder—a numbing blow—and he pitched headlong off the trail after the pronghorn carcass.

Dazed and battered as he was, with rocks cascading down around him and on him, Tal kept a grip on his lance, though the sword bounced free of its scabbard and clattered away on its own. The slope was not clifflike, yet it was sufficiently steep that Tal could only tumble end over end till he crashed into the thick underbrush at the base of the hill.

The brittle, autumn-dry brush tore mercilessly at him and here, at last, the lance eluded him and was left tangled in the first bush.

Stunned and semiconscious, Tal lay for a minute where he had fallen. He tried to think. *What had happened?* Something had happened. *He had to get up! He had to get away!* He shook his head and tried to rise, but his arms wouldn't lift him and he fell back.

Shouts of triumph and the sound of leaping, running footsteps barely penetrated to his conscious mind.

He was trying to get his feet under him when the four Acrobane warriors arrived at the base of the canyon wall where he had fallen.

Tal managed to sway erect, just as one of them, a burly,

bearded warrior half a head taller than Tal, grabbed him by the shoulders and flung him back hard against a jutting ledge of rock.

Still dazed from the club blows and the fall, Tal cried out and raised his hands ineffectually. The burly warrior stepped in close and drove his fist savagely into Tal's stomach.

Tal jackknifed forward and the warrior's next blow clipped him just above the left ear.

He went face down in the dirt and, barely conscious, was only faintly aware as his arms were wrenched cruelly behind him and lashed together with rawhide thongs. His knife was snatched from his belt and he was jerked roughly to his feet to stand, swaying weakly, glowering at his captors.

"Not bad, Dor," said one of the Arcobanes, walking around Tal to inspect him from all sides. "A bit thin, but he's young. He'll make a good slave."

"I'm not sure," said Dor, the bearded one. "He's got a mean streak to him—look at that fire in those eyes." He gathered Tal's whole face up in one massive hand and twisted it around so his companions could see Tal's eyes—a blazing, angry blue. "Ven Tamor may decide to geld him, if he keeps him at all."

Tal remained silent throughout this entire ordeal. The one thing he *must not* do was look toward the cave. If they had not yet discovered Alytha, they might be fooled into thinking he was alone.

"Let's go," said Dor, giving Tal a shove to indicate the direction. "That pronghorn will feast us all this night." He laughed and gave Tal a poke with his lance butt. "And that's twice you've fed us. Early yesterday we breakfasted on the buffalo cow you killed. You're almighty generous with your food!" And they all laughed.

The warriors led Tal up out of the canyon by the narrow trail across from the cave. None glanced toward the ledge where the cave was. Tal wanted desperately to look, but he did not dare. His stomach knotted with the fear that when they reached the Arcobanes' campsite he would find Alytha there, already a prisoner. Tal felt that he could survive anything they might do to him, but he could not endure the thought of Alytha in their hands.

Their camp was in a hollow of the rocks, sheltered on three sides by sheer granite cliffs. It was strictly a temporary camp, obviously a place where they had only bedded the night before. It was not a permanent hunting or scouting base.

And no one was there!

Tal felt so relieved upon not finding Alytha a prisoner that he said a quick prayer of thanks to Shandor. He knew that he was now a slave with, at best, a bleak and bitter future to face—but Alytha was free! Alytha was safe! Tal was content with that.

They moved out at dawn and Tal carried all their bedding and spare gear. His hands were never freed, except to eat and, twice a day, to relieve himself. And there were at least two swords kept on him at all times during these breaks.

The second night of Tal's captivity they camped in the mountains still, but on the third night they bedded down among aspens gone red-gold with autumn colors and in sight of a meadow where wild cows grazed with a scattering of buffalo.

On the fourth night they reached the settlement of the Arcobanes.

Ven Tamor, lance lord of Arcobane, was a huge, barrel-chested man with a matted gray beard and a shining, bald dome of a forehead. His keen, sharp eyes looked Tal over carefully when the prisoner was thrust before him.

"Thongor," he grunted, recognizing the tribal markings on Tal's headband. "He is young." Ven Tamor walked around the prisoner and examined him from all sides. "And strong." He pinched Tal's bicep between a gnarled thumb and forefinger. "He will make a fine slave. Shandor smiled on you, Vaj Durmo."

But even as Tal felt the iron slave collar snap shut around his neck, he could not repress another inner burst of thanks to the *true* Shandor—for Alytha was still free!

FOUR

Like slashing knife blades, the Ilrik battle cruisers darted toward the *X-97* but the starship was moving and, like the almost elemental force that she was, there was nothing that could stand against her.

A razor-thin line of brilliant cobalt blue lanced ruler straight out from a barbarian spaceship as her disrupters were triggered. A section of metal on the disc-shaped main hull of the *X-97* crisped up like charred paper and ripped a jagged tear in the smooth titan alloy surface.

Three more beams crisscrossed as fire was returned. The two Ilrik beams missed completely; the destructive lances crawled away in an absolutely precise line of intense blue that at last disappeared into the vastness of space, but the gunner on the *X-97* was more expert and his beam struck the Ilrik cleanly in the side. There was a tremendous, soundless explosion as the battle cruiser's propulsion units detonated.

"We need more power!" cried Dr. Palmerin. "We've got to enter subspace before the Ilriks can surround us!"

"The engines are building power," came the reply from the helmsman. "I'm pushing them as hard as I dare right now."

"Push them harder," Palmerin snapped. "I'd rather blow up than let the Ilriks take us."

Even as he spoke, the *X-97* shuddered convulsively from a second disrupter hit. Red and yellow tattletales blinked on all across the instrument panels.

Cursing, the weapons master sighted carefully through his

azimuth and pressed a series of buttons. He sighted again and cursed again.

"Missed, damn it!"

He took another reading and pressed the buttons again.

In the airless, lightless void beyond the hull a second Ilrik battle cruiser died as the beam from the starship lanced through its vitals. Space was littered with debris.

"Number two engine approaching overload!" called the helmsman, his eyes on a wavering needle gauge before him.

"Maintain pressure!" snapped Palmerin, his eyes on the same gauge. "It's now or never." Lanawe entered the bridge behind her father and stood close to him, as if to offer strength and support.

The X-97 was accelerating steadily, her nucleonic engines warping the very fabric of space itself till she could achieve that strange limbonic state of existing nonexistence called subspace.

"Number two engine at overload! Capacity critical!" said the helmsman, at exactly the same moment the pilot cried: "Subspace ETA twelve seconds!"

"Maintain pressure!" Dr. Palmerin was aware that Lanawe had put her hand on his shoulder. He was also aware that Alun Akobar had entered the bridge and stood to one side, watching.

The starship staggered again as she sustained a third disrupter beam—then, without warning, there was a strange tingling sensation that everyone experienced simultaneously. For a moment, everything else was forgotten as the crew members realized they were entering subspace!

The tingling was followed by a sudden sensation of vertigo, momentary nausea, a strange dizziness, and then it was over—except for an inexplicable ringing in everyone's ears.

"Subspace achieved at thirty-one oh one point six," said the pilot.

"Number two engine fusing!" cried the helmsman, as the needle gauge wavered well past the critical red line. "Nucleonic drive going infra!"

"Shut down pressure to number two!" said Dr. Palmerin. He whirled to the scan operator. "What's the status on the

Ilriks?"

"They ... they're gone." The operator's voice was scarcely more than a whisper. "And the stars—the stars aren't there anymore either...."

"We made it, Dad!" Lanawe hugged her father. "We made it into subspace! We're safe!"

Dr. Palmerin looked at Dr. Sequa, sudden concern in his pale eyes.

"Can we maintain subspace with reduced pressure on number two engine?"

"For a time." The Oriental ancestry of Sequa manifested itself in his present inscrutability. "Long enough to effect repairs."

Palmerin pressed an intercom button.

"Attention, Engineering section. Need emergency repair crew on number two engine immediately! Repair takes precedence over all other engineering functions except critical life support maintenance. I repeat: repair takes *immediate* precedence!" He turned back to the status boards on the bridge. "Damage report," he said crisply; then, to his daughter: "You'll handle all damages outside of number two engine."

As the damage reports were relayed and Lanawe made appropriate notes on her clip pad, she was aware that Alun Akobar had moved over to stand beside her.

Lanawe knew that Alun loved her and she also knew that it was assumed they would one day marry. She had never really stopped to analyze her feelings for him. That he was handsome she would readily admit—his blond, bronzed good looks had caused many females to consider how best to snare him—yet Lanawe could somehow not quite see herself as his wife. She had never decided whether or not she really loved him, nor had she ever considered the question very seriously.

Now, as she took charge of the repair operations, Alun attached himself to her and, when she had all the data, he volunteered: "The rupture of the food storage bins on level three is the most critical."

Lanawe felt a moment's irritation, but her only overt response was to lift one slim, black eyebrow before she replied. "Thank you for your opinions, Alun. However, I feel the atmospheric leak on hull level one should be sealed first. It's the only place where the automatic sealant units failed. I'm taking a repair team there now." She hesitated. "If you wish, why don't you take a second team and work on those food storage bins?" She glanced down at her notes again. "I feel that the spectroscopic sensors and the hangar bay doors can be repaired at our convenience."

While his daughter efficiently handled the repair problems, Dr. Palmerin turned his attention to the next most pressing question.

"Do you have the coordinates plotted?" he asked Tishir Sequa, who was busily running figures through his minicomp.

"Almost," Sequa assured him. "But the data are old, very old. If I make a mistake transposing digits. . . ."

Palmerin peered over his old friend's shoulder as Dr. Sequa worked out the coordinates the main computer banks would utilize to return the X-97 to Earth. Sequa was working from the original data and he had to be very careful to get his reference points precise. A mistake of one decimal point could result in an error of several thousand parsecs at their estimated destination.

"There!" The Oriental leaned back, a look of satisfaction upon his face. "The coordinates are done. I've checked every transposition out to eight places and I'm satisfied. If the original tapes were accurate, *this* will get us to Earth!"

Dr. Palmerin felt that a great load had been lifted from his shoulders. Calculating the coordinates was a job outside his area of expertise and therefore something which he could not control. And things he could not control made Fel Palmerin very nervous.

"So," he said, rubbing his bony hands together. "Now all we need do is program these coordinates into the computer and it will do the rest."

"Not precisely," said Dr. Sequa. "First, I've got to work out our trajectory, using the known coordinates for Aryor and the calculated coordinates for Earth. *Then* we can program the computer."

Even as the mathematician wrestled with his problems,

Lanawe Palmerin was facing a problem of her own—a problem named Alun Akobar.

"Alun." Lanawe's voice was chill. "I am going into the damage area. I have my assignment and I *will* carry it out."

"But it's dangerous," said Akobar, his hand still on her arm. "Let some of the others check it. You don't have to go yourself."

"I do have to go myself. It's my job, Alun, my *job!* We each have a job to do. I gave you an assignment repairing the ruptured food storage bins. Why aren't you there instead of here trying to prevent me from getting these repairs done?"

Akobar ignored her question and countered with one of his own: "Why do you always find things for me to do somewhere away from you? How come you never want me working with you on anything?"

"Because of the way you're acting right now," Lanawe answered. "You try to take over my life, Alun. You tell me to do this or not to do that, to go to this place or not to talk to a certain person. You act like you own me, Alun, and you don't. You act like we were married, or something." She ended lamely.

"But I want to marry you, Lan. Don't you know that? Don't you know that I love you, that I adore you?"

"But you don't *own* me, Alun!" Lanawe took a deep breath. "I'm very fond of you, but—" She hesitated. Akobar seized on it.

"'But—' what? You're 'fond' of me? *Fond* of me? Is there somebody else, Lan? Tell me if there is and I'll. . . ."

"Alun!" Lanawe's voice was a whiplash. "This conversation is pointless. I expect you to obey your orders as I obey mine. Your job is to repair the ruptured food bins. If you don't report there immediately, I'll call Security!" Her blue eyes were like rolled steel spikes as she waited for his answer.

Akobar stood without speaking for a moment, his brown eyes hurt and resentful. Lanawe took advantage of his silence.

"Go on, Alun," she said, in a softer voice. "It's important that we get these repairs made. We don't have much time."

Akobar was silent a moment longer, then he took a deep breath and sighed heavily.

"All right, Lan," he said, not looking at her. "I get the

message." He turned away to leave, but could not resist flinging back over his shoulder: "But when I find out who he is—I'll kill him!"

Hot anger flooded Lanawe, but Akobar was already walking away. Damn! She stamped her foot. The man infuriated her at times! She quirked her mouth as she turned toward the damage area. Sometimes, she thought, it would have been better if Alun had been left behind on Aryor.

She instantly regretted thinking this—but she was honest enough to admit that it was not the first time.

As she rejoined the repair team in the damage area, Lanawe tried to put Alun Akobar out of her mind, but she knew it was a problem that could not ultimately be escaped. In the end, she would have to face it, and deal with it, as best she could.

On the bridge, the Engineering section gave the first good news: "Number two engine repaired and fully operational."

"Thank you," said Dr. Palmerin into the intercom. "Coordinate other repairs through my daughter, who should be on hull level one." He turned to Dr. Sequa as he pressed the OFF button. "First big hurdle past."

"Second one, too," replied Sequa, looking up from the command console. "I've calculated our trajectory and just finished programming the computers. It's all out of our hands now. We've either got it made or. . . ." He shrugged.

Dr. Palmerin's knees felt weak.

"Then there's not much left," he said. Suddenly, a tremendous sense of exultation swept over him. It was as if all his lifetime had been rolled back and he was a young man again.

"Let's go to my cabin, Tishir," he said. "I feel like a drink."

Dr. Sequa smiled at his old friend. "That sounds very good," he said.

In his quarters, Dr. Palmerin took two crystal stemmed glasses of palest, translucent amber from the compartment behind his bed and carefully filled them three-quarters full of the dark red brandy in the cut glass decanter.

"To our success," he said, lifting his glass in a toast.

"Success," echoed Dr. Sequa. Then his eyes turned toward

the magnetically sealed compartment on the opposite wall. "To—our *ultimate* success." And he lifted his glass to the Chalice of Time.

"Yes," agreed Dr. Palmerin. He put out a hand and touched the cabinet. "I wonder—" he said, musingly. "I wonder what it will be like—on Earth."

"Different," said Dr. Sequa. He, too, walked over to the sealed compartment. "I only hope we can locate the Eternity Stone once we reach Earth."

"There shouldn't be any trouble there. You know how advanced Earth was a thousand years ago when the X-97 fled; just think how much farther along they must be today."

"True enough. But still—" Sequa hesitated. "Do you suppose they will help us search for the Eternity Stone?"

"I doubt there'll be much searching necessary," Palmerin commented. "After all, if more Earthmen had landed on Aryor within the last thousand years looking for the Chalice of Time, how far would they have had to search?"

"You've got a point." Sequa nodded sagely. He emptied his glass and Dr. Palmerin refilled it and his own.

The gray-haired scientist sipped his brandy and continued to stare at the sealed portal beside Dr. Sequa.

"I wonder how big it is," he suddenly said. "The Eternity Stone, I mean."

"Probably not more than a kilo and a half," Sequa replied. "Judging from the dimensions of the Chalice of Time."

Palmerin shook his head in wonderment. "And the two, when brought together, are supposed to release a force so powerful that nothing in the universe can stop it." He paused. "I wonder if that story's true. For Aryor's sake, I hope it is."

"Even if it's not, though I think it is, you realize that we're safe. We can always take refuge on Earth. It *is* our home planet."

Dr. Palmerin looked down at his drink morosely. "I don't like to think of it that way," he said, "but I suppose you're right. We are safe, unless"—he looked up at Sequa suddenly—"unless there's a government system on Earth that's worse than the Ilriks."

"What could be worse than the Ilriks?" Sequa countered,

but before Dr. Palmerin could reply the intercom "beeped" and a crisp voice said:

"All repairs complete, Doctor. Your daughter reports all damage control stations fully operational."

"Thank you," said Dr. Palmerin. Then he punched the button that broadcast his voice throughout the entire ship.

"Your attention, please. This is Doctor Fel Palmerin. The *X-97* has attained subspace. The flight data to return us to Earth have been programmed into the computers. I have just been advised that all necessary repairs are now completed. Nothing further can be done till we reach our destination: the planet Earth—the planet our ancestors fled in fear of their lives over a millenium ago.

"As all of you know, the *X-97* is fully computerized and self-operational from here to the already programmed orbit around Earth. All crew members are superfluous for the balance of our flight. As you know, it would be impossible to store adequate consumable life support supplies—food, water, and especially oxygen—for the duration of our projected voyage. As you also know, each couch is constructed with the electrochemical connections necessary to maintain a form of suspended animation called Cold Sleep. We shall all, at this time, retire to our couches and enter Cold Sleep, which will maintain us healthy and well whatever the duration of our trip. The computer will automatically awaken us from Cold Sleep when Earth orbit is achieved.

"I want to say to each of you that the efforts and sacrifices you have made are not unappreciated. We—you and I together—are the only hope for the millions of our people left in slavery on Aryor. I will not, and I know you will not, fail them."

Dr. Palmerin snapped off the intership communicator and turned to his old friend.

"Goodnight, Tishir," he said. "When the computer wakes us from Cold Sleep. . . ."

". . . Then our work really begins." Sequa nodded as he finished Palmerin's sentence, then, with a quick touch to his old friend's arm, he was gone.

Dr. Palmerin adjusted the controls on his couch and set the various indicators in the proper positions, as the ancient instruction tapes had directed.

Then, before he lay down on the couch, Dr. Palmerin went back to the brandy decanter and refilled his crystal stemmed glass. He very carefully placed the glass beside his couch and snapped an airtight protective cover over the top, so that when the computer called him back awake he could celebrate the success of the voyage.

He lay down full length on the couch and placed the receptors against each temple and over his heart, slipped his hands into the gloved slots, and gently depressed the ACTIVATE button.

His last thought, as the clear plastic cover sealed over his couch, was that he should have said good night to Lanawe.

FIVE

In his dream, Tal watched the high wheeling flight of a peregrine falcom as it soared in the arching blue heavens across which the rings were milk white bands of blinding brilliance. He envied the bird its freedom of flight and said a short prayer to Shandor, as he had often done before, for the gift of flying through the air as freely as the falcon flew.

A sadistic kick in his ribs brought him awake.

Instinctively, Tal rolled himself into a ball and away from the direction of the kick.

"Get up, you lazy dog!" snapped Vaj Durmo, who delighted in abusing any of the slaves who fell into his power. "We need firewood for breakfast cooking and fresh water for bathing."

Tal looked stolidly at Vaj Durmo, while the big Arcobane warrior unlocked the chain which passed through the ring in the side of his iron slave collar. Very quickly, Tal had learned one of the cardinal lessons a new slave must know: a slave does not glower, glare, or look sullen. Impassive or stolid are the only safe facial expressions.

Twice Tal had been beaten so savagely he felt sure he would die—simply for scowling blackly at his captors. He had not died, however, and he had learned quickly. He no longer glared or looked sullen when kicked, shoved, slapped, or spoken to sharply. To everything, good and bad alike, he remained stolid, impassive, and stoical. He became like an animal in his lack of emotional display.

He also learned to move with alacrity when spoken to, to

step aside quickly if meeting an Arcobane, and to expect a kick or a blow as the best reward for whatever he might do.

"Get some wood in my lodge for the breakfast fire!" Vaj Durmo shoved him bodily out of the quarters he shared with a dozen other male slaves.

Tal jogged to the village woodpile, his body shivering in the morning coldness, trying to warm himself as he ran. He gathered up the largest, driest pieces he could find, digging deep into the pile so that the damp ones on the outer edges would be gotten by another slave. He also remembered to get enough smaller pieces to serve as kindling in order to start the blaze properly.

After the morning meal and baths were completed, while the female slaves cleaned up, Tal and another male slave were sent to shovel out and clean the communal latrine.

Tal got assigned to such tasks on a regular basis when Vaj Durmo had a hand in it. Vaj Durmo had been one of the warriors who captured Tal that day in the hidden valley and, for some reason known only to himself, he had developed a fierce hatred for the tall, blue-eyed Thongor slave. More than once, in Tal's presence, he had urged Ven Tamor to geld Tal—but the burly Arcobane lance-lord merely ignored him.

As Tal worked in the latrine, his ragged clothes streaked with human excrement, he heard that which, no matter what he was doing at the time, never failed to bring a hard, cold knot to the pit of his stomach and to cause his breath to catch in his throat. It was the shout: "Hunting party coming in!"

Tal's hardest task, as a slave, was to remain stolid and impassive whenever that shout rang through the Arcobane settlement. When he heard it, his whole being teetered on a knife edge of heart-stopping fear and he desperately prayed to Shandor: *Don't let Alytha be with them!*

His own slavery Tal could stand—though he was constantly alert for an opportunity to escape—but he felt he would go mad at the thought of Alytha in their hands, especially Vaj Durmo's hands.

At the risk of a beating, Tal halted his work and watched as the line of warriors emerged from the trees and entered the compound. Carefully, searchingly, he scanned the group; and then they were all out of the trees and into the village and he could relax. Alytha was not there. They had not discovered her.

But there was someone else with them.

Two warriors of a breed Tal had never seen before. Tall they were, taller even than Tal himself, and strangely dark skinned. Their skin gleamed as if it had been oiled and their hair, black as Tal's, straight as a war lance, long as their waists, was thick braided into a single plait and was so oily it shone.

They wore breeches and boots of heavy skin tanned with the fur out and their tunics, made the same way, hung to their knees and had heavy, encompassing hoods flung back. Odd looking devices were strapped to their backpacks: round hoops of bent bone laced together with tight stretched rawhide strips in a lattice-work pattern. Their war spears were tipped with white bone and Tal noted that they carried them loose and easy in their hands. They were not only not arriving as prisoners, they were obviously arriving as friends and honored guests.

"Farades," said the slave who was working with Tal.

"Who?" Tal was puzzled. "What kind of people are they?"

"The Farades live on the borders of the Ice Region that circles the middle of the world—or so the shaman of my tribe taught me when I was a whelp. The Farades must be coming to invite us to Rendezvous."

"What is 'Rendezvous'?" asked Tal, but before he could get his answer, a violent blow across his shoulders knocked him to his knees.

"You lazy Thongor trash!" snarled Vaj Durmo. "I'll teach you to stand around like a freeman when you've been ordered to work!" He hit Tal across the back and shoulders with the haft of his war lance. He hit him again and again. He hit him so brutally and so savagely that he might have beaten him to death had not Ven Tamor himself ordered him to stop.

As it was, it was a day before Tal regained consciousness and almost a week before he was able to be on his feet. During that time, as he lay chained by the iron slave collar to the center post of the slave quarters, he made a promise to himself: one day he would kill Vaj Durmo.

During this same time, Tal had at last learned the identity and the purpose of the strange visitors who had come in with the hunting party that day.

They were Farades, from the equatorial Ice Regions, and they were there to invite the Arcobanes to Rendezvous. Once a year, for a week, there was a truce between the Farades and the Arcobanes. They met at a convenient place, called Rendezvous, and traded for supplies and handmade items each had that the other wanted. It was the high point of the year for the Arcobanes.

Tal could see the change spreading over the entire Arcobane village, almost as visibly as ripples spreading over a pond when a pebble is tossed in. There was excitement and laughter and eager anticipation on all sides. The warriors shouted at each other and indulged in rough horseplay. The women giggled and gathered in small knots to talk animatedly. The children shrieked and scampered about even more helter-skelter than usual.

The slaves were put to packing carefully handpicked items; then, all these would be unpacked and other, even more carefully handpicked items would replace them, only to be unpacked in their turn and replaced by still other items, or sometimes the original ones.

Tal was amazed at the effect the impending Rendezvous had on the Arcobanes. The whole village took on a certain carnival atmosphere that imparted itself, though only slightly, to the slaves.

Tal found himself wishing that Thongor had had some sort of festival like Rendezvous. It would have been a welcome break in the monotony of village life. As it was, war—in the form of raiding other tribes or resisting raids by other tribes—was the only break in the tedium for the Thongors.

When Tal was back on his feet and hard at work helping with the preparations for Rendezvous, he discovered that even Vaj Durmo ceased tormenting him. The burly warrior was too busy picking out lances and war clubs he had made that the Farades might find interesting.

The preparations took roughly two weeks. After a couple of days, the Farades departed and Ven Tamor sent three

Arcobanes with them. By the beginning of the second week they were back with more Farades. (Tal was unable to determine if these Farades were the same warriors or if they were strangers. Their dark, chocolate-brown skin and odd facial features made them all look alike to Tal, who had never before even imagined a nonwhite race.) In a day or two, the Farades left and two Arcobanes accompanied them. The location for Rendezvous had been decided.

Then, at last, came the day for which everyone had waited so impatiently. Ven Tamor called the tribe together, assigned slaves to the various families and unmarried warriors, and ordered them ready to move out. The shaman said a short prayer to Shandor and they were on their way to Rendezvous.

Tal was assigned to Kolu, a female warrior. The Arcobanes differed from the Thongors in this respect, Tal had learned not long after his captivity. They allowed females full rights with males in the warrior class. Any female who could fight—and was willing to do so—could be counted a warrior and treated as such in battle, on the hunt, or at tribal council.

And Kolu was as fierce a warrior as any who wore the tricolored bird symbol that was the Arcobane totem.

Kolu was no more or no less gentle in her treatment of Tal than any male warrior would have been, with the obvious exception of Vaj Durmo. She gave her orders explicitly and curtly, and struck him if he did not carry them out quickly enough to suit her. By the same token, when he was loaded with as heavy a pack as he could stagger under, she shouldered the remainder of the load with no more hesitation than the burliest male warrior would have shown.

There was much singing on the three day trek to Rendezvous, but none of it was done by the slaves. Each of them, by the time the first camp was made, gratefully unloaded their weighted packs, prepared the campsite, then the evening meal, and, after the warriors had eaten, they fought among themselves for the scraps.

At dawn, they were the ones the guards kicked awake, while the rest of the camp slept. They prepared the morning meal and, after the warriors had eaten, they ate. Then they repacked everything that had been used at camp, reshouldered their packs, and filed silently along the forested trail with the laughing, singing tribesmen.

Among the Arcobanes themselves it was a different story. They carried backpacks, too—though nowhere near as heavy as those borne by the slaves—but still they sang songs, made jokes, laughed often, and shouted friendly insults to each other. At the campsite, there were high spirits, good cheer, and a general atmosphere of gaiety and fun. After the leisurely evening meal, the Arcobanes gathered in small groups to talk excitedly about Rendezvous, then, one by one, they rolled up in their fur robes and slept.

When they awakened, shortly after dawn, the slaves had the morning meal ready. When it was done, the Arcobanes talked and laughed among themselves as they readied their personal packs. Then, taking up their loads once more, they marched off through the woods singing happy songs, accompanied by the grimly silent slaves.

Rendezvous was a large, open area right at the edge of the forest. Heavy woods covered the hills that flanked the area on two sides, the forest itself made the third side, while the fourth was flat, rolling prairie that became tundra and, eventually, merged into the equatorial ice band that girdled the globe.

The rings looked milk white in the cold, pale blue sky when the Arcobanes emerged at Rendezvous to find the Farades already encamped. Like the Arcobanes and the Thongors, the Farades lived in huts made of hides stretched over a light framework. However, the Farades' huts differed in many respects.

The dwellings with which Tal was familiar were conical, with an opening in the roof to emit smoke, and were usually divided into two or three inner compartments by hanging curtains. Frequently, the outsides of the dwellings would be painted with pictograms portraying either the prowess of the warrior who dwelt within or some bird or animal totem which the warrior particularly admired and desired to emulate.

The Farades' dwellings, on the other hand, were bulbous and squat, almost onion shaped. Their color was very dull, when compared to the Arcobanes' or the Thongors' huts. The ice dwellers' huts were smoke colored, some almost pure white, some a dirty gray that shaded to charcoal.

The Farades themselves were a source of never-ending wonder to Tal. He discovered that they were not all the rich, chocolate-brown of the ones who had come to the Arcobane village. Some were, of course, but others were almost as fair as he himself, and there were all gradations and shades between the two extremes.

Two things all Farades shared in common, however, was the oily sheen of their skin and the long, lustrous, straight black hair. It was the second day of Rendezvous that Tal learned the secret of the oily sheen.

He had noticed, whenever his duties brought him close to one of the dark skinned strangers, that the Farade had a distinctive scent—a spicy, not unpleasant, but certainly unusual fragrance. On this day, not long after the morning meal, Kolu ordered Tal to go to the hut of Fen Melton, one of the Farades, and tell him that she desired to see again the pelts they had discussed the previous evening.

Tal wended his way to Fen Melton's hut and rapped lightly on the drumskin by the doorway.

Instead of inviting him to enter, as a Thongor or Arcobane would have done, the brown skinned Farade came out. He had a small pot in one hand, filled with a clear, oily liquid, very viscous in texture, and perfumed with the now familiar spicy scent. As Tal stammered out Kolu's invitation, the Farade dipped one long fingered hand into the pot and began smearing the scented, oily liquid onto his face, covering every visible centimeter of skin; then he carefully rubbed it on his neck as far down as the open collar of his leather tunic. By the time Tal had finished explaining his mission, Fen Melton had noted, with some amusement, his interest in the strange ritual.

"You are wondering what I'm doing," he said, in his curiously accented voice. "I can see it in your face."

"Yes, I am," admitted Tal, quite frankly. He was still uncertain, since a blow or a kick was a slave's natural portion in life, yet the open, friendly manner of the stranger reassured him.

"It is bear grease," the Farade explained, extending the pot for Tal to sniff and touch the oily substance. "We render it from the carcasses of the great ice bears that we slay, and then we crush certain herbs and spices into it for the scent we desire."

"But why do you—" Tal suddenly stopped. A slave did not question a freeman. A slave did not even address a freeman except in direct response to a direct question or if bearing a message from another freeman.

"Why do I put it on my face?" Fen Melton finished for him, with a smile. "Because where we live, and where we hunt and fish and whatever else we might do, the wind blows always and it is cold—colder than you have ever seen, colder than you can even imagine! The wind cuts at you like a knife, rips at you with fangs and claws that are fiercer and more deadly than those on any of the beasts that roam the Ice Region.

"Our furs protect us as much as anything can, but our faces are exposed to the constant, never ceasing wind. The oil serves to keep us from freezing. If not for it, the wind, blowing off the ice, would peel the very flesh from our bones!" Fen Melton smiled at the fierceness of his description and the smile made his face warm and friendly. It had been a long time since anyone had smiled at Tal. This gave him the courage to say:

"I can't imagine anything being that cold."

"It is though," Fen assured him. "Just imagine the coldest night you've ever experienced; so cold each breath was like little knives ripping your lungs; so cold your fingers ached when you held them to the fire for warmth; so cold you huddled inside your robes and held yourself in your arms and still could not stop trembling. Now imagine it *twice* that cold, perhaps *three times that cold!* Now imagine the wind blowing, always blowing, blowing every day and every night, blowing endlessly through the great fields of ice, blowing across miles of empty, snow-covered desolation. That will give you some faint idea of the Ice Region and what it's like to live there." He smiled again.

Tal was awed. "I've never . . . heard words used like that before," he said. "When you describe the cold and the wind it's like I can actually *feel* it! It's . . . beautiful."

"Your mistress, Kolu, seeks my furs in trade," said the Farade, with another friendly smile. "But you have located

45

my real treasure. I am a poet. A poet and something of a philosopher, I am told, and—yes, I'm an historian. One of the very last of a dying breed, I'm afraid."

Tal was puzzled. "What is a . . . poet?" he asked. "And a . . . 'phil-' . . . 'philos-opher'? And . . . the other thing you said?"

"Historian." Fen Melton supplied the word for him. "A poet—the first I named—is someone who uses words. He takes them and polishes them and tosses them up in the air, just to watch them sparkle and twinkle as they fall. He takes words and shapes pictures out of them the same way a spearmaker shapes wood and bone into a smooth, straight shaft and a polished, keen-edged blade. He takes words and makes them obey him like a father makes his children obey. He uses words as tools and as decorations and, sometimes, as weapons."

Tal obviously did not understand, but the Farade went on with his explanation just the same. He had grown accustomed to not being understood.

"A philosopher is very much like a poet in his use of words, but he is more like a hunter. His quarry is an idea, rather than an ice bear, and he hunts it with words rather than a spear and a sword, but he is a hunter none the less. And when he tracks down his idea and uses his words to capture it, he must then take other words and construct from them a cage to contain his captive idea so that it can be displayed for the benefit and edification of his fellows—most of whom would not recognize an idea if one leaped on them in the dark.

"And the other thing: 'historian.' That is someone, like a philosopher, who also uses words to hunt—but not to hunt ideas. An historian hunts the past. He hunts for traces and images of what we have been. He hunts for the roots of how we come to be what we are today. He hunts for our origins in the misty eons of antiquity. And, when he finds some trace— old ruins, maybe, or broken weapons of a type no living warrior can employ—then he uses his words, like the philosopher, to build a cage to hold this one small trace out of all time beyond reckoning and to keep the trace safe till he, or some other, can dissect it, using words instead of knives, and learn from it more of the secrets of who we were and who we are and, perhaps, who we may become."

Tal was utterly baffled, yet enthralled. Never in his life had he heard anyone speak as this dark-skinned Ice Warrior spoke, the words rolling smooth and polished from his tongue yet touching deep chords of response in Tal. The words stirred images in his mind that made him wonder and marvel. He felt strange urgings and undefined longings that were new to him—yet seemed *almost* familiar. It was a unique experience.

But slaves are not made for unique experiences.

Even as Tal listened to Fen Melton's description of an historian, Vaj Durmo had rounded the corner of the Farade's hunt.

Now Vaj Durmo was not looking for Tal Mikar. He was, in fact, on his way to barter a sword he had taken from a dead Thongor for two or, hopefully, three warm pelts to keep off the winter's cold. But when he saw the slave, talking as a freeman would to the tall, slender Farade, it made him angry.

The first warning Tal had was when Vaj Durmo's fist exploded against the side of his head.

He sprawled sideways to the ground, instinctively rolling into a ball to protect himself as best he could. There had been a time, not too long before, when such a sudden, unprovoked attack would have brought an instant counterattack. But a slave learns quickly, if he would survive, that his only defense is hope.

Tal expected a series of brutal kicks—that was Vaj Durmo's usual reaction when he had knocked Tal from his feet—but instead a strange thing happened. The hulking Arcobane warrior stood perfectly still, not moving a single muscle. Slowly, warily, Tal raised his eyes. Then he saw why Vaj Durmo had ceased his attack and was standing so very still.

Fen Melton's dagger was resting point uppermost immediately below the warrior's chin, the point barely pricking the flesh.

Vaj Durmo looked very strained. He was unaccustomed to being thwarted in his purpose.

"Sir," he said formally, in a thin voice. "This is Rendezvous. Weapons are not permitted."

"They are permitted in defense of one's person or property," Fen Melton corrected him in his pleasantly accented voice. "You assaulted my guest. By Farade custom, that was the same as an assault on my person."

"That is an Arcobane slave," Vaj Durmo protested. "He can't be considered human. Slaves do not converse with freemen."

"This slave was sent to me by his mistress to discuss certain transactions she wished to conclude. We were discussing a corollary of those transactions when you attacked him without provocation. So far as I am concerned, you attacked a guest. Would you care to apologize to me personally, or shall I kill you now?" Fen Melton's voice was pleasant when he asked this, but Vaj Durmo's face went ashen gray.

"I . . . apologize, Farade," he said, though each word cost him some effort. "I apologize for disturbing *you*." He emphasized the last word heavily. Then his eyes turned to Tal and what they said, though silent, was not pleasant.

"Thank you, Arcobane," said Fen Melton, stepping back quickly. He made a gesture and the dagger disappeared. "I consider the matter closed."

But Tal knew it was not closed. He knew that as soon as Vaj Durmo could get him alone, the burly warrior would most likely try to kill him. Tal had been mulling over several possible escape plans and he decided that now would be as good a time as any. If Vaj Durmo attacked him—no, *when* Vaj Durmo attacked him—Tal determined that he would do his best to kill the Arcobane first, even if it meant his death rather than escape.

Fen Melton might have been reading Tal's thoughts, for he suddenly said: "I fear that one will seek recompense from *you* for his humiliation."

"I'm not sure what that means," said Tal, "but Vaj Durmo will try to kill me as soon as he gets the chance."

Fen Melton smiled. "*That* is what that means," he said. Then he cocked an inquisitive eyebrow at the slave. "What is your name?" he asked, and, when Tal told him, he said: "Don't worry about the Arcobane, Tal Mikar. I know how to prevent his taking his anger out on you." He smiled again. "Now run to your mistress and tell her I will be along in a little while with the pelts she desired. And, Tal"—he called, as the slave started away—"don't worry!"

The sun had not risen a span closer to the rings before Ven Tamor appeared at Kolu's hut. With him was a tall, dignified Farade whose lustrous black hair was touched by strands of gray.

"This is Ald Haslet," said Ven Tamor, by way of introduction to the female warrior. "He is lance lord of Farade. He had made a barter with me for your slave, Tal Mikar. I have sold the Thongor to Ald Haslet. He will go with them back to the Ice Region."

SIX

The *X-97* moved through subspace like a ghost ship.

On her main control deck, where Dr. Sequa had labored over the encoded coordinates and Dr. Palmerin had watched the Ilrik's battle cruiser detonate soundlessly in the void, there was a heavy silence.

Colorful tattletales flickered on and off in apparently random patterns across the banks of instrument panels. Small video monitors sprang to life, prompted by some inner electronic urgings, displaying columns of numbers and mathematical symbols that flickered back and forth across the screen to at last dissolve into schematics of wiring diagrams and energy flow indicators.

The life support monitors continued to hum and chatter to themselves—ceaselessly testing the atmospheric content, pressure, movement, temperature, radiation level, pollen count, and several other, more esoteric functions. Minute adjustments were made automatically, from time to time, as the monitors determined that one or more life support subsystems were not holding within prescribed tolerance limits.

The starship's sensor banks continued to probe outward on each of a hundred different scanner frequencies. The most minute and apparently trivial data was detected, recorded, computed, analyzed, coded, and programmed into the appropriate memory banks. The sensors did not differentiate between a speck of space dust a half millimeter thick and a planet-sized asteroid, except for computer navigation purposes. Everything was recorded.

The computer banks controlled the astral navigation with a nicety few human pilots could have managed. The coded symbols secreted on magnetic tape held the giant starship on an irrevocable trajectory that would, ultimately, intersect Earth—if Earth still existed. If any course deviation were necessitated by, say, a cluster of asteroids, a small solar system, a wayward comet, the tireless sensors would advise the computer; the computer would analyze the data, evaluate and implement the necessary course corrections, then return the X-97 to the proper trajectory plane once the obstacle was circumnavigated.

On the power deck, the energy systems were as near self-sustaining as imaginable. Wall-sized panels of instruments clicked and hummed as they worked endlessly to monitor and direct the controlled cataclysmic power of the immense nucleonic engines. Here, as on the control deck, flickering tattletales decorated the control boards in kaleidoscopic printouts of energy displacement.

But the X-97 was still a ghost ship.

All her circuitry and her instrumentation and her energy patterns were alive and functioning, but there were no people.

The winding, carpeted hallways were empty. The muted lights reflected off only polished steeluminium and plastiloid. The companionways were silent and brooding. The nul-grav lifts were desolate and still. The slidewalks no longer moved, their energy source having been evaluated as expendable and so deactivated. The recreation areas and mess halls were echoingly empty and lonely.

In the staterooms, in the sealed bunkbeds, in the stillness of Cold Sleep, the forty-odd humans lay as if ensorcelled.

No one moved, save for the still, small breathings. No one stirred, not even as a sleeper in a dream might stir. Not one eyelid fluttered. Room after room was silent, each human locked in his or her own cocoon of dreamless nonbeing.

Only the computers were alive and totally functioning. The human passengers would sleep the endless, silent, embryoniclike Cold Sleep till the scanner coordinates matched the preprogrammed coordinates Dr. Sequa had evolved. Then, when the computer decided the *X-97* had reached Earth—or, at least, where Earth should be—the crew would be automatically awakened.

Until then, the only sounds aboard all the vast starship were the clickings of the relays and the subdued hum of the life support systems.

Tal was not coming back.

Alytha had admitted that fact to herself many days before, but her admittance was an *intellectual* admittance only. In her heart, she still waited and hoped. And every day, night and morning, she prayed to Shandor for his return.

It was out of that waiting and hoping that she had devised a plan that let her go on living.

At first she had wanted to die, to join Tal in whatever the afterworld had to offer. She had prayed to Shandor for the release of death. But, gradually, she moved away from that notion. She was too much the primitive savage to be suicidal for long. The first lesson that all children of the wild learn is that survival is the only important thing.

For love of Tal Mikar she had left her father's hearth and the people of her blood. For love of Tal Mikar she had become an Outcast, one for whom all men were enemies. Now Tal was gone and Alytha knew he would not be back. She *knew* it, but she did not *believe* it.

On this day, several weeks after Tal's disappearance, Alytha was completing the last swing around her trap line.

She had followed Tal's trail and set the traps in the places he had marked. At first she had had difficulty propping up the snare boxes and looping the catch lines, but she had seen Tal do it often enough and she perservered.

Before long she set the traps as quickly and as skillfully as any hunter would, and her haul was good, in both furs and meat.

Alytha could have done almost anything she chose, even perhaps, have gone back to the Thongors, once she had faced up to the fact that Tal was not coming back. She could have done almost anything, but she chose to stay in the hidden valley. She chose it because it was her home, her home and Tal's home, and she would stay for the rest of her life . . . waiting for Tal Mikar to come back.

Today, the trap line had netted her two beaver, an otter, a squirrel, three rabbits, and a curious woodchuck, who had nosed too close while trying to figure out what the snare was. Alytha had killed them all and had slung each of them into her backpack, which she had fashioned from the hides of a pair of bobcats speared a few days after Tal had disappeared. All in all, she considered it a good day's work with the sun still only two lengths past the milk white rings. Time enough to roast a rabbit and skin all the other game before dark. If she were lucky, she might get some of the meat hung up to jerk before daylight failed completely. Tomorrow, she would jerk it all, plus scrape the hides.

With that thought in mind, and the thought of the wild tomatoes and wild onions she would eat with her rabbit for dinner tonight, Alytha stepped around a bend in the trail and squarely into the arms of a waiting warrior.

She had no chance to run, no time even for an outcry, as she was seized and hauled roughly off the trail into the brush. A second warrior had her disarmed in a moment and then ripped the backpack from her shoulders.

Alytha struggled and twisted and kicked and tried to bite the heavy hand that was clamped over her mouth, but the warrior shook her so savagely her head snapped from side to side. He released his hold on her mouth long enough to cuff her twice, reddening her cheeks, then he grabbed her again.

"Be silent, wench!" he hissed. "We want you alive. It's Tal Mikar we want dead."

For the first time Alytha became aware of her captors as other than beings to struggle against. She twisted her head around till she could see the face of the man holding her. He was Nol Garvin, a Thongor warrior she had known all her life.

Conflicting emotions suddenly churned within her: relief that her captors were Thongors and not enemy tribesmen, fear because they wanted to kill Tal, homesickness to see her father and her family again, fear because she had chosen to become Outcast and as such was removed from the tribe's protection, and an almost unbearable loneliness because of her separation from the fellowship of the tribe.

"There is no one else on the trail," said the second warrior, a Thongor named Gar Tanoll. "The wench is alone."

Nol Garvin turned Alytha so that she faced him, but he did not even momentarily release his grip on her.

"Where is Tal Mikar?" he demanded, shaking her again.

"He . . . is gone," Alytha finally managed to gasp, between shakes. "He has been gone for days. One morning he went to hunt and did not come back. I don't know if an animal killed him or if enemy tribesmen captured him or. . . ." She let it trail away.

"You're lying!" said Nol Garvin. He slapped Alytha again, once, twice, hard, stinging blows. "You're trying to hide him, to protect him!"

"N—No! No, I'm not!" Alytha insisted. "He's gone! I've been . . . alone . . . for days."

"We'll get the truth," said Gar Tanoll. "Let's take her back to our camp."

Alytha's hands were tied behind her with thin strips of rawhide and a noose was looped around her neck by which Nol Garvin led her.

They followed several twisting game trails and twice waded up winding streams. At last they emerged from a narrow canyon into a sheltered campsite, snug among a wilderness of fallen timber and fresh new growths. A small lean-to had been set up and the remnants of cooking fires told Alytha the Thongors had been there for some time.

They tied Alytha to a fallen log that weighed more than the three of them together and left her alone while they cooked and ate most of her game. They did not offer to feed her nor did they come near her. For her part, she leaned against the rough wood and tried to make sense out of all this. Why had they captured her? Why had they been so insistent on trying to find Tal? They wanted him dead, they said; but if him, why not her, too? They were both Outcasts—no longer Thongors. Why would they want to kill Tal, but take her prisoner?

And then the realization came to her and she wondered why it had not been immediately apparent. They were going to kill her, too, there was no doubt of that, but—oh, dear Shandor!—first. . . .

Nol Garvin left the fire and came toward her. Alytha shrank within herself at the thought of the ordeal she was about to face. The thought of death she did not fear so much, but the other—she shuddered involuntarily.

"Where is Tal Mikar?" Nol Garvin demanded, squatting before her. "You can't hide him forever."

"I've told you all I know. He went away one day to hunt and did not come back. I . . . suppose that he's dead." Her gray eyes welled up with tears. "I haven't . . . I haven't seen him for . . . a long time." She wept silently and bitterly.

"I think she's telling the truth," said Gar Tanoll. "Tal Mikar may already be dead."

"It doesn't matter," said Nol Garvin. "We have the girl and that's all that matters. The reward is ours."

His words slowly penetrated Alytha's consciousness and she looked up at him, his image wavering and swimming from her tears.

"What—" Her voice broke and she had to begin again. "What do you mean—reward? What reward?"

"Your father, Man Tavis, has offered a reward of a bearskin robe and a new dagger to the lance warrior who could find you and return you to him. He also offered a war lance and a new longsword for the head of Tal Mikar."

"But we are Outcast. When one is Outcast, one is beyond the tribe. We are to be as strangers." Her puzzlement was in her face.

Nol Garvin shrugged. "Your father offered the reward and we have earned it. If you would fathom his reasons, you must ask him when we reach Thongor again."

It was four days hard marching before they did reach Thongor. During all that time, Alytha kept going over in her mind all the possible motives her father could have for wanting her back. But try as she would she could find none of them that seemed to make any sense to her.

Man Tavis was not slow in telling her, however. Nol Garvin and Gar Tanoll were not out of sight with their reward, wrangling between themselves over who got the robe and who the dagger, when Alytha's father turned to her, a withering look in his cold eyes.

"Slut!" he said, and his heavy hand caught her savagely

across the cheek.

With her hands still tied behind her, Alytha could not keep her feet. The blow knocked her sprawling.

"Whore!" And he kicked her brutally with his sandaled foot. "Bitch!" He yanked her to her feet, her homespun robe ripping half off her from the violence with which he jerked her up. "Slut!" he said again, and slapped her heavily back and forth, right and left, forehand and backhand.

Alytha fell back against the wall trying to escape him, but Man Tavis moved in after her. With her hands tied behind her, the girl had no way to defend herself. She tried to call on Shandor for aid, but the terrible beating kept her from saying the words.

When her father had at last vented his fury, Alytha lay moaning and sobbing in a crumpled heap in one corner. Her nose was bleeding heavily, her lip was split in two places, one eye was swollen nearly shut, and her face, her exposed breasts, her back and shoulders were bruised and reddened. Stark fear was on her face as she cowered before her father.

"Slut!" Man Tavis called her again. "I do not know why, but Jad Thor still wants you. You are much cheapened in price, but he will pay a portion of what he offered before. He will claim you before first frost."

"I will not mate with Jad Thor! I belong to Tal Mikar!"

"Silence, whore!" Man Tavis kicked her savagely. "You are Jad Thor's! You are his forever!"

Alytha lowered her head and spoke, too softly for Man Tavis to hear, it is true, but still, through clenched teeth and broken sobs, she whispered: "I will never be Jad Thor's mate. I will die first. I swear it by Shandor—I will die first!"

SEVEN

It took the Farades six days to journey from Rendezvous to the Ice Region. For Tal, it was like a wonderland.

Each day they trudged deeper into a world he had never seen or even imagined existed. His universe had heretofore been bounded by the wooded hills and mountain fastnesses of the high country. The Thongors were clannish and had very little contact other than with the Arcobanes. Occasionally, it is true, one or two warriors would venture near to the Great Desert in the northwest and a few times had had brief encounters with the Kalathors, the dread nomad warriors of the Desert, but no one went south toward the Ice Region. That was a land unknown and unknowable, strange and legend-haunted and shunned.

Now, with wide eyes, Tal moved ever deeper into this eerie new world.

The country was barren of trees. Low bushes and stiff bladed grasses grew among the rocks and upthrust fingers of stone that jutted out at odd angles. The openness of the gently rolling, almost flat prairie was unsettling to Tal, whose eyes were adjusted to mountains and heavy stands of timber.

His lot among the Farades, while still that of a slave, was infinitely better than it had been among the Arcobanes. He still staggered under a pack twice as heavy as any freeman bore, he was still the first to rise and the last to eat, he still wore the iron collar that marked him as a beast of burden, but he did not have Vaj Durmo to torment him. That alone made his life as a slave almost bearable.

Besides which, he saw Fen Melton from time to time and the poet-philosopher-historian never failed to speak and smile. Alone, of all the people Tal had encountered since the morning he had left Alytha in the cave, only Fen Melton treated him like a human being.

But Tal's fears for Alytha were now doubled. When he had been an Arcobane slave he had dreaded the return of each hunting party, living with the constant fear that Alytha would be brought in a captive. Now, separated from the Arcobanes, his fears were worse because he would never know if Alytha were captured or if she were still free.

He prayed daily to Shandor for her safety and plotted ways to escape and somehow make his way back to the mountains and find her again. Yet step by step, day by day, he drew farther away from her; and there was no relaxation of the Farades' guard. By day he was constantly under a dozen pair of eyes, by night he was securely chained.

So as the rolling prairie gave way to the bleak tundra, and as the ground gradually became white with the permafrost, Tal felt his hopes wither and die within his heart. He felt that Shandor had abandoned him.

At last, ahead of them, he could see the blue-white rim of distance that marked the beginnings of the ice mountains and he knew that he could never make his way back to the site of Rendezvous, let alone from there to the Arcobane village, not to mention the winding trail from the village to his and Alytha's hidden valley.

As they approached the Ice Region, Tal learned another secret of the Farades. Since his first glimpse of them in the Arcobane village, he had puzzled over the odd hoops of bent bone, laced with a lattice-work of rawhide thongs, that were strapped to their backpacks.

As the permafrost thickened into a layer of perpetual snow on the ground, Tal watched in amazement as the Farade warriors unslung these cumbersome hoops and strapped them to their feet.

"They're called snowshoes," Fen Melton explained, as he showed Tal how to buckle a pair into place. "They keep us from sinking down as the snow gets deeper, and it will get deeper. They also—" Tal tried his first steps, promptly got one snowshoe tangled with the other, and went face first into the snow amid hoots of laughter from the Farades. "They also"—Fen Melton continued dryly, as if lecturing—"cause us to fall down a lot." He scooped up the red-faced youth with one strong arm. "Try it again," he said, calmly.

Tal tried it again, and then again. He fell down regularly at first, but gradually he got the hang of the spraddle-legged, high-stepping stride the awkward devices demanded. For a while he had trouble keeping up, but within a few hours he was trudging along as familiarly as the rest of them.

Tal was one of only three slaves in the Farade party ("We Farades don't exactly disapprove of slavery," Fen Melton had told him, "but we don't exactly condone it either."), but he was not especially overworked. The Farades had a looser social structure than the Arcobanes and a Farade warrior was not above preparing his own meal and even cleaning his own cooking utensils. While none of them except Fen Melton showed any overt kindness to Tal, still none of them was overtly cruel, either.

Being used to the harsh mountain winters in Thongor, Tal was not so severely affected by the cold as the Farades seemed to expect him to be. Still he accepted the furlined, hooded parka gratefully enough when it was offered to him.

The wind, however, was different from anything he had ever experienced before. It blew constantly, as Fen Melton had said, and its bite was sharper and keener than the edge to any wind Tal had ever felt in the high country. It made him snuggle deep within his new furlined suit and be thankful for its protecting warmth.

The Farades' village was reached just at dark on the sixth day. It was visible at first as a cloud of dense smoke hanging over a low mound of snow banked higher than the reach of a tall warrior. This, as they drew nearer, resolved itself into a retainer wall, laboriously hand hewn from foot thick slabs of ice. The wall, a barricade really, stretched on three sides of the village, while a series of hot springs provided the smokelike steam (and a natural barrier) on the fourth side.

Inside the retainer wall the strangely bulb-shaped huts were arranged symmetrically around the arable ground that was kept free of permafrost and snow by the hot springs. The

Farade women, who were uniformly tall, slender, and lovely, tilled their fertile ground, each working her family's individual plot, and planted the vegetables and fruit needed to supplement their men's steady supply of meat and fish.

Tal was the object of much curiosity upon his arrival. The Farade children especially crowded around him. Most of them, never having been to Rendezvous, had heard of white-skinned people only by word of mouth. They could not seem to get their fill of staring at him.

For his part, Tal was filled with equal curiosity. The Farades themselves were still a source of wonder to him and he marveled at their hardihood in living here amid the eternal ice and snow, even with the warm springs to provide natural heat and open garden land. He wondered why the whole tribe did not simply pack up and move to a more hospitable climate. He found an opportunity to put this question to Fen Melton.

"There are many reasons," Fen Melton replied. "Perhaps as many reasons as there are Farades. However, there are two basic reasons that I would guess are common to us all: one, is that Farade is our home; we have lived here for more generations than our singers can recount, since long and long before the ice came, when Farade was said to be a fair and pleasant land, warmed by the sun and cooled by something called the sea. The second reason is that we are safe here. No enemy can cross the ice in any direction without being under our eyes for at least a day, and no siege can take our village, for the ice wall protects us on three sides and the water that burns protects us on the other, and no warrior would choose to camp on the bitter snows—with no shelter from the undying wind—while we sleep warm and comfortable behind our ice barrier. No, Tal, this is a very good place for us to be.

"Besides, Farade is really more of a base camp than a real village. Less than half our warriors are in camp at any given time. Most are either out trapping—we all run trap lines—or fishing the ice lakes for the fish that swim below the frozen surface or hunting the great ice bear or the occasional herd of snow deer that migrate past or are gone on a trading expedition to the Arcobanes or the Falgons or the Lorwellans. Our women and our children and a few guards are most of what is in Farade at any one time." He paused and smiled wryly. "Which is one reason why we do not especially condone slavery."

Slavery was indeed not popular in Farade, as Tal soon found. There were less than a dozen slaves in the entire village and they were not treated as such—at least, they were not treated in the manner Arcobanes treated slaves. Tal was astounded to learn that besides the two male slaves he had met on the trek back from Rendezvous, there was only one other besides himself. The other slaves were all female house servants, cooks mostly, and seemed almost to be considered as members of the families to whom they belonged.

For the first few days after his arrival in Farade, Tal's life was simple, if confusing. He was communal property, as he had been in Arcobane, and Ald Haslet assigned him to various tasks and to various families as their need dictated. For one Farade woman he plowed ground all day, for another he chopped wood, for another he smoked deer meat for two days. Once, for three days, he went on a bear hunt with half a dozen warriors, but despite seeing the great shaggy ice bear from a distance, they never got close enough for a spear cast, and at last returned empty-handed to the village with Tal's eyes swollen and red from the snow glare and his light skin burned nearly as dark as that of his captors by the sunlight reflected off the ice sheet.

The day after his return from the unsuccessful hunt, while Tal was scraping and pegging out some hides to tan, Ald Haslet sought him out at the dwelling of the warrior to whom he was assigned that day. With the chief of the Farades was Fen Melton and the stately poet-philosopher-historian looked quietly pleased with himself.

"Thongor," Ald Haslet rumbled. "Fen Melton has paid the price I set on you. You are now his personal slave."

Tal bowed his head briefly, as he had learned to do from the Arcobanes, and made to rise to his feet.

"No, Tal." Fen Melton held up one hand. "Finish the hides you're working for Latheena. Her warrior won't be back for more days than those skins can wait. Come to my *yurt* when you're done."

Tal nodded again, not really trusting himself to speak.

While he would never stop looking for a chance to escape, he realized that Fen Melton was the best master a slave could hope to have. Until he won his freedom and could make his way back to Alytha, he could thank Shandor that he belonged to Fen Melton.

The sun was halfway between the rings and the ice mountains when Tal finished scraping and pegging the hides. He told the dark-skinned, almond-eyed Farade woman, Latheena, that he was done and that he was to report to Fen Melton's *yurt*.

The *yurts* were the name the Farades had given to the strange bulb-shaped dwellings they inhabited. So far, Tal had never been inside any except the slave *yurt* where he was chained each night by a bolt through his iron collar. The seven-centimeter-wide metal collar galled his neck, but he tried to ignore the pain. What he could not ignore was the sensation, experienced more and more frequently of late, of waking in the darkness of midnight with the feeling that the collar was so tight he could not breathe.

Tal tried not to think such thoughts as he wended his way to the *yurt* belonging to Fen Melton. He thumped lightly on the drumskin, then stood waiting expectantly.

The tall Farade pulled back the doorflap and smiled a greeting at Tal. "Come in," he said, with a gesture of welcome. "There is stew and herb tea on the grate. I have already eaten."

"Thank you," Tal murmured. He could not bring himself to say "Master" unless threatened with a beating. He helped himself from the stew pot and ate hungrily.

"I'm not quite certain how one should treat a slave," said the Farade. "I've never had a real slave before, only indentured servants, and I'm not sure just what to do with you."

While he spoke, Fen Melton took a long, slim tube with a hollow bowl on one end out of a special oilskin pouch. He packed the hollow bowl with finely chopped leaves of a rich, aromatic pungency. Then, to Tal's utter astonishment, he took a coal from the fire, lifting it with small metal tongs, and ignited the chopped leaves in the hollow bowl, while sucking on the end of the long, slim tube.

Tal stopped eating entirely and simply stared as he saw his

first pipe lit.

"What . . . are you doing?" he asked, forgetting once again that slaves do not question freemen.

"Smoking," replied Fen Melton, with a rich, deep chuckle. He exhaled and a cloud of white smoke billowed out of his mouth. He inhaled from the pipe and blew a smoke ring. The *yurt* began to have a pleasant aroma that was totally unlike anything Tal had ever smelled before.

"That's backy," the Farade explained. "The Lorwellans grow it and we trade them fish for it. It's one of life's great luxuries."

Tal shook his head in wonderment. "I've . . . never seen anything like that. It's amazing."

"Not really. Would you like to try it?" He offered the pipe to Tal, who took it gingerly. "Now just put it in your mouth and suck in your breath."

Tal did as Fen Melton instructed. The acrid smoke filled his mouth and his nasal passages and his lungs. He began to cough and choke and gasp. Tears streamed down his face. Great racking coughs shook his whole body. He tried to give the pipe back to the heartily laughing Farade, but in his haste he dropped it and Fen Melton had to retrieve it himself. His eyes continued to sting and burn and water while he coughed until his face was red splotched.

Fen Melton had obviously enjoyed the spectacle immensely. He waited till Tal had recovered his composure somewhat, then he said:

"That always happens the first time someone tries backy. It happened to me, too. Backy is something for which you develop a taste."

Tal finally managed to stop coughing long enough to say: "But why would anyone want to develop a taste for something like that?"

"Smoking is an old custom," Fen Melton replied. Suddenly he was the historian, lecturing the pupil: "I have found records of smoking that are the oldest artifacts I have. Let me show you." He went to a cunningly wrought cabinet, one of the few pieces of real furniture Tal had ever seen, and removed a packet wrapped in oilskin.

Carefully, almost reverently, he unwrapped the coverings

to reveal a small, handcarved box. He opened the box and tilted it for Tal's inspection, but without letting him touch it.

Inside was something even more amazing to Tal than the sight of Fen Melton smoking. It was a painting of a fair-haired woman in a strange garment and the woman held a thin, white tube between her lips. A tube from which smoke curled up.

Tal had seen many paintings—on the outside of his peoples' huts, on cave walls, on the shaman's medicine weapons—but never had he seen one with such vividness and clarity and lifelike qualities as this one. It was as if the girl were alive and staring up at him. Even the background details, a wooded hillside, an expanse of blue-green water, a sweep of blue-white sky, were meticulously drawn. Only one thing marred the absolutely lifelike perfection of the drawing. The unknown artist had failed to show the rings arching across the sky.

"Is . . . she smoking?" Tal indicated the slim tube in the girl's mouth.

"Yes," said Fen Melton. "There is more than one way to smoke. I use a pipe, but the backy can be rolled into small tubes and put in one's mouth and then set afire. I don't understand that method—a pipe is simpler—but they were called cigs. See"—he indicated a series of strange symbols drawn beneath the girl's picture—"that says: 'Enjoy Air-Filter Supreme Cig.' It was what the Ancients called the tubes of backy."

"That painting. . . ." Tal returned to his first source of wonder. "I have never seen a painting as real as that one looks."

"It is amazing," Fen Melton said, nodding in agreement. "The ancients had many arts and sciences which we have forgotten. Like the lettering there," he indicated the strange symbols again, "that is so neatly done. I have tried for hours and I cannot letter that perfectly. We have lost much."

"What is 'lettering'?" Tal had a little trouble with the unfamiliar word.

"Lettering is a form of communication called writing," Fen Melton explained. And Tal's puzzled look merely increased. "The Ancients had an art whereby they could mark down certain symbols and those symbols meant words, words like you and I are saying. Other Ancients could come along and see those symbols—those 'letters'—and understand the words the others had wanted them to know.

"For example. . . ." Fen Melton returned to the cabinet and brought out a square object about as thick as a dagger blade's width. "This is called a 'book,'" he explained, opening it to show Tal that there were a number of incredibly thin sheets inside, each covered with minute symbols in absolutely perfect lines. On one sheet was another drawing, equally as lifelike as the drawing of the girl with the cig, but showing a man dressed in a strange white robe standing before some kind of device Tal could not even remotely recognize. "Each of these letters makes a word and each word says something distinct. This was how one generation of ancients could communicate with another generation. This book, for example, is many thousands of years old."

"Where did you get it?" Tal was intrigued by the picture of the man in the white robe.

"I found it in some ruins. There are two other Farade historians and we occasionally travel to one or another of the places where the Ancients lived and try to dig up artifacts and books and things. Then we bring them back and study them until we understand them."

"Can you . . . can you understand all those symbols?" asked Tal, incredulously.

"Not all of them," admitted Fen Melton. "I have translated a great many, as have Jan Heron and Dav Rambo, but there is still so much, so very much, that we don't understand. But slowly, bit by bit, we're learning; and slowly, piece by piece, we're putting together the story of the Ancients. I may never know it all—I'm sure I won't—but my children may, or my children's children."

"But why do you want to learn about the Ancients?" asked Tal. "Of what use is it to you—or to anyone?"

"It could be a great deal of use." The Farade stretched out his long legs and relit his pipe. "The ancients knew so many things, things that we have forgotten. For instance, did you know they could fly?"

Tal choked on the bite of stew he was putting into his

mouth.

"That's right." Fen Melton smiled at Tal's expression of incredulity. "They had devices which lifted them into the air like birds. I have read of them in several of my books and I have seen pictures of the flying machines."

Tal was certain now that his new master was one for playing practical jokes. He did not laugh, for a slave does not laugh at a freeman, but he could think what he pleased in his mind.

"They also had weapons that could kill from a great distance. Weapons that could kill a thousand warriors at a single cast. These weapons caused tremendous explosions and fires. It would seem there was no protection against them."

"What kind of weapons were they?" asked Tal, his curiosity as a warrior getting the better of his disbelief.

"I don't know," Fen Melton admitted. "We know they existed. We know what they could do. We know that by using them, the Ancients destroyed themselves and all their secrets. But what they were, none of us historians has been able to discover."

"What do you mean about the Ancients destroying themselves?" Tal had finished the stew and had drunk the last of the herb tea. He did not know what to do with the utensils, so he left them where they were and turned his full attention to Fen Melton.

"I mean just that. There was a war, a tremendous war. I don't know even a portion of the story, but I know that it was the most terrible war in all our history. It involved every nation in the world and—every person. When it was over, the world was almost destroyed.

"The Ancients had smashed all their machines. They could no longer fly. They could no longer travel under the water like a fish. They could no longer talk to each other across a hundred days' journey by their science-magic. Their great cities lay empty and deserted and the wind blew through them with the sound of weeping ghosts and only death and silence grew where once the Ancients' magic had held full sway.

"All this the Ancients did with their wonder weapons.

They had the world, the sky, the stars—but they destroyed it all. And we, we are what is left. We are the pitiful remnants of their greatness left to scratch and grub amid the ruins like children playing in a dungheap!"

Fen Melton's voice had become quite bitter toward the end of this speech and he put the pipe down abruptly, turning away from Tal as he sought to recover control of his emotions.

After a few seconds' hesitation, Tal said, softly: "I . . . uh . . . have finished and I . . . uh . . . would put away the dishes if I knew where to put them."

"What? Oh, the dishes—" Fen Melton made a gesture of dismissal. "Don't worry about them. Ilola will get them in the morning. Go to bed now." He indicated a pallet by the door.

Tal hesitated. There was no slave chain there, yet that was the sleeping pallet indicated by his master. Slowly he walked to the furry pile and lay down, wondering all the while how Fen Melton planned to secure him to prevent his fleeing during the night. The tall Farade laughed at the obvious expression on Tal's face.

"In my *yurt* you will not be chained," he said. "I do not believe in chaining a fellow human to a post."

Tal was dumbfounded. "But—" he began, then he realized what he was about to say and shut up.

Fen Melton laughed again. He also had realized what Tal had nearly said.

"But what will keep you from running away?" he asked, finishing Tal's statement for him. "If you fled, we could see you for two days' journey in any direction across the ice. It would be a simple matter to pursue and recapture you. Also, if you fled, you would need a heavy parka, provisions, and snow shoes—none of which is left unguarded. If you decided to murder me in my sleep, it would accomplish nothing save your own death by torture on the morrow. Aside from preventing your fleeing, which is useless, or preventing your trying to kill me, which is pointless, why should I chain you to a post each night? In fact, if Ald Haslet will permit me, I hope to remove the iron collar from around your neck. No one should wear metal next to their skin in this climate."

Tal lay down on the pallet and pulled the furs over him. He lay awake for a long time after Fen Melton had retired. Tonight marked the very first time since his capture by Vaj Durmo that he had slept free and unchained. It was a strange feeling and he said a prayer of thanks to Shandor for the blessing.

He realized Fen Melton spoke the truth. His chances for escape were virtually nonexistent *at this time*. But if the Farade meant what he said, especially about removing the slave collar, then Tal had a renewed hope that Shandor had not abandoned him. Sometime, sooner or later, an opportunity would present itself. The absence of a slave chain was the first, even slight, relaxation since his capture. It was not much, but it was a start. Tal would wait and watch and be ready. . . .

The next morning Tal found that his new master meant exactly what he said. Fen Melton escorted Tal to the *yurt* of the Farade metalmaster, where the iron collar was struck from his neck with three sharp blows from a mallet and chisel. For the first time since his capture, Tal felt human again.

He found life as Fen Melton's servant to be quite easy. The scholarly Farade made few demands and never struck Tal or any of the other servants. The others, and there were three, were all indentured Farades, Tal soon learned, who were working off a debt of one sort or another. Ilola was the cook and chief housekeeper, a matronly lady of fifty summers or more. She was working off a debt incurred by her son, who had been slain by an ice bear before he could repay it. Waneena was younger than Ilola, probably not more than a dozen summers older than Tal. She had the straight dark hair and smooth brown complexion of all the Farade women.

The third servant was an old Farade named Bal Taslor. The old man had been a warrior, and a fierce one, but time had gradually dimmed his eyes and slowed his spear cast and weakened his arm till he could no longer hunt for himself. Many tribes, Tal's own Thongors, for example, would merely have let the old man starve. But Fen Melton took him into his *yurt* and cared for him and fed him. In return, Bal Taslor did small chores for Fen Melton, chores that were too heavy for Ilola or Waneena to handle easily.

When Tal joined the household, old Bal Taslor resented him sharply. It did not take the youth long to find out why. The old warrior saw Tal as a threat. The younger man could do anything the old man could do, plus many things he could not. He feared that Tal would replace him in Fen Melton's service and that their master would cast him out to starve.

However, Fen Melton soon set the old man's mind at rest. He kept Tal with him. They went almost everywhere together and the tall Farade seemed to take a great delight in explaining history to the youth.

Then, on the third day after Fen Melton had purchased him, the scholar told Tal what he had in mind.

"When I bought you from Ald Haslet I felt you were exactly what I needed. You are young and strong and healthy. My friends and I have need of someone with just those qualities. Jan Heron and Dav Rambo and I are planning an expedition into the Ice Region — farther in than anyone has ever been before. You will go with us."

Tal's pulse quickened and his blue eyes sparkled. This promised adventure and excitement, something slaves never experienced—plus one thing more: a chance for escape! Surely, somewhere on that trek, there would be an opportunity!

"There is a legend," Fen Melton went on, "of a great city buried beneath the ice many days' march to the southeast. It is that city we seek. Jan and Dav will be ready by dawn tomorrow. That is when we leave." He hesitated. "This is your chance, Tal, to see things no other living man has ever seen. Think on it."

Tal nodded and looked up at the arching rings spanning the blue-white heavens, trying to control the excitement rising faster and faster within him. Alone on the ice with three Farades who were scholars before they were warriors! Alone on the ice with the parkas, provisions, and snowshoes he would need to escape! Alone on the ice with no slave collar!

Tal said a prayer of thanks to Shandor and grinned wolfishly as he did. Fen Melton was right: This *was* his chance!

EIGHT

Something that was not human kept watch. A mechanical heart beat within the ghostly silent *X-97* as the never stilled computers kept their ceaseless data flow analyzed, encoded, and recorded. Photoreceptors scanned the sensory input and determined which data were electronically shunted to which storage tapes. The constant scanning was done with a faultless precision no human eye or mind could have equaled.

Suddenly there was a change in the quietly humming computer banks. A random bit of datum, correlating with a preprogrammed bit of datum, produced a matching data set and tiny tattletales flickered to life across an almost dead instrument console.

Artificial gravity was reinserted into the "active" program, the ship's lighting became brighter and higher, the life support systems surged back toward optimum.

In the various crew's compartments, where only the silent breathing of the dreamless Cold Sleep had been, new sounds began. Softly pinging alarms sounded, the receptors retracted from the temples and from over the heart, the gloved slots sent awakening tingles into the sensitive nerves of the fingertips.

Slowly, sluggishly, Dr. Fel Palmerin awoke. His eyes felt gummed and he was stiff and sore all over. He had the dull, subliminal headache that he always got if he slept too long.

He eased himself up onto the edge of his bunk and groaned aloud from the effort. He cradled his head in his hands for a few minutes, as if the very effort of holding it were too much for him.

He took several deep breaths and finally got himself together enough to punch for a refresher cup. Two sips of the steaming beverage, which the servall dispensed almost instantaneously, and he could feel his head clearing and his sluggishness dispersing.

He punched the computer terminal for grid coordinates and the line of lettering that spelled itself across the fresnal screen made his throat constrict with excitement:

"GRID COORDINATES OPTIMAL FOR SUBSPACE RETRACTION. TERMINAL DESTINATION ETA 47:01.3."

"By God, we made it!" he croaked. "We made it!" His ascetic face creased into a huge grin as he realized that within a matter of hours they would be orbiting Earth itself—their ancestral home world. "We made it," he whispered.

Carefully, almost reverently, he removed the air-tight sealed cover from atop the translucent amber, crystal-stemmed glass and lifted the brandy to his lips. "We made it," he said again, and drank a toast to himself and to his vision.

Less than an hour later he was on the bridge with Lanawe, Tishir Sequa, Alun Akobar, and almost all their small, select group of refugees.

"We will emerge from subspace into the real space-time continuum in nine point three minutes," Dr. Sequa said, busying himself with the hooded viewer at his computer station. "If all corrdinates are accurate as programmed, we should be within visual scanning range of Earth. We should be able to insert ourselves into an orbit around the planet and contact the representatives of their world government. Do you realize. . . ." His voice quickened with excitement. "Do you actually *realize* that in scarcely more than an hour we will be *communicating* with people on Earth! Communicating—for the first time in well over a thousand Earth years! It's almost unbelievable."

"Will we be able to communicate?" asked Lanawe. "I mean, surely there will be language differences."

"Oh, that's no problem," Sequa assured her. "We will simply monitor their dominant language groups, let the computer analyze them and prepare working translations, then beam them directly onto the optic nerve at the proper rhythm to insure their encoding in your memory cells. You'll talk like a native in about twenty minutes."

"Subspace retraction in eight seconds," said the pilot.

"Get ready," Sequa said, unnecessarily. He did things to his control console, peered anxiously into his hooded viewer, did other things, peered again.

Suddenly everyone experienced a very slight tingling sensation. This was followed by an abrupt feeling of vertigo, brief nausea, and unsettling dizziness, and then an inexplicable ringing in everyone's ears.

"We're out of subspace," Sequa announced. "Let's see— Earth should be visible at thirty-seven twenty-one mark four and eighty-eight ninety-seven mark two." He punched numbers as he said them. "Let's get her on the main. . . ." But he never finished the sentence.

The planet that suddenly appeared on the main viewer struck silent all conversations on the bridge. All eyes stared in utter amazement at the world revealed there. Lanawe Palmerin was the first to recover her voice.

"But . . . *that* can't be Earth! Can it?" she cried. "If it is— what's happened there in the last thousand years?"

The drums beat rhythmically and the dancers stamped their feet and swayed their bodies in the ancient ritual of the wedding dance.

Pale as death, Alytha stood within the hut that was Jad Thor's and wondered, as she waited for her new husband, why Shandor had abandoned her.

She knew he had abandoned her, because she had prayed to him repeatedly throughout the marriage rites—standing grim and silent beside Jad Thor. She had prayed for deliverance, for escape, for death, for *anything* to prevent the marriage. But Shandor had turned away his ears from her prayers.

Jad Thor, a hulking warrior whose gigantic chest and huge arms openly proclaimed him the strongest man among the Thongors, had claimed Alytha as his own and now she waited in his hut while he conveyed the agreed upon gifts to

Man Tavis, her father, gave the traditional gift to Sar Lon, the lance lord, and made the expected offering on the altar of Shandor. Of course, he would be obliged to drink a flagon (or two) of wine at each place of offering.

But the time passed quickly and Alytha knew he would come, and knew he would come soon.

Jad Thor did not disappoint her.

Even as she tried to plan an escape, having given up on asking Shandor's help, Jad Thor's great form suddenly filled the door to his hut and he entered.

His face was flushed from much wine and his eyes were hot with desire as he looked upon Alytha. He licked his lips, wiped his hands on his tunic, and took a step toward her.

"You're beautiful," he said, his voice a low rumble. "You're the most beautiful woman in Thongor. And you're mine!" he took another step toward her.

"I am not yours, Jad Thor," Alytha said, her voice firm despite the trembling of her flesh. "I am Tal Mikar's mate. I will never be yours."

"You *are* mine!" roared the giant warrior, as he rushed at her like a springing panther.

He caught her up in his burly arms and bore her effortlessly toward his sleeping pallet. His hands ripped at the front of her tunic, baring her breasts. He shoved her down and tore the cloth off her arms—and off the thin blade in her right hand that now stabbed upward into the iron muscles just below Jad Thor's rib cage.

His eyes opened very wide in surprise and he grunted once and then again as Alytha stabbed him a second time.

A lesser man would have already been dead, but Jad Thor was the strongest warrior of the Thongors and he did not die easily.

He spun around, still clutching Alytha and her bloody knife, and flung her from him with all the violence of his powerful frame.

She crashed against the far wall of the hut and fell to the dirt floor half stunned. Jad Thor was on her in an instant, springing across the space with unbelievable vitality.

Alytha tried to roll away from him and his clutching fingers tore at her already ripped tunic. The cloth held for an instant, then it split out and the girl rolled free, naked except for a brief loincloth.

She sprang away, her knife ready, and Jad Thor came after her. But he was staggering now. Blood stained the front of his tunic and ran down both legs of his breeks. Bloody froth bubbled between his lips with each breath he took, but still he came after her.

Alytha tripped over the sleeping furs and the warrior sprang like an attacking animal. One hand seized a perfect, naked breast, but the other hand, banded with muscles like plastic steel, closed upon her slim, white throat.

Alytha stabbed her knife into his back between his shoulder blades. Once, twice, three times she drove the blade home. She was desperate now, fighting for her life in earnest. She had no thought but the death of Jad Thor, even as her senses darkened and the blood pounded in her temples.

Suddenly the choking hand stiffened, then relaxed and fell limp. Jad Thor's huge body became simply so much lifeless weight.

Alytha tore his fingers from around her throat and choked and coughed as she began to breathe again. From somewhere deep within her, she found a wellspring of strength sufficient to roll Jad Thor's body off her.

Hastily she got to her feet. She discovered she could barely stand. She felt utterly exhausted, though the whole fight had taken only a matter of seconds and had been almost totally silent.

She knew one thing even in her exhaustion and panic: she must flee, and flee very soon.

Dazedly she staggered across the floor to where the pieces of her torn robe lay scattered, but a moment's examination convinced her they could not even be resewn into a serviceable garment.

Quickly she looked about for something to wear, for the loincloth she had on was scarcely large enough to cover her pubis, but before she saw anything even remotely suitable, a "rap-tap-tap" sounded on the drumskin and a chorus of drunken voices began to shout: "Come out, Jad Thor, and show us your bride! We want to see the bride!" And there was much laughter.

74

Alytha never hesitated. Like a startled deer she wheeled and sprang behind the curtain that separated the cooking area from the sleeping quarters. It took only a second to wrench the cover off the fireplace, actually only a square stone box open on both ends, and to wriggle through the still warm ashes to the outside.

Most of the Thongors were still shouting and dancing around the council fire in the revelry of the wedding feast, but Alytha knew a sentry would be at each gate of the palisade. At no time, under no circumstances, were the gates left unguarded.

Her bare feet made no sound on the hard-packed ground as she sprinted for the palisade at the curve farthest away from both gates.

She never slackened her pace when she reached the wall, but simply sprang like a gazelle, one bare foot smacking into the palisade of rough-trimmed logs at a point a good meter and a half off the ground and serving as impetus to get her hands hooked over the sharpened spikes at the top.

She held the bloody knife between her teeth by its handle as she swung herself up and over the wall. Even as she went over, she heard a terrible outcry behind her and she knew Jad Thor's body must have been discovered.

She hit the ground outside the palisade running. Speed was her only hope now and she was determined not to be recaptured.

With no food or water, unarmed save for one slim, blood-stained dagger, totally naked except for a very brief loincloth and a thick dusting of gray wood ash, Alytha fled into the darkened forest outside the Thongor village.

"That's Earth, all right," Dr. Tishir Sequa assured the group assembled on the bridge of the *X-97*. "Unless all our computer circuitry has totally malfunctioned."

"But Earth isn't a ringed planet," Lanawe Palmerin protested. "According to the tapes, only Saturn, the sixth planet, and Uranus, the seventh, had rings around them."

"Earth *wasn't* a ringed planet, you mean," Sequa corrected her. "The tapes also indicate that Earth had a satellite called the Moon. I submit that the rings Earth now has are the remains of the fragments of her former satellite."

"What happened to cause it to fragment?" Lanawe persisted.

"I don't know," said Sequa, quite honestly. "But probably the same thing that happened to the continents. Look at this." He touched a button and the picture on the main viewer suddenly split in half.

One side of the screen showed Earth as they had seen it, mottled blue and green and brown, with heavy swirls of white clouds, all banded with the milk-white rings set forty degrees off the equatorial axis. The other side showed a computer image of Earth as it had looked a millenium ago when the *X-97* had warped out of orbit on the journey that was to take her to Aryor.

"See the difference in continental outlines?" Sequa continued. A tiny green dot appeared which served as his electronic pointer. "That continent *there* is completely gone and a whole new continent shows up *there*, where Earth used to have nothing but an ocean. *That* continent, called—oh, what was it?— 'Americ' or 'America,' or something like that, is pretty much the same shape, but it seems to be all desert now, where before it was green and fertile."

"Speaking of green," put in Alun Akobar, "why is the top and bottom of Earth white in one picture and green in the other?"

"There *were* polar ice caps," said Sequa. "Now there's tropical jungle at the poles according to the spectroscopic readouts. The frozen arctic regions are now located in what used to be the equatorial zone. A reversal of magnetic polarity must have occurred—among other things."

Lanawe was still wrestling with the concept. "But what could have caused it? I mean, a planet doesn't undergo that much change in only a thousand years. It had to be caused by something."

"That is true." Dr. Sequa stroked his smooth chin, but it was Fel Palmerin, Lanawe's father, who supplied the answer:

"The war."

There was a chorus of audible sighs and muttered agreements as those assembled remembered their oft-told legends of the war that had been threatening to destroy all of

Earth when Shara Vralon and a handful of her followers had taken the Chalice of Time and fled Earth aboard the just completed, still untested *X-97*.

It was obvious, when Fel Palmerin said those two simple words, that it could only have been the war that so drastically altered the surface appearance, magnetic polarity, weather conditions, and other life attributes on Earth—not to mention the reduction of her planetoid sized satellite to a thin web of rock particles orbiting in a pair of matching rings around the globe.

"How are you doing monitoring their language patterns?" Dr. Palmerin asked. "Have they beamed any signals at us yet—welcoming or otherwise?"

"No," replied Dr. Sequa. "And I don't think they will." He hesitated. "There are no radio waves being broadcast on any known frequency. There are no video broadcasts. There are no hologram signals. There is no communication of any sort taking place."

All eyes swiveled from the twin pictures of Earth to stare at the Oriental, but it was Lanawe who said what was in all their minds:

"You mean there's no life on Earth?"

"Oh, no." Sequa leaned back in his chair. "There's life—and human life. The whole planet's pretty sparsely settled, it's true, but there's maybe a million humans down there." He hesitated again. "The problem's not a lack of life; the problem is a lack of communication equipment."

He turned back to his hooded viewer as if to verify what he was about to say before he continued:

"Sensors have monitored the whole planet. The most sophisticated energy source on Earth today is a wood burning fire."

The silence hung heavy on the bridge till Fel Palmerin said, "So they're savages."

"Just about," agreed Dr. Sequa. "Early bronze age, I'd say. Swords and spears and tanned animal hides for clothing. Probably human sacrifices. Not much help to a shipload of refugees from the Ilriks."

"Maybe not," agreed Dr. Palmerin, but he pressed on quickly, before his old friend's pessimism could become infectious: "But we weren't counting on *them* for help. We're looking for the Eternity Stone. It's all the help we'll need." He made his voice deliberately cheerful.

"But how do you expect to find the Eternity Stone?" Alun Akobar asked.

"That's easy enough," Dr. Palmerin replied, with a heartiness he did not feel. "Tishir, can you monitor verbal languages enough for the computers to work out a translation? I mean, without them being broadcast by radio?"

Dr. Sequa considered for a moment. "Well . . . yes, I suppose so. It'll take a little finer tuning and will require more time, but . . . yes, I can do it."

"Excellent! While you're doing that, Lanawe and Alun can get the shuttlecraft ready for our first trip down. We'll take the Chalice of Time with us. We'll leave as soon as you have the language tapes ready. Lanawe and Alun and I will go, along with twenty of the crew. Lan and Alun can select them later. But we *will* find the Eternity Stone. It's the only hope Aryor has!"

NINE

Tal's heart lifted with each step they took away from the Farade village.

As he raised his snowshoe-clad feet high in the odd gait those devices required, he kept the thought ever in the forefront of his mind that his chances for escape improved directly the greater the distance they traveled into the Ice Region.

Fen Melton led the way. His tall figure was wrapped in a heavy parka and he had rubbed his face with the aromatic ointment that had so intrigued Tal at Rendezvous. Tal himself was liberally smeared with the bear grease which he now found to be absolutely essential against the never-ceasing wind.

Behind Tal came Jan Heron, a Farade warrior even taller than Fen Melton and so thin he looked emaciated. His long face was set in such a perpetually mournful cast that, had Tal not known better, he would have thought the man mourning the death of a dearly loved one. Actually, Jan Heron had a very lively sense of humor.

Dav Rambo, the last man in the group, was half a head shorter than Tal and very burly. His barrel chest and thick shoulders filled his parka till the fur seemed about to split. He walked with a steady, measured stride. His snowshoes made a solid scrunching sound with every step he took.

Each man bore a heavy backpack loaded with supplies and equipment. In addition, Tal had a harness affair buckled across his shoulders and around his waist, which was attached to a small sled on which more supplies were securely lashed.

Fen had declared their intention, the morning before they left the Farade village: "We will search out vast new areas of the Ice Region. We will either find the lost city of the ice or we will put to rest forever its legend." They had come with supplies enough, supplemented by their hunting, to last them three or four months.

Around the campfire their first night the three scholars had been ecstatic about the possibilities of locating the lost city.

"Do you realize," said Jan Heron, "that it may well be a site not touched since before the ice came!"

"True," agreed Dav Rambo. "In it we should find enough artifacts to keep even the three of us happy for the rest of our lives." And all three laughed heartily.

After they had eaten and all, except Tal, had filled their pipes with backy, Fen Melton leaned back and sang them a song of his own composing. His oddly accented voice was rich and melodious and Tal found himself fascinated. The Singers of the Thongors and the Arcobanes chanted epic ballads, but he had never heard singing like this before. The song was a sad one, not the tragic sadness of a defeated nation but the solitary despair of one lonely man. Each verse ended with the refrain:

"I'm nobody's lover, nobody's friend—
"Just me and death and the dark-blowing wind."

All the next day on the march Tal found that he was humming the tune beneath his breath as he walked, repeating what he could remember of the words. Fen Melton seemed delighted at Tal's unconscious mimicry and promised to teach him more songs.

For the first three days the party did nothing but march steadily through the unbroken fields of ice. Then, shortly after breaking camp on the fourth day, their search began in earnest.

Each icy hillock now had to be explored carefully. Picks were brought out and cumbersome hand augers. Each likely looking site had to be thoroughly checked out before they could move on.

Specimens of the rocks found below the ice were taken and Jan Heron, who was an accomplished artist, Tal discovered, made sketches and maps indicating the areas where each specimen was gathered.

This method of exploration took up so much time that in the next week they did not travel as far as they had in the first three days. But this did not bother the three Farades. They seemed perfectly happy with their fruitless searching.

Tal was still racking his brain for a plan of escape. A guard was posted all night, every night—the three scholars rotated shifts—and Tal had no access to any weapons. Jan Heron he was sure he could kill or cripple with his bare hands; Fen Melton would be tougher, yet Tal was confident that in a pinch he could still win. Dav Rambo was another matter entirely. Him, Tal did not want to face without a weapon.

Of course, an accident could always happen, Tal realized. There were deep fissures in the ice. If he could catch them just right, he could hurl Dav Rambo into one, break Jan Heron's neck, and then have only Fen Melton to face. It would require extraordinarily quick reactions, and a very great deal of luck, but it could be done.

Suddenly Tal's bloody thoughts were interrupted by a sharp, anguished cry from Jan Heron.

The young slave flung down his pack and lurched through the crusted snow toward where the Farade lay—a dark crumple at the foot of the glacier face he had been trying to climb.

Fen Melton was the closest and he was there first. Tal arrived to see him cradling Jan's head in his lap and trying to extract a very small spear from the Farade's shoulder. The small spear was not as big around as Tal's finger and had colored feathers laced to the end of it.

"What happened?" demanded Dav Rambo, as he slogged up, his snowshoes splattering snow in all directions in his haste.

"Someone cast this spear into Jan," said Fen, indicating the embedded arrow.

"Who?" demanded the burly Farade, sweeping the area with his eyes. But there was absolutely nothing to see, just the vast open ice plain.

"I don't know," gasped the wounded man, who was obviously in great pain. "I was climbing the glacier to make a sketch of this whole section of ridges when I heard a funny sound—sort of a twang—and that little spear was just suddenly sticking all the way through my shoulder." As he spoke, Fen and Tal had been helping him to his feet and supporting him as they returned to the campfire where they had recently made their noontime meal.

Gently, almost tenderly, Fen Melton removed the arrow. He was forced to break it in two, since the chipped flint arrowhead could not be withdrawn through the wound.

Dav Rambo, his spear couched and ready, searched the area around the glacier thoroughly, but finally returned to the campfire without having found any trace of the mysterious attacker.

Jan Heron was not hurt badly, though the wound itself was painful, and he was soon sitting, propped against the sled Tal customarily dragged, carefully examining the two pieces of the weapon that had wounded him.

"Whoever threw this must not be very large," he suggested. "It is a great deal smaller than even our littlest child's spear."

"They may be small," commented Tal, "but they're obviously very strong."

"I see what you mean," agreed Fen Melton. "It took a tremendous amount of strength to hurl that lightweight spear completely through Jan's shoulder."

"That is true," said Dav Rambo, testing the heft of the arrow in one meaty palm. "I doubt that even I could do that, and certainly not from any distance away. Yet there was no one close at hand, for we all reached Jan within seconds."

Involuntarily, all eyes swung back in the direction of the glacier where Jan had been wounded, but there was nothing to be seen except the barren, unending expanse of the ice fields and nothing to be heard but the ceaseless, unending moan of the wind moving restlessly through the vaulted caverns of ice.

It was a very subdued camp they made that night. Dav Rambo and Fen Melton alternated watches and Tal was up and down all night tending Jan Heron. The tall, dour-faced

Farade developed a mild fever toward morning and Tal had his hands full keeping the fur blankets wrapped securely around him.

The next day dawned crystalline clear and cold—so cold that each breath Tal took cut his lungs like knife blades. When they broke camp, Jan Heron was strapped onto Tal's sled and the extra supplies were divided between the three men.

Before the day was over, however, the Farade scholar had thrown off his fever and appeared to be mending, though still weak. In fact, he insisted on getting off the sled and walking for a while toward the end of the day, an idea Tal greeted with grateful alacrity.

Camp that night was almost as subdued as the night before. Again Fen Melton and Dav Rambo alternated on guard while Jan Heron slept. Tal slept, too. In fact, he was so exhausted he fell asleep as soon as he rolled himself into his furs. This night he would not have escaped had the three Farades all marched away and left him alone.

The next day dawned cold and bleak with scudding gray clouds moving in to blanket the blue sky and to hide the milk-white rings. The three Farades, familiar with the weather patterns in the Ice Region, looked at the sky and shook their heads, muttering to themselves. Tal, who knew nothing of storms or the like on the ice, nevertheless felt a sinister unquietness in the air—a vague feeling of foreboding to which he could not put an actual name.

This day was more like the last few before the mysterious attack: the Farades returned to their mapping and exploring and sample gathering. Again the crude augers were forced down through the ice and snow to determine what detritus lay below it, again the picks hammered away at the hillocks of ice to see if anything resembling ruins were encased in the suggestive humps and tells.

When they pitched camp that evening they were not a third of a day's march from their camp of the night before, but in spirit they were light years away.

Everyone's morale was up and Fen Melton sang a lilting, happy tune while the three Farades smoked their pipes after eating. For two days now they had seen no one and had had no more trouble. Except for a few snowbirds, a half dozen snowshoe rabbits, a distantly glimpsed ice bear, and the tracks of some snow deer, they might have been the only living things in all that vast and terrible expanse of ice.

Jan Heron declared himself fit to stand watch that night, but Fen Melton thought he should rest first. It was finally decided that Fen would take the first watch, Dav Rambo the second, then Jan Heron could stand the last watch before dawn.

Tal lay awake for a long time that night listening to the wind. Its sound was a low and mournful threnody that somehow reminded him of Fen Melton's song at their first camp. He thought, as he drifted softly off to sleep, that he had never heard a more lonesome sound than the wind as it blew endlessly through the ice fields.

He awoke sometime in the still, black hours of the predawn. At first he could not determine what had wakened him. He lay, listening for some strange or unusual sound, but there was only the eerie, awful silence.

And then he knew.

The silence.

The wind had stopped!

Tal raised himself on one elbow and looked around. The fire was banked down to hardly more than embers. Jan Heron dozed near it, propped against Tal's sled, his spear lax in his hands. What little firelight there was cast weird, flickering shadows against the hillocks of ice and snow.

Tal suddenly blinked several times and shook his head. For just an instant it had seemed as if one of the ice hillocks had moved. . . .

Then it moved again and Tal recognized the danger.

"Look out!" he yelled, even as the figure, clad in furs as white as the snow on which it lay, rose up and hurled an ice chunk with sufficient strength and accuracy that it caught Jan Heron squarely on the forehead and sent him sprawling backward before he could even react to Tal's shouted warning.

Half a dozen shapes sprang up, seeming almost to materialize by magic, so closely did their furs blend into the snow cover, and leaped for the just awakening camp. But quick as they were, the black-haired Thongor was quicker.

In one bound Tal had recovered the spear dropped by the unconscious Jan Heron. His training as a lance warrior now got its first test in actual battle.

The spear stabbed out and caught the warrior who had flung the ice chunk full in the chest. The bronze tipped spear went through the man's heart, impaling him as much by his own forward motion as by the strength of Tal's arm. Then Tal yanked the spear back and swung the shaft sideways like a club into the charging warrior on his right.

With wind knocked out of him, that warrior doubled over on the ground even as Tal hurled the spear to completely transfix the warrior who was leaping in on his left.

Shandor! It's good to hold a weapon again! thought Tal, as he realized he had effectively removed three attackers in scarcely twice that many seconds and without moving from where he crouched beside the crumpled body of Jan Heron.

The other attackers were into the camp now and one of them, a squat, burly warrior, slashed out with a wicked stone knife as he hurled himself at Tal.

Tal got the man's knife arm twisted away and they rolled over and over in the snow, each straining to overpower the other, each fighting for his life.

Dav Rambo was on his feet now and his spear lashed out to impale a warrior who would have stabbed Tal in the back. In a moment Fen Melton was beside him and their great swords made short work of the attackers who seemed to have no better weapons than sharpened stone daggers.

Tal twisted his opponent's head back with one hand, while he held off his knife wrist with the other. All their rolling and twisting had ceased. The two warriors lay still now, their mighty muscles corded into knots as they strained against each other. The attacker had his free hand around Tal's throat and was slowly choking the life out of him even as Tal forced his head back and back farther.

Then, with a distinctly audible "crack," the vertebra snapped and the warrior was dead.

Tal rolled free of the jerking corpse and came to his feet to find the attack over.

Fen Melton had a gash on one cheek and a shallow cut

across the back of his left hand, plus several slashes across his fur parka where only its thickness had saved him from more serious harm.

Dav Rambo had a slash across his left forearm, plus numerous cuts on his heavy parka.

But of the attackers there was no trace except for eight corpses and dark blood splashes across the trampled snow. The swift, silent, deadly ice men had disappeared as completely as if they had never been. Tal knew it was their white fur cloaks that enabled them to become virtually invisible, but the effect was uncanny nonetheless.

"How is Jan?" asked Fen, moving quickly to the fallen Farade's side. Dav, in the meantime, hastily piled more coals on the fire to make it leap up, even though dawn was staining the distant sky with a glow that looked like blood seeping through the lowering clouds.

Tal knelt beside the two Farades, but his attention was still out on the ice fields. His fighting blood was up and he was as alert and wary as a hunting panther.

Jan Heron moaned, shook his head, and tried to rise. There was a bloody welt on his forehead where the ice chunk had struck him. He groaned again and finally managed to sit up.

No one seemed to notice when Tal appropriated a spear and one of the attacker's stone knives. He prowled the edge of the camp peering out over the lightening ice. He was armed now and he knew one thing for certain; no one would disarm him again without slaying him first. By Shandor, his days as a slave were over!

But no one showed any interest in disarming him. Dav Rambo began heating water to bathe their wounds while Fen Melton assured himself that, aside from a splitting headache, Jan Heron was all right.

Tal joined Dav Rambo at the fire and began preparing breakfast, but he kept his weapons close to his side.

"They seem to have come from nowhere," Fen Melton remarked. He rolled one of their late opponents over onto his back so they could get a better look at him.

The warrior was short, nearly a head shorter than the Farades, and round, plump, and yellow as a butterball. Not Oriental yellow, which has a brownish cast, but true honey-butter yellow. His hair was long and lustrously black like the Farades, but woven into it were bones and teeth to make a strange and archaic design. This motif was repeated in a series of tattoos across the dead warrior's face.

"I have never seen people like these," Fen Melton said, examining the corpse very carefully. "What do you make of these strange markings he has apparently cut into his own face?"

"Most interesting," said Dav Rambo, looking at them while he was washing and bandaging Fen Melton's wounds. "I wonder why anyone would want to mutilate themselves in such a way."

"It must have been very painful," commented Fen. "Are any of the others marked the same?"

Tal left off his breakfast preparations to examine three of the other corpses and to comment that each was tattooed identical to the first.

"Perhaps it indicated the tribe to which they belonged," Jan Heron suggested weakly. Of the four, he was the most seriously injured. Tal, except for some bruises on his throat and a slash on one sleeve of his parka, was unscathed.

"I suspect that may be true," agreed Fen Melton, who had now joined Tal at the task of preparing breakfast. "But I wonder what tribe they are. They are utterly new to my experience."

By the time the harried party had completed their morning meal, the sun was well above the rings, though hidden in the heavy gray clouds that seemed to have taken over the world in a foglike haze, reducing visibility by a considerable extent. It was only after they had eaten that the others became aware of the fact that had first awakened Tal from sleep.

"The wind has stopped," said Fen Melton, his head snapping erect as he listened intently.

"It *has* stopped!" cried Dav Rambo. "We've got to find shelter—and fast!" He began throwing their gear together in almost desperate haste. Fen Melton assisted him and even Jan Heron, weak as he was, tried to do his part.

Tal was puzzled by their obvious fear.

"What's so terrible about the wind stopping?" he asked, but even as he asked he was busily packing their gear.

87

"A storm is brewing," Fen Melton explained. His oddly accented voice was totally calm, yet he worked with almost frantic speed. "A great ice storm will break soon, maybe in an hour, maybe in a day. The wind will, quite literally, peel the flesh from your bones. Our parkas will not stop it, will not even slow it. If we are not under cover—ice caves perhaps, dug into some snow banks at the least—we will surely die."

With most of their supplies packed, Tal and Fen quickly divested the stiffening corpses of their late attackers of the snow white fur parkas and hooded cloaks they had worn. These were quickly added to their own gear and camp was struck.

Weak as he was, Jan Heron tried to walk, but after an hour he could not keep up. They either had to leave him or he would have to ride on the sled.

"I'll not drag him a single step," said Tal. "I am no slave now. You want to drag him, you drag him."

There was a moment of sharp tension as Dav Rambo turned. He was the one Tal watched. It was from him that trouble would come.

"I will pull the sled," Fen Melton suddenly said, stepping forward. "Tal has pulled it long enough." But Dav Rambo was not to be dissuaded.

"Since when does a *slave* say what he will and will not do?" he demanded, fingering his spear.

"I, too, have a lance," Tal replied evenly. "Come and see if you can make me drag the sled."

Dav Rambo took a step toward Tal, but before he could take a second there was the sharp "thwang" of a bowstring and a stone-tipped arrow suddenly bloomed wetly red out of his chest. He stared down at it stupidly for a moment, seeming to be infinitely baffled by how it came to be there, then he crumpled forward on his face in the snow and the feathered shaft was seen protruding half its length from between his shoulder blades.

Tal and Fen Melton hurled themselves prone on the ground, but there was nothing to be seen. The gently rolling snow banks and ice hillocks disappeared into the wet gray fog without revealing a trace of the enemy.

Tal realized, with a start, that there might well be a

hundred of the warriors within spearcast of them at this very moment; but their snow-colored furs protected them so completely they were virtually invisible.

"We've got to get to some kind of shelter," rasped Fen Melton. "And I don't mean just from the storm. Whoever these people are, they're still with us."

There was another "thwang" and an arrow thunked solidly into the sled by which the three defenders crouched.

"These are the same ones who attacked me!" cried Jan Heron. "That little spear is exactly like the one they used."

"Only they don't throw it like a spear," said Tal. "I'm not sure how they do it, but—*there!*" His arm shot forward in a lightninglike movement and his spear pinned a screaming warrior to the ice.

Tal was on him in an instant, the captured dagger not necessary to finish him off; the spear had done its work thoroughly. Tal retrieved his weapon and wheeled to scan the surrounding ice, but there was no more movement of the sort that had betrayed the ice warrior.

"We've got to pull out of here," he said, as he rejoined the two Farades. "I'm going to take a portion of the supplies and move on. I suggest you do the same."

"You're right," agreed Fen Melton. He turned to Jan Heron. "Can you make it? And I don't mean on the sled."

"I don't have much choice, do I?" replied the dour-faced scholar. With a sigh, he lurched to his feet and set off across the snow.

Just as they dipped over the crest of an ice hillock—almost as a parting afterthought—another arrow swooshed out of the fog and imbedded itself in Tal's backpack. Quickly he swung about, but their invisible foes were nowhere to be seen.

They made poor time. As they marched, they swiveled their heads from side to side till their necks were sore, but there was nothing to be seen. Only the endless ice and snow, lying bleak and desolate in the dirty gray fog that had shrunk the confines of their world almost claustrophobically.

Jan Heron was barely able to stagger on after an hour or so. Fen Melton supported him on one arm till he, too, was near exhaustion. Tal hesitated as long as he could, but at last he stepped back and relieved Fen of the burden. He supported the injured Farade till they stopped briefly in the early afternoon to eat some dried meat.

They sat, while they gnawed on the leathery jerky, with their backs together so they could watch in all directions at once. But for all their watching, they might easily have been the only living things upon all the vast expanse of ice. Even the animals had disappeared. Sensing the impending storm, they had all sought shelter somewhere. Even the great ice bear would not willingly be abroad in the face of one of the storms such as now threatened. To Tal, it seemed that the very air became thicker and heavier with menace. There was something in the atmospheric pressure that made him nervous and uneasy. Knowledge that they might well be under surveillance by an invisible enemy at that very moment did not help quieten the uneasy feeling at all.

"Whoever these people are," mused Fen Melton, while they ate, "they can't pursue us much longer. They're going to have to get under cover before the storm breaks. And it's going to break very soon."

"What about us?" demanded Tal. "Do you have any idea where we can take shelter?"

"Not exactly," admitted Fen. "But, did you notice how rough and uneven the ground has become? How it definitely slopes up? I believe we're coming into some foothills. If we are, there should be ice caves ahead of us somewhere—somewhere close, I hope. They should provide us with adequate protection."

They had finished their brief rest by now and were wearily struggling to their feet again. Fen Melton bent to help Jan Heron rise.

"If that's the case," said Tal, "then our attackers, whoever they are, may be planning to hole up in the same caves."

"That's possible," admitted Fen. "However, I doubt it. I'm sure by now they've all gone to ground somewhere."

Even as he said this there was the "thwang" of a bowstring somewhere out in the perceptibly thicker gray fog and a stone-tipped arrow sank half its length into his right thigh.

With a yell, the tall Farade sprawled out on the ice, clutching his leg with both hands. As he fell, he knocked Jan Heron from his feet, thereby saving the man's life, for another arrow just clipped the edge of his parka as he fell.

Tal threw himself prone, but there was no real protection. What galled him most of all was that there was no way to fight back. How does one fight an invisible enemy?

Fen Melton clutched his leg tightly, but the blood was already congealing in the bitter cold. The arrow had gone in directly and he judged that the point was against the bone. That meant that he could not break it in two and extract each half as he had done for Jan Heron. Nor could he pull the barbed stone tip back out through his flesh.

He explained all this to his two companions in quick, gasping sentences as they lay huddled on the ice. Throughout it, Tal kept his eyes roving through the fog that was now definitely a mist, a fine sleet, still seeking some sign of the enemy.

"What it means," Fen Melton said between clenched teeth, "is that I can't go any farther. I'm staying here. You two are going to have to leave me."

"I'm not going to leave you!" said Jan Heron. "This seems a good place to die."

"Listen!" said Tal, holding up his hand. "Is that the wind picking up again?"

There was a moment of startled silence, broken only by the rising threnody of the wind as it indeed picked up again. The sleet began moving, diagonally at first, then in almost horizontal sheets. It rapidly congealed into ice pellets that stung like flung rocks when they struck exposed skin. Tal pulled his parka hood closer over his head.

"It's the storm!" said Fen Melton. "It's starting! You've got to get to shelter!"

"I'm not leaving you!" Jan Heron repeated.

"We've got to try to move you!" said Tal. "Can you walk at all?"

"No—no, I can't!" Fen mastered his pain with a visible effort and put his hand on Tal's arm. "Listen," he gasped, "there's nothing you can do! Jan and I simply can't go any farther, but there's a chance you can escape." He fumbled with his backpack for a minute, then thrust one of the snow-white, hooded garments of their attackers into Tal's hands.

"Put that on," he instructed, over the ululation of the rising wind. "Get to one of the caves. You're free now. If you survive the storm, bear to the north and west. When you see the smoke from the water that burns, be careful! You don't want to be captured by another Farade.

"Once you skirt our village—and, remember, you are visible for two days in any direction—bear almost due west and you will be out of the tundra in five or six days' march. From there, you're on your own. Here—" He thrust all their supply of beef jerky into Tal's pack. "Jan and I won't be needing this. Now go—quickly!"

Tal hesitated. It was an illogical emotion, he knew, but he felt almost as if he were deserting his friends. It took an effort of will for him to remember that he had been brought here a slave and that escape was what he had planned all along. He smiled bleakly at his own foolishness as he wrapped himself in the white fur cloak.

"Go quickly," said Fen. "As your master, I give you your last order: save yourself!"

Tal looked at the dark face just visible beneath the hood. Whatever else he had been, Fen Melton was a warrior! Tal touched his arm briefly.

"Shandor be with you," he said, then he moved away from them into the face of the howling storm. In a moment, they were lost to his sight as if they had never been.

TEN

The great bulk of the *X-97* dropped rapidly away to stern as the small shuttlecraft swooped downward toward the atmospheric envelope of the planet below.

Lanawe Palmerin was at the controls and her father sat beside her. The interior of the shuttlecraft was open, except for the enclosed head, and Alun Akobar, along with nineteen other crew members, was strapped into contour couches behind the two Palmerins.

Each of the party was quite fluent in over two-thirds of the languages spoken on Earth—Dr. Sequa had not had sufficient time to prepare mentapes on *all* the languages—and they were each armed with a neuron gun. The weapons were, of course, stored until planetfall was accomplished.

"Do you really think we'll be able to locate the Eternity Stone?" Lanawe asked her father, in a voice too low for the others to hear.

Dr. Palmerin gave a dry laugh.

"I didn't really think the *X-97* would ever break orbit at Aryor," he admitted. "Once it did, I never really thought we'd be able to return to Earth. Now that we're here—well, I'm ready to believe almost anything is possible."

The little jetboat dropped into atmospheric resistance. Skin temperature began to rise and Lanawe activated the coolant circuitry.

"But how do you propose to find it?" persisted the girl. "I know you said you had a plan, but I'd feel better if I had some idea of just what it is. We don't know where to look. We'll have to search an entire planet. In fact, we don't even know exactly what we're looking for. We don't know how big the Eternity Stone is, we don't know what shape it is, we don't know what color it is. It could be as big as a mountain or too small to be seen by the naked eye. And we have a whole world to look for it in. I'd say, all things considered, that's a pretty big order."

"True," Dr. Palmerin agreed. "But I think we know more about the Eternity Stone than you think. For example: the legend says that when the Eternity Stone is placed within the Chalice of Time, a force will be unloosed that nothing in the universe can stand against. Now, we have the Chalice of Time. From the dimensions of it we can deduce that the Eternity Stone probably weighs no more than a kilo and a half, is roughly point two eight meters thick, and is round or, at least, rounded on one end. The legend also says that the Chalice of Time will glow and vibrate when it passes within a few kilometers of the Eternity Stone and the glow and vibration will increase the closer it gets. If we can't find native Earthmen who can guide us to the Eternity Stone, and I really believe we can, then I think we can ultimately find it on our own by using the Chalice of Time."

"But that's just a legend," protested Lanawe. "How can you be sure the Chalice will really glow and vibrate? And exactly how close do you have to be?"

Dr. Palmerin chuckled again.

"The *whole* story is a legend," he reminded her. "All of it—the Eternity Stone, the power, Earth itself—was all a legend. We've come this far believing the legend, and it's been right this far, so we might as well go on. Besides, we really don't have much choice. As to your last question: I have no idea how close we have to be. The legend isn't specific there. We're going to have to do it by trial and error."

The little shuttlecraft was now fully airborne and Lanawe touched the controls that swung the delta wings forward for greater stability and aerodynamic maneuverability. The world below them had ceased to be a planet and had become a landscape toward which they were dropping at about thirteen hundred kilometers per hour. The rings were well outside their trajectory and were now above them, milk white bands arching across the purplish-blue heavens.

The ground below was mottled green and brown, mountains and forests, and toward the distant horizon it gleamed a blinding white. Sunlight reflected off the equatorial ice belt.

"Well, I guess it's the best we can do," Lanawe said. "And you've been right so far. We'll just have to keep on."

"True," agreed her father. "However, as I said, I'm sure we'll be able to find a native or group of natives who will guide us to the Eternity Stone. It's like I said to Tishir: if anyone had arrived on Aryor within the last thousand years looking for the Chalice of Time, how many people would he have had to ask to find out where it was?"

"I see your point, but answer this: once he found it, would we have let him have it? Of course not! It was a sacred symbol to us. What makes you think any of the Earth natives will joyfully hand over the Eternity Stone simply because we ask them to?"

Dr. Palmerin looked very grave as he replied, "I don't expect them to simply because we ask them. I *hope* they will, but I don't expect them to. I expect them to hand it over because we have neuron guns and personal deflector shields." He paused. "Tishir said this culture was early bronze age. What can a culture like that do against neuron guns and deflectors?"

He and Lanawe had been conversing in tones too low for the others in the party to hear. Now, Dr. Palmerin turned slightly and raised his voice so all the crew members could hear:

"We're on the final approach now. I think our first objective should be to establish some form of friendly intercourse with the natives. Before we do, I think we should observe them carefully to determine which tribe to approach first and to determine the best method for approaching them. With that idea in mind, I want Lanawe to circle wide and let's get some idea of what's happening down here before we set down."

Lanawe whipped the little shuttlecraft around in a tight bank when they were less than a kilometer off the ground. The sensory data were played back on the big screen set overhead so that all the crew members could see exactly what

Lanawe and her father saw in their viewer in the center of the instrument panel.

Of course, the sensors told them only a part of the picture. As they flew, everyone peered out of the ports equally as much, if not more, than they scanned the technically more accurate but aesthetically less satisfying sensor input.

They were flying over a heavily wooded mountain area. Great cliffs towered up almost as high as their flight path, then fell away to achingly beautiful valleys where thin silver ribbons of waterfalls traced their paths through the heavy greenery.

Once they flashed over a rude, palisaded village. Lanawe slowed their speed and they circled—the viewscreen set on maximum magnification.

The natives, who appeared to be panicked by the sleek, silver jetboat, wore homespun and leather garments. The men wore tunics, breeches, and boots. The women wore long robes. The men all appeared to be armed with swords and long, slim spears—obviously javelins. There was no indication of body armor of any sort. The people were Caucasian, but heavily tanned, and both men and women wore their hair long, the men to their shoulders, the women longer yet. The men appeared, for the most part, to be clean shaven. Most of the tribe had dark brown or black hair, but there were a few, a very few, people with light brown hair and there was one red head. There were no blonds in the village.

After a couple of spirals—the sensors automatically recorded everything for future evaluation by the computers aboard the X-97—Lanawe leaned into the joystick and the shuttlecraft peeled off and headed on over the mountains.

A babble of excited voices rose from the crew members as the village disappeared behind them. The Aryorians were nearly wild with excitement at seeing their first real Earth people. Their enthusiasm was dampened somewhat by the fact of the obviously primitive life-style they led. Despite what Dr. Sequa had told everyone before they left the starship, it had not really hit them till they actually *saw* the people of their ancestral home world living in hide-covered huts behind wooden walls and carrying bronze swords.

The wooded hillsides flattened below them and became

gently rolling foothills and then flat, less heavily wooded land. In a short time, the plain became sparsely wooded, then only an occasional tree dotted the rolling, grass covered prairie.

As they flew, they passed over an occasional party of hunters or, less often, a lone warrior bound on some business of his own. In each instance the warriors took immediate cover, such cover as they could find, and made gestures with their spears which were unmistakably threatening in nature.

"The natives don't appear to be overly friendly," commented Lanawe.

"It's not surprising," remarked her father. "You realize that in the present state of their culture all warriors outside of their own tribe are potential enemies. They live in a very hard, very savage, very brutal world. Constant vigilance is the price not just of their liberty, but of their very lives."

"It must be terrible to have to live like that," said Lanawe with revulsion.

"It's less terrible than what life is like on an Ilrik slave world," said Dr. Palmerin. That statement effectively terminated the conversation till he said, "Bear about ten degrees starboard. Let's have a look at the ice."

Indeed, the flat, grassy prairie had been altering under them. The grass became browner and more sere. At last, it gave way to true tundra, then to the beginnings of the snow fields.

The day was waning fast, but from their height they still had close to an hour of sunshine. The westering sun cast an orange-red glow over the ice except for one region, a few hundred kilometers ahead of them, where they could see roiling gray clouds all the way down to the ground.

"Bad storm up ahead," said Lanawe. "Want me to climb over it?"

"Might as well," agreed her father. "I'm reasonably sure we're not going to find life on the ice, anyway."

"I don't know," commented the girl, gesturing out at a slight movement below and to one side of them. Magnification on the viewscreen revealed a great, lumbering polar bear. "There's life for you."

"I don't mean that kind of life," replied her father. "I meant sentient life forms. We aren't going to find any people out here."

The little jetboat rose nearly two kilometers before they got above the ice storm that was howling along below them. From their altitude, the clouds were a brilliant, blinding white where the waning sunlight struck them and a murky grayish-black where it did not.

They had hurtled along for over a hundred kilometers before Lanawe said, "Why don't I head back? There's nothing out here."

"Okay," agreed Dr. Palmerin absently.

He glanced routinely at the sensor input as Lanawe stood the jetboat on her starboard wing in a stomach-wrenching turn that reversed their course. Suddenly his attention was riveted by a display on the screen.

"Circle again," he said. "Infrared scanners are picking up body heat." He adjusted calibration. "Mass is adequate for a man—a group of men." He adjusted again. "There are three men in a cluster surrounded by twelve or fifteen others. Wait, one of the three is moving away. I think he's escaping from the others."

"In that storm down there? Why would he be escaping?"

"Look at the pattern," he gestured at the small screen as he talked, but the crew members all saw the same display on the big screen overhead. "See how those men are fanned out there and there. They've almost got the three surrounded. Those two are close together and"— he made another adjustment—"bio-scanners indicate that they are both injured. The third member is escaping." On their screens the Aryorians saw the irregular blob that the infrared scanners identified as a man move diagonally away from the other two.

"If that storm weren't blowing like twenty devils down there, our boy wouldn't get through the circle of enemies that has him surrounded. Right now though, unless he accidentally steps on one, he has a very good chance of making it."

Lanawe held the shuttlecraft in a lazy spiral above the storm as their scanners followed the invisible drama two and a half kilometers below them on the ice fields.

"This may be an excellent opportunity for us," said Dr. Palmerin, excitement in his voice. "If we could pick that fellow up off the ice—literally rescue him from a near certain death—he might be persuaded to tell us something about the Eternity Stone."

"If he knows anything about the Eternity Stone," added Lanawe.

"Well, that's true," agreed the old man. "But it's a starting point, and it gives us an edge. Can you fly this thing through that storm down there?"

Lanawe frowned. "I don't know," she admitted. "Sensors indicate the winds at a steady hundred and ten kilometers per hour, gusting to a hundred and forty-five. Surface temperature is minus thirty. It'll be a damned rough ride."

"Let's try it," urged her father. "It may not come to anything, but. . . ." He shrugged.

The jetboat made one more spiral while Lanawe got a locating fix on the moving blob of light that was her target, then the stub-winged silver shuttlecraft dropped down into the roiling storm clouds and disappeared like a stone sinking into soft mud.

Lanawe's estimation of a rough ride was a definite understatement. The jetboat leaped and pitched, yawed and heaved, slipped sideways in sudden wind gusts and dropped violently in sudden air pockets.

She fought the controls in a literal physical battle. The restraining seat straps held all the passengers secure, yet they were all jerked and snapped back and forth as the shuttlecraft plunged madly about in the storm-racked sky.

It took more than Lanawe could do to maintain her bearings on the heat blob their scanners had singled out for them. Within a very few minutes it had become a sheer matter of staying in the air, without attempting to reach a predetermined target.

"It's no good!" she rasped, between clenched teeth. "The wind's too violent! I can't hold her!"

"Take us out," ordered Dr. Palmerin. "We'll try to pick him up after the storm blows itself calm."

Lanawe hauled back on the joystick, but the response was sluggish. She tapped the thrust lever, but it was already onto full. She adjusted the fuel mixture, then pulled back on the joystick again. The response was negligible. She reached for the power boosters and saw that they were on. Still the shuttlecraft would not respond to the joystick.

"I can't get her nose up," Lanawe finally said, in a voice too low for the crew to hear. "I think the lift vanes have frozen over and I think we've picked up a coat of ice that's made us too heavy. I can either try to fly out through the storm or try to set her down and wait till it blows over."

"What's the terrain like down there?"

Lanawe adjusted the scanners for topographical readout. An outline of the surface immediately below them printed itself across the screen.

"It's a little rough," she said, "but it shouldn't be any trouble. There are no cliffs or anything below us."

"What about those hills there?" asked her father. "The ones it looks like our boy is making for."

"They're almost a kilometer off our starboard bow. They won't affect our planetfall. Right below us are some rills, but the highest is less than a meter. We should be able to set straight down."

"Let's do it then." Dr. Palmerin raised his voice so all the crew members could hear. "We're going to make planetfall. We will wait out the storm, then we're going to pick up a native. Maybe—I repeat, *maybe*—he can tell us something about the Eternity Stone. Take us down, Lan!" None of the anxiety Dr. Palmerin felt was echoed in the crisp tones with which he addressed the crew.

The buffeting and tossing of the little jetboat increased the nearer she got to the surface. Lanawe had her hands full trying to bring her down in anything like a banked descent. The wind gusts picked up markedly at ground level.

But Lanawe Palmerin was the best pilot on Aryor. She wrestled the joystick back and forth with delicate precision as she anticipated each yaw and pitch of the slewing aircraft. They were only a few dozen meters off the surface, yet she was as calm and steady as if they had all of space surrounding them.

The ports were now iced over so that only a glazed whiteness was visible through them. All their scanning sensors were set for reading directly below them, so the sensory input was nil. In essence, the crew was virtually blind, but they still felt the distant "thump" as the jetboat touched down.

A great cheer went up from all of them, even staid Dr. Palmerin. They might be sealed inside their jetboat while a howling ice storm raged outside but they were back on Earth! Earth—which their ancestors had fled more than a millenium ago! Earth—their legended homeworld that many Aryorians had come to believe way only a myth. Earth—the quasi-holy resting place for the matching half of their sacred Chalice: the Eternity Stone!

Shara Vralon's children had come home.

"Can we unstrap now?" asked Alun Akobar, his hands already on the release catches of the magnetic webbing.

"Sure," said Dr. Palmerin. "Only don't take any strolls outside." Everyone laughed.

The landed shuttlecraft rocked and vibrated from the force of the wind howling outside, but there was no longer any danger. The crew poured themselves refresher cups and a few broke out sandwiches and sweet rolls. The atmosphere was one of gaity and holiday fun. Their troubles were over; they were back on Earth.

"I wonder why the *X-97* hasn't tried to raise us?" commented Dr. Palmerin. "They were supposed to maintain an open-line monitor on all our transmissions."

"I think it's magnetic fluctuations from the rings," Lanawe said, sipping the refresher cup Alun had brought her. She tried, tactfully, to ignore his presence hovering beside her. "They interfere with transmission of radio waves. They played hell with my radiocompass when we dropped past their orbit."

Dr. Palmerin grunted and flicked on the transmit switch.

"Shuttlecraft One to *X-97*, do you copy? Over." Only the crackle of static answered him. "Shuttlecraft One to *X-97*, do you copy? Over." Only static. "Fel Palmerin to Tishir Sequa, over." Nothing but static.

"Damn!" said Palmerin. Then, after a second, he regained his composure. After all, he reminded himself, he was the leader of this group. They depended upon him. "Oh, well," he said, shrugging. "There was nothing to tell them anyway, except that we were down safely."

The storm howled and shrieked around the jetboat for

most of the night. After everyone had eaten, Dr. Palmerin suggested they try to get a little sleep. Tomorrow, he pointed out, might be a very big day.

Alun Akobar tried to talk to Lanawe, but the black-haired girl always managed to be busy or to be with one of the groups avidly discussing what it would be like to walk the surface of the Earth after more than a thousand years of exile. Finally, in anger, Alun retired to his couch and thereafter refused to speak to anyone for the balance of the night.

At last, despite their excitement, the crew members returned to their couches and slowly, one by one, drifted off to sleep. Only Fel Palmerin remained awake in the end. He sat silently in the subdued light, his eyes brooding on the box that contained the Chalice of Time. He was afraid—deathly afraid—that all their efforts, their schemes, their hopes would come to nothing. It was so slender a thread, so very slender a thread, from which to hang the fate of a whole civilization.

The morning broke clear and cold.

The sun turned the snow fields a blinding, dazzling, eye-hurting white. The sky was deep cerulean blue, with the rings bands of burnished silver touched with rose. The temperature was minus fourteen degrees and the wind was an easy, steady nineteen point five kilometers.

"What we're going to have to do," explained Dr. Palmerin, as the crew pulled on their thermal suits, "is remove the ice from the lift vanes, the directional vanes, and the exhaust vents. It won't take long. It'll give us all a good chance to stretch our legs."

Only one crew member would remain aboard and that one, a girl named Varel, was most indignant about missing her opportunity to set foot on Earth.

"But the *X-97* might punch through the interference and reach us," Dr. Palmerin explained. "So someone's got to be here to monitor the radio." He clipped his snow goggles into place.

"Should I break out the neuron guns and personal deflectors?" asked Lanawe, gesturing toward the arms locker.

Dr. Palmerin considered a moment.

"No," he finally decided. "There's no one in sight. And besides, we'll never be more than a couple of meters from the hatch and we'll leave the outer door open."

When the hatch dilated, sheet ice had to be broken free before they could emerge. Dr. Palmerin was the first out. The snow scrunched almost musically beneath his boots. One by one, the others followed him outside except for poor disappointed Varel. Truthfully, most of the crew members simply gamboled about in the snow, as happy as children let out of school. Only Fel Palmerin, his daughter, Alun Akobar, and a couple of others worked on removing the ice from the shuttlecraft. The others enjoyed a snowball fight and made short, exploratory forays.

"Don't go too far," Dr. Palmerin warned, as a pair of crew members wandered away. "We need to stay close."

"We will!" one called back, less than a second before the arrow whistled out of nowhere to pass almost completely through his chest.

Dr. Palmerin was staring directly at him when it happened, but it still took several seconds for it to register. The last thing he was expecting was an armed attack.

"Inside quick!" he yelled, wheeling to leap for the hatch.

He stopped abruptly, facing two white fur-clad warriors whose drawn bows leveled arrows directly at his chest.

Suddenly the entire party realized they were surrounded. No one moved. No one spoke until Dr. Palmerin, clearing his throat, said, in one of the Earth dialects he had learned via mentapes: "Greetings. We come as friends."

Without warning the short, butter-colored native who seemed to be the leader struck the old man a savage blow across the face that knocked him sprawling onto the snow.

One of the warriors sprang through the open hatch a moment before Varel, who had been watching out the port, could close it. The hatch contracted and there was nothing till, faintly through the metal skin, those outside heard a girl's scream of anguish. Varel had died without ever setting foot on Earth.

The warrior who had entered the shuttlecraft now appeared at one port. He banged on it, but it would not open. He tried another. Soon they heard him banging on the inside hatch, but he could not discover how to open it. He had effectively trapped himself. He returned to the port and beat on it further.

He and the leader communicated by signs while Lanawe and Alun helped Dr. Palmerin to his feet. The old man was bleeding from a split lip.

At last, angrily, the leader made a sharp gesture and, without a word having been spoken, the prisoners were marched away across the ice.

ELEVEN

The ice cave was not deep, but it provided Tal all the shelter he needed to survive the storm. He had burrowed into its depths, protected from the wind, and had wrapped himself securely in his borrowed cloak. He had chewed a strip of tough jerky before he finally allowed himself to sleep.

He had never before experienced a storm on the ice, so when the great fireball descended, with much roaring and hissing, Tal merely thought it another manifestation of the storm. He scarcely let it disturb his sleep.

It was not till the dawn broke clear and cold, etching all the world with hard-edged clarity, that he saw the strange silver bird resting upon the ice about twice as far from him as a strong man could cast a lance.

At first, Tal wondered what it was. He lay very still, almost completely covered by the snow that had banked against his ice cave, warm and secure within the hooded fur cloak from the dead warrior, and watched it to see what it would do.

He was soon very glad that he had decided to lie still and watch.

A section of snow-covered hillock raised itself a little way off the ground and scuttled forward, dropping down again almost immediately. In a second, another clump of snow did the same thing. Then a third and a fourth moved.

Tal realized these were the warriors that had pursued him and the Farades for days across the ice. Their white fur cloaks made them virtually invisible against the snow.

Far off, on the other side of the strange silverbird, Tal saw a flutter of movement, then two long, stiff dark objects were brought into view. After a moment, Tal realized these were the bodies of Fen Melton and Jan Heron. The two Farade scholars had not survived the storm.

A movement by the strange silver bird now swung Tal's attention back to it and attracted the attention of the Ice Warriors, also.

One section of the ice that coated the bird's gigantic side suddenly changed color; it seemed to be much lighter than it had been and dark shapes could be seen moving behind it. Then, with a sharp, flat sound, the ice was shattered, falling away in chunks. A large, square hole was now revealed in the bird's side and the figures of several humans were visible.

Fascinated, Tal watched as a tall figure stepped out onto the snow. The person was not wearing a bulky fur parka. Instead, his slim, erect figure was covered in a snugly fitted garment that seemed all one piece from head to toe. The garment was black, with contrasting scarlet piping edged in gold. Part of the garment made a tight hood around his head and strange looking amber colored lenses fitted over his eyes.

After walking back and forth for a few moments, the figure was joined by another and then another. All were dressed identically but some, Tal could tell by the snug fitting uniforms, were female. There appeared to be twenty or twenty-one of them altogether.

In all his life, Tal had never seen a tribe like this one. He knew the great bird had not been there when he had escaped through the storm the night before—he now guessed that the roaring, hissing fireball had marked the bird's descent somehow—and he knew the strangely dressed tribesmen had not been there, either. How they had arrived and who they were was an utter mystery to him.

Four or five of the people, including the one who had first emerged and whom Tal therefore judged to be their leader, went to one wing of the bird and began removing chunks of ice from it. Tal could not comprehend exactly what they were doing, but they seemed very intent upon it.

The other tribesmen, however, ignored the bird and acted more like children at play. Some gathered up handfuls of snow and flung them at one another, others wandered about apparently aimlessly, pointing off at unseen things across the snowfields.

Tal did not see a single spear or sword among them. None of the warriors appeared to be standing guard. By Shandor, they were either incredibly stupid or so awesomely powerful they had nothing to fear!

He learned which it was almost immediately.

Two of the tribesmen started to walk away and their leader called something to them in a language Tal did not understand. One of the warriors turned, called back an equally enigmatic answer, and suddenly took one of the short spears directly through his chest.

The ice warriors sprang erect now, their strangely curved devices used for launching the small spears were bent and the tiny, deadly weapons were leveled at the party of strangely clad warriors.

The leader yelled something and whirled as if to spring for the open door in the bird's side, stopping only when he realized the ice warriors had them effectively surrounded.

There was a moment of sharp tension, then Tal heard the leader say, quite distinctly: "Greetings. We come as friends." The leader of the ice warriors, without speaking or changing expression, suddenly struck the other a savage blow across the face. Tal recognized the gesture. It was a warning that the other's leadership was ended and that they were helpless prisoners totally at the mercy of their captors.

Suddenly one of the ice warriors sprang through the door in the side of the bird. Tal had seen the sudden movement in the shadowed interior that had attracted him. Almost immediately a section of the bird's skin rolled down and effectively sealed itself shut. The door had disappeared as if by magic!

From inside the bird—Tal realized he was going to have to stop thinking of it as a bird, though Shandor knew he could not imagine what else to call it—came a sudden muffled shriek. It was the death scream of a woman.

After a moment the ice warrior's head appeared in one of the round things Tal had been thinking of as eyes. He seemed to be trying to open it, but that produced no results. He repeated the process at another one of the "eyes." Then he disappeared from view.

The Ice Warriors seemed very interested in all this, but still no one spoke.

Presently Tal heard a dull booming from the area where the door had been. He assumed the warrior was trying to beat his way out through the skin. This soon stopped and the warrior's head reappeared in one of the "eyes."

He and the leader of the Ice Warriors made signs to each other for a moment, then the leader made a sharp gesture and all the prisoners were marched away toward the distant hills off to Tal's right.

Tal fetched out a hunk of beef jerky and chewed on it while he watched the group troop away across the snow. He had no idea who the party of warriors from the great bird had been, but he had a good idea what their fate was going to be. He noticed the Ice Warriors had taken the bodies of the two Farades and the slain bird man with them. This suggested possibilities that he did not like to consider.

The party had not quite disappeared from view over the first hill when Tal saw one of the black-clad tribesmen stumble and fall. As he did, he fell against two of his captors.

There was a momentary scuffle and in the distraction of the moment, one slim black-clad figure struck the rearmost guard savagely in the stomach, then brought a knee up viciously into the warrior's face. Then the slim black figure was racing madly across the snow toward the silver bird.

As Tal had expected, a dozen of the little spears were fitted to their launching devices and aimed at the fleeing prisoner. Then, to his surprise, he saw the leader of the Ice Warriors make a sudden, sharp gesture. The weapons were lowered. The leader made several other signs—Tal began to wonder if the Ice Warriors even had a spoken language—and two of the Ice Warriors flung aside their weapons and set out in a run after the escaping prisoner.

The black-clad warrior had drawn close enough that Tal could see she was female, and very beautiful. That was evidently why the leader of the Ice Warriors wanted her recaptured rather than killed. And the two warriors pursuing her were rapidly closing the distance between them.

It seemed the leader of the Ice Warriors had implicit faith in his men's ability to overtake the girl, for Tal saw the rest of the guards and their prisoners disappear from sight in the direction they had originally been going.

The girl was having a hard time running in the snow, but the Ice Warriors seemed right at home. They were steadily gaining on the girl.

She soon became aware of this and, apparently remembering the warrior that was still trapped inside the bird, she suddenly altered course and headed almost directly for Tal's ice cave.

The Thongor cast one glance in the direction the main party of Ice Warriors had gone and he saw they were now completely out of sight. That left only him and the two who pursued the girl.

The closest Ice Warrior was just reaching out for the girl when Tal's lance erupted from the ice cave and drove its bronze tip completely through the man's heart. They were so close that when the dead warrior fell he was almost at the entrance to the ice cave.

Without hesitation, Tal launched himself at the second warrior. They went down onto the snow and rolled over and over. Tal had the advantage because he sprang with his captured stone knife already in his hand while the Ice Warrior had been running empty-handed. The stone blade came down once, twice, and Tal sprang to his feet to face the frightened girl.

Only she was not quite as frightened as Tal had thought she would be. He turned to find himself facing the bloody tip of his own lance, which the girl had wrenched from the chest of the dead Ice Warrior. The girl held it as if she knew how to use it and the fierce light in her blue eyes told him she would not hesitate to do so.

"Keep your distance!" she said, the lance tip never wavering from its position.

"Why are you threatening me?" asked Tal. "Didn't I just save you from the two Ice Warriors?"

"Yes, you did," said the girl. "But until I find out who you are and what you want, I'm not going to trust you at all. No one will take me unarmed again!"

"That's wise. If your warriors had been armed when you

came out before you might have escaped the Ice People. They are great cowards."

"My father felt that we were safe." The girl grimaced as she thought of this. "I'm afraid all of us have much to learn about what life is like on Earth today."

"Your father is the leader of your tribe?"

The girl considered this and then smiled. The smile made her enchantingly lovely.

"I guess you could say that," she admitted. "His name is Dr. Fel Palmerin and he *is* the leader of our expedition. I'm Lanawe Palmerin. We're from Aryor." She added this last even though she knew it would mean nothing to Tal. She was aware of the primitives' strong territorial sense and she felt sure he expected such a place name as part of her introduction.

"I am Tal Mikar of Thongor. What do you plan to do now, Lanawe Palmerin?" He stumbled a bit over the unfamiliar name.

"Call me 'Lanawe,'" she said, with another dazzling smile. "First, I've got to get inside the shuttlecraft. There are weapons there that I can use to rescue my father and the others."

"You can't rescue them by yourself. The Ice Warriors would simply make you a prisoner again."

Lanawe laughed sharply. "Let me get my hands on a neuron gun and a personal deflector and we'll see about that!" She looked toward the jetboat. "Do you want to help me, Tal?"

Tal looked in the direction she did, but he had to admit none of this made any sense to him. However, there was one thing of which he was sure: he had known this girl, Lanawe Palmerin, before—or had known someone very closely related to her.

There was such a strong sense of familiarity about her that Tal was visibly relaxed, even though the lance was still leveled at his stomach. Somehow he felt sure that Lanawe would not harm him.

"What is it you want me to help you do?" he asked.

"I'm going to open the shuttlecraft hatch. There's a warrior inside. We're going to have to . . . take care of him.

I've got to get the weapons that are in there."

"If these weapons are so strong, how do you know the Ice Warrior won't have them ready to use against you?"

Lanawe considered how to answer that. She finally said, "Well, they're locked up and hidden. I don't believe he can find them."

Tal looked at her carefully. There was a glint to her blue eyes and a set to her jaw that struck a very responsive chord; but one that he could not quite put his finger on. Suddenly he laughed.

"You are crazy to think of rescuing them yourself, but I will help you." He laughed again. "Maybe I'm crazy, too. Come on." He headed toward the shuttlecraft.

Lanawe had to trot to keep up with his long strides and in a moment they were standing outside the now contracted hatch. The Ice Warrior was watching them through the port—had, in fact, been watching throughout their entire encounter.

The trapped warrior had not taken his bow and arrows into the jetboat with him, but he did have his stone knife and this he brandished at them.

"Can you . . . handle him?" asked Lanawe, looking uncertainly at Tal.

"I can handle him. How do you plan to get inside?"

By way of answer, the girl touched a hidden button and the hatch dilated soundlessly. It beckoned wide and inviting and dark. Tal hesitated.

"Are you going in or not?" Lanawe demanded.

"I'm going in," Tal assured her. He studied the situation for another moment, then backed away several steps. He hesitated just a second longer, then took two running strides and sprang through the hatch, landing well inside the jetboat.

The Ice Warrior, who had been poised to seize him as he entered, was utterly startled. Not so startled, however, that he did not launch himself at Tal immediately.

They came together, each grabbing the other's knife wrist, and braced their strength against one another in the narrow aisle between the passengers' acceleration couches. Each was a big, strong man and each was equally matched by the other.

Then Tal hooked his foot behind his opponent's heel and shoved him hard. The Ice Warrior fell backward, tumbling over the bloody corpse of Varel. Tal leaped for him, but the Ice Warrior was on his feet in an instant. In that same instant, however, his foot slipped on the girl's blood spilled on the deck plates. Before he could recover, Tal had him. Two corpses lay on the deck.

Tal turned to find Lanawe opening the arms locker.

"Here!" she cried, tossing him a wide belt set with strange ornaments. "Put that on."

Tal looked it all over and fingered it for several seconds before he shrugged and buckled it around his lean waist. It fitted snugly but comfortably over his parka and hooded cloak.

"Why are we wearing these?" he asked Lanawe, as she buckled a similar belt around her waist.

"They're personal deflector screens," she explained. Then, at his blank look, she elaborated. "They're sort of like a shield. They keep weapons from hurting you in a fight."

"But they aren't wide enough to be any real protection," protested Tal. "Unless a warrior happened to hit one of the little jewels on the front, it would serve as no protection at all." He thought the girl was being a bit foolish. Shandor knew women did not understand weapons at all.

"Let me show you." She stepped up to Tal and touched a button that looked like an ornament to him. Instantly he felt the briefest tingle from head to toe. He started involuntarily and stepped back, holding his arms out and looking at himself in alarm to see what was causing the tingle that he could feel even through his furs. So far as he could tell by looking, everything was the same as it had been.

"What did you do?" he cried. "What do I feel?"

While he was distracted by the strange and unaccustomed tingling, Lanawe had seized his spear from where it leaned against the bulkhead. "Tal," she said quietly and, when he turned toward her, she jabbed it with all her strength straight into his stomach!

Only it never touched his stomach.

The bronze tip stopped exactly two and one-half centimeters from the fur parka. It stopped abruptly, as if Lanawe had shoved it against a solid wall. The parka was never touched.

Tal's reactions were trigger-quick. He seized the lance and tore it out of her hands. He sprang for her like a hunting panther, but Lanawe had anticipated this reaction. One slim finger activated her deflector and when Tal's hands closed on her throat, he received a sharp, mildly painful electric shock at every point where their shields touched.

They both cried out and sprang apart. Tal looked horror struck. What was happening to him was so far beyond his experience that he found it difficult to cope. He was in over his head.

"Let me explain, Tal!" cried Lanawe, reaching out toward him but not touching him. "These belts are personal deflector screens. Nothing larger than air molecules can penetrate them. That's the reason the spear failed to hurt you. That's why you got a shock when you touched me; our screens interacted. You're safe from any weapon on Earth so long as your screen is activated."

Tal slowly regained his composure as she explained to him what was happening.

"You felt the *thrust* of the spear—the deflectors don't cancel out inertia—but you weren't hurt. A really strong blow—like from a club or an axe—might knock you down, but no actual damage would be done by the weapon itself. If a bear or a tiger grabbed you, the screen would protect you from their fangs and claws, but you'd probably be killed from the battering around. The deflector screens will *work* against such dangers, but they aren't really designed for them."

Tal examined himself, and Lanawe, but so far as he could see they looked the same—except for the belts each of them wore.

"The personal deflectors were designed to protect from a neuron gun, which blasts the nerve centers but has virtually no impact force. It's an ideal defense against that, though the Ilrik's disrupters soon tore through them!" She ended bitterly. "Do you feel okay now? Not mad at me anymore? Well, push that red button there—no, that one. Now—your deflector screen is off."

"How do I . . . make it work again?" asked Tal, obviously

intrigued.

"Push that red button in and turn it slightly. Like that," she said approvingly. Tal looked very pleased when the tingle reasserted itself. He deactivated the screen, activated it again, deactivated it—

"That's enough!" said Lanawe. "The energy cells don't last forever. Here, take a neuron gun." She handed him a pistol that tapered to a silver cone at the muzzle. There was no opening for a projectile. A knob was set on the very top of the pistol and a long, narrow gauge beside it was graduated in almost infinitesimal markings. There was no trigger as such, but a button was located approximately where the thumb would fall if the pistol were held in the right hand.

"What is this?" asked Tal, examining it curiously. His experience with the deflector screen had given him a new respect for the girl's weapons.

"This is a neuron gun," explained Lanawe, demonstrating with her own pistol. "You activate it *this* way—" She twisted the knob and a light began to glow under the graduated gauge. "You can set it for any force from mild vibration to kill. The brighter the light, the stronger the beam. The red strip is your charge. When you're down to *this* point, the weapon requires recharging. You fire it by pressing this button with your thumb."

Tal looked interested. "Is this one of the weapons that can kill at a distance?" he asked, weighing the neuron gun in one hand.

Lanawe was startled. "Why . . . yes, you could say that. But what do you know about weapons like that?" She looked at him narrowly.

"I know the Ancients had them," he said. "Fen Melton told me about them."

"Who is Fen Melton?"

"He . . . was someone I knew. Do these weapons kill thousands of warriors and cause explosions and fires?"

"No. They kill, or disable, only one person at a time, and there is no physical damage. They beam sound waves along the nerve endings and affect the nerve centers. That's why we call them neuron guns."

"And this bird—" Tal gestured at the shuttlecraft. "It flies through the air?"

"Yes." Lanawe was the one intrigued now. "You seem to know quite a lot about us."

Tal shrugged. "Fen Melton told me of such things. Besides, this skybird wasn't here when I escaped in the storm last night, but it was this morning. The only way it could have gotten here was to fly." He shrugged again. "You must be one of the Ancients."

Lanawe took a deep breath and considered for a moment. "You . . . might say that. Or, more nearly, I'm a direct descendant of those you call the Ancients." She hesitated. "I'd like to meet this Fen Melton."

"He is dead. The Ice Warriors took his body, and that of Jan Heron, when your party was captured."

"And that reminds me," said Lanawe. "We've got to get on with our rescue. Here—" She handed him several more neuron guns and several spare deflector screens. "We'll take these and follow the Ice Warriors, as you call them. I think they're in for a real surprise!"

"Will you fly the skybird after them?" Tal was obviously hoping she would say yes.

"I'm sorry to disappoint you," she told him, with a short laugh. "But I'm afraid the shuttlecraft would destroy our element of surprise. I will take this, though." She fished a portable infrared scanner out of its rack. "It will make trailing them easier and will also prevent them from ambushing us."

As they set out on the trail of the Ice Warriors, now almost an hour old, Lanawe explained how the infrared scanner worked. She explained how the blue dots that appeared on the eight-centimeter-square screen were footprints whose body heat was retained against the snow.

It was soon evident to Tal that Lanawe felt the same sense of familiarity around him that he experienced around her. Her attitude, mannerisms, and way of touching him as she spoke all indicated that she felt totally at ease with him.

Lanawe herself wondered about this. She caught herself reacting to Tal with a sense of familiarity that she would never have used with Alun Akobar. She had to remind herself that he was an ignorant, savage barbarian who had already killed three men in the hour or so that she had known him and had bodily attacked her. Yet, to her, Tal seemed like someone she had known for a lifetime, like an old lover whom she had not seen in far, far too long. It was a very strange sensation and Lanawe did not even pretend to understand it—but she found it most interesting.

Suddenly, the images on the screen demanded all her attention.

"Activate your shield!" she hissed, and Tal hastened to comply. This time, the strange tingling felt very reassuring to him.

"They are to our left," said Lanawe, swinging the scanner back and forth. "There are two of them and they are between four and five meters away." She indicated the direction.

And from that direction the arrow came whistling to bounce harmlessly off Tal's chest. The momentum of the impact stung a little, but no injury was done. He laughed out loud at his sudden invincibility.

"Watch this," said Lanawe. She twisted the knob atop the neuron gun about halfway, leveled the weapon in the direction from which the arrow had flown, and depressed the button with her thumb.

There was a soft, high-pitched hum that set Tal's teeth on edge and suddenly a snow bank ahead of him erupted into life. The Ice Warrior sprang up, clutching his head. He shrieked once and fell backward into the snow, his body jerking and twisting.

The second Ice Warrior got off an arrow that bounced harmlessly off Lanawe's screen before the girl cut him down with her neuron gun.

Tal was absolutely fascinated by the weapon.

"These are wonderful!" he said, looking from the pistol to the dead warriors. "The strongest warrior could not escape one of these. From how far away will they kill?"

"They'll kill at a range up to ten meters. They'll stun as far away as thirty meters. They won't do much at all beyond that."

"If there is another ambush, I wish to use the . . . neuron gun," Tal had a little trouble with the unfamiliar term.

"Bloodthirsty, aren't you?" remarked Lanawe; then, when Tal frowned uncomprehendingly, she said, "Never mind.

116

Come on. And I promise: the next ambush is yours."

But there were no more Ice Warriors lying in wait before them. They trudged along for endless hours, never seeming to gain on the moving war party ahead of them. They stopped briefly and Lanawe gave Tal a thick, pulpy cube from a sealed packet in her tunic.

"Eat this," she said. "It contains all the vitamins, minerals, and protein you'll need for the next twelve hours. Besides it's very filling."

Tal chewed on the cube and found it very sweet and a trifle tangy. He thought it very good. Far superior, in his opinion, to the dried beef on which he had been subsisting. He decided to try for a little information.

"Where is this Aryor you come from?"

"Far away," Lanawe said. "Farther than any man of your tribe has ever been."

"Did you come in the skybird all the distance?"

"Not precisely. We came in another vessel, even bigger; the skybird was inside with us. We used it, only after we got here, to explore the area."

"Where is your other vessel?"

Lanawe hesitated, but she decided to tell him the full truth.

"It's up in the sky," she said, indicating the direction with one gloved finger. "Above the atmosphere. Above the rings."

Tal was silent for a moment and Lanawe suspected he was doubting her story, then he said that which led her to decide she had completely underestimated his natural intelligence:

"Is your home then on another world in the sky? One of the little lights that we see at night?"

"W—Why yes, it is. What do you know of other worlds in the sky?"

"Not much," Tal admitted. "Only old legends." He took a sip of water from the canteen Lanawe proffered. "Come now. The trail grows cold."

For the balance of the afternoon Lanawe puzzled over his remarks, but she did not question him. Her full attention was needed for tracking the Ice Warriors.

It was less than an hour short of dusk when they reached the Ice Warriors' village.

Like the Farades' village, it was surrounded by an ice wall.

The buildings themselves, however, were quite different from the Farades' *yurts*. These buildings were fashioned from great blocks of ice like the wall. They were curved into rounded domes with smaller, rounded entrances that were little more than tunnels. Flues were formed into the tops of each and Tal was amazed to see smoke emerging from houses built of ice.

"Igloos," muttered Lanawe. "I'll be damned!"

Tal said nothing, but carefully scanned as much of the village as he could see. He was evaluating it with a warrior's eye.

"There is only one gate," he said, at length. "I see two warriors in that ice tower. Since the wall is curved, they have only the one watch. There are no others on guard."

"Yes, there are," contradicted Lanawe, indicating the infrared scanner. "There are two more who make an erratic swing around the wall on the outside, moving in opposite directions. One should emerge to your left in a moment—*there!* See him? The other one will come around from the right."

"That device is wonderful!" Tal enthused. "No warrior could hide from it. Your people must be the greatest warriors on your world."

"No," said Lanawe, bitterly. "No, we're not." She shook her head briskly, as if to clear away the memory of the Ilriks' screaming death ships. "Let's move a little closer. When it gets dark we'll take them."

Tal wished for a beclouded night, but Shandor was not with him. The sky was clear and cloudless and the shifting ringlight made the snowscape almost as light as day.

"We might as well go," said Lanawe. "The two outer guards are on the far side of the village. You've got the white snowsuit on, so get as close to the gate as you can. I've shown you how to operate the neuron gun, so take out the two guards in the tower. I'll take care of the other two while you get the gate open. Okay?" She sounded almost cheerful.

Tal nodded grimly and activated his deflector shield. Moving as silently as the shadow of a shadow, he crossed the ice. When he was less than a spear cast from the tower he halted and leveled his neuron gun. Almost he wished for a lance, but he depressed the button and heard the high-pitched hum.

One Ice Warrior toppled from the tower without a sound, but the second managed to get out one lusty yell before Tal's alien weapon cut him down.

Then Tal was at the gate, hammering frantically at the lock to force it open. He heard Lanawe's neuron gun hum behind him and heard the soft hiss and thump of an arrow bounding ineffectually off her shield. He wheeled, as the gates swung open, and he and she both shot the second outer guard.

In a moment they were through the gate and rushing into the village.

A hail of arrows fell around them, stinging like wasps as they bounded harmlessly off their screens. Both their neuron guns kept up a steady, deadly humming and the Ice Warriors melted back before them.

The prisoners were soon evident, herded together with their hands tied, in the center of the village. The frozen corpses of the two Farades and the corpse of the dead Aryorian were there, too; as were half a dozen cooking pots attesting to the fact, which Tal had already guessed, that the Ice Warriors were cannibals.

"Lan!" shouted Dr. Palmerin. "Over here! Quickly!"

Lanawe and Tal moved virtually without resistance toward the prisoners. The Ice Warriors, demoralized by the fact that their weapons had no effect upon the two, and routed by the death that struck so swiftly and without a weapon cast, broke and fled. In a matter of moments the village was deserted except for the prisoners and the two rescuers.

"Are you all right, Dad?" asked the girl, as she freed her father from his bonds. Tal, having deactivated his deflector, was doing the same for some of the other prisoners.

"I'm okay now," the old man said, then he looked quizzically at her companion. "I see you've made an acquaintance. Would you do the honors?"

"Certainly. Dad, this is Tal Mikar, lance warrior of Thongor. Tal, this is Dr. Fel Palmerin, chief of our people from Aryor, and my father."

"I am honored, great chief," said Tal, with grave dignity. "Your daughter is a credit to yourself and to your people. She is a fit mate for a warrior."

"She won't be a mate for any warrior here!" put in a hot, angry voice and Lanawe said: "Tal, this is Alun Akobar."

The two young men stood facing each other. Tal was taller than Alun and wider in the shoulders, but Akobar outweighed him by at least nine kilos. They made an interesting contrast: Alun blond and bronzed, elegant in his form-fitting black jump suit with the scarlet triangle and the golden sunburst on the chest; and Tal, shaggy and barbaric, with his fur hood thrown back from his rudely bobbed black hair.

Then, instinctively, Lanawe put her arm through Tal's and said, "Let's get back to the shuttlecraft. We have lots to do."

And even as the former prisoners were buckling on the deflector screens Lanawe had brought and were checking the charges in their neuron guns, they did not fail to notice the gesture she made nor the familiarity with which Tal accepted it, as if it were completely natural. Dr. Palmerin wondered at it and whatever Alun Akobar thought he kept to himself.

Alytha was frightened.

She had climbed a tree once and peered along her back trail. There, coming as swift as a pack of hungry hounds, were a dozen lance warriors of Thongor. She dropped back to the game trail she was following and fled along it like the very wind.

But she knew she could not elude them. A lance warrior could track a snake across bare rock. And she knew she could not outdistance them. A lance warrior who could not run for a day and a night and a day without rest would never last among the Thongors. And already Alytha knew she was nearing the absolute end of her strength while her pursuers had not yet even begun to sweat.

As she ran, she tried desperately to think of a plan of escape, but nothing occurred to her. There was no hope for her so far as she could see. She was destined to be recaptured.

So lost in thought was Alytha that when she rounded the curve, she almost ran headlong into the pack of wild dogs that were tearing at the bloody, unrecognizable haunch of something that had fallen into the quicksand which lay to one side of the trail at that point—a place known locally as "Devil's Slough."

The dogs wheeled, snapping and snarling, and several started toward the girl, bellies down, fangs bared. It was that movement that gave Alytha her mad plan.

Without stopping to even consider what she was doing—if she had hesitated, her courage would have failed her—Alytha uttered a piercing shriek that she knew the trailing Thongors could hear and ran headlong at the wild dogs.

Her shriek and her sudden charge were so unexpected the dogs shrank back momentarily and in that moment Alytha reached the bloody haunch on which they had been feeding and sprang like a panther for a liana that looped down over the Devil's Slough.

Breathing a prayer to Shandor that the vine would hold her weight, Alytha went up it hand over hand to an overhanging limb. There she put the second part of her plan into action. With the dagger she had used to slay Jad Thor, she hacked off a lock of her soft brown hair and let it fall onto the haunch to which the wild dogs had now returned.

It was only then that she discovered that her loin cloth had fallen off as she had scrambled madly up the vine. It now lay, half buried in the quicksand of the Devil's Slough by the edge of the trail.

She had not planned that, but it added the perfect final touch. The Thongors should draw the inevitable conclusion. They would consider Alytha dead and so she would be forgotten.

Naked as the day she was born, Alytha scrambled through the branches and came to the ground some distance away from the trail. Resolutely she strode off into the forest. There would be time enough to fashion garments when she reached her destination. She was going back to the little valley where she and Tal had made their camp. She was going home.

TWELVE

Tal slept comfortably inside the shuttlecraft and awoke to the smell of breakfast cooking in the small galley. It reminded him of how very hungry he was.

They had taken a few quick minutes to bury the bodies of Fen Melton, Jan Heron, and their own fellow crew member—after Lanawe had charred them beyond recognition with a thermite bomb to prevent the Ice Warriors disinterring them and eating them later—then they had headed back toward the jetboat.

It had taken over half a day for Tal and Lanawe to reach the Ice Warriors' village, but they had been following an uncertain trail and continually scanning for possible ambushes. They returned to the shuttlecraft in little more than three hours.

The four bodies there, Varel and the three Ice Warriors, were buried after they had been charred too badly to serve as food. The mess aboard the shuttlecraft was cleaned up.

Alun Akobar made it very plain that he did not care for Tal, but Tal took no offense. He judged that Akobar was not enough of a warrior to pose any real threat to him and he also knew that Akobar's own people were not greatly impressed by his blustering.

Tal also noticed that Alun tried at every opportunity to give the impression that Lanawe was his woman, but Lanawe made it indelibly plain that she was no one's woman. Tal found this little byplay between them somewhat amusing.

All the crew members took to their reclining couches and prepared to sleep the balance of the night. Lanawe offered to help Tal make himself comfortable in one of the two empty couches, but Tal politely declined.

"Sleep better on floor," he said and, suiting action to words, he curled up in the corner not far from Lanawe's pilot's chair. He drew a fold of his fur cloak around him and appeared to go to sleep almost immediately.

He was awake long enough, however, to hear Lanawe and her father exchange several words in a totally alien language that he did not understand at all. He was shrewd enough to deduce that they were most likely talking about him, but he had no idea what they said.

What they said was in Aryorian and Dr. Palmerin asked his daughter what she planned to do with their barbaric friend.

"Tomorrow, I'm going to tell him about Shara Vralon and the Eternity Stone. Then I'm going to explain why we're here and see if he can help us in any way."

Dr. Palmerin lifted his eyebrows and quirked his mouth. "Well," he said, "we've got to start somewhere, I suppose."

Awake now, with the smell of hot food in the air, Tal wondered again what the two had said about him the night before.

Lanawe joined him where he squatted against a bulkhead. She had two trays heaped up with reconstituted eggs, synthetic sausage, and slices of bread substitute. In a fitted receptacle molded into each tray set a steaming refresher cup.

"Let's eat, Tal," she said, giving him her enchanting smile as she handed him his tray. "We've got a big day ahead of us."

"What is this?" Tal asked, frowing suspiciously at the refresher cup.

"It's good. It's hot, but it's good. Try it. Like this." Lanawe demonstrated how to blow on the steaming beverage and then sipped it, making smacking sounds with her lips to indicate its tastiness.

Tal tentatively copied her, then raised his eyebrows in pleased surprise as the stimulant sent new vigor and alertness coursing through him. He fell to with a will and proved himself an excellent trencherman.

"Tal," Lanawe began almost hesitantly. "I wonder if you

could help us."

"What help do you seek?" he asked, suspecting, from her tone, that she was leading up to whatever she and her father had discussed the night before.

"Well . . . we're searching for something—we're not sure exactly what—and since this is your country, not ours, we thought—we hoped—you might help us find it."

Tal considered. "You have two problems," he finally said. "One: if you are not sure what you seek, I could not help you find it. Two: this is not my country. I was brought here a slave to the Farades. My country is far and far away, in the mountains." He gestured vaguely to indicate direction.

Lanawe was perplexed. "You were a *slave*? There is slavery here on Earth?"

"Why, yes," said Tal, looking surprised at her reaction. "Isn't there slavery on your world?"

"Not till the Ilriks came," she said, bitterly.

"Who are the Ilriks?"

"I will explain in a moment. But first, tell me how you came to be a slave here so far from your home."

In a few terse sentences Tal told her of his love for Alytha, daughter of Man Tavis, and of her love for him. He told her how they fled the tribe of Thongors to become Outcasts. He told her of their lovely little valley, where Alytha now waited alone, and of how the Arcobanes captured him and made him a slave. He told of how he was sold to the Farades and of how he came to be alone upon the ice fields after the Ice Warriors attacked Fen Melton's expedition.

Lanawe was silent for several minutes after he had finished. They were done eating and, with refresher cups to sip, had moved to the pilot's and copilot's chairs for relative privacy. Outside, the ice was being cleared, under armed guard, so the shuttlecraft could lift off. Alun Akobar was working on his project, though he spent at least half his time glaring through one or another of the portals at Tal and Lanawe. The Aryorian girl seemed very pensive.

"You've had a hard time of it, Tal," she said gently. "What do you plan to do now?"

"Go back to the valley and find Alytha." He hesitated, and shot her a quick, appraising glance from his volcanic blue eyes. "Could this skybird fly me to my valley?"

"I'm sure it could," Lanawe told him. "And, if you help us, we'll be happy to take you there."

"Help you," Tal echoed. "You mean help you find this thing you are seeking that you don't know what it is?"

"Yes, that's what I mean. Let me explain, Tal. You asked about the Ilriks. Well, they're part of the explanation, too. It's a long story and a tragic one. But, first, to put it in a perspective you can understand, let me ask you something. You asked me once if I were one of the Ancients. Tell me what you know of these Ancients."

Tal shrugged. "Not much. My people have legends about the great warriors of the past, stories of men flying like birds from one great wizard-city to another, children's stories of great boats that flew up to the points of light in the sky. Shandor knows these are all fantasy, though.

"Fen Melton told me the Ancients really had machines like this skybird and had other machines that could go underwater like fish. He told me they also had terrible weapons that killed thousands of people at a single cast. These weapons killed at great distances and caused explosions and fires. Fen Melton said that with these weapons the Ancients destroyed themselves and all their secrets."

"Fen Melton was correct," Lanawe asserted. "Now let me tell you *my* story, Tal.

"Long, long ago, more than a thousand years ago, Earth was the center of a rapidly expanding solar system wide empire. The blazing heat of Venus, the dead Moon, the frozen wastes of Mars, the asteroids—all had been explored and settled, by miners if not by colonists. Scientists were building a starship. It would take humans to another star, the longest journey in our history.

"Lan Regas was the ruler of Earth. He loved a girl named Shara Vralon, who loved him, too. Lan Regas was a tyrant— a terrible, cruel man who extorted high taxes, tortured captured enemies, and ordered whole cities leveled to the ground. The longer he reigned, the more terrible he became.

"Lan Regas was the master of something called the Science of Infrastatics. Even today we do not fully comprehend what this science was, how it operated, or what it would do; but we do know that it gave Lan Regas more power than any human has ever wielded, before or since. He had almost the power of a god.

"Shara Vralon opposed Lan's cruelties. Gradually she came to oppose everything about him. They who had been lovers were now enemies. Shara led an armed revolt against Lan. She stole some of his own Infrastatic weapons to use against him.

"This is the war which Fen Melton described to you. It was the most destructive event in all Earth's history. Whole continents disappeared, new ones were forced up from beneath the sea, the Moon itself was smashed into rubble and this rubble became the rings which surround Earth today. In fact, if our instrument readings are valid, Earth's magnetic poles were reversed and her orbit was severaly altered. This changed her climate drastically. For instance, all this—" Lanawe waved her hand at the ice outside the jetboat—"was once a tropical zone. At the North and South Poles, where tropical jungles grow now, there used to be only ice and snow.

"At last, seeing that the war was hopeless and that Earth was doomed to revert to barbarism, Shara, who was a scientist herself, stole the newly completed starship, the *X-97*, the only ship of its kind in the universe. With ten thousand of her devoted followers—all that could be packed in the *X-97*—she fled Earth and set course for Alpha Centauri. With them, they took only one Infrastatic weapon: it was called the Chalice of Time. They took the one weapon . . . and a legend.

"The *X-97* reached Alpha Centauri at last. They found no habitable planets, so they went on. They explored Aldebaran's solar system, among others. At length they reached Aryor, which orbits a star not even visible in Earth's skies. Aryor became their home.

"Those who accompanied Shara Vralon on this odyssey were sturdy, hardworking types and the colony on Aryor prospered, grew, and at last spread over three separate solar systems. They were a peaceful, nonaggressive people much given to scientific research.

"Then, without warning, the Ilrik barbarians swept in from the rim of the galaxy. They are not human, though they are humanoid, and all things that live are their enemies. They swept over our outer colonies like fire burning up dead grass. None of our weapons could withstand them. Long ago we switched to the deadly but nondestructive neuron guns. These stun the Ilriks, but do not kill them. This had led us to theorize that the Ilriks have a different nervous system than humans'.

"On the other hand, their disrupters cut through our personal deflector screens like a knife through butter. One after another of our worlds fell before them till soon only Aryor was left free."

"Why didn't you use the Infrastatic weapon against them?" asked Tal. "I thought you said these weapons were the most powerful ever devised."

"I'll explain: the Chalice of Time is essentially only *half* a weapon. Lan Regas used his science to create something he called the Eternity Stone. We deduce it must have been what was called a Doomsday weapon, because the legend Shara Vralon took to Aryor said that if the Eternity Stone were placed within the Chalice of Time, a force would be unloosed that no power in the universe could withstand.

"That's why we're back on Earth, Tal. We returned in the old starship *X-97* to obtain a weapon we can use to defeat the Ilriks. We've brought the Chalice of Time back with us. We want you to help us find the Eternity Stone."

THIRTEEN

Tal tried not to let his fear show as Lanawe adjusted controls on the instrument panel before them and as the thrusters built up pressure like a million screaming demons behind them.

Dr. Palmerin had graciously relinquished the copilot's seat to Tal and Lanawe was preparing the jetboat for lift-off. Tal had at first objected to the light nylon safety webbing, but when Lanawe assured him it was genuinely necessary he acquiesced.

Tal did not try to understand his feelings toward the dark-haired, blue-eyed beauty. He was not in love with her, but the physical attraction was very strong. And not just the physical attraction: it was the sense of having known her before that intrigued him so much. There were certain gestures Lanawe made, certain mannerisms that were intrinsically a part of her, yet were so eerily familiar to Tal that he knew exactly what she would do and just how she would do it.

Like the way she had of cocking her head slightly and lifting one eyebrow as she listened to something interesting. How he had known she did that, Tal did not know, but when she had reacted with just that expressive mannerism, as he told her that he had indeed heard of the Eternity Stone, he had known at once exactly how it would be.

"There are legends among my people," he had said. "Mor Haskin, our shaman, has spoken of the Eternity Stone. He called it the Accursed of Shandor. I do not know if he could tell you more of it than that, but if we can fly this skybird to the Thongor village you can ask him."

"I thought you wanted to return to your valley and Alytha." Tal was not experienced enough in the ways of women to recognize the signs, but Lanawe Palmerin was physically attracted to him even more powerfully than he was to her. She did not have the memory of another love to offset her urgings.

"I do," Tal had said promptly. "The only way I could direct you to the Thongor village would be to try to find my way back to the Farade village, from there to Rendezvous, from there to the Arcobane village, from there to Alytha's valley, and from there to Thongor. So we can pick up Alytha on our way to search for your weapon."

"Here we go, Tal!" Lanawe warned, as the jetboat lifted off in a slow, steady climb.

Tal blanched and his knuckles whitened on the arms of the copilot's chair, but he gave no other sign of fear as he felt the vertiginous thrust of acceleration push him deeper into the foam cushions.

Lanawe deliberately held the shuttlecraft in a slow, gentle trajectory. She was capable of standing the little stub-winged craft on her tail or of spinning her in a stomach-wrenching bank that few eagles could duplicate, but she sensed how frightened Tal was at his very first flight and so she made it as gentle and as easy as she could.

Gentle and easy was not how Alun Akobar made it when Lanawe, after consulting with her father, had told the other Aryorians her plan, shortly before the lift-off.

"How do you know you can trust this—savage?" Akobar had demanded. "How do you know he is not trying to lure us into some kind of trap? What do you know about him, anyway?"

"I know he saved my life and helped save yours!" Lanawe had retorted hotly. "And he's given us a lead on the Eternity Stone. I say trust him!"

"And I say no!" Both Alun and Lanawe were speaking Aryorian so Tal could not understand their words, but their voice tones, their expressions, and their gestures conveyed the message very clearly.

"Perhaps Alun Akobar and I should take a walk upon the

snow," suggested Tal gently. "I think, if we did, there would be no more objections." There was a glimmer like hard steel in his cold blue eyes.

"I'm not going anywhere with you!" Akobar had insisted. "You want to kill me—you all heard him! You want to kill me so you can have Lan for yourself! Well, I'm not going anywhere with you!"

"Then you'll stay here by yourself!" Dr. Palmerin had said. "Because we're going to Thongor to try and get information about the Eternity Stone."

Alun Akobar had not said anything else, but his face had been dark with fury. He was very careful, however, to keep well away from Tal Mikar. It was not exactly that he was afraid of the tall barbarian, but there was something about the lithe, pantherish warrior with the cold blue eyes that hinted that Tal had no civilized compunction about killing. He would slay Alun Akobar as quickly as look at him.

Now the shuttlecraft was hurtling through the cold clear air at the height of a kilometer off the ground. Tal was absolutely fascinated by the view. The horizon had rolled back so far to his right that he could see, dim in the distance, where the ice fields gave way to the gray-brown tundra. And ahead of them, hazy in the sky, hung the steam that could only come from the water that burns, which marked the site of the Farade village.

Tal pointed it out to Lanawe and explained what it was. In only a few minutes the jetboat flashed overhead and the girl brought it around in a series of wide banking curves while Tal got his bearings.

He had not realized how different everything looked from the air. It took him several minutes to get himself oriented in his mind—while the dark-skinned Farades howled and brandished their spears threateningly at this apparition from the sky—then he gestured definitely toward the distant tundra.

"That way lies Rendezvous," he said, and Lanawe leaned into the joystick, sending the shuttlecraft off in the direction indicated.

He had her slow their speed to about a hundred and sixty kilometers per hour so that he could scan the country below them for landmarks. This backtracking from the sky was something totally new in his experience.

Then the prairie, which had long ceased to be tundra, rolled up to break like surf against the green wall of the forest. There, in a cove formed by two arms of the woods encroaching out into the blowing grass, Tal recognized Rendezvous.

Again Lanawe circled the jetboat while Tal considered directions. It was harder here, because from above the rolling green forest was simply one great mass of greenery, tangled unrecognizably. Nothing that Tal might have observed along the trail would be of any use to him with his new perspective.

But then, just as he was about to suggest that Lanawe land, their very height provided the help he needed. In the distance, across the forest, Tal saw a cliff face of rotted granite and recognized it as the last campsite before Rendezvous.

By now, Tal had gotten the idea of how to backtrack by air, so as the jetboat circled there, Tal looked for the stream that had been their first camp. In only a few minutes scanning he found it.

Here was where the offworld science came to his aid. As they circled over the stream, Tal indicated the general direction of the Arcobane village and Lanawe snapped on the infrared scanner—a much larger version of the model they had carried when tracking the Ice Warriors.

Soon the heat seeking sensors zeroed in on the cooking fires and massed body heat of the Arcobane village.

The Arcobanes reacted exactly as had the Farades when Lanawe circled their village. For a minute Tal's eyes narrowed as he remembered Vaj Durmo, then he indicated the direction they should take and they set out for Alytha's valley.

In a short time they reached the aspen grove where Tal's captors had camped the last night before they reached their village. From here on, the country was rolling blue mountains, and Tal felt that he had come home.

Provisions had been broken out and they had eaten about the time they reached the site of Rendezvous. It was falling dusk as Lanawe gently set the shuttlecraft down in the valley where Tal and Alytha had thought to make their home.

"Alytha! Don't be afraid! It's Tal! I've come back! Alytha?" But the cave was empty when Tal reached it, except for a family of foxes who had made their den there, telling him that it had been abandoned for some time.

Their small store of provisions had been broken into, by animals, not men, and spare traps and a war spear Tal had made still leaned against one wall. But Alytha was not there.

The only traces of cooking fires were old. There were no fishing lines set. No traps baited and ready. No sign that anyone had been in the valley for weeks, perhaps months.

Tal was utterly forlorn. He walked disconsolately along the stream and through the woods, calling Alytha's name pitifully, futilely. Tears ran open and unashamed down his cheeks.

The Aryorians were forgotten. The Eternity Stone was out of his mind. His only thought was that Alytha was gone.

Through all his weeks of captivity and slavery, two thoughts had sustained him: the image of Alytha safe in this valley and the knowledge that one day he would return to her here. Now he had. And Alytha was gone.

"Perhaps it's the wrong valley, Tal," suggested Lanawe softly, coming up behind him in the darkness. "Remember, from the air things look different than they do on the ground."

"It's the right valley," said Tal, in a broken voice. "It's the right valley. Everything's here—our camp, our supplies, our traps. Everything except Alytha. Only Alytha is gone." His wide shoulders shook with sobs.

Lanawe reacted instinctively. She put her arms around Tal and held him close against her and stroked his shaggy head with one slim, white hand. She kissed his cheek and his eyes and his mouth and whispered soft words of reassurance and comfort.

And as she held him she marveled, in one part of her mind, at how *familiar* his body felt in her arms—as if she had held him before, but long and long ago. And the desire for him was like a hot flame burning in her loins, a flame she could scarcely contain.

For his part, Tal let himself be comforted. This time he did not puzzle over the aching sense of familiarity Lanawe bred in him. This time it did not even occur to him. Alytha was gone and all his senses were tuned to that grief. Lanawe's ministrations were accepted, but not responded to. Under the circumstances, she had not really expected them to be.

A few yards away, standing by one of the huge evergreens, Alun Akobar watched them and in his eyes smoldered the fire of a hatred that only blood could quench.

They spent the night in the valley. Everyone except Tal slept in the shuttlecraft. Tal went back to the cave, but he did not sleep. Long into the night Lanawe, watching from a port, saw his lonely silhouette against the sky, illuminated by the shifting ringlight.

At dawn, only the grim set of his square jaw and the dark circles under his red-rimmed eyes bespoke his grief of the night before.

After a hearty breakfast, which Tal hardly touched, the jetboat lifted off and swung away in the direction of the Thongor village.

Tal was impressed anew by the wonders of the offworlders' science. The journey that had taken him and Alytha many days of bitter marching now flashed by in an hour or two. Well before noon the Thongor village lay below them, its palisaded tepees surrounded by growing fields. With an ache in his throat, Tal looked at the ironwood grove where he had so often trysted with Alytha in happier days.

The women who worked in the fields outside the palisade scattered and ran for the gate as the shuttlecraft swooped in, barely a dozen meters in the air. Lance warriors gathered from all sides, their eyes on the sky monster, their mouths open in fierce war cries the people inside the jetboat could not hear. Among them, Tal saw Sar Lon, lance lord of Thongor, Man Tavis, Alytha's father, Mor Haskin, the shaman, Sol Makor, the singer, and others whom he had known, admired, and loved throughout his life. These were his people! And Outcast though he had become, Tal felt his heart swell with pride when he saw them standing there brave and unflinching before the sky monster, even though it was obvious the palisade would be inadequate protection should the flying thing attack them.

"Land here, near the gate," he directed, and Lanawe brought the jetboat down precisely where he indicated. All the Aryorians crowded to the ports on the side next to the village to stare warily at the villagers who crowded the palisade to stare warily at them.

Tal took a personal deflector from the arms locker and buckled it around his lean waist. He had to tighten it considerably since he no longer wore his thick fur parka.

"Let me go out first and talk to them," he said. "They are my people and they will know me." He looked at Lanawe. "When I signal, you come out. They will see that you are a girl and so will not fear you. But do wear your deflector screen!" he admonished her.

Then he turned to Dr. Palmerin. "You come out next, sir. As the leader of your people you can negotiate directly with Sar Lon. After you two have talked—only after you have talked should the others come out. My people are very suspicious of strangers. And all of you"—he took in everyone by his raised voice—" wear your deflectors and carry your weapons, *but make no move unless threatened.* Understood?"

Everyone nodded assent and Tal activated the deflector screen, feeling the protective tingle run from head to foot.

He had deliberately instructed Lanawe to land with the hatch *away* from the palisade, so that when he dilated it to emerge, no warrior could cast a weapon inside.

A great shout went up from the Thongors as Tal stepped around the nose of the shuttlecraft and the warriors recognized him.

"Outcast!" screamed Man Tavis and hurled his heavy lance at Tal.

Tal instinctively dodged, but not quickly enough. The war lance hit his chest squarely over his right lung and bounced harmlessly off to clatter on the ground.

Tal was staggered by the force of the blow, but otherwise he was not harmed. The Thongors were taken aback.

"You'll not be lucky again!" roared Man Tavis, seizing a war lance from his neighbor. "This one is for your heart!" And he hurled the spear full at Tal's breast.

Tal never slowed his steady walk toward the gate, but he braced himself for the impact, which nearly knocked the wind from him as the lance bounced off the invisible deflector screen.

Sudden silence fell on the warriors of Thongor. What apparition was this that walked like a man in the guise of the Outcast Tal Mikar, yet which lances could not pierce? Many a hot-blooded warrior murmured incantations to Shandor to protect them and Mor Haskin made a cabalistic sign to ward off evil.

"Sar Lon, I would parlay!" called Tal, as he reached the gate, which was now securely locked on the inside.

"Begone, you mountain devil!" the lance lord replied. "You who have taken the form of our Outcast warrior have no place here! Begone, or we shall call down Shandor's wrath on your evil head!"

"I am no mountain devil!" responded Tal. "I am indeed Tal Mikar, who voluntarily became Outcast through love for Alytha." Man Tavis roared at this. "I have journeyed far since leaving Thongor and have found some of the Ancients still living. Our legends tell of the flying boats of old, do they not?" He looked from Sol Makor to Mor Haskin. "Here is one as proof.

"I do not seek to return to Thongor. My home is not here. I seek to parlay with you, Sar Lon—and with you, Mor Haskin—for knowledge which the Ancients desire. Then we shall be on our way."

He waited, silent while the warriors of Thongor considered his words. He saw Sar Lon frown massively as the lance lord listened to whispered exhortations from first one and then another. Only Man Tavis said nothing. His eyes were glittering slits of pure hate as he looked at Tal.

"Where are these Ancients you speak of?" demanded Sar Lon at length. "Are they in the skybird behind you?"

"Yes," answered Tal, motioning for Lanawe to join him. "But do not bother to cast your spears at us. We wear a weapons device of the Ancients that no blade can pierce." He tapped his deflector belt as he said this.

By this time Lanawe Palmerin had emerged from behind the shuttlecraft and a murmur went up from the onlookers.

"She looks like any other woman!" protested Sar Lon. "How do you know she is one of the Ancients?"

"Because I fly the skybird!" Lanawe answered for herself. "And because Tal has seen our magic weapons that can kill at a great distance." The warriors instinctively stepped back from the palisade, but Lanawe lifted her empty hands. "I come here without weapons!" she said quickly. "I come here protected only by the same device that protected Tal from the thrown spears. I come here because we seek information. Will you parlay with us?" She stood silent now beside Tal.

The warriors hesitated only a moment longer, then Sar Lon said: "I will parlay. Outside the gate."

"With Mor Haskin!" added Tal, and the grim lance lord nodded.

"Shall I call Dad?" asked Lanawe, in a soft aside to Tal, who shook his head negatively.

"Not yet," he said. "First we talk to Sar Lon."

The palisade gate opened a mere crack and the lance lord sidled through, followed closely by Mor Haskin, the Thongor shaman. Sar Lon held his great sword unsheathed in one hand and his war lance ready in the other. He was taking no chances. Mor Haskin held a magic talisman, the most potent in his medicine bag. He put more faith in it than in Sar Lon's sword.

The two Thongors stopped before Tal and Lanawe. They peered at them keenly, trying to determine if they were in truth human or if they were mountain devils taken human form. At last Sar Lon seemed satisfied.

"Parlay," he said, bluntly.

"We seek knowledge of a thing only Mor Haskin would know," said Tal. "We seek the Eternity Stone—that which is called the Accursed of Shandor." Both Thongors paled at this. "But I seek other knowledge for myself. Have you seen Alytha since the time we stood Outcast?"

"Aye," said Sar Lon. "She was in our village till two nights agone."

Lanawe saw Tal's mighty shoulders tense under his sueded leather tunic, but he gave no other sign.

"Tell me," he said, and Sar Lon began:

"Jad Thor still desired Alytha though she be not virgin. He offered rich prizes to any warrior who would track her down and return her to him. And even richer prizes if they brought your head as well.

"Alytha was captured and returned to Man Tavis, who wedded her to Jad Thor. On their wedding night, but two nights past, Alytha killed Jad Thor with a dirk and fled into the wilderness. We gave pursuit and as we drew near we heard her scream in mortal pain. We arrived to find wild dogs feasting on the part of her that had not yet disappeared into Devil's Slough.

"So both Jad Thor and Alytha are now dead and, till your return, we thought the matter laid to rest."

Tal's blue eyes narrowed and the muscles in his jaw stood out in great ridges as he listened to this. Then he shook his head sharply.

"I do not believe Alytha dead," he said, between clenched teeth. "I know not why, but I feel she lives. And by Shandor's blood, I'll find her!"

"*We* will find her, Tal," Lanawe said quickly. "You know what our scanners can do. You yourself said no one could hide from them. We'll use them to search for Alytha."

Tal looked at her. "You would do this for me?" he asked.

"Yes. Help us find the Eternity Stone and I promise you, we'll use every device we have to track down Alytha."

Tal nodded his head. "Good," he said, then he motioned for Dr. Palmerin to join them.

"The chief of the Ancients will join us," he told Sar Lon. "Then we will speak of the Eternity Stone."

In a few moments Dr. Fel Palmerin had joined the quartet of figures standing before the gate. Sar Lon carefully looked over this chief of the Ancients. Dr. Palmerin wore his black uniform with the striking scarlet and gold emblem on the chest. His white hair was brushed back and he looked every inch a dignified, civilized patrician: tall, slim, and elegant.

Sar Lon, by contrast, was bulky and shaggy; his hair unkempt and shoulder length, a bearskin cloak flung over his leather tunic, a necklace of human teeth half hidden in the matted hair of his bared chest.

"Why do you seek the Accursed of Shandor?" asked Mor Haskin. "It is a thing to be shunned, to be spoken of in whispers. A thing from Hell itself. A thing which even mighty Shandor feared and abhorred."

"We seek it to remove it from your world," said Dr. Palmerin. "It is a weapon the Ancients built that we, their children, can use to destroy our enemy far and far from here.

"We come from Aryor, which is one of the points of light in the sky. Do not your legends speak of the fact that the Ancients had great skyboats that flew up to the stars? Well, what think you of that in which we arrived? You saw it fly through the air. My daughter here controls it. We flew in a much larger version of it from Aryor to here—to Earth—to find the Eternity Stone and take it back to Aryor with us. If you think the Eternity Stone is a thing accursed and a thing to be feared, then realize that you need fear it no more. If you can tell me where it is, we will remove it completely and forever from your world."

Both Thongors were silent as they considered the off-worlder's words. Sar Lon was lance lord, true, but this was a medicine affair and he waited for Mor Haskin to speak. At last, the shaman did so:

"Your words have a ring of truth, old one. This much I can tell you: Shandor took the Accursed with him to his wizard-city of Shalimar, said to lie somewhere within the lostness of the Great Desert. There the Accursed is said to be hidden to this very day. I can tell you no more than that."

"But where is this city called Shalimar? Can you direct us there?"

"It lies in the Great Desert. I can tell you no more than that."

"Fen Melton spoke once of Shalimar," said Tal. "He told me it was in the heart of the Great Desert, which had once been called Northern Americ or Northern Amerigo, or some such."

"The Arcobanes live nearer to the Great Desert than we do," suggested Mor Haskin. "And they are known to trade with the Kalathors, the desert warriors. Perhaps the Arcobanes can give you more knowledge."

"The Arcobanes!" Both Lanawe and her father turned to Tal. "Weren't they the ones who . . . ?"

"Yes," said Tal. "They were. And we passed their village yesterday. Come, I will direct you there again. And on the way you can use your magic machines to help me find

Alytha."

At the sound of Alytha's name there was a sudden roar of rage from the palisade gate. Man Tavis emerged, a long sword in his hand and madness in his eyes.

"You will die, Tal Mikar!" he screamed. "You took my daughter from me and you will die!"

Sar Lon and Mor Haskin leaped aside, for a berserk warrior is believed to be sacred to Shandor. Only Tal stood his ground. Lanawe and her father recoiled from the screaming attack.

Tal stepped in to meet the descending sword and caught the old warrior's wrist in an iron grip. For a moment they stood locked together, a savage and primitive tableau, then the sword clattered to the ground and Man Tavis' fury broke on the solid stone of Tal's strength and fell into glittering shards of grief.

The old man sank slowly to his knees, sobbing in anguish, fury, and pain. His love for his daughter and the guilt he felt at being an instrument in her death, the guilt he had projected outward onto Tal Mikar, left him a broken, empty figure, older than his years. He called Alytha's name again and again through his weeping.

Slowly, gently, Tal knelt beside him and took the bereft old man in his arms. "I, too, love her very much," he said. "You have other daughters. I have no one now. But I do not believe Alytha is dead. I will search for her with the Ancients' help, and when I find her, we will spend our lives together. And where we live, Outcast or not, there will be a place at our hearth for Man Tavis."

Uncomprehendingly, the old man looked up at Tal and allowed himself to be helped gently to his feet. With swimming eyes he stared at the man he had tried to kill.

"Go back to your other daughters," said Tal, softly. "I will find Alytha for you."

He deliberately turned his back and walked toward the shuttlecraft, followed in a moment by Lanawe and her father.

FOURTEEN

The shuttlecraft swung in a wide, low arc over the quicksand bog called Devil's Slough. Lanawe had landed there and a diligent search had been conducted before Tal was convinced that there was no trace of Alytha.

"We will search for Alytha today," he announced flatly. "Tomorrow I will direct you again to the Arcobane village."

There was some protest to this high-handed decision, but Tal remained inflexible. If the offworlders wanted his help in relocating the Arcobane village, then this day would be devoted to searching for Alytha. Alun Akobar looked very smug and knowing when Tal took this position, but he refrained from commenting.

"Alytha would try to make her way back to our valley," decided Tal. "We will search in that direction. Circle wide and use your scanners that can find a person even when they are hidden."

Lanawe snapped on the infrared sensors and swung out in a series of wide arcs over the timbered mountains.

Several times the heat-seeking sensors picked up the body heat of a human being hidden in the foliage. In each instance they dropped down to investigate, hoping they would find Alytha. They found frightened warriors who, twice, hurled lances at the jetboat. Once they found a woman cowering behind a heavy stand of undergrowth, but she was a wandering Arcobane woman. Of Alytha there was no trace.

At one point they picked up a varied mass of heat that Lanawe at first thought indicated a village ahead of them. A moment later she discovered her error as the shuttlecraft hurtled out over a hot springs area where naturally heated geysers turned the air steamy and humid. She started to pass on when a shadow moved across the rocks below her.

Curious, Lanawe brought the jetboat around and made another pass over the hot springs area.

"I thought I saw something—*there*," she said to Tal, pointing.

Everyone on that side of the jetboat joined Tal in scanning the rocks and bubbling geysers below. There, in the direction Lanawe indicated, a fluffy tailed rabbit sprang up and hopped frantically to another place of safety.

"I guess that's what I saw," she said, with a sigh. She made one more pass over the hot springs area, then swung out on a new trajectory.

Behind her, hidden in a crevice between two boulders and therefore invisible from the air, a slim, lovely girl listened to the diminishing sounds of the jetboat's thrusters. At last, convinced it was safe, Alytha peeped out from her cover next to one of the bubbling hot springs. Reassured, she scuttled on across the rocks, her naked figure blending against the stony landscape as her body heat had blended with the heat from the hot springs around her. Still clutching her dagger in one hand, she disappeared into the forest.

Several kilometers ahead of her, and high in the air, Tal Mikar breathed a short prayer to Shandor for aid in his search. He still had no basis, save his intuitive feeling, for believing that Alytha was alive. Yet somehow, in his heart, he was certain that she was not dead. He was certain they could find her if they searched diligently.

But by the end of a day of diligent searching, they had found no trace of her at all. It was very disheartening, but Tal still would not admit that she was dead.

Lanawe landed the shuttlecraft in a small clearing beside a stream of running water. There, under armed guard, the Aryorians went down to the little stream and bathed. The men bathed first with Tal, Dr. Palmerin, and another man standing guard with neuron guns. Then the three guards bathed quickly while others stood guard. Back aboard the shuttlecraft, some of the men prepared their evening meal while the women bathed.

Tal was amused that the men prepared the food. He refrained from sneering at them, but barely. Among his people, no warrior, unless he were a slave, did such menial tasks. That was woman's work.

When all the offworlders were aboard again and the meal was served, Tal was pleased that Lanawe again chose to eat with him. He noticed Alun Akobar watching them as they ate. It occurred to Tal that sooner or later he was going to have to kill the blond offworlder.

"Will you direct us to the Arcobane village tomorrow?" asked Lanawe. She tried to make the question sound casual. She did not want to sound as if she were pressuring Tal.

"Yes. I will take you there," he answered, looking down at his tray of reconstituted chopped steak, instant potatoes, and dehydrated corn. "We will go to the Arcobanes. I will stay with you till you find the Eternity Stone."

"Then what?"

"Then I would like you to return me to Alytha's valley. Will you do that?"

"Of course, Tal. But why are you so sure Alytha is still alive?"

"I do not know," he admitted, shaking his head ruefully. "I only know that if she does not live, then I have no desire to live. After you have found what you seek and have returned to your own world, I will begin my quest. I will find Alytha or die in the attempt."

"If she lives, Tal, I believe you'll find her." Lanawe instinctively reached out and touched Tal's hand. It seemed the most natural gesture in the world to her and, equally natural, was Tal's response: his hand closed over hers and gave her fingers a gentle squeeze.

Across the shuttlecraft, Dr. Palmerin observed this and lifted one eyebrow, but he did not comment. He shot a quick glance at Alun Akobar, but for once the other seemed not to have noticed.

Tal was up at dawn and emerged into the dew-sparkled clearing while the others still slept. His keen blue eyes scanned the surrounding forest, then he saw a sign that evidently satisfied him for he set off silently into the woods.

Perhaps an hour later, Lanawe awoke and went to the head to relieve herself. Returning to her couch, she glanced at the corner where Tal had curled up to sleep the night before. He was not there.

"Dad!" She quickly roused her father. "Tal's not here. I think he's gone."

"What—gone?" Dr. Palmerin was on his feet in an instant. "Are you sure?" He looked quickly around the interior of the shuttlecraft, scanning the faces of the sleeping crew. "Maybe he went outside."

"I *know* he went outside," said Lanawe, as she and her father dilated the hatch and stepped to the ground. "There's the trail across the grass where he went into the forest. I just want to know if he's coming back."

"Of course not!" said Alun Akobar, emerging behind them. "He's gone and you can kiss him good-bye—along with any chance we had of finding the Arcobanes."

"You can't be sure that he's gone!" protested Lanawe hotly. "You have no idea what he's doing."

"I have a pretty good idea what he's doing. He's abandoned us. He got everything he wanted except you. There's no reason for him to hang around."

"He'll be back," Lanawe said definitely. "You watch. He'll be back."

"I hope you're right," said her father. "We might never find the Arcobanes without Tal's help."

"He'll be back," Lanawe repeated. "I *know* Tal. He won't leave us stranded here. I'll guarantee it."

"What do you mean, you 'know' him?" demanded Alun. "You only met him two days ago. You can't know much about him in that length of time."

"I do, though," Lanawe insisted. "It's like . . . it's like I've known Tal for years. I know what he'll do. I know how he'll react to different things. I sometimes feel I know what he thinks. It's a weird feeling."

Before she could say anything else, and before Alun Akobar could frame the rejoinder that was on the tip of his tongue, Tal Mikar emerged from the woods with the carcass of a small antelope across one brawny shoulder.

"Good hunting this morning," he remarked. "I saw the

spoor of this forked horn and realized I was hungry for fresh meat." He flung the carcass down. "We'll eat well today."

"I knew you'd come back!" cried Lanawe, flinging her arms about his neck and giving him a hearty kiss. "I told them you would!"

Tal appeared puzzled by her behavior. "What made you think I wouldn't come back?" he asked.

"I never thought you wouldn't come back," she replied, "but—" She turned to gesture at Alun Akobar, but he was not there. He had gone back inside the jetboat. "Oh, well," she said. "It doesn't matter." She looked at the carcass of the deer. "What are you going to do with that?"

Tal laughed. "Me? Nothing. Dressing meat is women's work. I'll hang it for you."

"For me? Now wait a minute!" Lanawe backed up, her hands out in front of her. "Hold it right there, friend. I don't know a thing in the world about dead animals." She looked at the still bleeding carcass in sudden distaste.

"What do you mean, you don't know about them? Who dresses the animals the warriors kill on Aryor?"

"Uh . . . I don't know. I mean . . . I don't *know!* I've never seen a dead animal before."

Dr. Palmerin came to his daughter's rescue: "We have a different society on Aryor. Our men are not hunters. Animals are raised and killed by people who are especially trained for that purpose. When Lanawe, or almost anyone on Aryor, desires fresh meat, they simply order it from the market and it is delivered via pneumatic tube. Most Aryorians never saw any form of death—until the Ilriks came."

Tal looked at Lanawe in absolute amazement. "You mean . . . you don't know how to skin and dress a forked horn? You really don't?"

Lanawe shook her head in mute horror. "I really don't."

"Come." He took her by one hand and with the other he almost effortlessly slung the antelope carcass across his shoulder again. "All women need to know this."

With Lanawe very reluctantly in tow, Tal crossed to the edge of the forest and strung the carcass up to a low hanging limb. He quickly severed the jugular through to bleed the animal completely. Lanawe choked and turned away, biting her fist to keep from retching.

"What's the matter?" asked Tal, genuinely puzzled.

"I can't stand the sight of blood," said the girl, still looking away, her mouth twisting in revulsion. "I never could stand it."

Tal lifted his eyebrows in surprise. He shrugged, then turned his attention back to the antelope. With quick, expert strokes of his knife he deftly opened the belly and exposed the viscera. Before he could do more than that, Lanawe had pulled away from him and was literally fleeing for the sanctuary of the shuttlecraft.

Most of Tal's kill was quick-frozen and stored in the freeze-locker aboard the jetboat. However, there were juicy antelope steaks for everyone who desired one for breakfast. Lanawe breakfasted on a single refresher cup and this time did not sit with Tal.

In a short period of time they were airborne again and following Tal's directions toward the Arcobane village.

"The Arcobanes are different from the Thongors," he explained to Lanawe and her father as the jetboat hurtled along above the timbered mountains and out across the forested valley floor. "My people are warriors, but our womenfolk work in the fields and raise our crops and tend our flocks. The Arcobanes have no flocks and only very few fields. They are *all* warriors, the women as well as the men, if they desire to be. No one ever steals an Arcobane woman for a mate. They are as vicious as she-panthers.

"The Arcobanes acknowledge only power. They respect only power. Show them you are strong and unafraid and they will welcome you to their huts. Show the least sign of fear and they will kill you, or make you a slave!" His blue eyes narrowed as he said this, and Lanawe knew he was remembering his own experiences in the Arcobane camp.

"Where we approached the Thongors warily to reassure them, we must go boldly to the Arcobanes. I will need a neuron gun in addition to a deflector screen. As I said, the Arcobanes respect only power."

Tal had the neuron gun and was buckled into his deflector screen by the time Lanawe brought the jetboat in a sharp banking sweep over the Arcobane village.

The warriors scattered for their weapons and the palisade gate swung ponderously shut. A line of warriors, their number bristling with heavy war spears, appeared in ragged formation along the top of the stockade.

The shuttlecraft settled gently to the ground in front of the main gate. Again, Tal had instructed Lanawe to land with the hatch away from the village.

"Wait till I signal you," he told them, just before he dilated the hatch. "And when you come, come armed. Walk bold and unafraid. Let them see that all of you bear weapons. Only then will they respect you."

As Tal walked around the bow of the shuttlecraft he scanned the ranked warriors for some sign of Vaj Durmo. He spotted the burly warrior almost immediately and Tal's volcanic blue eyes smoldered with a savage fire.

"Ven Tamor!" he bellowed. "I am Tal Mikar, who was a slave here once! Come down! I would talk with you!"

"I have nothing to say!" answered the lance lord. "I know not how you fly through the air, but begone or we will make you a slave again!"

Tal laughed harshly. "You will not see that day, Ven Tamor! Vaj Durmo took me by a cowardly blow from behind. Let him come out now and face me again. He can bring his finest war spear. I will use *this*!" Tal lifted the neuron gun. "I challange Vaj Durmo to single combat!"

Tal stood waiting, a scornful smile on his lips. He knew the Arcobanes could see that he bore neither lance nor sword, yet he challenged one of their mightiest warriors to single combat. They were considering all the implications of that.

"Is Vaj Durmo too cowardly to face a lone man armed with such a small club?" he taunted. "Look, I'll put one hand behind me to make him less fearful. I swear by Shandor that I will slay Vaj Durmo with only this one hand!" He lifted the hand that held the neuron gun and gestured with it.

"I will meet you, little man!" roared the hulking Arcobane. "And I will hurt you much before I let you die!"

While Vaj Durmo was making his way to the gate, Tal looked full at Ven Tamor.

"After I have slain the fool," he said, "I would talk with you, Ven Tamor. I have friends—" he gestured at the shuttlecraft—"who seek information from your shaman."

Before the lance lord could reply, the palisade gate opened and Vaj Durmo came out, war spear couched in one hand, long sword naked in the other.

"I will see that you do not run away from me!" the big warrior yelled, hurling his lance so that it should transfix Tal's upper leg.

Tal gritted his teeth and let the heavy, bronze-tipped war spear glance off the deflector. He knew from the force of impact that he would carry a tremendous bruise on his right thigh for several days.

There was a moment's stunned silence, while the Arcobanes gawked and Tal waited for feeling to come back to his numbed leg, then he slowly lifted the neuron gun and leveled it at Vaj Durmo. The high pitched hum of the weapon was lost in Vaj Durmo's scream of agony as he seized his temples, spun around on his heel, and sprawled dead before the palisade gate.

"Now, Ven Tamor!" roared Tal. "Come down! I would talk!"

"If we come down, you will slay us all," the lance lord protested.

"Does the hawk kill all the rabbits that creep in the forest?" demanded Tal, scornfully. "Besides, if I wished, I could slay you all where you stand. Come down. I am weary of waiting. And bring your shaman with you!"

Tal signaled for Lanawe and her father to join him. They came, with neuron guns plainly visible on their hips. And Fel Palmerin bore in his arms a haunch of the antelope Tal had slain.

When Ven Tamor emerged, accompanied by a wizened little man whose accouterments clearly marked him as a shaman, Dr. Palmerin placed the meat on the ground before him.

"We make you a gift," he said, "to prove our good intentions."

Ven Tamor's eyes narrowed and Tal saw that the old man had nearly undone all his efforts, so he added quickly:

"And to prove our superiority as hunters! Have you a gift of an equal amount of meat to offer us?" He saw his words thrust home. They were established as mighty hunters as well as mighty warriors. He thanked Shandor that the old man had brought the meat. It had worked to their advantage after all.

"This is your shaman?" he asked, looking at the wizened little man.

"Yes," said Ven Tamor. "This is And Lalon. He is a great wizard."

Tal snorted in derision.

"If he is a wizard, I'm a warty frog. Listen, old man, we come seeking information. If you can tell us what we need to know, well and good. If not, it will only be what I expect. If you do not speak the truth, you will die as Vaj Durmo did." He gestured with the neuron gun significantly.

"What information do you seek, outlander?" asked And Lalon, seemingly unperturbed by Tal's threats.

"We seek the Eternity Stone. That which is called the Accursed of Shandor."

Both Arcobanes instinctively shrank back and And Lalon made the same cabalistic sign Mor Haskin had used. It meant nothing to Tal, but Lanawe and her father recognized that this primitive witch doctor had made the sign of the double helix—the DNA code.

"The Accursed of Shandor is forbidden. No man may see it and live!" And Lalon intoned this dire pronouncement in a deep, sepulchral voice.

Tal laughed. "Then the Accursed of Shandor will do what the tribe of Arcobanes could not do! Do you know its location?"

"It lies in the city of Shalimar—Beloved of Shandor. Shalimar lies far and far away, in the heart of the Great Desert. No man has seen Shalimar in a thousand years or more, except perhaps the Kalathors." And Lalon paused.

"You think the Kalathors might be familiar with Shalimar?" Tal prompted. The old witch doctor shrugged.

"The Kalathors are like the wind. They go where they will. They cross and recross the Great Desert as the sun crosses and recrosses the rings as it sweeps through the heavens. They may have seen Shalimar; they may have not. If they have, they will tell no man who lives. The Kalathors give away nothing."

"You have spoken well, old man," said Tal. "We will seek the Kalathors' aid in finding Shalimar."

"Then you seek death, outlander!" hissed And Lalon. "For the Kalathors will slit your throats and take your woman"—he gestured sharply at Lanawe—"and leave your bones to whiten in the sands of the Great Desert."

"Who are these Kalathors?" asked Dr. Palmerin, but Tal waved him to silence.

"That may be true, old man," he said to the Arcobane shaman. "I know the Kalathors are said to be the greatest warriors on earth, but we will seek them out and they will deal with us." He laughed again, not a pleasant sound. "And we will seek out the Accursed of Shandor even in the ruins of Shalimar. This we will do!"

Suddenly the old witch doctor stretched out one hand toward Tal and his face took on an expression of anguish.

"I sense peril, outlander," he said, his eyes wide. "I feel death in the air. It comes with your presence and abides with you as close as a shadow. Its chill is on you all." He stopped and peered deeply into Tal's eyes.

"No," he said, contradicting himself. "No, not all. For you," his hand clutched at Tal's arm, but the deflector held him off, "I see not death, but something more!" Genuine terror was in the old man's look. "For you, I see—the *undeath*. . . ." His voice trailed to a whisper.

Tal angrily shook off And Lalon's hand, frightened in spite of himself.

"What is this gibberish, old man?" he demanded in a harsh voice. "What are you babbling about?"

And Lalon frowned massively and seemed to shrink inside his cloak. He shook his head several times before he answered: "I don't know. I don't understand what I sense. All I know is what I feel. About the others I sense the shadow of death, but for you. . . ." The old man was visibly afraid.

"About you," he continued, looking directly at Tal with horrible intensity, "what I sense is something else; something so utterly terrible I cannot put a name to it. I can only call it— the *undeath*!" He turned away, but looked back over his shoulder to say: "Go with Shandor, outlander, and pray that he can help you when the *undeath* is upon you."

Then And Lalon turned and walked directly toward the gate into the village. Ven Tamor hesitated only a second, then followed him, leaving Tal and the two Aryorians standing alone in the mid-morning chill that heralded the winter nearly upon them.

FIFTEEN

Tal crouched behind the boulder in the cold darkness that immediately preceded dawn. His right leg pained him no little bit, being still stiff and sore from where Vaj Durmo's lance had struck, and he stretched it as best he could, being careful to make no sound.

He and Lanawe, her father and Alun Akobar, plus a half dozen other Aryorians were hidden on a hilly slope above the Kalathors' encampment, waiting for dawn so they could make their move.

They had spotted the encampment the evening before. Lanawe had held the shuttlecraft too high for its true nature to be made out and they had used scanners to locate the desert nomads.

The camp was not a big one. There were less than thirty tents and no more than a hundred horses picketed nearby. Over the largest tent floated a black banner with a golden labrys etched on it.

"Who are these Kalathors?" Dr. Palmerin had asked again, as the jetboat had circled high above the fringes of the Great Desert.

"The Kalathors are the fiercest warriors on earth," Tal had explained. "They are nomads of the Great Desert. No one knows much about them. They are very secretive and very terrible. They do not live in villages like the Thongors or the Arcobanes or the Farades. They live in tents that they fold up and take with them. When they make camp, they may remain for a day, for a season, or for a year. Then one morning, their tents will be gone and the Kalathors with them. One thing is certain, however: for so long as the Kalathors choose to remain at any given spot, they are the absolute masters of that area. The unchallenged lords of all they survey.

"Part of their power comes from the fact that they ride upon the backs of large, four-legged animals called horses. I have never seen a horse, but members of my tribe who have been to the Desert say that this is so. They say the Kalathors move like the wind across the sands and rocks. They say that warriors on foot have no chance at all against mounted Kalathors."

"But will these Kalathors aid us in finding Shalimar?" Dr. Palmerin had asked. "If they're as fierce as you say, what makes you think they'll help us?"

"I don't know that they will," Tal had admitted. "If they do, the only thing that will persuade them will be our utter lack of fear. Like the Arcobanes, the Kalathors are great respecters of courage. If we show them that we are unafraid, and that their weapons can't pierce our deflectors, then we may win them over. But if they think we are in the least afraid, they will kill us all, most probably by torture."

Lanawe had shuddered. "You paint an awfully encouraging picture," she had commented.

Tal had shrugged this away. "I only tell you what I know of the Kalathors. We must be bold, or appear to be, if we would have their help at all."

The nomad encampment was at the base of a series of rocky, treeless hillocks that bordered the Desert itself. Lanawe had very deftly cut the motors and glided the jetboat into a dead stick landing in a secluded canyon a couple of kilometers from the encampment. They had decided to move out—a select, handpicked company—and be in position to enter the camp just at dawn.

Now, as Tal watched, the edges of the milk-white rings turned rosy pink as the sun announced that day was at hand. The rings always gave the first indication of dawn, reflecting back the sunlight before it touched the horizon at all.

Tal rubbed his sore leg and waited as the rings turned fiery red and the horizon turned pink and silver and pastel blue.

He knew it would not be long before the big test would be upon them.

He was aware that the Kalathors knew the Great Desert as well as he knew the mountain trails around his home village. Since the Desert covered nine-tenths of what had been the continent of Northern Americ, he was also aware that the Aryorians' chance of finding the ruins of Shalimar without the help of the Kalathors was negligible. Even with the instruments aboard the shuttlecraft, they might search for years without coming near Shalimar. Besides, Tal had heard legends—mostly from Fen Melton—that said the Great Desert housed the ruins of thousands of cities. Without the Kalathors to guide them, the Aryorians might spend a lifetime searching one ruin after another without ever knowing which was Shalimar.

Full dawning dispelled these meditations from Tal's mind as he watched the Kalathor encampment slowly coming to life. The fierce nomads had posted only a half dozen guards. They slept secure in the knowledge that no one attacked a Kalathor—anywhere, ever. A pack of snarling, yelping dogs circled through the camp. They were the first domesticated dogs Tal had ever seen, though he was bitterly familiar with the packs of wild dogs that roamed at will over the mountains and through the forests.

The Thongors had goats and chickens, as did the Arcobanes, while the Farades had shaggy, oxlike cattle for meat and milk, but the Kalathors domesticated goats, dogs, and horses.

These last were a source of great curiosity to Tal. He was eagerly looking forward to seeing one of the nomads mount and ride one of the beasts.

Finally he decided it was time. Stories were whispered about the way Kalathor women were kept and treated—they were said to be less than animals—so he had cautioned Lanawe and most of the others to stay hidden while he, Dr. Palmerin, and Alun Akobar made the initial approach.

With that end in mind, the three rose from the rocks and began a leisurely descent of the hillside, acting for all the world as if they were merely out for a morning stroll.

The dogs gave the first warning. The pack began to bark

and yelp and yap and headed straight for the intruders. A Kalathor sentry was not far behind and Tal got his first close look at the desert nomads.

The Kalathors were generally shorter than the peoples with whom Tal was familiar. None was as tall as Tal himself and many were considerably shorter. They looked chunky and solid, definitely not fat, and were burned a swarthy brown by the sun. They wore tight fitting breeks of tanned leather stuffed into high topped boots that came to mid-thigh. Their silken tunics were loose fitting with belled sleeves, flowing collars, and open necklines that exposed much of their chests. Flowing cloaks swung from their shoulders and almost touched the ground. Each Kalathor wore a broad brimmed hat woven of some reedlike material that closely resembled straw and each wore about his neck a colorful bandanna to protect his nose and mouth from the savage Desert sandstorms.

A longsword and a wicked looking dagger were thrust into this Kalathor's sash, which served as a belt and, not coincidentally, was the same color as the bandanna around his neck. In his hand he held a labrys, the double-headed battleaxe that was the symbol of his clan. Tal winced inwardly when he saw it. He was not at all certain what would happen if a deflector received a solid blow from one of those heavy, razor-sharp axes. He preferred not to find out the hard way.

The Kalathor said something in a language that Tal did not understand and the Thongor felt his heart sink. If they could not communicate, the Kalathors could not help them at all.

"What clan is this?" Tal demanded, in the pidgin language the Thongors used for trading with other tribes. His one hope was that the Kalathors might barter often enough to have a smattering of this "trader's language."

Apparently they did, for the sentry stopped and looked at them with suddenly narrowed eyes.

"Axe clan," he said, in a guttural dialect. "Adfor is clan chief."

"We would talk with Adfor," said Tal, never slowing his advance. One of the dogs made a sudden nip at his leg, but the deflectors brought it up short. Surprised by something totally new in its canine experience, the dog yelped and sprang away. Tal did not break stride nor appear to notice.

"Stop!" said the Kalathor, lifting his axe meaningfully. "You can come no farther."

"Step aside, dog!" snapped Tal, never slowing. "Our business is with your master!"

The Kalathor swung the labrys high above his head and Tal fired his neuron gun, set on the lowest possible charge. The Kalathor started violently and sprang back, the battleaxe falling to the ground as he clawed at his head.

Other Kalathors were approaching at a run and Tal knew the next few minutes would be critical. By prearranged signal, both he and Dr. Palmerin suddenly seized the arms of the Kalathor guard who had first intercepted them. The electrical impulse field of the deflector screens used the man's body as a compatible conductor and he received a painful, and totally unnerving, electrical shock.

With a strangled cry he lurched away and fell prone before the approaching warriors.

"Hold!" roared Tal, flinging up one hand dramatically. "We would speak with Adfor!"

The Kalathors stopped, intrigued as much by his apparent fearlessness as by the strange malady that seemed to have affected their fellow.

"I am Adfor," said a burly, barrel-chested individual in the van of the warriors. "What do you seek in our camp?" His tone was bellicose.

"Does Adfor discuss his business in front of these dogs?" demanded Tal, in an equally haughty tone. "If he does, then he is no part of a clan chief!"

"Adfor discusses his business where he pleases," said the ruler of the Kalathors. "You tread on dangerous ground, mountain man."

Tal laughed scornfully.

"The only danger here is to those who make empty threats against their betters," he replied. "See you what has happened to the desert jackel who would have stopped us from speaking with you?" Tal jerked his thumb at the sentry who was just regaining his feet and who was still trying to figure

155

out what had happened to him. "We can just as easily deal with any warriors in your clan, so you would be well advised to consult with us, Adfor of the Axe Clan."

Adfor hesitated for a second and one of the other warriors, one Tal suspected of having ambitions to be clan chief, stepped into the hesitation.

"Let a *real* warrior show you how it is done, outlander!" he cried, and in one swift movement that was too fast for the eye to follow, sent his axe hurtling straight for Tal's chest.

There was no time for Tal to dodge, no time for any action at all, not even to brace himself. The axe struck solidly and jarred Tal back two steps by the force of its impact, but it fell to the ground without penetrating the deflector.

There was sudden silence. The Kalathors had seen the axe strike blade first. By rights it should have split Tal's chest like rotten wood; but it had not. There was no mark on him.

Slowly, deliberately, Tal moved the setting on his neuron gun up two notches. Slowly, deliberately, he raised his arm and took aim. The high pitched hum made everyone jump, everyone but the ambitious warrior. He gave a strangled cry and fell forward on his face in the dirt, not dead but stunned.

"Now, Adfor," said Tal, in a cold voice. "I think we should talk—in your tent."

The clan chief nodded and led the way to the large central tent where the labrys pennant fluttered in the morning breeze.

Inside, he clapped his hands smartly and two women appeared from behind a curtain. Their appearance confirmed what Tal had heard about the Kalathors. Both women were totally naked and their backs and bare buttocks showed evidence that they had been whipped, and whipped often. Their manner was totally subservient and they seemed to be in abject dread of Adfor, cringing each time he came near. Tal was forcibly and bitterly reminded of his own recent slavery among the Arcobanes and the Farades.

"We would break our fast," Adfor commanded them. "Bring refreshments."

The clan chief motioned them to be seated at a low table which was so close to the ground that large pillows served as seats. A decanter of dark red beverage sat in the center of the table and Adfor poured each of his guests a metal cup full from the decanter.

He noticed their hesitation as they took the wine and completely misinterpreted it.

"There is no poison," he said, curtly. "In the clan chief's tent, your lives are sacred to Shandor. Besides, no Kalathor would stoop to poison when he could still lift an axe or a sword."

"It is not that we thought of poison," said Dr. Palmerin, speaking for the first time. "It is that our weapons of defense do not allow for drinking or eating."

Adfor looked puzzled. "What weapons of defense do you mean?"

"The best way I can answer that is to demonstrate." Dr. Palmerin held out his arm. "Touch my hand," he said. "Go ahead. It's all right."

Hesitantly, Adfor reached out his own hand and touched the old man's, or tried to. The deflector screen stopped him a half centimeter or so before he touched the skin. His hand apparently hovered there in mid air, yet all Adfor's strength could not force it to make contact with Fel Palmerin's frail wrist.

The old man did something below the level of the table and instantly the Kalathor's hand was on his bare skin. Adfor looked dumbfounded. Before he could react, Dr. Palmerin had triggered the deflector again and Adfor's hand lifted, apparently of its own accord, till it was once more not touching Dr. Palmerin's.

"Now do you see what I mean by weapons of defense?"

The clan chief was nothing if not shrewd.

"You mean you have some kind of invisible shield that prevents anything from touching you?"

"Precisely. Nothing larger than air molecules can pass through it."

Adfor suddenly looked keenly at Tal. "That was why Cron's axe didn't hurt you." He made it sound like an accusation.

Tal nodded, but he did not answer. He thought it best to let Adfor think that the deflectors made them invincible. He did not want to admit that the momentum of the thrown axe had knocked the wind out of him, left a tremendous ache in his chest—and the knowledge that tomorrow he would have a bruise to match the one Vaj Durmo had given him on the right thigh—and almost knocked him off his feet. Better that Adfor thought it useless to raise any weapon against someone shielded by a deflector.

Before anything else could be said, the two slave women returned, each bearing a silver tray heaped with figs, dates, olives, fresh baked bread, honey, and brimming mugs of steaming, aromatic spiced herb tea.

"You are guests in the clan chief's tent," Adfor repeated. "Here you are sacred to Shandor. You may take off your invisible shields and break your fast."

Tal was the first to do so. He snapped off the deflector and took a sip of wine. It was sharp on his tongue and pungent in his throat. He coughed and nearly choked. Somehow he had expected something very, very sweet and very thick, but the wine was neither.

Dr. Palmerin and Alun Akobar quickly followed suit and for the next several minutes the four men devoted themselves to the pleasant task of depleting the foodstuffs the slave girls had provided.

Then, as they relaxed over the cinnamon and clove scented tea, the Kalathor chief opened the parlay:

"And why did you come so boldly into my camp seeking me?" He leaned back against the pillows and waited for their reply.

"We seek your help. . . ." Dr. Palmerin began, but Tal instantly amended that to: "We seek your *advice*."

"Uh . . . yes. . . ." Dr. Palmerin acknowledged Tal's correction. "Yes, we seek your advice. We search for something that we believe only you can guide us to. We are aware that no one knows the Desert like the Kalathórs and that which we seek is lost somewhere in the vastness of the Great Desert. We believe you can guide us to it."

"And what is this mysterious place you wish to be guided to—Shalimar?" And Adfor laughed.

Dr. Palmerin blinked and came up short. He frowned in puzzlement and looked from Tal to Alun Akobar and back to Tal again.

"Why . . . yes, that's exactly where we wish to go. How did you know?"

"What?" roared Adfor, leaping to his feet so suddenly he upset the table. The crash and his shout brought two armed guards bounding into the tent, axes at the ready.

All three intruders hastily activated their deflectors and Tal crouched low, his neuron gun swiveling to cover the guards.

"It's all right!" Adfor waved for everything to stop. He motioned the guards to leave, for Tal to replace his weapon, and for the slave girls to repair the havoc he had wrought. Significantly, all three visitors kept their deflectors activated.

"What's wrong?" asked Dr. Palmerin, uncomprehendingly. "Why did you get so upset?"

"Why?" Adfor seemed scarcely able to believe his ears. "Why did I get upset? Because you said you wanted to be guided to Shalimar. Don't you know—Shalimar is the Beloved of Shandor? *No one* goes to Shalimar. No one. Ever."

"I did not know that," Dr. Palmerin said. "I did not know it was forbidden to go there."

"Shalimar is the Beloved of Shandor," Adfor repeated. "You should know that, mountain man!" He directed this last at Tal.

"I had never heard that it was forbidden," Tal answered boldly. "I knew that it was Shandor's beloved city. I knew that it was lost in the Desert. I knew that *no man knew its location*." He emphasized this heavily. "But I did not know that it was forbidden."

Adfor narrowed his eyes and looked sharply at Tal, who returned him look for look.

"I still do not know that it is forbidden," Tal said, deliberately. "But I do wonder if Adfor knows the way to Shalimar. This talk of it being forbidden could be to cover the fact that a man who should know the Desert thoroughly does not know the location of so famous a place as Shalimar."

The clan chief took a step toward him, one fist clenched in anger.

"You are a guest in my tent or I would have your tongue cut out!" he growled, but Tal laughed scornfully.

"So long as we wear our invisible shields you will do nothing but talk, sand runner. And I say again: I doubt your knowledge of Shalimar's location."

"I know its location, mountain man! It lies far and far away in the Desert, buried in the sands, forgotten by all save the Kalathors and the wind and the spirit of Shandor."

"If you know where it is. . . ." Dr. Palmerin seized on this. "Could you . . . could you direct us there?" His eagerness was on his face and in his voice.

"It is forbidden," Adfor repeated. "Shalimar is the Beloved of Shandor. No one goes there."

Tal had been considering carefully as Adfor spoke. He knew his only hope for finding Alytha was through the offworlders, and to have their help he must first aid them in locating the Eternity Stone. He decided to try a long shot.

"That warrior who threw the axe," he began, almost musingly. "What was his name? Cron? He has a strong arm." Tal deliberately lifted the cup of spiced herb tea and pretended to sip it, but the deflector screen stopped the cup before it touched his lips. "He is also headstrong, Adfor. You hesitated, and while you hesitated, Cron acted. I think he would like to be clan chief." Tal set his cup down and smiled at Adfor. "I think he plans to challenge you soon. I could see it in his eyes."

The clan chief did not speak, but his face darkened with suppressed anger. Tal smiled again and went on:

"Now I know you're a mighty warrior, Adfor. No man becomes clan chief of the Kalathors unless he is terrible in battle. Therefore, I know you would neither need nor desire any help, or protection, on that day when Cron challenges you; but think of this, Adfor. Consider how doubly fierce your warriors would be in battle—say, in their next clan raid, perhaps—if your leaders were all wearing our invisible shields."

"What are you saying?" demanded Alun Akobar, breaking silence for the first time. "The deflector screens are not yours to bargain with or offer!"

"Quiet!" snapped Dr. Palmerin, speaking in Aryorian, which neither Tal nor Adfor could understand. "This is his show. If it gets us the Eternity Stone, I'll give him anything he wants—including your head!" To Adfor, the old scientist said, "Of course, we did not expect you to guide us without payment. A dozen personal deflector screens would be small recompense for your trouble."

Adfor considered this. He looked slyly from one to the other of his guests as he weighed their offer.

"As I said," Tal repeated, "you would neither need nor

desire such a shield when Cron challanges you, but it would make the Axe Clan the terror of the Desert if her warriors could not be harmed by any weapon."

While Adfor still considered, stroking his lean jaw with thick, strong fingers, a sudden shout from outside caught their attention. Before anyone could react, a bedlam of yells and shouts and curses erupted and then, penetrating it all, came the high-pitched hum of a neuron gun!

"Lanawe!" Tal yelled and in an instant had bolted through the tent flaps, followed more slowly by the others.

It was indeed Lanawe. It had been nearly an hour since her father, Tal, and Alun had disappeared amid the welter of tents and Lanawe decided it was time to investigate. She picked another crew member, Varn Virgilus, and the two of them had simply stood up from behind their boulders and sauntered into camp.

When Tal burst through the tent flaps, it was just in time to see Lanawe and Virgilus each leveling down on a charging Kalathor warrior. One already lay stunned and moaning on the ground.

One burly warrior, beefier than Cron or even Adfor, swung back his double-headed axe prepratory to hurling it at Lanawe. Without pausing to think, Tal snapped up his neuron gun and fired almost instinctively. The warrior went down like a polled ox and Tal suddenly realized the setting was on full. He had killed the man.

The startling and unknown nature of the neuron guns caused the attack to falter and Dr. Palmerin seized the opportunity to hastily assure Adfor that the two newcomers were members of his own people.

"Stand back!" Adfor bellowed, gesturing the Kalathors aside. "These are our guests, too!"

"Does the Axe Clan host any who wanders out of the Desert?" asked Cron, quite loudly. Adfor faced him boldly.

"The Axe Clan hosts whomever Adfor chooses," he said, belligerently. "Does Cron object?"

The two warriors faced each other for several seconds, then Cron shrugged and turned away. The time had not yet come for him to challenge Adfor—but it would come, and soon. Tal knew this and Adfor knew this. As Cron turned away, Adfor glanced meaningfully at Tal and pursed his lips.

"Adfor!" the shout came from a knot of warriors clustered around the burly Kalathor whom Tal had killed. "Adfor! Judd is dead!"

"Dead?" The clan chief swung around to face Tal. "The other warriors you felled are not dead. Why is Judd dead?"

"I struck too hard," said Tal, reaching for a simile the Kalathor would understand to explain a phenomenon Tal only barely understood himself. "You can knock a man down with your axe, you can knock him unconscious, or you can split his head like a melon—all depending on how hard you strike. It is the same with our weapons." He gestured with the neuron gun. "I saw your warrior about to hurl his axe and I struck harder than I intended."

Adfor nodded his head at this explanation and looked at the neuron gun with new interest.

"And you could strike hard enough to kill Judd from that far away?" Tal nodded. Adfor continued: "And do your invisible shields protect you from weapons like that?" He indicated the neuron gun.

"Yes, they do," said Dr. Palmerin, quickly. "If your man had been wearing a deflector screen, he would not have even known that Tal had . . . uh . . . struck him."

Adfor stood with narrowed eyes for another moment, then he gave an abrupt jerk of his head to indicate that they should reenter his tent. Lanawe and Virgilus went inside with them, though the Kalathor guards lifted their eyebrows at the sight of a female enjoying equal status with the males.

Inside, Adfor had the slave girls bring more spiced herb tea. This time it was Lanawe's eyebrows that lifted as the totally nude girls served the hot, aromatic beverage. After they had departed, Adfor reclined on a pile of cushions.

"You wish to go to Shalimar," he said, carefully, in a calculating tone. "Very well. I will guide you. In exchange for—" He held up a hand to stop Dr. Palmerin's sudden exclamation. "In exchange for twenty of your invisible shields and half that many of your death weapons."

Tal opened his mouth to protest, knowing full well the Kalathor expected to haggle and was actually prepared to settle for a considerably smaller quantity, but before he could speak, Fel Palmerin said, "Done!" And the pact was made.

SIXTEEN

Tal had always thought of the Great Desert as a barren, lifeless place of rocks and drifting sands. He was surprised at the amount of life that existed there.

It was not a true desert in the old sense, Dr. Palmerin had explained to him. While most of it was bare rocks and drifting sands, as Tal had expected, there were many isolated rills of greenery where a forgotten streamlet trickled through a narrow cut in age-old rocks or where a small spring bubbled for a distance on the surface before sinking down again into the depths below.

Always it was the water that signaled life. There would be a thin cluster of grass, maybe trees or occasionally flowers, but only where there was water. A few birds would be there and sometimes rabbits or squirrels if the area of moisture were large enough.

Other than that, away from the water, the only life signs were lizards, snakes, and rock scorpions—some as long as Tal's foot. This alone was life. The rest was desolation.

The party rode in a straggling line. Adfor in the lead, followed by Dr. Palmerin, then Tal, then Lanawe, then Rylleh, Adfor's shaman, then Cron, then the dozen Aryorians and the half dozen or so Kalathors who made up the bulk of the expedition. Nearly half the Aryorians had remained behind with the shuttlecraft, the Kalathors refused to even come near it, while a chosen few rode in search of Shalimar.

Lanawe had tried desperately to get Alun Akobar to remain behind, even imploring her father to appoint him leader in their absence, but Akobar could not be swayed. If Lanawe were going into the Great Desert and if Tal Mikar were going with her, then Alun Akobar intended to be there, too.

For Tal, the horse had been the hardest part.

When he had seen them at the edge of the camp, he had been intrigued and had hoped to see a Kalathor mount one and ride it. The thought never crossed his mind that *he* might be riding one soon.

His first close view of the horse herd was unsettling. For one thing, they were bigger than they had appeared at a distance. Also, they were livelier: tossing their heads and prancing about nervously. For another thing, they smelled.

True, it was not an unpleasant odor, but it was a distinctive *horse* smell that triggered latent racial memories in Tal. And all the associations of the smell were not good.

Later that first day, Tal got to see a Kalathor ride. The stocky horseman put one foot in the stirrup and swung gracefully astride a golden palamino with flowing mane and tail. It seemed he had barely settled into the saddle when the horse reared onto its hind legs, pawing the air with its front hooves, causing Tal and Lanawe unconsciously to flinch back.

Then the horseman was off like a shot, galloping across the rocky plateau, wheeling as gracefully as a bird in flight to thunder back toward the encampment. At one point, the rider rose in the stirrups and the palamino soared lightly over a small clump of brush. Tal thought the feeling of being airborne on the back of a galloping horse must be wonderful.

He got his chance to find out shortly.

Several of the Kalathors asked Tal and the others if they would like to ride, but all declined. The horse was unknown on Aryor, so the offworlders were no more familiar with one than Tal was.

Dr. Palmerin brought the rest of the party that was with him into the Kalathor camp and both groups got an opportunity to warily appraise each other.

Most of the day was spent in making preparations for the trip. Adfor insisted that all the Aryorians could not go—Tal knew he feared an ambush and massacre—but he did leave the ratio at roughly two to one. The biggest single detail to be wrangled out was who among them was going to go.

When Dr. Palmerin suggested that they use the shuttlecraft, Adfor was openly skeptical. A tent made of metal, big enough to hold them all, that flew through the air? Tal could see that the Kalathor clan chief was reassessing his new charges.

Even when Adfor, and ninety percent of the Kalathor warriors, had scrambled up the rocky hillside and back to the valley where the shuttlecraft was berthed, the burly clan chief was not impressed.

But when Lanawe lifted the jetboat off in a blasting acceleration that sent the stub-winged craft knifing skyward, the Kalathors were impressed.

Or, more precisely, terrified.

Adfor made the sign of the double helix and threw himself down on the ground with his hands over his head. Rylleh, the Kalathor shaman, also made the sign of the double helix, but he alone of the Axe Clan stayed on his feet. He intoned a mighty, rolling prayer in a rich, sonorous language that none of the strangers understood. Evidently the language of the Kalathors was one tongue Tishir Sequa had not programmed on a mentape.

Lanawe landed the shuttlecraft close in to the Kalathor encampment, there being no further need to conceal it. Adfor led the others as they walked back and he was obviously still shaken.

Rylleh put a curse and a spell on the devil machine, the strongest at his command, and Adfor pronounced it anathema.

Dr. Palmerin sought to get him to explain his violent and unreasoning fear and hatred for the jetboat, but Adfor would only shudder, make the sign of the double helix, and mutter the one word: "Anode!"

Palmerin was unable to find out anything beyond that. He could not even determine if the word "Anode" designated a person, a place, a thing, an event, or was simply a curse. The one thing he was able to determine utterly beyond question was that neither Adfor nor any other Kalathor would come within a dozen meters of the shuttlecraft, let alone consider setting foot aboard it.

That was how Tal Mikar, former lance warrior of the mountain tribe of Thongor, found himself in a rope corral facing a sorrel mare with white stockings.

When it was definitely established that the expedition to Shalimar would go by horseback, it was discreetly suggested that the newcomers learn something of the art of horsemanship. Understandably, none of them had been exactly eager to be the first pupil. Finally, almost out of desperation, Lanawe Palmerin offered to take the first ride.

Tal's mountain-warrior chauvinism would not allow him to stand to one side while a woman did something he was fearful of, so he laid a hand on Lanawe's arm.

"I will do it first," he said. "The others can observe how I learn."

Now, most unwillingly, he found himself walking toward the little sorrel mare.

He had observed the Kalathor rider before. The man had taken the reins in his left hand, seized the saddle horn with the same hand, seized the cantle with his right hand, put his left foot in the stirrup, and swung aboard. That part seemed simple enough.

Tal had been assured that this mare was a gentle horse, quite suitable for a beginner, and not at all likely to rear up as the palamino had done. Tal was quite certain he did not want to try *that* particular trick yet.

Now, with everyone's eyes upon him, he took the reins in his left hand, seized the saddle horn with the same hand, seized the cantle with his right hand, lifted his left foot—and found the stirrup a good twenty centimeters higher than he could reach.

He tried to jump up and stick his foot in the stirrup. Unfortunately he missed the stirrup and succeeded only in kicking the sorrel mare in the ribs with the toe of his boot. The mare shied away from him and Tal took two hopping steps after her and tried again—with the same results.

One of the Kalathors stopped Tal's fruitless one-legged pursuit of the mare and offered his hands as an assist up. Grudgingly, Tal accepted.

Once in the saddle Tal became aware of several things, all

of them unpleasant. The mare was fatter than she looked, the saddle was more slipperly than Tal had imagined, and it was an immense distance to the ground. Tal decided that he did not care for horseback riding at all.

Then the mare took a few tentative steps and Tal discovered the worst was yet to come.

He *bounced*.

The Kalathor had sat astride the palamino as if he and the horse were one entity, moving only in rhythm with the horse and that in perfect synchronization. By contrast, Tal bounced up and down with teeth-rattling force. He also swayed from side to side, out of time with the bouncing, and was certain at every moment that he was about to part company with his mount.

He got a death grip on the saddlehorn and squeezed more tightly with his knees. This helped the bouncing and swaying somewhat and gave him a much more secure feeling. He guided the mare about and found that she responded easily to pressure of the reins.

One of the Kalathors rode up beside him and gave him pointers on his riding. Tal learned to shift his weight as the horse's front feet came off the ground. He learned to let his body translate the bouncing and swaying into a rhythmic rocking that was mated to the horse's own movements.

By late afternoon, Tal was making fair strides toward becoming a horseman.

Not all the Aryorians were faring as well.

Lanawe and Alun Akobar had proved to be as adept as Tal himself, but Dr. Palmerin and one or two others who had been selected to go on the expedition could never seem to get past the bouncing and swaying. Everyone, except the vastly amused Kalathors, was thoroughly delighted when the day's riding adventures were done.

The expedition was to leave at dawn. While the Aryorians and the Kalathors shared a communal evening meal, the naked Kalathor slave women were busy preparing dried meat, waterskins, pemmican, and other provisions that would be taken.

The Aryorians and Tal slept aboard the jetboat. Dr. Palmerin had armed the entire contingent that was to go with neuron guns and personal deflectors. He also gave each of them a supply of the nutrient cubes that Tal and Lanawe had eaten while trailing the Ice Warriors, plus an assortment of stimulants. A compact but very complete medical kit was assembled.

When Tal awoke the next morning, he was so sore he could scarcely move.

His legs ached in every muscle, as did his back and shoulders, and the insides of his legs and his buttocks felt positively raw. It was agony just to get up off the deckplates and make his way, limping, to the head.

Slowly, one by one, the others awoke. Tal was gratified by two things: one, that the others were obviously as stiff and sore as he was; and two, that he had awakened first and had walked some of his stiffness out before the others got up.

They breakfasted with the Kalathors while dawn was still painting the rings with a rosy pink and then, with first true light, they rode away into the Great Desert. Adfor rode in the lead, followed by Dr. Palmerin, then Tal, then Lanawe, then Rylleh, Adfor's shaman, then Cron, then the dozen Aryorians and the half dozen or so Kalathors who made up the bulk of the expedition.

That first day out was one of the most terrible in Tal's memory. Each movement of the little sorrel mare—he had chosen the same mount—sent fresh agony through his legs and buttocks. Soon the pain moved on up his back into his shoulders and finally into his head. The blazing sun, reflected mercilessly off the rocks and sand, did nothing to ease his throbbing headache. The heat was stifling.

By the time a brief halt was called for food and water, Tal and most of the Aryorians were barely able to stay in the saddle. The sun beating down on their unprotected heads had as much to do with their condition as the unaccustomed riding.

"We must have something to protect our heads," Dr. Palmerin said, during their brief rest. "Something like the hats the Kalathors wear."

"But what?" asked Lanawe, shading her eyes with one hand. "We don't have anything."

"Yes, we do," said Tal. He walked up to his sorrel, untied

one of the straps that secured his saddlebags and other gear, and pulled loose the tightly rolled blanket such as each rider carried. "We can fashion head coverings from our blankets."

"You can't make a hat out of a blanket!" scoffed Alun Akobar. "Besides, a blanket keeps you warm. In this heat, we'd roast if we wrapped up in blankets!"

"We're not going to wrap up in them or make hats out of them," replied Tal. He drew his dagger suddenly and Alun Akobar stepped back so quickly several of the Kalathors laughed.

The desert riders were as curious as everyone else when Tal took his dagger and cut out a rough square of material a little less than a meter each way. Then he cut a long, narrow strip of blanket, about seven centimeters wide by a meter and a half long. The square of material he placed over his head, with the front edge protruding a couple of centimeters past his hair line and the rest hanging down across his shoulders. The strip he wound around and around his head, covering the beaded headband and securing the makeshift burnoose in place when he tied it.

"The mountain winters are cold in Thongor," he explained, as he quickly cut out a second square and another strip. "Our warriors make these hoods of bearskin and wear them for protection when the dark winds blow and the wolves howl in the winter night."

He turned to Lanawe and carefully fitted the burnoose in place for her. The girl was delighted with it and the idea was readily adapted by the other Aryorians. Even Alun Akobar made one, though he did it reluctantly.

The balance of the day was not as bad as the first part. The burnooses helped considerably and Tal felt his headache reduce to manageable limits. When Adfor signaled a halt for the evening, all the new horsemen heaved great sighs of relief.

The camp that night gave Tal an eerie feeling of *déjá vu*. He was accustomed to trees and rocks and mountains hemming him in on all sides. The campfire was in a small shelter of tumbled boulders, yet mostly the area was open, making the fire look lonely against the vastness of the surrounding night. It reminded Tal, starkly and vividly, of the camps Fen Melton had set up when he had accompanied the Farade scholar on his ill-fated expedition into the Ice Region. The memory made Tal unaccountably sad and led, by a chain of association, back to Alytha.

Without explanation, Tal got up from the fire and walked out to stand alone in the desert night. Lanawe watched his figure disappear into the darkness and she bit her lip, frowning worriedly. Both her father and Alun Akobar watched her, but whatever each of them thought, each of them kept to himself.

Tal was much less stiff the next morning, though nearly as sore as he had been. The second day's journey was almost a duplicate of the first. The Great Desert stretched endlessly in all directions, its harshness broken only rarely by oases of green.

They saw the city on the third day.

At first, Tal thought they were seeing mountains, hazy in the distance, then he realized the outlines were too regular and too even, too square and angular to be mountains. He pointed them out to Lanawe, who rode beside him.

"That must be a ruined city!" the girl cried, excitedly. "I wonder if it's Shalimar!"

She kicked her pony past Tal and past her father till she caught up to Adfor.

"Is that an old city?" she asked, pointing at the distant ruins. "Like Shalimar?"

Adfor grunted assent. The Kalathor still did not like the idea of a woman treating him as an equal.

"What city is it?" Lanawe persisted. Her father, by this time, was looking at the distant ruins with interest. "Are we going there?"

"Not going there," said Adfor, sharply. "Old city. No good. Nothing there. Going to Shalimar." And he spurred his horse away from her to indicate that he had terminated the conversation.

The ruins were in sight most of the day and the Aryorians and Tal swiveled in their saddles to watch them as long as they could. At last, when the sun was already well below the rings, the last glimpse of the ancient towers was lost in the distance.

The next day they saw more ruins, which they again skirted by a wide margin. The fifth, sixth, and seventh days of their trek were marked by an endless expanse of rocks and sand, and the first cacti Tal had ever seen, with absolutely nothing to break the monotony of the landscape. On the eighth day they came quite close to another ruined city.

They rode close enough that Lanawe, Tal, and the others could see the jagged, broken walls and tumbled down heaps of rubble that marked the old buildings. They were too far away to make out many of the details, but it was obvious that over the centuries the wind and the blowing sand had taken their toll of the ancient structures.

When they made camp that night it was less than a kilometer from the ruins.

"Not safe to camp closer," Adfor advised them, as they ate their evening meal. "Bad things live in the city. Rats that run in packs like wolves and sometimes wild dogs."

"And people?" asked Dr. Palmerin. "Are there any people that still live in the cities?"

"No people. All the people gone long and long ago. Nothing in the cities now but rats." Adfor sipped his spiced herb tea. "Sometimes not even rats, but we still don't camp too close. You never know. . . ." He left the sentence unfinished.

The nearness of the ruined city made everyone restless that night. Gradually, however, the days of riding took their toll, and, one by one, the travelers drifted off to sleep.

Tal sat alone by the banked campfire. He was in a blue mood this evening, his thoughts far away, with Alytha in a cool green valley surrounded by towering mountains.

Finally, to take his mind off his memories, Tal got up and walked away from the campfire into the cool darkness of the desert night.

He walked in the general direction of the ruined city, but stopped when he was still more than a dozen meters from the nearest mound of rubble. There, alone in the night, he seated himself on a smooth slab of stone and stared out at the oddly wavering shadows cast by ringlight.

The night air was quite chill, but it was early enough in the evening that the ground still retained quite a lot of heat from the day.

Tal found that his memories of Alytha were just as strong

alone here in the darkness as they had been when he sat by the campfire. He was in a depressed mood that was not natural for him. Try as he would, he could not take his mind away from the vision of the slender, gray-eyed mountain girl.

His black study did not affect his habitual alertness, however, and he heard the footsteps from the direction of the camp long before his eyes picked out the dark figure approaching. He rose to his feet and turned to face Lanawe Palmerin just as she reached him.

She made a small, sharp intake of breath as Tal rose nearly in front of her.

"You startled me!" she said, instinctively speaking in a near whisper. "I didn't see you." In the darkness, her hand reached out and took his for reassurance of safety.

"I'm sorry," said Tal, in an equally soft voice. He took a step nearer to her. "I heard you coming." He put his other hand on her arm and Lanawe moved closer yet.

"I've been worried about you, Tal," she said, looking up at him in the oddly shifting ringlight. "You've seemed unhappy and sad."

"It's nothing," he said, shaking his head. "I'm all right."

And the truth was that he *was* all right now. Lanawe's presence made Alytha recede into the background of his mind. Somehow, it seemed utterly natural that Lanawe should be there with him, alone in the ringlight. She seemed to *belong* with him. It was a sense of familiarity that Tal found both overwhelming and incomprehensible, yet completely natural.

It was equally natural when he pulled her against him and kissed her soft, warm lips.

The kiss was gentle and tender and Lanawe responded. They looked into each other's eyes for a moment, then kissed again—an open-mouthed kiss of pure passion that made Tal's blood sing in his veins.

He felt the slender, yielding body crushed hard against him and all the loneliness and desire rose up within him in one great throbbing need that would not be denied.

The need was equally strong in Lanawe, for when Tal's questing hands moved across her body he found the magnetic seams of her garments already loosed and his hands moved onto her naked flesh.

Beneath his thin-soled boots, Tal could feel that the ground was rocky. He lifted Lanawe easily in his strong arms and walked to the edge of the rocky outcropping and laid her gently on a bed of soft sand.

He had not had a woman since the morning he had left Alytha in the mountain cave. His passion was an eagerness that made him tremble as he touched the silken softness of her skin. Lanawe moaned softly and reached up for him, her passion as fierce and as eager as his own. He rolled awkwardly against her and she moved to accommodate him, moaning again in pleasure and biting her lip as he made penetration.

It was an act of passion and tenderness, of fierceness and gentleness, for them both. From the first movement, Lanawe anticipated Tal's every body shift. It was almost as if she could read his mind and moved to meet each changed position. It was almost as if her body could anticipate where and how he would next touch her. It was almost as if they had made love together many times before.

Tal's orgasm was quick, but Lanawe's was started before his was done. Each of them had done everything with smooth precision to bring the maximum satisfaction to the other. For Lanawe, who had had several lovers, it was the best she had ever experienced. For Tal, who had been virgin when he took the equally virginal Alytha, it was unbelievably good.

Afterward, they lay cradled in each other's arms. The cool desert night felt good on their sweat-sticky bodies.

"Where did you learn to make love like that?" asked Lanawe, half teasing. "You must have worn out all the women in your tribe just practicing."

Tal chuckled, shaking his head. "You are the second. I have only loved Alytha before this." At the mention of her name, Tal felt sharp twinges of guilt over what he had done. He was too much the primitive barbarian for guilt to be a major factor in his thinking, but he did feel touches of it because of Lanawe.

Lanawe felt the change in his attitude that the mention of Alytha's name produced. Not for the first time she wondered at this sensitivity Tal evoked in her. She could sense subtle mood changes in him more readily than she could detect major emotional changes in others. She did not understand this feeling at all, but she understood Tal.

"Don't feel bad over what we did," she said, touching his cheek gently. "A human body must have sexual release just as surely as it must have food. This does not mean that you love Alytha any the less." She kissed him quickly. "This is a thing shared just between us, a moment of time that is ours alone."

She kissed him again, then quickly rose to her feet, adjusting her garments back into position. By the time she was presentable, so was Tal. She kissed him yet again, her body clinging to his with a memory of what they had shared and a promise that it could be shared again. Hand in hand, they walked back to camp.

The Kalathor sentry watched them come out of the shadows. It took very little imagination for him to figure out what they had been doing. He smiled to himself.

He was still watching when he saw Alun Akobar step out of the shadow of a tent to confront them.

"Where have you been, Lanawe?" he asked, through clenched teeth.

"I've been walking with Tal," the girl replied coolly.

"I don't think you should be alone with him." Akobar's face was ugly with anger. "You don't know if he can be trusted."

The exchange had been in Aryorian, which Tal could not understand, but tonal inflections told him most of it. He stepped in front of Lanawe.

"You are in our way, little man," he said, although Alun Akobar was not small. "Step aside."

"Nobody's talking to you!" snapped Akobar, and he made as if to shove Tal aside. It was a natural enough mistake.

Tal's hand closed on Akobar's wrist and the Aryorian was jerked sharply forward to meet Tal's other fist, which exploded in the pit of his stomach. Caught completely off guard, Akobar doubled over, and had enough sense not to try to get back on his feet. He knew without a doubt that Tal Mikar would kill him if he got up.

"I've tried to discourage your attentions, Alun," Lanawe said to him, "but you've ignored my hints. All I can say now is that I prefer the company of Tal Mikar to you or to any other man I've ever known."

She turned and, in full sight of the awakening camp, kissed Tal lightly on the lips.

"Good night," she said, and walked away to her tent.

SEVENTEEN

At first it looked like any other ruined city.

As usual, Tal was the first to spot it. The first of the non-Kalathors, that is. Adfor had been staring at it for over an hour before it caught Tal's eye.

They were ending their second week of steady riding. Everyone, even the offworlders, had adjusted to the pace. All of them, with the single exception of Dr. Fel Palmerin, were as at home in the saddle as were the Kalathors. Dr. Palmerin still sat stiffly in the saddle and still bounced high with each step his horse made, but he never complained and he never lagged behind.

Slowly, the ruined city grew as the small caravan wended toward it. It was past the noon break before it became obvious to them all that Adfor was heading directly for this ruin, not skirting it as he had done all the others.

Lanawe had learned the futility of trying to question the Kalathor clan chief. Adfor simply refused to recognize any woman as having the right to question any man. So she made a quick suggestion to Tal and he kicked the little sorrel mare into a canter. In a moment he caught up with Adfor.

"We seem to be heading toward that ruined city," he said. "Are we?"

"Yes. That is Shalimar—Beloved of Shandor."

The Kalathor looked neither to the left nor to the right as he said this and his nonchalant manner caught Tal off guard. It was a moment before the impact of what Adfor had said finally hit him.

"Shalimar?" he said. "You mean . . . we're there?"

"Camp there tonight," was the laconic reply.

Tal wheeled his pony around and relayed the massage to Lanawe and her father. Within minutes the entire party knew it.

An immediate change swept over the band. The off-worlders' spirits lifted, their voices rang out in shouts and laughter, their whole manner became excited and almost festive. The end of their terrible quest was almost in sight. Somewhere—in the ruins ahead of them—lay a millenia-old legend that was their one chance to save their world from the Ilrik invaders.

To Tal, Shalimar meant something else entirely. It meant the Aryorian's help in finding Alytha. It meant a new chance at life and freedom for them both.

Slowly, as the sun dipped below the rings, the ruins grew closer.

Shalimar was not as large as some of the other ruined cities they had passed. The overall area, Tal judged, was scarcely more than a kilometer square. It had been Shandor's retreat, his place to come to when the pressures had grown too great, and he had built it for grace, tranquility, and serenity—modeled, Tal had been told, on an even more ancient place with the same name.

Only one or two buildings were left reasonably intact. Most had long since fallen into mounds of indistinguishable ruin, many nearly covered by drifting sand and blowing dirt. There was an almost palpable feeling of desolation to the place.

The clatter of the horses' hooves on manmade concrete streets had a strangely frightening sound.

There was no life at all in the ruins of Shalimar. No birds, no small animals, no insects. There were not even any rats.

"How do you know this is Shalimar?" asked Dr. Palmerin, when Adfor reined in at a great central plaza. "I mean . . . there's nothing here that identifies it as Shalimar."

Adfor looked at him coolly, but before he could speak, Tal heard himself saying: "It is Shalimar."

Everyone turned to look at him. The surprise on their faces simply mirrored the surprise Tal himself felt.

"How do *you* know this is Shalimar?" asked Lanawe softly, her eyes searching Tal's face. The strangely intuitive feeling that she got from Tal was signaling confusion. She could sense it in every gesture he made.

"I . . . I don't know." Tal frowned and looked around him at the desolated city growing black shadows in the lengthening twilight. "There's something . . . something about this place. I . . . I can't tell you. . . ." He shook his head. "But I *know* that it is Shalimar! I don't know how, but I know it. This is Shalimar!"

"It *is* Shalimar, mountain man," said Rylleh, the Kalathor shaman. He reined his pony next to Tal's and looked at him with piercing eyes. "I see something in your aura," he said, almost musingly. "Something I do not understand. This night I will offer up prayers to Shandor, here in his beloved Shalimar, and will cast the bones and read them. This thing I see about you portends much. I must pray long about it."

The shaman's words had a dampening effect on the rising spirits of the expedition. Or perhaps it was merely their reaction to the unearthly stillness of Shalimar.

The campfire shed a warm orange glow over the rocks and scrub bushes around the plaza. A standing wall still flanked one side of the area, which was about ten meters square. The tents had been erected near this wall and the campfire built in front of them. The wall was almost three meters high and somehow the party seemed more secure with its heavy stonework at their backs.

Rylleh did not eat that night. Instead he retreated to the shadows and squatted alone there in the darkness. His long cloak folded around him still, with his wide brimmed hat tilted over his eyes, he could almost have been mistaken for a boulder, so motionless did he sit.

Later, after everyone had eaten and most had rolled up in their blankets for the night, the old shaman came back and squatted by the campfire. He prepared a cup of spiced herb tea, dropped in a pinch of powder from some source of his own, then slowly sipped the now heady mixture.

He unfolded a beautifully tanned piece of buckskin and uncovered a handful of whitened bones. These bones had a mystical significance and Rylleh had gathered them from many sources. A few had been bequeathed him by his father.

Now the old shaman shook the bones loosely in both hands and scattered them across the buckskin on the ground. He looked at the way they fell, their relationship to each other, the direction certain ones of them pointed. He studied them for many minutes, his brows knitted in concentration. He carefully rearranged one or two of them and studied this new pattern an equally long time.

He was casting them for the third time when he became aware of a shadow beside him. He spoke without looking around:

"What do you seek here, mountain man?"

"I seek to know what you see in your dead bones, wizard," replied Tal. "And to know why you said what you said before we camped."

"What I see in the bones is not for such as you. And I spoke what I did because of what I saw in your aura." The old man refilled his cup with spiced herb tea and to it again added the mild hallucinogen he always carried.

"And what did you see in my aura?" Tal pressed. "You play with words, wizard. Is it to hide the fact that you have nothing to say?"

Rylleh lifted his eyes to look directly at Tal and Tal shook within himself at what he saw in the old man's hawklike gaze.

"There is something about you, mountain man," Rylleh said, in a low, heavy voice. "Something I sense, but do not understand. It was in your aura today. There are great forces for which you are the locus. I cannot put a name to these forces, but I can feel them about you as surely as I can feel the wind before a storm breaks over the Desert.

"The bones can tell the shape of things to come and can explain the ultimate end of things which have happened in the past. The bones say that you were born to be here, at this place, at this time. There is a destiny you must fulfill, mountain man, and the bones hint that it is a terrible destiny. More than this I cannot discern. But the bones speak of death." He gestured toward first one of the white slivers on the buckskin, then toward another.

"*That* one," he said, "by pointing north, tells of the death of someone great. A clan chief, perhaps." He glanced toward Adfor's sleeping figure. "*That* one, by crossing this other, speaks of evil and famine loose in the land. And *that* one...." His voice died suddenly as he bent over the tumbled bones.

Tal waited for him to continue, then, when he did not, he asked impatiently, "What about that one? What does it foretell?"

Rylleh slowly raised his head and Tal saw that his eyes were full of fear. His voice was a hoarse whisper.

"That one speaks of *my* death, mountain man. I will die here, in the heart of the Great Desert, and will never again see the tents of my clan nor know the embrace of my children. I will die here, near this place, and my bones will whiten in the Desert sun and the vultures will feast upon my entrails." He looked back down at the bones.

"But even that is preferable to what I see for you. The bones speak of something *like* death, but *not* death." He touched the magic symbols reverently, being careful not to disturb their pattern. "It is something I have never seen before. There is no word for it. I would call it only—the *undeath*."

Tal's flesh crawled as the Kalathor shaman repeated the same words said by the Arcobane shaman. There was no way Rylleh could have known what And Lalon had told Tal and Tal's barbarian superstition made his hair literally stand on end.

He looked at the old shaman for several heartbeats, then he turned and walked away. And that night he did not sleep.

At dawn, Shalimar took on a whole new aspect.

With the rings a golden glow across the clear blue sky and the sun still half hidden by the horizon, the tumbled down ruins took fire from the morning light and for a short period of time the party could almost recreate in their minds some sense of what the city must have looked like when it was newly built and alive with people.

To Tal, most of all, the city spoke. While the others prepared breakfast, he and Lanawe stood on the outskirts of the central plaza and he pointed out the salient features to her as if he were a resident of the city and she was a tourist.

"There was a tall building *there*." He pointed. "With balconies along two sides. See? You can see part of the wall there and that abutment—see?—is the base of the lowest tier of balconies. Over there," he gestured, "was a large dome. It seems to be all gone now. But I'll bet the tower still stands." He wheeled and gestured and, sure enough, a slim tower thrust itself skyward above the level of rubble around it.

Tal was excited as he pointed out various buildings. There was an almost feverish glint to his eye. Lanawe was worried about this reaction and her worry was reflected in her face and in her voice.

"How do you *know* all this, Tal? Have you been to Shalimar before?"

Tal looked at her and then out at the ruins, then back at her again.

"I don't know," he said. "I mean, *no*, I've never been to Shalimar before and yet . . . and yet I *know* how everything should look; I *know* how everything used to look; I *know*. . . ." He stopped. "I don't understand it, Lan. I've never seen Shalimar before and yet . . . and yet, I feel that, somehow, I *know* it.

"It's like you. I never saw you before that day on the ice, but when I saw you, the moment I saw you, I knew that I'd known you before. I knew that I'd known you always. That's the way it is with Shalimar."

Lanawe instinctively put her hand in his.

"I . . . understand. In a way," she said, frowning as she searched for exactly the right words to say. "I . . . feel like I've known you all my life, it seems." She laughed lightly. "I've never felt so *close* to anyone, felt as if I *knew* anyone, felt . . . I don't know . . . so much a *part* of anyone before. Does that make any sense to you at all?"

"Yes. Yes, it does. It's like the way I feel. About you . . . and about Shalimar." He looked back at the ruins. "I had never heard the name 'Shalimar' till Fen Melton told me some old legends. The name meant nothing to me when I heard it. It was just a word. But now that I'm here, in the midst of it, it's almost like coming home."

After the morning meal, the Aryorians got ready for a systematic exploration of the ruins.

The legend, which had proven accurate so far, said that the Chalice of Time would glow when it came near the Eternity

Stone. Unfortunately, the legend did not specify how close it had to be brought for this phenomenon to occur. Dr. Palmerin determined it would have to be a trial and error method.

The offworlders split themselves into three groups. Dr. Palmerin, Lanawe, Tal, and Alun Akobar made up one group. They took the Chalice of Time with them and began the actual search for the Eternity Stone. The other two groups were delegated the task of carefully sectioning out the ruins and clearly marking the boundaries of each section so that the search party could be certain no part of the city might be overlooked.

The Kalathors watched all these preparations with mingled curiosity and amusement. These strangers certainly had unusual notions, they reasoned. The searchers' actions made no sense to them at all.

They found the crypt in the middle of the afternoon.

Alun and Lanawe were moving rubble ahead while Tal moved stones for Dr. Palmerin. Suddenly the girl shouted: "Dad! Dad, come here!"

The excitement in her voice caused both her father and Tal to come dashing to where she and Alun stood, panting, before a massive doorway.

The door was more than half below ground level, with four steps leading down to it. It was set in a massive stone and metal wall that might once have been the foundation and lower floor of a quite imposing structure. Now, however, mounds of ruin were heaped atop it, though the wall in which the door was set seemed utterly impervious to the ravages of time and the elements.

The door was over two meters high and nearly a meter and a half wide. It was set so flush with the wall that a fingernail could scarcely be put in its crack anywhere. And there was no knob, lock, bolt, hinge, or any other conceivable device whereby the door might be opened. It was sealed and sealed solid.

There was a curious symbol carved on the door, at about eye level for a tall warrior, and a single line of oddly curved markings just below that. Other than this, the door was smooth and unmarked. But it was the first still recognizable door they had seen in Shalimar.

"What do you make of it, Dad?" asked Lanawe, as her father examined the strange portal.

"I don't know," the old man admitted. He held the Chalice of Time against the stone, but nothing happened. He moved it around and around, but the results were negative. "We need to find some way to get in."

But getting in proved to be something of a task. First Alun, then Tal, then both together, then both of them and Lanawe strained against the door, but it was solidly set. They might as well have been trying to push down a mountain.

Tal motioned the others back, then seized a fallen block of stone. Straining, groaning, his muscles cracking with the effort, he swung the massive stone over his head and hurled it with all his strength against the door. The stone shattered and the door was unmarked.

Then Tal picked up a section of metal girder about a meter long and attacked the recalcitrant door with every intention of battering it down. In ten minutes the girder was bent, his hands were bleeding, and the door was unmarked.

Now Alun Akobar motioned Tal back. The offworlder placed a thermite bomb against the door and ignited it. When the blinding flame died down, the stone and metal casing was scorched and blackened, but the door was unmarked.

Lanawe tried firing her neuron gun at it, but with no real hope of success. Neuron guns were designed to affect the human nervous system, but she felt she had to try something. The door was unmarked.

"Maybe there's a secret catch," suggested Alun, and he and Lanawe began to carefully work their way around the edges of the door.

While they were doing that, Dr. Palmerin climbed atop what must have been the upper portion of the structure and began searching for a second entrance. As he searched, he moved the Chalice of Time back and forth, always hoping, if the Eternity Stone were within, it would trigger a latent signal.

He determined that the area roofed over was between thirty and thirty-two meters square. When the rubble was all cleared away, or enough of it anyway, he could easily make out the square configuration of the building. The wall came up not quite a meter and then formed a large, rectangular platform. There was no other entrance save the one doorway.

Dr. Palmerin got on his hands and knees and moved the Chalice of Time along until he had covered the entire surface area. There was no reaction to indicate the object they sought was within.

The examination took him well over an hour, by which time the three young people had given up all hope of forcing the door or of finding a hidden catch. While Palmerin was conducting his painstaking search, Tal, Alun, and Lanawe had completely circled the structure, moving rubble back from the edges and making absolutely certain there was no other entrance.

When he had completed his search of the top, Dr. Palmerin passed the Chalice of Time to Lanawe and she and Alun recircled the building, carefully testing every outside centimeter to see if a response would be triggered.

While they did this, Tal returned to the doorway.

His blue eyes clouded over as he stood before the portal. *There was something here—*

His mind reached out for an answer that lay right on the fringes of his awareness, but which twisted away from him and darted back into the shadows. He tried to ferret it out, but he could not put a name to it. *But there was something— something here. . . .*

Camp that night was quiet and subdued. The Aryorians had been elated when they had finally reached Shalimar, but the day's fruitless searching had somewhat dampened their ardor. They were all tired and sore from the clambering, sliding, climbing, and rock moving they had done all day. The evening meal was quickly eaten and everyone rolled up in their blankets for a good night's sleep.

But Tal Mikar was awake.

Despite the fact that he had scarcely slept the night before, Tal found that he could not get the strange doorway out of his mind. There was something about it that pulled at him with an almost physical force.

None of the others had seemed to feel it. Not Lanawe, whom he had half expected to react as he did; not Dr.

Palmerin, and certainly not Alun Akobar. For some reason the sealed crypt exerted its influence only on Tal.

His was a simple, direct mind. A mind not suited for puzzling out strangenesses. More for him was the tracking of a fluffytail through the snow or reading the signs a forked horn left as it passed through the mountain forest than the unraveling of mysteries of the sealed crypt.

It baffled him and Tal did not like being baffled. At last, convinced that he was not going to be able to sleep, Tal threw off his blankets, seized his sword and lance, and walked away from the firelit central plaza into the shadowed ruins. Only Rylleh, the Kalathor shaman, saw him go and the strange old man kept his own counsel.

The ringlight cast weird, moving shadows among the tumbled ruins, but Tal paid them no mind. He knew where he was going and went directly there, without pausing or turning aside.

He descended the four steps and stood before the sealed crypt. The one line of unknown writing was invisible, but the strange symbol glowed very softly with some magic light of its own.

Tal put his hands out till they touched the cool stone, then squatted slowly, letting his hands slide down its glass-smooth surface, till he knelt before it.

Something still pulled at his mind, but he could not put a name to it. There was something he knew about this door, about this crypt—but what? What was it?

Was it something Fen Melton had said, some legend or other he had told him around a campfire in the Farade village? Was it some old story he'd heard the shaman tell when he was a boy back in Thongor? Was it something else? Something from the same source that made him feel so close to Lanawe Palmerin?

All these questions circled in Tal's brain like vultures circling a carcass before they feast. He did not know the answer to any of them. He did not know if they even had answers. All he knew for certain was that something about the sealed crypt called out to him.

He never knew when he slept, but dawn found him curled up before the crypt door, with only a stone for a pillow, shaking from the chill of the night. Bleary-eyed, he staggered back to the encampment and gratefully accepted a refresher cup from the female who was helping Alun Akobar prepare breakfast.

The second day of searching was a repetition of the first. Only Tal did not stay with Dr. Palmerin's small group all day. Several times he returned to stare at the sealed crypt, but the doorway remained as enigmatic as ever.

Everyone was tired and short tempered at the evening meal. Adfor reminded Dr. Palmerin that he had guided him to Shalimar and asked for his payment. Dutifully, the old man removed the agreed-upon number of neuron guns and personal deflector screens. The Kalathors gave every indication of planning to ride away at dawn.

"You can't leave us here," Dr. Palmerin protested. "We could never find our way back across the Great Desert to our own people." Actually, the Aryorians had maintained radio contact with the jetboat and Dr. Palmerin knew it could reach their position in less than a day, but he did not want the Kalathors to leave just yet. He felt that their presence provided better security while they searched than would be the case if only the Aryorians were there, even including those from the jetboat.

Adfor shrugged. "I bargained to take you to Shalimar. Nothing was agreed beyond that. You are here now. We will ride back."

"What payment would persuade you to stay for this many more days?" Fel Palmerin held up the fingers of both hands. "Would another payment equal to the one we have just made help you to decide to stay that many days?"

Adfor considered this. The stocky nomad carefully weighed the tactical advantages that would be his with even more of the magic weapons. He nodded slowly.

"We will stay," he said.

The third, fourth, and fifth days were equally fruitless. By this time, all of Shalimar had been sectioned and mapped, and a goodly portion of it had been explored. The searching was the hardest part. The Chalice of Time was passed along over the ground and over the rubble and over every conceivable hiding place much the same way a metal detector or a radiation detector might have been used. It was slow, tedious, time-consuming work. But no one knew of an easier way.

In the late afternoon of the sixth day, Tal left the searchers and went back to the sealed crypt. He could never be away from it for more than an hour without the urge to see it again compelling him to leave whatever he was doing and go there.

He was standing before it, wrestling again with its enigma, a worried, puzzled look on his face, when the sound of footsteps running through the rubble caused him to come alert, lance at the ready.

Lanawe Palmerin was running toward him, her black hair blowing in the wind, her face alight with excitement.

"We've found it, Tal!" she shouted, as she neared him. "We've found it! We've found the Eternity Stone!"

EIGHTEEN

It scarcely seemed a thing worth a trip halfway across the galaxy.

The Eternity Stone was roughly oval, with rounded ends. To Tal, it looked like nothing in the world so much as an enormous egg. He almost smiled when he saw it.

Only no egg ever looked quite like the Eternity Stone. Its surface was impossible to look at directly. When one stared at it, one involuntarily glanced away. Its outline was clear, its shape was easily discerned, yet somehow one could not look directly at it.

"The Accursed of Shandor bends away the eye," said Rylleh, offering an explanation for the optical phenomenon they all experienced. "It is not good to look too long at a thing so hated by Shandor."

Despite its peculiar optical qualities the Eternity Stone could be readily touched, handled, and moved, although its weight was such that two strong men could scarcely shift its mass.

But the material from which the Eternity Stone was shaped had a most unusual thermal quality, also. It was neither hot nor cold nor lukewarm nor cool. Even where it was exposed to direct sunlight, after the rubble was cleared away from it, it took on no warmth and reflected no heat.

"It's very interesting," commented Dr. Palmerin, as a sling was rigged so the treasure could be carried back to the central plaza. "I've never seen anything quite like this."

There was no question about it being the Eternity Stone.

The legend had said that the Chalice of Time would glow when brought close to the Eternity Stone and that receptacle, now held by Dr. Palmerin, radiated an almost blinding light.

The thin, highly reflective metal from which the bowl was formed, soft gold on the outside, nontarnishing silver on the inside, was now brighter than the brightest glow-bulb aboard the *X-97*. And the tiny recesses around the inner edge, which looked as if they might once have held jewels, glowed in a flickering pattern of ever-changing colors. For all the world, thought Lanawe suddenly, like tattletales on a control panel.

It was full dark by the time the Eternity Stone was transported to the central plaza. Everyone was too excited to eat, but Dr. Palmerin ordered the evening meal prepared. He took a refresher cup and stepped aside to counsel with his daughter, Tal, Alun, and two or three others whose opinions he valued.

"We have a choice," he said, speaking slowly. "Should we try placing the Stone within the Chalice while we're here, in Shalimar, or should we transport them separately back to Aryor and do it there?"

Tal frowned. "What," he asked, "exactly is supposed to happen when you put them together?"

"That's the nub of the problem," answered Dr. Palmerin. "Nobody knows what will happen, or even what is supposed to happen. All we know—and remember, until an hour ago all this was only a legend to us—is that when the two devices come together, a weapon is supposed to be unloosed that no power in the universe can withstand."

"Do you suppose that means an explosion?" asked Lanawe. "Could the Eternity Stone be a bomb and the Chalice of Time a triggering device?"

"It's possible," agreed her father. "But somehow I doubt it. Remember, the weapon, of which these are the two halves, was built during the war of rebellion when Shara Vralon opposed the tyrant, Lan Regas. At that time, the dominant weapons were based on the Science of Infrastatics. They were not simple explosive devices.

"Of course, no one today knows or understands anything about Infrastatics. We do know that it was infinitely powerful. Whole continents were displaced by it and a satellite nearly a third as big as Earth itself was reduced to rubble and became the rings we now see overhead.

"Yet, Infrastatics could be controlled and handled. It does not say for certain, in any of our legends, but I've always deduced they were nonexplosive weapons. Of course," he elevated both eyebrows, "I could be totally wrong. We might trigger a bomb that would utterly destroy this entire solar system."

"It . . . is not a bomb," said Tal, slowly, speaking from the same unknown reservoir of knowledge by which he had identified the city as Shalimar. "I do not know what it is—and I *fear* it!—but it is not a bomb."

Lanawe looked at him and saw that he was suddenly pale. His blue eyes looked huge in his face and cold sweat stood out on his forehead.

"Are you all right, Tal?" She put her hand on his arm as she asked this. He nodded slowly, several times, before he spoke.

"I'm . . . all right," he said. "But I feel . . . I feel something *evil* about . . . that thing." He looked toward the Eternity Stone, resting squat and stolid not far from the cooking fire. "I felt it suddenly, just a few moments ago. That thing should never have been found! It is a thing of evil that no living human being should even be near!"

Dr. Palmerin cleared his throat.

"Yes, well . . . I'm sure that's all well and good, Tal, but—" he cleared his throat again—"That *thing,* as you call it, is the only hope we have of saving our world from total slavery by the Ilriks. If Aryor is ever to be free again, we must use the Eternity Stone by whatever means is possible."

"Besides, Tal," Lanawe said comfortingly. "Now that we have the Eternity Stone, we'll soon be leaving. It will be taken completely away from your world and whatever you fear from it will be gone then."

"I'm curious about something," said one of the other Aryorians, thoughtfully. "Have you ever considered the names? The 'Chalice of Time.' The 'Eternity Stone.' Don't these strike you as odd names to give to a weapon?"

"They do, indeed!" said Dr. Palmerin. "And it's something Tishir Sequa and I have often discussed. There is a connective element in both names—a temporal element: the Chalice of *Time;* the *Eternity* Stone.

"I've wondered, quite honestly, if the weapon is some sort of time device. Perhaps even something strong enough to alter the very time fabric of the universe itself. I've wondered if the temporal qualities of the two names are supposed to suggest that."

"Or, possibly," said another Aryorian, "it could open a doorway—a sort of time portal—through which we could obtain help from the past. Or, perhaps, alter the past in some way so as to eliminate whatever the threat is in the present."

"I think we're speculating rather far afield," commented Lanawe. "I think we should simply consider our options. One, we can test the weapon here and now, by simply placing the Stone in the Chalice; two, we can call the jetboat, get them out here to Shalimar, and then test the weapon; three, we can call the jetboat, get them out here, load the weapon aboard, fly to the *X-97*, and test the weapon there; or, four, we can load everything aboard the *X-97*, return to Aryor, and test the weapon against the Ilriks."

"That last would be our best bet," said Alun 'Akobar. "That way we'd be certain of destroying the Ilriks. After all, how do we know how many times the weapon will work? I mean, if we try it now, that one time may be it—and we'd have nothing to use against the Ilriks."

"How will we use it against the Ilriks?" asked Lanawe.

Alun opened his mouth to reply, then stopped suddenly. "I . . . well . . . I don't know," he finally admitted.

"That's my point," said Lanawe. "*Nobody* knows. We've *got* to test the weapon some time before we go up against the Ilriks with it. If we don't, we're worse than helpless."

"Then let's take it up to the *X-97* and test it there," suggested one of the others. "There are instruments aboard her that your father and Dr. Sequa could use to examine the weapon very carefully before they tried it out."

"True," agreed Lanawe, "but what if the weapon creates some displacement when tested, either physical, like an explosion, or temporal, like Dad suggested, or electrical, like shorting out all the circuitry aboard the *X-97*? What then? The inside of a spaceship in deep space is an extremely dangerous place to test a new and totally unknown weapon."

"You seem to have already made your choice," said Dr. Palmerin, smiling slightly. "But I'll give you a chance to clear the field. What are your arguments against calling the shuttlecraft out here and then testing the weapon?"

Lanawe grinned at her father.

"You're right," she said. "I have made my choice. And to answer your question: I think there's a very good chance all or some of us may be killed when we test the weapon. But there's no reason why any more should be endangered than have to be.

"I think we should call the shuttlecraft, tell them what we've found and what we're about to do, but tell them either to wait till they hear from us again or to approach this area with extreme caution. That way, even if all of us are killed, they might be able to figure out what we did wrong.

"Also, if we get the jetboat out here before we test the weapon, and then if there's some form of explosion that destroys everything, that would leave Dr. Sequa and the others stranded in orbit aboard the *X-97* with no way to ever get down to Earth."

Dr. Palmerin nodded thoughtfully.

"I think your reasoning is good," he said. "I'll get on the radio and call the others back at base camp, then we'll see just what we have here."

Somehow, during the quick meal that was eaten, Tal could not shake the sense of impending evil that hung over him like a raincloud.

It was not an actual sense of fear so much as it was a feeling of dreadful anticipation. As if something profoundly evil were about to manifest itself. Not necessarily something threatening, but simply evil—the essence of evil—the very soul and embodiment of evil.

Tal finally put his food aside, untasted, and walked to the very edge of the firelight. He wanted to go back to the crypt. There was something about that enigmatic sealed door that drew him, even more strongly at this precise moment.

However, there was something else—a feeling that he must somehow face this evil, a feeling that he had somehow been born for this very manifestation that was about to occur—

that kept him here, at the edge of the firelight, and would not let him go to the crypt.

"They do not understand that which they are about to do," said a voice beside him. Rylleh stood there, a grim, unreadable figure in the shifting ringlight.

"Do you understand it, wizard?" Tal challenged, angry because the old man had managed to surprise him.

"I understand enough to know that this is a thing that should not be done." Rylleh hesitated. "I also understand that this is something that was foreordained to happen so that certain other things, necessary things, might come to pass."

"You talk in riddles, old man. Speak plainly."

Rylleh simply looked at him for a moment before he said, "The ways of a man upon the Desert are a riddle to a hawk riding the wind, but to other men they are plain." Then the old man turned and walked away.

None of this did anything to relieve Tal's sense of impending evil. The sealed crypt called to him, but the knowledge, that came from the unknown source somewhere within him, that he was somehow a part of the forces at work here this night kept him where he was. He knew, with some deep and profound knowledge, that the real drama—for which all his life up to this point had been mere preparation—was going to unfold within the next few minutes.

Since he was far back at the edge of the plaza, Tal clambered atop a tumbled down section of masonry so he could have a clear view of the proceedings. Lacking the scientific training of the Aryorians, he had nothing but his barbarian's instinct to rely upon, and it held no threat of explosion or other physical danger, only the overwhelming sense of impending evil.

From his vantage point he saw Dr. Palmerin bring the Chalice of Time forward and place it on a smooth stretch of tile near the exact center of the central plaza. The other Aryorians were motioned back, except for Alun Akobar and two others who were actually going to move the Eternity Stone. Lanawe Palmerin stood beside her father.

Sweating, despite the coolness of the desert night, the three offworlders squatted and seized the oval smoothness of the Eternity Stone. Its size and shape precluded their obtaining a firm grip, but they managed to wrestle it off the ground and headed toward the Chalice of Time with it.

As the Stone came closer, the glow from the Chalice became as bright as the noonday sun. When the Stone was less than a meter away, the Chalice began to hum with a soft, low sound. At the same moment, the inside of the Chalice suddenly went dark. It was not that it simply ceased to glow. It actually became a black void, a point of nothingness, in the center of a circle of flickering, varicolored lights that chased themselves around the inner rim.

The humming rose several octaves as the Stone came into position over the Chalice. Carefully, their faces eerily lit by the blinding glow from the receptacle, the three men lowered the Eternity Stone into the Chalice of Time. The rounded end of the oval egg exactly fitted the interior of the bowl.

There was sudden silence and sudden darkness.

Lanawe, her father, and the others, hastily backed away from the area of the now strangely quiescent artifacts.

Softly, ever so softly, a glow began to emanate. This time it came from both the Chalice and the Stone. It was totally unlike the original light the Chalice had emitted.

As the glow brightened, the outlines of the Stone balanced upright in the Chalice began to blur and melt. It became impossible to look at them without the eyes watering and a sudden sense of vertigo overwhelming one.

Somehow, in the midst of the strangely opaque glowing, it seemed as though the shape of the Chalice began to blend and change, to enlarge and expand, to contract and swell. The shape that reformed itself was much lower and longer, a horizontal abstraction rather than a vertical one.

Then the glow began to fade, again so softly that it was almost imperceptible. The light became dimmer and seemed to be absorbed directly back into the shape that now remained on the flagstones of the central plaza of the city of Shalimar, Beloved of Shandor.

A naked man lay there on his back, his face turned up to the ringlight.

Of the Eternity Stone and the Chalice of Time there was no trace.

Slowly, hesitantly, Lanawe, her father, and one or two

others approached the apparent corpse.

Only, when they came closer, they could see that the man was not dead. His deathly pale chest, white as the finest alabaster, rose and fell in a slow, steady rhythm. A tiny blue vein in his throat could be seen beating beneath the milk-white skin.

He was very tall, fully two meters, but whippet thin. There was not the color of blood about his body, yet the muscles looked like bands of rawhide. His bone-thin body looked as if it possessed almost abnormal strength. His hands were big and coarse, though white as the rest of his body, and Lanawe noticed, irrelevantly, that he had stiff-looking hairs growing in the center of each palm.

His thin, fine-boned face looked aristocratic, with its high-bridged aquiline nose, flaring nostrils, and thin-lipped, finely chiseled mouth. His ears were definitely pointed on top. His high cheekbones and sharp chin made his face look even longer, but he was still a decidedly handsome man. *Although,* Lanawe added mentally, *almost surely a cruel one.* She wondered at the strange tingle that ran through her as she thought this.

The man's hair had once been black as midnight, but was now shot through with gray and, in some places, with pure white. It was brushed back from the face in a smooth sweep of iron gray. Yet the face did not look as old as the hair indicated. The man looked to be early middle-aged, certainly no older.

The Aryorians knelt by the recumbent figure and, almost fearfully, Dr. Palmerin placed a hand on the man's chest. His dead white skin was almost painfully hot.

"Who . . . could he be?" asked Lanawe, hesitantly.

"Or *what* could he be?" countered Alun Akobar.

As if in answer to this last question, the man's delicately veined eyelids opened, and everyone shrank back involuntarily.

The eyes were blood-red and feral.

It was not that the eyes were bloodshot. They were truly red, with a gleaming spot for the iris—like the iris of an animal's eye in a flash picture. The eyes were totally inhuman. If a tiger had looked out at them, its gaze would have been no less alien than that evil red stare.

"I am Anode," said the man, in a hoarse whisper. "I . . . thank you for bringing me back. Much . . . much reward shall be yours." The speech seemed to exhaust him.

"I'm Dr. Fel Palmerin, from Aryor. Who are you? Where did you come from? Are you hurt? Can we help you?"

"I am Anode," the man said again, in an almost soundless whisper. "For freeing me . . . I will give you the world—in time. But now . . . I must sleep. To regain my strength . . . I must . . . rest. . . ."

The feral eyes closed and the man slept.

"Get a sleeping bag from my tent," commanded Dr. Palmerin. "This man seems to have a raging fever. We've got to keep him warm."

"Where did he come from?" asked one of the Aryorians. "And what happened to the Eternity Stone and the Chalice of Time?"

"That's what I want to know," echoed Alun Akobar. "Is *he* the weapon that was supposed to be unloosed?"

"I don't know," admitted Dr. Palmerin. "You all saw the same things I saw. If anyone has an explanation for them, I'd welcome hearing it."

"I don't have an explanation," said Lanawe, thoughtfully. "But I do have a suggestion."

By this time, Anode had been wrapped carefully in Dr. Palmerin's own sleeping bag and nothing was visible of him save only the milk-white face and the iron gray hair. The Kalathors were some distance off, Tal Mikar stood to one side on a jumble of fallen masonry, and only the Aryorians stood close to the sleeping figure of the man Anode. They all turned quizzically to Lanawe.

"Do you remember when we tried to get Adfor to fly in the jetboat and he refused?" she asked, in a soft voice, speaking Aryorian so that no one else could understand her words. "He and Rylleh cursed the jetboat and said the name 'Anode.' It didn't mean anything to me then, but now. . . ." She glanced significantly at the sleeping figure. "I suggest we keep the identity of our . . . visitor . . . a secret until we can learn more about all this."

"You've got a good point," said her father. In spite of all their worries and perplexities, he managed a quick smile. "It seems you've had all the good ideas tonight."

"But what about our weapon?" persisted Alun. "We came all the way back to Earth to find a weapon to use against the Ilriks, a weapon 'nothing in the universe could withstand.' What do we end up with? One man—and him more dead than alive!"

"I don't know. . . ." said one of the other Aryorians. "Did you see those *eyes*?" He shuddered. "Nothing human could look at the world through eyes like that."

Lanawe turned away, looking immediately for Tal, and seeing him gone from his perch.

The sight of Anode excited her like nothing she had ever experienced before, yet it was an excitement she did not like. He aroused her sexually with the strongest desire she had ever felt, yet there was a feeling of ugliness and cruelty that he aroused, also—and she found herself fighting both urges.

Lanawe did not consider herself perverted sexually in any way, but when she had looked into Anode's feral red eyes it was as if something slimy and abominable had turned over in her soul. She felt a sudden rush of sexual fantasies of the most cruel, sadistic images. This strange influx of passion had frightened her and she struggled against it.

That was why she now sought Tal Mikar. Himself as cleanly elemental as a timberwolf, the feelings he aroused in her, while strong and sharp, were yet simple feelings of straightforward sexual desire.

When she saw that he had abandoned his vantage point, she knew immediately where he had gone.

Without another word, she stepped away from the Aryorians and headed toward the sealed crypt. Only Rylleh saw her go and that strange old man said nothing.

Nor did he give any sign when, a few moments later, he saw Alun Akobar follow Lanawe into the ringlit ruins.

As she had known he would be, Tal stood before the door to the sealed crypt. The soft light from the enigmatic symbol carved on the door cast faint illumination over his lean, young face. He turned at the sound of her approach.

"Lanawe," he said, and took a step toward her. Before he could say anything else, she was in his arms. All the fierce, irresistible passions Anode had stirred were boiling up within her and she had to have release.

It was almost as if she were a different woman from the one Tal had loved before on the desert sands. Then it had been a gentle, tender thing, an act of love. Here it was hot lust aroused to full frenzy—all passions aflame.

Tal's arms went around her and her kiss was open-mouthed, tongue-thrusting. Her hips ground against him almost painfully. At the touch of his hands her whole body began to tremble.

This time she did not loosen the magnetic seams of her black jumpsuit—she literally ripped it off and flung it aside. In the faintly wavering ringlight her body was as white as Anode's had been and her hair was as black as sin.

She was pulling Tal down atop her almost as soon as he had loosened his breeks. Her desire could not be contained a moment longer and her sudden, sharp cry of pleasure could almost have been heard at the encampment.

Before, their loving had been gentle and tender and sweet. This time, Lanawe fought and bit and scratched, her instincts taking over and pulling something primeval up from her soul. She moaned and cried and laughed and groaned from the sheer excess of animal lust that consumed her.

Tal responded with a fierceness to match her own. Never with Alytha, or the one time before with Lanawe, had he ever considered lovemaking as a rough, brutal act; but he made it so now because that was what Lanawe demanded. He thrust savagely to meet her equally savage hunching, and the cries she made sounded like two beasts rutting.

It was this that allowed Alun Akobar to get as close as he did.

He was close enough, scarcely two meters away, to see them clearly where they lay on the steps to the sealed crypt. He knelt behind a fallen archway and looked down at them and the light in his eyes was scarcely less feral than that which had been in Anode's.

The final cry of ecstasy did indeed reach the camp, however faintly, but was heard by no one save Rylleh, who never slept.

"Lanawe?" Tal was puzzled, and also quite breathless from the sudden frenzy. "What . . . brought that on?"

"I—" The girl suddenly seemed to be aware of her own

nakedness and hastily covered herself with her clothing. "I . . . I don't know. I mean—" She seemed dazed, confused, as if she'd just awakened from a bad dream. "I'll . . . talk about it later." She scrambled to her feet and literally fled.

Tal stood watching her go. Her sudden, unaccountable lusting puzzled him. It was totally out of character for the cool, rational, self-contained Lanawe Palmerin. It was simply not something she would do.

Nor was her confused, frightened reaction afterward any more in character. She was not a person to be confused or frightened, and certainly not over a question of sex. Her whole attitude was almost as if she had become someone else.

Tal shook his head as he readjusted his clothing. It seemed his life was more and more full of puzzlements. And he did not like puzzlements.

He turned back to the door of the sealed crypt. Somehow it seemed different now. There was a feeling of sadness, almost of loss. Something had gone out of the night that could not be regained.

The stone struck him with no warning.

Alun Akobar had lifted it over his head in both hands and hurled it with all his strength at the back of Tal's skull. Tal went down without making a sound.

Alun did not have his neuron gun with him, but he did have a hunting knife. He leaped down beside Tal and plunged the knife into his back up to the hilt. Once, twice, three times he stabbed him. Then he rolled him over and stabbed him again, just below the vee of his breastbone.

Quickly, he got his hands under Tal's armpits and dragged the bleeding body several meters away to a large crack between two fallen buildings. He wedged Tal's body into the crack, as far as he could, then he tumbled in dirt and rocks and sand and stone till it was completely covered.

Carefully, he spilled sand over all the spots of blood and did his best to wipe out all traces of where Tal's body was buried. Then, feeling quite pleased with himself, he returned to the camp.

Only Rylleh saw him enter.

NINETEEN

The animal was dead when Alytha removed it from the simple snare she had set, a snare that Tal had taught her how to build one day that seemed so long ago.

The animal was a fluffytail, and Alytha busily set to skinning it with the knife that was her sole possession. The skin was small, but once tanned would make a loin cloth for her.

She crouched beside the embers of a fire, over which she had a large section of the fluffytail spitted, and carefully scraped the inside of the hide as clean as she could. Dusk was creeping through the tumbled boulders where she had made her camp and the firelight etched her nude body with a golden sheen.

Alytha was still as naked as she had been when she swung to safety across Devil's Slough. The nights had been cold, but she had snuggled deep into dried leaves and, on two occasions, into heavy sand, and had kept a fire burning all night.

It was two days after she had hidden from the great silver bird that had swooped low over her as she crouched by the hot springs, when Alytha decided to set her first trap.

Today was the third day she had been trapping. She hoped to have luck for the next couple of days, then she would have enough pelts, although small ones, to fashion herself a rude loincloth, a short tunic, and a pair of sandals.

Once she was even partially clothed, Alytha knew she would feel easier in pushing on to the valley. She estimated that she was nearly halfway there now, but she felt reluctant to go farther without any clothing at all.

Alytha was a barbarian and the question of modesty was not the same for her as it would have been for, say, Lanawe Palmerin, who came from a much more civilized society. However, there is something in the very fact of nakedness that imparts an innate feeling of vulnerability. It was this vulnerable feeling that preyed on Alytha's mind. With her brief scraps of clothing she would be scarcely more covered than she was now, but the psychological benefits of those bits of tanned skin would be immeasurable.

After she had eaten, and had pegged the latest hide to dry beside the others, Alytha carefully gathered firewood to keep her fire burning throughout the night, then snuggled herself deeply into a nest of leaves and leafy branches.

It was not the best bed in the world and, as before, she awoke shivering with cold several times during the night, but for Alytha it was enough. It was enough because she was free. She was free and returning to Tal.

The next morning after warming herself over the replenished fire, watching the chillbumps chase themselves across her belly and down her thighs, she breakfasted off the remains of the fluffytail and a handful of berries, then set out to check her snares.

She stopped at the watering hole, about half a kilometer away from her campsite, and took a long drink. One of the first rules of wilderness living is not to camp too near a water hole. Everything that lives must have water and everything that moves will, at one time or another, come to the nearest water hole. If one would live long in wild country, one will know all the watering holes but one will not camp by them.

The two Arcobane warriors who watched Alytha drink knew this rule equally as well as she did.

These two, and a third, had camped the night before about as far on one side of the water hole as Alytha had on the other. Each had been equally ignorant of the other's presence and it was the merest chance that brought them to the watering hole at so nearly the same time.

The two Arcobanes froze into immobility when Alytha

emerged from the brush. They could scarcely believe their eyes: here was a startlingly beautiful girl, stark naked, alone in the forest!

A naked woman was perhaps the last thing they had expected to see at the water hole that morning, yet they had approached it warily. One never knew when a night feeder might be enjoying a belated meal there. It was this natural prudence that had led them to survey the water hole and its environs from a vantage point of concealment before they ventured out to drink.

Now, from their well-concealed position, they watched Alytha kneel by the stream. Her long, wavy brown hair fell forward across her shoulders as she drank. When she stood up, her hair fell across one shoulder and hung almost to the nipple on her perfect breast.

When she had disappeared into the forest, moving at right angles to the direction of her camp, Vaj Kulan, the bigger of the two Arcobane warriors, and brother to the newly slain Vaj Durmo, seized Kyl Theron's shoulder.

"Did you see that girl?" he demanded, his eyes hot with lust. "She was naked as a newborn child!"

"I saw her," Kyl Theron agreed. "But it could be a trick, or a trap. Why would a woman like that be out here in the woods alone, and with nothing on?"

"I don't know. But trap or not, I'm going after her!"

Alytha checked her first snare and found nothing. She carefully avoided touching it and went on to the next. It, likewise, was still set and had not been investigated at all, so far as she could tell. Halfway to her third snare, she came upon a cache of nuts and stopped to eat.

For better than half an hour she gorged herself on the rich nut meats. Some poor squirrel was going to have a hard winter she knew. Several times, while she ate, she had the feeling she was being watched, but she saw nothing and heard nothing.

After she had eaten, she gathered more of the nuts in a sack improvised from a large leaf, and went on her way. Her third snare was also untripped.

Annoyed now, Alytha turned to retrace her steps to the campsite. Vaj Kulan stood in the trail directly in her path.

Alytha's reaction was almost instinctive. She knew, without stopping to think about it, that she could not outrun him. Her only hope was to kill him, and to kill him quickly.

She flung the leaf-sack full of nuts at his head in almost the same instant that she saw him. His instinctive reaction was to throw his hands in front of his face, exposing his belly to the knife which struck like a poised snake.

Vaj Kulan would have died at that moment if not for Kyl Theron.

The second Arcobane materialized from the brush beside the trail and seized Alytha's knife arm in a heavy, calloused hand. He easily disarmed her, tossed the knife aside, and twisted her arm around painfully behind her back. He reached around, seized her other arm, and twisted it behind her, too. Alytha cried out, once, at the sharp pain.

Vaj Kulan stepped close to her and looked her up and down with an insolent, lusting leer. He reached out and put his hands on her breasts. Alytha tried to twist away, but Kyl Theron held her too tightly. Vaj Kulan laughed at the expression of disgust on her face.

Deliberately, he reached down and cupped his hand between her legs, forcing them apart. Alytha looked away and he laughed again. A nasty, evil sound.

"That's enough," said Kyl Theron. "Let's get her back to camp."

"I'm for that!" agreed the other. "I'm going to enjoy this one. I want her first in my sleeping fur." He laughed again, his eyes hot and dark.

"I think we ought to take her to Ven Tamor," Kyl Theron argued. "I think this is one he'll want for himself."

"He can have her—after I'm done with her!"

"Ven Tamor won't like that. I think this one is pretty enough that he'll want to be first."

"Ven Tamor is in Arcobane, and I am here!"

Nothing more was said on the way to their camp. Alytha's heart sank. Never, not even when Tal had disappeared, had she felt so helpless. She knew what was in store for her at the Arcobane camp and she would almost have preferred death. But there was nothing she could do. The big warrior who had captured her never relaxed his grip for an instant. There was nothing for her to do except to face what was coming.

Ren Sagvor, the third Arcobane, had a mess of fish broiling by the time they reached the camp.

"Where have you—?" he started to ask, then broke off suddenly when he saw Alytha. "What in Shandor's name have you got there?"

"Breakfast," said Vaj Kulan, with another of his nasty laughs.

Ren Sagvor subjected her to the same humiliating scrutiny that Vaj Kulan had. His reaction was the same.

Kyl Theron released her arms, but before she could move away, the other two seized her—only they did not seize her arms.

Alytha tried to pull away from them, but their hands were everywhere: on her breasts, on her belly, between her legs, on her buttocks. There were only two of them, but they seemed to have a hundred hands apiece.

And always there was the nasty, leering laughter.

At last, sobbing in anger, frustration, and shame, Alytha was forced down to the ground, flat on her back, with Vaj Kulan atop her, his knees holding her legs apart.

"I think we'd better take her to Ven Tamor," Kyl Theron protested again. "He'll want this one unhurt."

"What I'm going to do won't hurt her," answered Vaj Kulan, reaching beneath him to loosen his buckskin breeches. "Or, at least, it won't show."

"Ven Tamor will have to take thirds," agreed Ren Sagvor, breathing hot and heavy. "Or maybe fourths?" He gave Kyl Theron a knowing wink.

"I have nothing to do with this," the other said. "What you do with her is up to you. And you'll be the ones to answer to Ven Tamor!"

Alytha's cry of pain and Vaj Kulan's cry of pleasure were blended into one sound, but Kyl Theron turned away and walked to the far side of the camp.

The eyes took some getting used to.

Anode had been moved into Dr. Fel Palmerin's tent and his recovery was rapid. He had slept for two days and two nights, then awakened and seemed much refreshed.

Dr. Palmerin, Lanawe, Alun Akobar, and one or two other Aryorians were gathered in Dr. Palmerin's tent to talk with Anode now that he was awake.

Only Tal Mikar was missing.

He had not been seen since the night the Eternity Stone had been placed in the Chalice of Time and Anode had materialized. Lanawe had searched the entire ruins of Shalimar, but there was no trace of him.

She had enlisted her father, Alun, and the others, and they had searched again, but Tal was not to be found. The Kalathors knew nothing of his whereabouts and none of the horses was missing. That meant if he had left Shalimar, he had headed off into the Great Desert afoot.

It was as if the ground had opened up and swallowed him.

Anode's awakening did a little, but only a little, to take Lanawe's mind off Tal.

He sat, propped in a reclining position on a makeshift couch, in the center of Dr. Palmerin's tent. Even now, there was no color at all to his features—only the bone-white complexion, the white streaked iron-gray hair, and the eyes, the feral red eyes.

"I am Anode," he said, in a rich, well modulated voice. "I thank you for freeing me from the prison in which I was sealed by Shandor the Unspeakable more centuries ago than I can tell."

Lanawe still felt the strange excitement Anode generated in her. Even through her fear for Tal, the strong, animal sexuality that Anode aroused in her made her go all hot and wet inside.

"I'm afraid we are at a loss," said Dr. Palmerin, hesitantly. "You see, we came from Aryor, a planetary system halfway across the galaxy from Earth, to find the Eternity Stone." He paused nervously. "Our legends . . . on Aryor . . . said that if the Eternity Stone was placed in—"

"—In the Chalice of Time," Anode finished for him. "Good! Excellent! Shara got away after all." Then he looked directly at Lanawe and smiled. "But of course she did." His voice held just a hint of mockery, as if cynicism lurked immediately below the meaning of everything that he said.

Dr. Palmerin caught his smile directed at Lanawe and

cleared his throat discreetly.

"Perhaps we should introduce ourselves. I am Dr. Fel Palmerin. This is my daughter, Lanawe—" But Anode interrupted him.

"I know who she is," he said, and smiled again. It was not really a pleasant smile. Lanawe thought once more that he was almost certainly a cruel person.

"Shara Vralon escaped in our starship. That much I learned even while Shandor the Unspeakable worked his magic on me. He used his knowledge of Infrastatics, which was admittedly greater than my own, to seal me away in an alternate universe. I was trapped below the level of the solid vibratory rate and the alternate reality displacement that I caused manifested itself in our continuum as the object called the Eternity Stone.

"One reason for that name was because time, as it is measured in this universe, does not exist below the level of solid vibration. For me, but a moment had passed after Shandor completed the circuit till you broke it. Yet, at the same time, I was fully aware of every second of every day of every century of the unutterable amount of time that I was imprisoned.

"You set me free from a living death that was more horrible than any living entombment could be, because so long as I was imprisoned, I was immortal! My solitude would never be broken and would never end. It is a frightful thing to be the only living creature in your own private universe."

"But why were you imprisoned? And how? And who did it? I mean, I've heard you say—we've all heard you say—that someone called Shandor the Unspeakable did it. Our legends speak very little about someone called Shando or Shandor, the legends differ, who was some associate of Lan Regas. The Earthmen have a deity they call Shandor. My daughter tried to ask Tal Mikar about the similarity in names once and he became angry about it. He said Shandor was Shandor, and that was that. But what do you think? Is this Shandor the Earthmen worship and Shandor the Unspeakable and the Shandor of our legends all the same person?"

Anode chuckled and elevated his eyebrows.

"You certainly are full of questions," he said, "but I'll do my best. First, I know nothing about what the Earthmen believe today, but it seems likely we're talking about the same Shandor. Why? Because, on Earth, at least, he won. And time can turn a winner into a legend and a legend into a god.

"But let me begin at the beginning. In the year two thousand four hundred twenty A.D., as the centuries were then reckoned, when the tyrant Lan Regas ruled all the world, a handful of brave souls who loved freedom more than their lives revolted against his iron rule. They were led by the patriot, Shara Vralon, who had once been Lan Regas' lover.

"The real power behind Lan Regas' dictatorship was the scientist called Shandor. The dictator's slaves named him Shandor the Unspeakable. He was master of the Science of Infrastatics. His powers and his weapons were almost beyond conception. He built this city of Shalimar for his own pleasures, which included the most horrible tortures ever devised by a sick mind.

"I was also a scientist who worked with Infrastatics. I was not so knowledgeable nor so powerful as Shandor, but I was still, *am* still, a great scientist. Almost daily my knowledge was increasing. In my areas, my experiments with Infrastatics went far beyond anything Shandor had attempted. I was rapidly becoming his only serious rival.

"When Shara Vralon and her small but dedicated band of patriots revolted against Lan Regas' tyranny, I was enlisted in their cause. I tried to be, for Shara, what Shandor was for the tyrant. I knew that in the end it would be the power of my science against Shandor's that would decide the issue. The ultimate master of Infrastatics is the master of the world.

"The war was long and bitter. I developed weapons to counter Shandor's weapons and he developed weapons to counter mine. Our struggle completely changed the face of the Earth and utterly destroyed the moon, leaving only the rings that you have seen.

"Many people joined Shara and me. They named me Anode the Mighty and called Shara their savior. But many more were afraid. For them, slavery had become so much a way of life that they were frightened of obtaining their freedom.

"I developed a machine that would hold one immobile

below the solid vibratory level. I also developed a device for breaking this statis field. This was the Chalice of Time, which I entrusted to Shara Vralon's keeping. I did this because I learned that Shandor the Unspeakable was working on a similar device and I knew that once he perfected it I would be his primary target. I wanted something to insure my escape.

"As the war dragged on, our side began to suffer reverses. After all, it was inevitable that we would. Lan Regas had the resources of a whole world to draw on, while Shara had only what little she could beg, borrow, or steal. Our cause began to look lost.

"That was when work was started on the *X-97*, the first starship. True, we had had interplanetary flight for several hundred years and had thoroughly explored our solar system, but no attempt had ever been made to go to the *stars*. Now, in our duress, we felt that this was our only hope. A place of escape where Lan Regas' stormtroopers and Shandor's Infrastatic weapons couldn't reach us. So we built the *X-97*.

"The war went on while the *X-97* was being built. By this time, we were reduced to fighting only to buy time to make good our escape. If we couldn't be free on Earth, we would be free in the stars or we would die in the effort. We felt that death was preferable to further slavery.

"Lan Regas had learned of the starship and a desperate battle was launched. We were working from my, *our*, secret headquarters at the North Pole, a place we called Rynn. Shara and the others were making their escape up to the *X-97*, using an Infrastatic Teleporter, at the moment the attack came. I stayed behind to hold off the attackers and to give Shara and her people time to get away.

"I used all the weapons at my command, but in the end Shandor was too strong. I was captured by a statis field and imprisoned in the 'other universe' that manifested itself as what was called the Eternity Stone. This Stone was the spatio-temporal displacement from *that* universe of the volume of space I occupied in it.

"But even as a prisoner I learned of Shara's escape. What I didn't know, what no one could know, was the ultimate end of her flight. Would the *X-97* reach a safe, habitable world or would the crew die somewhere in the cold emptiness of deep space? An eternity is a long time to wonder such things."

Anode was silent, but his story had been so powerful and compelling that half a minute elapsed before his listeners were aware that he was through.

"But what happened here on Earth?" asked Dr. Palmerin. "I mean, with the rebels gone, what brought down the government?"

"Exhaustion and internal decay," said Anode. "Lan Regas had burned up the resources of a whole planet in fighting us. He had spread himself to the very limits. His troops were depleted, his power was weakened, his forces were exhausted. And then Shandor disappeared.

"Many people said that he died. Others said that he was off somewhere experimenting. The more knowledgeable ones said that Lan Regas had had him murdered, after his usefulness was over, because he had become too powerful. For whatever reason, Shandor the Unspeakable was never seen again. And Shalimar fell into neglect.

"Without Shandor behind him, Lan Regas soon found himself helpless. One by one, the scattered remnants of humanity fought for their autonomous rights. Society fragmented, and the altered planetary weather cycle abetted the fragmentation.

"Within a hundred years of Shara's departure, all of Earth was reduced to rampant barbarism. In some cases to little more than stone age savagery. Lan Regas won, but he paid a high price for his winning."

Again there was silence. Anode's story had moved the Aryorians deeply. It corroborated so much of their own prehistory that, till now, had been no more than myths and legends.

"And then you came," said Anode. "I sensed you from afar. Actually, it was the power of the Chalice of Time that I felt. And at last you set me free. What price can I offer? How can you be repaid?"

"We need help," said Dr. Palmerin simply. "Or, should I say, Shara Vralon's descendants need help. You see the *X-97* did reach safety. A world called Aryor—halfway across the galaxy from Earth—became our home. Shara Vralon's people lived to walk the fields of a free planet again.

"In time our society spread to three worlds. We had a happy, stable culture. It was not utopia, by any means, but it was a good life. Our people were happy.

"Then the Ilriks came. They were aliens. No one had seen them without their space armor. They are true barbarians. Nothing can withstand them. They have defeated and overrun our three worlds. Aryor is a slave world now.

"But we remembered the legend of the Eternity Stone and we had the Chalice of Time. So we, a mere handful of us, used the old *X-97* to flee from Aryor to Earth, the same way Shara Vralon had once used it to flee from Earth to Aryor.

"We didn't know what we would find when we located the Eternity Stone. We only knew we had no other choice." He paused. "Will you help us? *Can* you help us?"

"I can and I will," said Anode firmly. "Tomorrow we will leave for Rynn. There I have many Infrastatic weapons waiting in secret chambers. I can repair any that need it and I can build what we need that might not be there. We will wipe the Ilriks from the galaxy. You will never fear them, or any other thing, again!" And his feral red eyes blazed in his bone-white face, shadowed by his white-streaked iron-gray hair.

In the jubilation that followed his words, there was only one who remained grim and quiet. At that moment, more than anything else, Lanawe Palmerin wanted to know the whereabouts of Tal Mikar.

TWENTY

In the darkness there was a light.

A Presence was where before had been only Aloneness. Life had come back to the haunts of death.

Tal Mikar feels hands upon his body. The stones, dirt, and rubble are raked and shoved away. The hands gently bring him out of the grave where Alun Akobar has left him. Tal feels the coolness of the nightwind on his face.

Soft, gentle, healing hands cleanse the dirt and blood from around his terrible wounds. Ointments and lotions are applied and Tal feels their soothing, comforting touch spread new life through his body. The pain vanishes.

Cool water is pressed on his lips, dripping from a golden cup. Tal feels the delicious coolness cross his parched lips and touch the dried membranes of his mouth and throat. This is the most delicious drink Tal has ever tasted, bringing with it a restoration of life.

A hand appeared through the loosely packed dirt.

For a moment it scrabbled about uncertainly, then it scratched and clawed at the rubble that entombed it. Its movements were weak and feeble, but they were movements. Life existed there yet.

In a moment another hand clawed out through the sand and loose rocks. Another time of weak scrabbling and a dark, shaggy, blood-spattered head appeared. Tal paused to rest.

Then, slowly and laboriously, he dragged himself out of the grave where Alun Akobar had thrust him. His skull was bloody and matted with filth around the wound. His upper body was literally covered in blood, yet enough life was left that Tal dragged himself forward till he fell free and lay in the open outside his grave.

But the exertion had exhausted the small reservoir of strength implanted by the dream and he lost consciousness.

The Presence sensed this loss and knew that the feeble spark of life It was maintaining was almost gone. It also knew that if true death claimed Tal Mikar, then all would be lost at this point.

Gently, easily, the Presence stole into Tal's mind and touched the dreaming memory circuits to force up the images It must use to save both Tal and Itself. Tal dreamed . . . .

Soft, gentle hands cleanse the dirt and blood from around his terrible wounds. Ointments and lotions are applied and Tal feels their soothing, comforting touch spread new life through his body. The pain vanishes.

Cool water is pressed on his lips, dripping from a golden cup. Tal feels the delicious coolness cross his parched lips and touch the dried membranes of his mouth and throat. This is the most delicious drink Tal had ever tasted bringing with it a restoration of life.

A rich, heady aroma fills his nostrils. It is a meaty broth of some kind. Tal slowly sips its warm, rich heartiness. With each sustaining swallow he feels more strength return.

Strong hands are on his arms. Tal feels himself lifted to his feet. Strong arms support him as he takes his first faltering steps. He will make it!

Tal's eyes blinked open.

There was life in them, but no sentience. Only the Presence kept the tiny flicker of vitality from being extinguished. The Presence had a *need* and it was only that which kept the shadow of life in Tal.

But whatever kept it, it was there. Slowly, like some broken mechanical toy, Tal moved. He raised himself on his hands and knees, then, slowly and unsteadily, he swayed erect onto his feet.

For a moment he remained there, moving his head blindly from side to side like some great bear sniffing the breeze, then, his destination apparently determined, he stumbled forward in a lead-footed shuffle, like someone with both hamstring muscles cut.

Two steps he took. Four. A dozen. Two dozen. And then he stopped. Immediately before him were the four steps leading down to the door of the sealed crypt. He had come unerringly to *here*.

He hesitated now, as if considering how to negotiate the steps. Almost experimentally, one knee bent—and Tal fell headlong to the bottom.

For several minutes he lay there, blood seeping from his newly opened wounds. The Presence worked with him almost desperately, afraid that It had lost him so close to Its goal.

But Tal's strong young body had some resilience left in it. Once more his blue eyes flicked open, though they were still dull and empty and void of rationality. Tal was scarcely more than an automaton, but he still lived!

Once more, slowly, painfully, he got onto his hands and knees. This time he leaned against the door to the sealed crypt and used it as a brace and a support. He managed to get his feet under him and used the door to lever himself erect.

The power that impelled him came from within the sealed crypt. The power that had drawn him since he first came to Shalimar was there and now, with the spark of his life-force at its lowest possible ebb, its pull was a thing he could no longer actively resist.

Tal pressed himself against the sealed door as if he were going to insinuate himself through its molecules. His body thrust itself against the door with the last of its failing strength. His body, against the door, looked like a chip of metal clamped against a magnet.

The Presence was baffled. It had done so much, extended Itself so far, to get Tal here. It would not be defeated now! There had to be a way—

And then the Presence realized what was wrong. It realized that *It* was the factor preventing Tal's entry. It realized that It would have to release him and hope that the faint flicker of life would last unattended for a few seconds more. It would have to release Tal and trust to whatever gods there might be.

The Presence withdrew.

For only a second Tal remained, fixed against the door,

and then it was as if the solid door that was neither stone nor metal nor wood had become a thing made of quicksand; for Tal sank into it completely, as if both he and it were totally insubstantial.

In a moment he was gone, absorbed by the door, and everything was as it was except that it was as if Tal Mikar had never been.

"We must leave Shalimar," said Anode, his feral eyes burning as they rested on Lanawe Palmerin. "This was the city of Shandor the Unspeakable and the aura of his power is not entirely gone. I must be away from this place!"

"Very well," agreed Dr. Palmerin. "I'll call our jetboat. It's back at the edge of the Great Desert, but it can reach us in less than a day."

"Do not call it from here," said Anode, in his strangely mocking voice. "Let us ride forth from this place immediately. I would put Shalimar behind me."

Dr. Palmerin nodded and went out to begin preparations for breaking camp. Only Lanawe and Anode were left in the tent.

Anode looked at the girl and an almost gloating smile spread slowly across his bone-white face. Lanawe felt her breath catch in her throat and felt her pulse quicken with the sudden, wild passion Anode always aroused in her.

As much to cover this feeling as anything else, she demanded in an annoyed tone: "Why are you looking at me like that?"

Anode's smile became a chuckle, rich, deep, and full of an almost palpable cruelty.

"Do you really not know?" he asked softly. "Do you really . . . not know?"

"I don't have any idea!" she snapped. She had seen the look of lust in men's eyes before, but nothing like the laval gaze of Anode's blood-red stare. He laughed again.

"In time you will remember," he said. "In . . . a very short time." His chuckle faded back into the gloating smile. "I had forgotten how appearances deceive you. What is . . . obvious to me is still obscure to you . . . but *you feel it!* I can tell that. You sense it." His inhuman eyes almost glowed. "In time . . .

you will remember." And he laughed again.

Lanawe tore herself away from his hypnotic gaze and literally fled from the tent, her face flushed, her breathing ragged. Never in her life before had anyone affected her the way Anode did. He both repelled her and attracted her and at the same time he called up a latent vein of cruel and perverse passion that lurked beyond a threshold within herself that she had never crossed over before. And the desire! The very thought of Anode roused a sexual hunger in Lanawe that could scarcely be contained, an elemental force that completely swept away her cool, dispassionate ego and left only the hot, panting essence of female sexuality behind.

All around her the camp was abustle as tents were struck, packs were filled, bedding and other items were gathered and sorted. Alone with her confused thoughts, Lanawe turned away from the stir of activity. She passed a knot of Aryorians and heard her father saying: ". . . weapons that can defeat the Ilriks. He says that in his city of Rynn there's everything he needs. Once we're away from Shalimar, he wants me to call the shuttlecraft and we'll. . . ." But she did not even pause.

She walked out into the ruins and strode away from the central plaza as purposefully as if she knew precisely where she was going.

And, in a way, she did.

She stopped before the door to the sealed crypt. Here was where she had last seen Tal Mikar. From this spot he had apparently vanished from the face of the earth.

She walked down the four steps and stopped before the strangely marked door. What was it that had drawn Tal back here so many times? What attraction had it held for him?

She looked down at the flagstones before the door. There were dark stains there that she had not noticed before. Then she saw that there were a few dark smears on the surface of the door itself.

Lanawe frowned as she examined them. She did not believe they had been there all along. Were they blood? Could they be blood?

She touched one brownish stain, but it was several days old and it merely flaked away. It might have been blood. It might have been dried mud. It might have been something else.

Sadly, her shoulders slumping in dejection, Lanawe turned away from the sealed crypt. With heavy steps, she returned to the camp that was by now almost ready to move out. Alun Akobar saw her coming and he smiled. In Anode's feral red eyes there was no humor, but he, too, smiled. Only he knew what powers were brought so sharply into focus by the slim, dark-haired girl who walked into camp with downcast eyes.

TWENTY-ONE

Soft, gentle hands cleanse the dirt and blood from around Tal's terrible wounds. Ointments and lotions are applied and Tal feels their soothing, comforting touch spread new life through his body. The pain vanishes.

Cool water is pressed on his lips, dripping from a golden cup. Tal feels the delicious coolness cross his parched lips and touch the dried membranes of his mouth and throat. This is the most delicious drink Tal has ever tasted, bringing with it a restoration of life.

A rich, heady aroma fills his nostrils. It is a meaty broth of some kind. Tal slowly sips its warm, rich heartiness. With each sustaining swallow he feels more strength return.

Tal's eyes opened.

The room was warm and a soft, golden glow like a summer sunset lay over everything. There was a feeling of almost palpable power in the air.

The golden man lay on a raised dais at one end of the room. Two large cones were suspended directly over him, with their open ends down. The source of the light and the warmth came from there. The golden man appeared to be sleeping.

Again Tal moved.

His body turned, stimulated more by the Presence than by any volition of his own. He got his hands under him and dragged himself forward. He left a trail of blood behind him.

A square black box was affixed a meter or so away. On its top was a red button. Tal dragged himself slowly toward the box. His eyes were glazed over.

The golden man did not move. His nude body, beneath the light bath, gave no signs of life. His hair, a lighter golden-yellow than the golden-bronze of his skin, was like a skullcap sculpted of the finest metal. His body, over two meters tall were he standing, was a marvel of physical perfection, with rippling muscles like bands of plastic steel beneath the bronze lacquer of his skin.

Tal had almost reached the box. One hand, like a talon of death, went out and came down on the button. There was a sudden, low humming as if scores of powerful motors had abruptly come to life. The honey-colored light from the two cones above the golden man suddenly turned rosy, then a pale pink, then pure white, then an electric blue as the dynamos' power surge built.

But Tal did not see any of this. When his hand fell upon the button, the Presence withdrew and Tal's body lay lifeless and bloody upon the floor.

Ven Tamor was furious.

"You bloody, filthy, rutting dogs!" he roared. He struck Vaj Kulan an open handed blow that sent the big Arcobane warrior sprawling. "Are you chief of the Arcobanes that you take your women where you please?" He swung a mighty blow at Ren Sagvor that knocked the man from his feet. "Is Kyl Theron the only one of you who respects my wishes?" And the chief kicked Vaj Kulan savagely.

All this time, Alytha stood beside Kyl Theron. Her head was down and her soft brown hair tumbled across her face. Her lithe, nude body still bore the weals her attackers had left there.

The Arcobane lance lord continued to berate the two warriors. As Kyl Theron had predicted, Ven Tamor did not appreciate that they had taken it upon themselves to violate the girl. Only Kyl Theron escaped the lance lord's wrath.

Neither Vaj Kulan, nor his late brother, Vaj Durmo, were liked by the other warriors, so all the tribe gathered close to watch his chastisement. This fact cost Vaj Kulan his life.

Kyl Theron had released his hold on Alytha. He still stood beside her, but, after all, inside the palisade, in the midst of the

Arcobane village, surrounded by the entire tribe, what reason did he have to hold her? How could she escape? What could she do?

What she could do suddenly became quite evident.

Alytha spun on the balls of her feet and drove one slim elbow squarely into the diaphragm of the warrior to her left. The man doubled over, all the wind knocked out of him. When he did, he released the war lance he had been holding. It was this that Alytha wanted.

Before Kyl Theron could react, before anyone could move, before, in fact, the warrior who had released the lance had doubled over, Alytha had the two-meter-long shaft in her hands and had driven the bronze tip completely through Ren Sagvor's heart, so that the point stood out the middle of his back all sticky red.

She leaped around the doubled over, winded warrior, spinning him with her as she leaped so that he fell in front of Kyl Theron, who was springing to recapture her. Both warriors went down in a tangle together, but Alytha stayed on her feet. Only now she had the warrior's sword naked in her hands.

She sprang forward and made one wicked swipe that caused Ven Tamor to jump back. Her backstroke came down precisely where she had planned and Vaj Kulan screamed as the heavy blade bit into his genitals.

Alytha spun again and leveled the bloody blade at Ven Tamor. No one moved except Vaj Kulan, who lay twisting and screaming on the ground, blood gushing between his clutching fingers from where his manhood had once been.

"It is my right," said Alytha, fiercely, the blade never wavering. "The wrong was done to *me!* Mine is the right of vengence!"

"I am lance lord of the Arcobanes," said Ven Tamor.

"And I am the one with the sword."

There was a moment's hesitation, then the lance lord nodded. "Yours is the right," he said, and Vaj Kulan's screams were suddenly stilled as Alytha brought the sword down in one swift, savage, deadly, final arc.

Again the naked girl faced the lance lord of Arcobane with a bloody sword in her hand. There was a deathless resolve in her gray eyes and Ven Tamor knew this was one who would die before she surrendered her sword. And he knew that she would not die alone.

"What is your name, girl?" he asked roughly.

"I am Alytha, of the Thongors, mate to Tal Mikar."

A sudden murmur ran through the crowd of Arcobanes. Tal Mikar's last visit was still a topic of much conversation and speculation.

"Welcome, Alytha," said Ven Tamor. "You fight like a true lance warrior. We of the Arcobanes would welcome you among us. You could be lance warrior among my people and win much honor and riches. The people of Arcobane, totem of the gray wolf, ask you to join us."

The tribe shouted its approval. The Arcobanes respected courage above all else, and a woman who could fight was treated the same as any other warrior.

"I . . . cannot," Alytha finally said. "I seek my mate Tal Mikar. I must continue my search for him."

And Lalon, the Arcobane shaman, stepped forward and raised one hand for attention.

"Your mate has been to Arcobane not long ago. He came with a strangely dressed woman and an old man, in a thing like a silver bird that flew on wings of flame. They sought the Eternity Stone, that which is called the Accursed of Shandor." He made the sign of the double helix. "Your mate used a magic weapon to slay Vaj Durmo, brother to the warrior you just killed. Your mate also worked some magic that made Vaj Durmo's lance not harm him. They left us in their skyboat to seek the Kalathors at the edge of the Great Desert."

"Then it is to the Great Desert that I must go," said Alytha. "For I will find Tal Mikar."

"You are a brave warrior," said Ven Tamor. "We of the Arcobanes honor you. Stay with us a few days and hunt with us. We will give you clothing to wear and food for when you resume your quest. Till then, fight and hunt with us as a lance warrior!"

Alytha considered a moment, then slowly nodded and lowered her sword. The Arcobanes roared their approval.

And so Alytha, Outcast of the Thongors, became a lance

warrior for Ven Tamor.

Tal awakened as if from a deep sleep.

His first sensation was that there was no pain. He opened his eyes and found himself nearly blinded by a yellow light that seemed to fill his whole world. He winced and turned his head away.

As if his movement activated a switch, the light dimmed, then went out. Tal saw that he was lying on his back on a dais below two large cones, which were suspended from the ceiling, open ends down, and it was from them that the golden light had emanated.

Tal swung his feet down and sat up. He still had on his boots and homespun breeks, but his tunic was gone. His upper body was bare. He looked down at himself and saw a faint white mark below the vee of his breastbone.

"Your wounds are healed," said a resonant, mellifluous voice and Tal jerked his head around sharply.

The golden man stood before him—only he looked more bronze than gold when not under the light. He had dressed himself in a simple, but functional outfit: black boots, brown breeches, a heavy black belt with pockets on it, a cream colored tunic edged with brown piping, and a short brown jacket that matched the breeches. His blond hair was thick and full and worn loose and natural. Only his eyes were strange.

They looked like twin pools of flake gold, constantly stirred by tiny whirlwinds. There was a strange, hypnotic quality to them that gave Tal pause when their gaze fell upon him.

The man was a head taller than Tal, broader across the shoulders and thicker through the chest, but with a lean waist and long, powerful legs. His chin was square, his mouth firm, his nose short and straight. He looked handsome, but in a rugged, masculine way. There was an aura of vital dynamism about him.

"Who . . . are you?" asked Tal. "And . . . where am I?" He looked quickly around the room.

There was a moment's hesitation, then the bronze man said: "I am Shandor."

Tal could not have been more surprised had the stones stood up and spoke to him.

Shandor?

Shandor was a god. Gods do not suddenly appear and speak to people.

"I am Shandor," the bronze man said again, his flake gold eyes sparkling. "I have slept for eons—kept alive by the power of my Infrastatic Stimulator. I am awake now because Anode has been freed from the Eternity Stone. The power of evil is loose again in the world and I must do what I can to stop it."

Tal still stared at Shandor blankly, uncomprehendingly.

He tried to remember what had happened. He remembered the man that had appeared when the Eternity Stone was placed within the Chalice of Time. He remembered the urge he had felt to return to the sealed crypt. He remembered Lanawe Palmerin seeking him out there. He remembered her wild, lustful passion, so much out of character for her. He remembered . . . something . . . striking his head. . . .

And he remembered pain and blood and fragmented dreams. But his head had been hurt. . . .

Tal raised his hands to his head and ran his fingers through his thick, black hair. There was no blood. There was no wound. There was no pain. He looked back at Shandor and tried to understand.

"Your wounds have been healed," the bronze man said again. "The Infrastatic Stimulator regenerated your body tissue and fluid. This was how it kept me alive, only in your case it was speeded up drastically." He smiled. "I was not sure you would survive, you were so nearly dead, so I cloned you and was preparing to do a neural scan for programming when you passed the critical point."

"Clone?" Tal was lost. "What are you . . . ?"

"This." Shandor opened the cover on a two-meter-long sealed tank. Inside, bathed in the now familiar warm honey colored lights lay—Tal!

"But . . . that's me!"

"It is a clone. An exact replicate formed artificially from a single cell of your body." Shandor closed the cover. Tal felt better not looking at—himself. "The body is alive, yet not alive. It lacks the mind and will, memories and personal behavior patterns that go to make up *you*, the separate, distinct, and unique entity that is Tal Mikar. But it is alive in the sense that the Infrastatic Stimulator has kept all the organs and tissues healthy and functioning. In fact, the clone's body will probably still be there a thousand years from now, intact just as it is." He smiled again. "An immortality machine is quite handy sometimes."

Tal smiled, too. There was something reassuring about the simple presence of the big bronze man. Shandor seemed utterly capable of meeting any situation and coming out the winner.

"And I *am* Shandor." The voice compelled belief. "I am the Shandor of your legends—and I'm sure there must be legends. The last Infrastatics War was the stuff from which legends are made."

Tal nodded slowly, still trying to take it all in.

"Yes, there are legends," he said. "They only tell of Shandor the Mighty and his wonderful deeds." He paused. "Lanawe and her people have . . . other legends. Shandor, or someone called Shandor, is in them, too." He looked at the bronze man with suddenly suspicious eyes."

"Is Lanawe the one who freed Anode?"

"You mean the one who put the Eternity Stone in the Chalice of Time? Yes. Or, at least, her father did. They came from the stars to find the Eternity Stone here on Earth."

"From the stars," repeated Shandor, and his flake gold eyes glittered with pinpoints of light. "Shara's children have come home."

"Then it's true—what Lanawe said?" Tal's accusation was sudden.

Shandor had turned a comfortable chair to face Tal, who still sat on the edge of the dais. He now handed Tal a thin cup full of a steaming, savory brown liquid. He held a similar cup in his own hand.

"This will refresh you," he said, "and restore your spirit." He seated himself in the chair and sipped his beverage. "Now what was said whose truth you question?"

Tal held his cup, but did not drink.

"Lanawe told me how Earth once had a great civilization, a wonderful civilization, but was ruled by an evil dictator named Lan Regas, who had an associate named Shandor. Shara Vralon fought for their freedom, but in the end she was defeated. She and her followers fled to the stars—to a world called Aryor—with the Chalice of Time. That—and a legend about the Eternity Stone, how it made a weapon when put in the Chalice. Lanawe and her father returned because they have need of such a weapon."

Shandor considered for several minutes, his flake gold eyes hooded. At last he said: "The basic facts are true, but the interpretation is wrong. Lan Regas was not a dictator. He and Shara Vralon were lovers. Together they rediscovered the Science of Infrastatics, in the year two thousand four hundred twenty A.D., as we then reckoned time.

"Without understanding the power they held, they managed to free Anode from the prison where I had put him after the First Infrastatic War. Anode is a master of the science and he almost devastated the Earth and her solar colonies before I was awakened to challenge him.

"Lan Regas would not condone what Anode and Shara were doing. He resisted their evil and thereby aided me. In the end we won, but more damage was done in the Second Infrastatic War than was even done in the First. I imprisoned Anode in another dimensional plane, his own private universe. The projection from that dimensional plane, or the displacement caused by inserting Anode into it, infringed upon our space-time continuum and produced the effect called the Eternity Stone. The Chalice of Time was a triggering device for freeing him, a key to unlock the gates to Hell. Shara Vralon took it and fled to the stars. I could have destroyed her starship as they flew away, but—there had been enough killing.

"I thought perhaps time would reform them or their descendants, if any survived. And I felt the Eternity Stone was safely hidden here in Shalimar. Besides, I took other precautions. When I went under the Stimulator, I set a mind key to recall me if the Eternity Stone became inactive, in other words, if Anode were freed.

"But the mind key became partially deactivated over the centuries. It was only functional enough to arouse my consciousness, not my physical body. I managed sufficient astral projection to reach out for help. That's when I found you. Your head had been struck by a large, heavy object—there was a massive skull fracture—and you had been stabbed several times, once in the heart.

"I did everything I could on the astral plane to maintain your life-force. I even allowed you to absorb a portion of my own essence through dreams I implanted, dreams where you were eating broth and taking nourishment. I kept you alive this way till I could get you into my laboratory where you manually activated the Stimulator to awaken my physical body. I got you under the Stimulator, but I was afraid I was too late. It can Infrastatically mend bone and flesh, but it is not magic; it cannot restore life once a body is truly dead. That's why I artifically cloned your body and Infrastatically aged it so that it reached your present growth level. I was on the verge of making the neural recordings so I could transfer your memory patterns and your instinctive reaction pattern, which was as much of *you* as would be left, to the clone, when you regained consciousness. Had I been a few seconds later, you would not have survived."

Tal looked around him again.

"You mean I'm inside the sealed crypt?" At Shandor's nod, he asked: "But how did I get through the door? We did everything we could to open it or to smash it, but nothing affected it."

"It's not really a door," said Shandor. "It's a force field. Nothing can penetrate it. Absolutely nothing. I sealed the entire laboratory that way. It was almost a million years after the First Infrastatic War before there was the Second. If there were to be a Third, I could not judge how long it might be. I wanted my laboratory safe."

"Lanawe said that it was a thousand years ago when Shara Vralon left Earth and fled to Aryor."

"A thousand years since she left," mused Shandor, his golden eyes hooded. "That's a thousand years *her* time. It must be well over a hundred thousand here on Earth. Perhaps two hundred thousand. Perhaps more. There's no way to be sure."

Tal blinked. "What do you mean? She said it was a thousand years. It doesn't matter whether it was *there* or *here*.

A thousand years is a thousand years."

"Not exactly. You see, I helped design the *X-97*. I built her nucleonic engines. We called them a 'warp drive,' because they warped the fabric of space *and time*. Moving beyond the speed of light into subspace, strange things happen to your time sense. A few hours to you on the ship might be years to those who remained planetside. You might come back, still a young man, to find your great-great-great-grandchildren welcoming you home."

Shandor laughed ironically. "For whatever purpose your Lanawe needed the weapon she thought the Eternity Stone would make, the threat is now past. Whatever she feared has been dead and dust for centuries on her home world. It was all for nothing." He shook his head. "All for nothing."

Tal lifted the savory beverage and sipped it. He still felt unsure, disoriented. The drink, however, was exactly what he needed. It imparted an almost instant feeling of relaxation and tranquility, plus sending strength back into him as if it were a hearty meal. After the third or fourth sip, a feeling of mild euphoria set in. Tal did not put the cup down till it was emptied. He looked up to see Shandor smiling at him.

"I told you it would restore your spirit," said the bronze man. "Now tell me a little of yourself. Your name I picked from your mind on the astral plane. I know a great deal about who you have *been*, but I know very little about who you are *now*."

Tal frowned and then shrugged. "I don't understand," he said. "I am who I have always been. I am Tal Mikar, lance warrior to Sar Lon of the Thongors." He stopped suddenly. "If you've been sleeping all this time, how do you speak my language so well?"

"On the astral plane, all language is universal," said Shandor. "I took the essentials when I touched your mind and extrapolation was simple. I'm sure Anode speaks whatever language, or languages, his Aryorian friends speak."

Tal still frowned. The explanation made no sense to him, but he did not press the point. Instead, he quickly told his tale to Shandor. He omitted nothing, except only the two times he made love to Lanawe Palmerin. When he had finished, he saw that Shandor's flake gold eyes were sparkling and alive with interest.

"So it begins again," he said. "There must be a Third Infrastatic War. But this time—Anode must die! He is the embodiment of ultimate evil and I cannot allow him to live." He paused. "But I do not know if he can be killed."

"Anything that lives can be killed," said Tal. "A sword blade through the guts would be all it takes to kill Anode."

"It's not that simple," said Shandor. "A knife blade through the heart means death for most people, yet you have survived that. There is a natural law at work here that I am not sure I am powerful enough to circumvent."

"I don't understand," said Tal. "You kept me from dying. You gave me new life. You've kept yourself alive for . . . a long time. These are all natural laws. What's so hard about killing Anode?"

"Let me try to explain," said Shandor. He exhaled sharply before he said: "Let's see. How much do you know about karma?"

"Karma?" Tal elevated his eyebrows. "I've never heard of it."

"Karma is a very important part of what I'm going to try to explain to you. Karma is like . . . well, it's sort of like a debt. Say you owe me something. . . ." He paused. "What symbols does your tribe use for exchange? Do you use money or do you barter—use trade goods and the like?"

Tal shrugged. "We use furs or fresh meat, sometimes, or maybe weapons."

"All right. Say you owe me ten furs and a new sword. We'll call that debt your karma. Today, you give me three furs. Now your karma is less. Tomorrow, you give me two furs. Your karma is even less. The next day, you *take from me*, six furs and a lance. Now your karma is greater than it was before, greater even than at the beginning. Do you understand?"

"Yes," said Tal, frowning. "But when I took the furs and the lance, why wouldn't you come after _me_ with a sword?"

Shandor laughed at Tal's barbarian instincts.

"In your village, I probably would," he admitted. "But this was just an illustration. I want you to understand that karma is like a debt you owe to someone, only you don't pay it with furs. You pay it by living right, by doing good. When you do good, you reduce your karma—or build up a balance toward future karmic debts. When you knowingly and deliberately do evil, you add to your karma. Do you follow me so far?"

"I guess," said Tal, with a shrug. "But what's the point to it? I asked you a question about natural laws and I get this lecture on debts and karma. What's the connection?"

"The connection is that karma is one of the *essential* natural laws we were talking about. You mentioned my keeping you from dying, my restoring your health, my own preservation for thousands of years. These are *superficial* natural laws. The Science of Infrastatics can circumvent them easily.

"You see, Infrastatics has to do with the vibrational level at which the atomic structure is held stable. Make a modification to the vibrational level and a modification to the basic atomic structure results. An example would be to rearrange the atomic patterns so that a heart wound heals itself or a fractured skull knits together or the process of age and deterioration is retarded. These are all simple—simple, that is, for Infrastatics—scientifically applied methods of altering the *superficial* natural laws.

"But there are *essential* natural laws that neither Infrastatics nor any other power on Earth can alter. Karma is one. Agape love is another. Wholeness, the Law Of One, is still another. I do not know if I can circumvent these laws enough to kill Anode. I do not know if I can."

"If karma is like a debt, what are the other two you mentioned?"

"Agape love is an ancient term," said Shandor, slowly. "It means simply to love completely, selflessly. It is not a love like you felt for Alytha. It is not the love of a parent for a child or a brother for his family or a son for his parents or a friend for his friend. It is all of that and more, much more. It is absolute love. The love that would do no harm to any living thing. It is a love best expressed by a man long, long ago—almost twenty-five centuries before the Second Infrastatic War. In that incarnation, which was his last on this plane, he was called Jesus. As his enemies put him to death—to a very painful death—he said: 'Forgive them. For they know not what they do.' That is agape love."

"It doesn't sound very practical," said Tal, doubtfully. "I still think a good sword and a stout lance make a better answer."

"Perhaps. For Tal Mikar. But you are more than Tal Mikar. You are part of the Law of One. That's the third *essential* natural law.

The Law of One is really the first law. Its essence is that *all* life-force is basically part of the same substance. Not that we are 'brothers under the skin,' but that we are *one*. You and I, Alytha and Lanawe, Sar Lon and Ven Tamor, Lan Regas and Shara Vralon—and Anode, too—are all a part of the elemental life-force that *exists*. We are part of it as are the animals, the birds, the fish, even the trees and flowers and grass. Everything that lives is part of us and we are part of it.

"When we kill, it should only be to sustain life. We must kill to live, whether we're carnivores or vegetarians, but the life-force we ingest is not lost. It goes back into the Whole by sustaining our own life-force. The bodies that we sustain this way are mortal. They, too, in time, will go to feed the life-force of other bodies. It is the soul that is immortal and, in moving from body to body, works out its karma.

"It is when we deliberately and knowingly do evil to another living thing that we violate the Law of One. Again a quotation from an ancient writer says it best. This man, a poet in that incarnation, was called Aden Romine, and he wrote:

> *The pain we lay upon the soul*
> *Of our brother's heart fills us.*
> *The grief he bears, we, too, must bear*
> *And the death he dies kills us.*

"You see, Tal, it was a violation of the Law of One that led, in the beginning, to the First Infrastatic War." Shandor suddenly stopped. "I hadn't intended to tell you all this," he said. "We have a great deal to do and very little time in which to do it, but I think it's important that you learn exactly what we're up against. Let me tell you the history of the Infrastatic

Wars."

Before he did, however, Shandor refilled his cup and Tal's with the savory brown beverage. Then, reseating himself, he began:

"Earth once boasted a great civilization. This civilization had flying machines, devices that could talk over great distances, all manner of marvels. Many you can't even imagine. Earth had once been a desolate wilderness peopled by savage animals and even more savage man-things. Gradually, century by century, man built himself a civilization that was truly fantastic. The capital of that great civilization—certainly its greatest power—was called Atlantis.

"Two lovers lived in Atlantis: Thon and Keena. Anode and I lived there, too. We were, Anode and I, just working out the mechanics of what would become the Science of Infrastatics. At that time, Anode and I appeared no different than anyone else.

"The *essential* natural laws were being propounded by teachers in Atlantis' finest schools. Thon and I, who were close friends, joined a group called the Sons of the Law of One. We took vows to harm no living thing unnecessarily. In fact, much of my work with Infrastatics was designed to repair hurt things by modifying their atomic structure—as I did with your wounds.

"We did not know, until later, that a subculture existed in Atlantis that denied the essential natural laws. They called themselves the Children of Belial and they were devoted to a completely hedonistic, totally selfish life-style. Their belief was simply to do whatever pleased them at the moment and to ignore the consequences.

"Anode, who was my colleague, joined the Children of Belial. He started using Infrastatics to provide a perverted pleasure for this group. Then, worst of all, he persuaded Keena to join them.

"The problem with hedonism is that it takes greater and greater 'thrills' to keep you stimulated. In time, Keena became as utterly depraved as anyone in the group, and she became Anode's lover. Together, they plotted the evil that brought destruction upon them all.

"The idea, I later learned, was Keena's. The Children of Belial had become quite sadistic, torturing animals by Infrastatically dissolving the bones inside their flesh or causing their brain to alter its atomic structure. Keena decided to lure Thon, who knew nothing about this side of her nature, to a meeting of the Children of Belial and they would torture him for their amusement, as they had been doing the animals. Anode loved the idea.

"It was done and my friend was betrayed to death by someone he loved and trusted. The ultimate investigation exposed the Children of Belial. Attempts to imprison Keena led Anode to use Infrastatic weapons that no one could resist or withstand. No one except me.

"I countered with my own Infrastatic weapons. The powers that we loosed on each other shook the Earth to its very core. Atlantis split asunder and sank forever. New continents were created. The whole face of the world was altered.

"When it was over, civilization was utterly destroyed. Mankind had been reduced to the level of the animals—if not below. But I had imprisoned Anode in an Infrastatic force field for his final defeat. The Law of One would not allow me to take his life—I do not want that karmic debt—but I left him immobile, impotent, and imprisoned.

"But I did not feel safe, so I placed myself under the Infrastatic Stimulator. I knew that if Anode should free himself, I had to be there to stop him again. It seems he and I have a karmic link, we are bound one to the other.

"Anyway, the world again became a desolate wilderness peopled by savage animals and even more savage things that had once been men. Then again, century by gradual century, man built himself another civilization that rivaled that of Atlantis. The greatest power in this civilization was called America.

"This civilization ultimately branched out and reached the moon, a satellite Earth had in those days. Colonies were set up on all the planets of this solar system. It seemed science had gone as far as it could go—and then two young scientists, Lan Regas and Shara Vralon, rediscovered the science of Infrastatics.

"Remember I told you that these bodies which we sustain are mortal and will ultimately perish, but that the soul is immortal and goes from body to body as it works off its karma—the debts of evil deeds it owes, which it can only repay through good deeds?

"After Thon was killed by Keena, he reincarnated in another body, a primitive tribesman called simply Urg. Keena, too, reincarnated, but she missed Thon in that lifetime. You see, Tal, the souls *will* ultimately reincarnate together, but it may take many lifetimes. Each soul must make progress in its own fashion before they are ready to attempt again to resolve their karmic debts to each other.

"Time after time, down through the centuries, Thon and Keena reincarnated in other bodies. Sometimes one made progress, sometimes the other did. Sometimes one or both lost ground. Because it is the deeds we do in each lifetime, Tal, that add to or subtract from our karmic debt. Each lifetime we must either progress, regress, or stagnate. But the final result came about that Thon reincarnated in the person of Lan Regas and Keena reincarnated in the person of Shara Vralon.

"Now the stage was set again. Now they had their second chance. Lan and Shara were lovers. Together they rediscovered Infrastatics. Together they could work wonders for the good of mankind. But, together, they managed to release Anode from his prison.

"That was when the physical changes produced by Infrastatic stimulation for prolonged periods of time became evident. Anode was something not quite human. But physically and mentally he outstripped every living mortal.

"He tricked Lan and Shara at first. He pretended to be friendly and helpful. But a change had been wrought in his basic metabolism. Anode could no longer live on food such as ordinary people ate. He derived his physical sustenance on an emotional level. Fear, terror, anger, hatred, lust—all the baser emotions were quite literally food to him. Death, particularly death by torture, was an exquisite delight for him and one such death could sustain his life for days. He became what the Ancients would have called *nosferatu*, a 'vampire'— but one that lived off evil itself rather than off blood.

"Soon Shara Vralon fell under his spell. The good karma she had accumulated over many lifetimes was not enough. She gave way to lust and again took Anode as her lover. Once more Infrastatics was perverted to provide unnatural pleasures.

"This time Lan Regas was not fooled as Thon had been. He broke away from Shara, though he never stopped loving her and wanting to help her. But Anode became so incredibly powerful that Lan was virtually helpless. What little Infrastatics he had mastered was child's play compared to what Anode commanded. Everything seemed lost at this point, and all through a blunder of mine.

"I had not prepared a device sufficiently strong enough to awaken me from the Stimulator. I did not know then that the power of the Stimulator accumulated geometrically rather than mathematically. Therefore, I remained in my state of suspended animation while Anode ravaged the world and her colonies in space.

"Finally, more by accident than intent, Lan Regas stumbled upon a way to free me. Like Anode, I, too, had been altered physically. Like him, I now had greatly increased physical strength and intellectual capacity. Like him, I, too, no longer lived on ordinary food. My hunger is an intellectual hunger rather than an emotional one. Where Anode feeds on emotions of fear, pain, and suffering, I live on thoughts of deep and profound philosophical truths. There is much to be said for such a diet.

"But we had very little time left. Anode and his minion, Shara Vralon, had become almost omnipotent. There was very little that could touch them, but still I launched my counterattack.

"The powers we had used to sink Atlantis were as nothing compared to what we used now. The moon was destroyed and the fragments made Earth a ringworld. Whole planets were shifted in their orbits. But in the end, we won; and Anode was imprisoned inside the Eternity Stone while Shara Vralon took the Chalice of Time and fled to the stars.

"But the Earth had been devastated. All man's great works were left in ruins. His second great civilization, like the first, crumbled about his ears. He was reduced, once again, below the level of the animals. The world reverted to savagery.

"Most of the Second Infrastatic War was fought in space, which is why Earth received no more damage than she did. Enough was done, however, that her orbit tilted and her magnetic polarity was reversed.

"As I told you earlier, when I returned to the Infrastatic Stimulator, I set a mind key to awaken me if the Eternity Stone were deactivated and Anode were freed. You know the results.

"What you do not know is that the karmic debt must still be worked out. Thon, who had been Lan Regas, reincarnated many times here on Earth. It would seem, from what I learned on the astral plane while seeking help, that Keena, who had been Shara Vralon, must have done the same on Aryor.

"While I was on the astral plane, I saw the Akoshic records. Keena's soul, that which had also been called Shara Vralon, is even now returned to Earth, reincarnated as Lanawe Palmerin.

"And Thon, he who had been called Lan Regas, has reincarnated at this time, too. And his name, in this incarnation, is Tal Mikar.

TWENTY-TWO

They found the corpse on the first morning after they left Shalimar.

It was Varn Virgilus, one of the Aryorians, and his neck had been broken.

"But look at those marks on his neck," said Dr. Palmerin. "Those are the oddest looking bruises I ever saw."

"Those are fingermarks," said Adfor. "Your warrior was killed. His neck was broken by a very powerful man."

"Killed?" Dr. Palmerin looked aghast. "But who—?"

"Don't know," replied Adfor. "Perhaps the White Death from the Desert."

"The what?"

"Our people have a legend, old as time. It tells of a terrible monster that Shandor chained up in the Great Desert many years ago. This monster looks like a man, but is pale as the face of death. It is called the White Death."

Instinctively all Aryorians looked toward Anode, but he had his burnoose low over his face. Nothing was visible save his burning red eyes. Only the Aryorians knew of Anode's oddly pale complexion—the Kalathors had only seen him briefly and then just by firelight—and they wondered exactly who, or what, they had found in Shalimar.

Lanawe thought about it again that night when she took Anode his evening meal, which he ate in the privacy of Dr. Palmerin's tent.

"What are you staring at, pet?" he asked, in his faintly mocking voice.

"Your hair—" She looked puzzled. "I thought—it had white streaks in it. Now it just looks gray."

Anode laughed. "Eyes play strange tricks sometimes."

The next morning there were two corpses, both Aryorians. One had had his neck broken, like Virgilus, the other was almost totally dismembered. Lanawe gagged when she saw the remains.

She turned away and stumbled back into camp. Something made her stop—some force she could not control—and made her turn toward her father's tent.

Anode stood there, just within the entrance, smiling a cool, sardonic smile. And his hair was only lightly flecked with gray!

Lanawe turned away, shaken to her core by the wildly erotic feelings Anode aroused in her. It was as if the very essence of sensual lust poured into her from his feral eyes.

Dr. Palmerin returned to camp stunned. It was decided to bury the bodies at once and move on. The Kalathors were afraid to stay here. The camp was alive with the sibilant whisper: "The White Death. The White Death from the Desert!"

As the dispirited expedition rode on that day, Lanawe noticed that Anode rode close to Cron and talked to him in a low, droning voice. Several times she saw Cron look into the shadows where Anode's face was hidden and it seemed as if the Kalathor was terrified, but he continued to ride with and talk to Anode.

After the noon rest, Lanawe saw that Cron had led others of the Kalathors to ride with Anode till that strange man, if he were a man, was the center of a milling throng of horsemen. He talked to each man in the same low, droning voice he had used when he talked to Cron. Of the Kalathors, only the shaman, Rylleh, and the clan chief, Adfor, did not ride with Anode.

It was a very subdued, very quiet camp that evening. Lanawe took Anode's meal to him and she confirmed what she had seen that morning: his hair was very dark, just lightly flecked with gray.

"I don't understand about your hair," she said, feeling embarrassed for the hot emotions that were stirring inside her. "It seems to get darker by the day."

"Rest and . . . nourishment . . . restore one's vitality," he said, smiling and showing his sharp white teeth.

Lanawe felt the lust rising in her. No one, ever, had aroused such savage desire in her as did this stranger.

"Who are you?" she asked, and Anode laughed his low, evil, almost taunting laugh.

"I am Anode," he said, in a sensual whisper. "You remember me, don't you?" His feral red eyes literally burned in the softly lit tent. "There is much about me that you remember." Lanawe felt as if his eyes had grown to immense size. "You remember my voice and you remember my words." Lanawe looked into two huge furnaces, each large enough to swallow her, each blazing with an unholy blood-red flame that consumed but did not destroy. "You remember my touch. Most of all, you remember my touch."

She was only dimly aware that Anode was bending over her, kissing her, one powerful hand closing on her breast.

She felt the fierce hot flame of passion blaze up within her. At that moment, more than anything else in the world, she desired the feel of Anode's flesh on hers, the touch of his body, the animal mating urge of pure, unreasoned lust.

But even as she felt herself responding to his embrace, felt herself loosening the magnetic seams of her tunic, a sudden vision of Tal Mikar flooded into her mind and it was as if a chill wind had blown upon the warmth of her desire.

She pulled back from Anode, breaking free both of his embrace and of his hypnotic hold on her. It was as if she saw him for the very first time. She saw that he was truly evil, a living embodiment of all the basest emotions and desires that human flesh is heir to.

With an inarticulate cry, Lanawe tore herself from Anode's still reaching arms and fled blindly out into the desert night.

The first person she saw was Adfor, the clan chief. The burly Kalathor lay in a pool of blood, his head split open by the gore-dripping axe in the hands of Cron.

Horror-stricken, Lanawe stopped and Cron took a step toward her, his axe raised, but Anode's voice lanced out through the night: "Leave her! She is mine!"

He stood in the tent opening, dressed all in black, with his skull-white face and hands clearly visible. "I am the White Death from the Desert and I claim this one as mine!"

Alun Akobar emerged sleepily from his tent just as Cron turned away from Lanawe. Before the nightmare could register as reality, before the girl could gather breath enough to scream, Cron swung his axe almost offhandedly and Alun Akobar went down, the scream in his throat bubbling wetly, his chest bloody and shattered.

Then the Kalathors were everywhere—ripping, slashing, killing. One Aryorian got his neuron gun into action quickly enough to slay a charging warrior, but he, too, was brought down, even as he was buckling on his deflector.

The slaughter was over in minutes, but many of the Aryorians were only wounded. Their screams became truly horrible as the Kalathors vied with each other to see who could inflict the most excruciating tortures.

Helpless, numb with shock, Lanawe felt Anode's hands seize her arms like bands of steel. Helpless, step by step, she was forced to walk across the death camp, past the corpse of Adfor and, just beyond that, the bloody, dismembered body of Rylleh, to where her father lay.

Dr. Palmerin was still alive, but in great pain. One leg was obviously broken and both arms were slashed by wicked, bleeding wounds. He was held by two Kalathors as Anode and Lanawe came to him.

"L-Lan . . ." he managed to gasp. "Lan, I . . . I. . . ."

"And now the pleasure begins," said Anode, who turned Lanawe so she could see his face, alight with an almost religious fervor, and his blazing red eyes, and his hair—black as midnight without the slightest touch of gray!

When Shandor deactivated the force field, Tal's first thought was for the camp. But the ruins of Shalimar lay desolate and empty.

"They have been gone for some time," Shandor told him. "They left while you were still under the Stimulator and near to death."

Tal soon learned that the search the Aryorians made of Shalimar's ruins could have been scarcely more than a perfunctory glance. Under the stimulus of Shandor's belt

238

controls, force fields dropped, sometimes after first vaporizing tons of rubble, and vast laboratories, armories, and vehicle hangars were revealed.

"The important things in Shalimar I preserved," Shandor explained. "I did not want to be unprepared again if the need arose."

While Shandor busied himself with the weaponry he felt would be needed to contain Anode, Tal wandered morosely through the ruins. Where before he had returned again and again to the sealed crypt, now he found that he repeatedly made his way to the central plaza where the Aryorians' camp had been.

He had a great deal to think about.

Shandor had really shaken him when he had said that Tal was the reincarnation of Lan Regas, who was the reincarnation of someone named Thon from a place called Atlantis. That was an awful lot for Tal to swallow at once.

He had never, before the day, heard the word "reincarnation" nor had he ever considered the concept. His was a barbarian's mind: simple, direct, and straightforward. A philospher he was not, had never been, and did not desire to be.

Yet what Shandor had told him made a certain sense.

It explained the strange familiarity he had felt for Lanawe. It explained the way she had felt about him. It explained his familiarity with Shalimar, a strange familiarity for one who had never been there before. And it explained his preoccupation with the sealed crypt: because deep in his unconscious mind, in the part that had been Lan Regas, he remembered the day Shandor had gone into it and had sealed the force fields into place.

All this was not to say that Tal accepted the idea. These were merely arguments his mind presented to show where Shandor's story might fit. He mulled it over and over again as he roamed the ruins. And he thought of things to ask Shandor as his mind threw up puzzles he could not solve on his own.

"What about Alytha?" he asked, as he ate the meal Shandor had prepared for him. The bronze man sipped a cup of the savory beverage Tal had learned was called simply *glow*. "If I'm Lan Regas and Lanawe is Shara Vralon, then what part does Alytha play in all this? Who was she before?"

"I don't know," Shandor admitted. "When I was on the astral plane, I gleaned nothing of Alytha from my brief contact with your mind. I would have to return to that plane and consult the Akoshic records before I could answer."

"Was there ever a triangle? You've spoken of Thon and Keena, Lan and Shara, me and Lanawe. Was there ever anyone else? Ever a third party?"

"No. Not on Thon's part. His love for Keena, *your* love for Keena, outlasted a hundred lifetimes. But maybe, as your soul progressed, it grew away from Keena. That happens sometimes in working out karmic relationships. Alytha may be a coupling for this lifetime only, or she may be an indication that your karmic debt to Keena is nearly paid off, that you've forgiven her in your heart, and are ready for a more rewarding relationship with someone else. I rather suspect it's the latter."

"But you've told me that Keena—and later Shara Vralon—was evil, perverted, and cruel, right?" At Shandor's nod, he went on: "But I know for a fact that Lanawe Palmerin can't stand the sight of blood. I killed a deer once and would have shown her how to dress it, but she ran away. She would not speak to me and would not eat for some time afterward. Lanawe doesn't seem to have any of the qualities you said that Keena and Shara had."

"That's good," said Shandor, sipping his *glow*. "It means that Keena's soul has made much progress since I knew it last. That is the most hopeful thing you've told me."

"One more thing," said Tal, suspiciously. "You said you don't eat real food anymore, but you seem to drink plenty of *glow*."

Shandor laughed.

"I do that," he acknowledged. "But *glow* is not a food. It is a mild narcotic that is pleasant to my taste. I did *not* say that I no longer ate food. I said that I no longer required it to sustain my body. I can eat anything you can—so can Anode—but the food is not absorbed by our bodies. It does nothing for us. I drink *glow* because I like its taste, nothing more."

Most of the next day Tal spent prowling among the ruins

while Shandor completed his preparations. Tal returned once more to the central plaza and squatted there with his back against the wall where the tents had been pitched.

He missed Lanawe, he suddenly realized. He missed Alytha, but he missed Lanawe equally as much. He sat silently in the warm sunshine and thought about her, remembering her black hair and blue eyes and her slim figure, almost boyish compared to Alytha's.

He remembered the last time he had seen her, when they had made love on the steps to the sealed crypt. He thought again how her sudden, hot lust had been so out of character for the coolly dispassionate Lanawe Palmerin.

But not for Shara Vralon!

The air suddenly grew colder, as if the sun had gone behind a cloud although it still shone down the same as before. Tal's head jerked up and his eyes opened wide as if he had heard a sudden sound, although there was nothing save the silence.

It was not out of character for Shara Vralon—or for Keena.

Tal did not like that idea at all. He remembered Lanawe's confused actions after her animallike passion had spent itself. She was confused as if she had not done such a thing before *or as if she suddenly found herself in a strange place and in a strange body!* Her confusion might well have been the reawakening of the Keena part of herself.

Tal would have liked to ask Shandor about this, but that would have meant telling the bronze man about his sexual relationship with Lanawe. Somehow, even for Tal's barbarian mind, that was an invasion of privacy he could not do.

But he did consider several things.

Something had impelled him to leave, to get away, when he had seen the strangely bone-white figure materialize from the Eternity Stone. Something within him had told him to leave and to go to the sealed crypt. *Could that have been his Thon-Lan Regas memory urging him to flee from Anode and seek Shandor's help?*

If it were, then the sight of Anode might well have triggered latent memories within Lanawe Palmerin, too. The sight of Anode might well have brought her Keena-Shara Vralon memory to the forefront and driven her to a lusting that was alien to Lanawe herself.

It was a theory that explained Lanawe's behavior, which had so puzzled Tal before. It was a theory that tied in directly to what Shandor had told him. But it was a theory that Tal did not want to believe. It was a theory he wanted to reject.

Because if the theory were true, then it was *all* true. And that was something Tal was not yet prepared to accept.

He got up, angry with himself for his dark musings, and stalked off into the ruins like some disconsolate spirit. What he needed, he decided, was something to get his mind off all this.

His wish was granted almost immediately.

A low, sleek, metallic shape suddenly slid across his peripheral vision. Tal whirled, his dagger out and ready.

The machine—he saw now what it was—had Shandor inside. Its top was a clear plastic bubble with polarized touch panels to keep out the sun's rays and with room for about six passengers inside. The body of the vehicle was sleek silver, tapering front and back. Twin air scoops were recessed on each side of the slim front and directional air foils made fins across the back.

The vehicle hung, apparently suspended by nothing at all, about a meter off the ground. As Shandor swept it up to a stop beside Tal, the younger man saw the sand kicking back from the rear jet exhausts.

The little craft stopped before Tal and waited there, hanging in midair, while Shandor touched a button on the control panel. When he did, a section of the curved plastic bubble hinged up like a wing unfolding, and a section of the metal side retracted within itself, leaving Tal an easy entry.

"Got the skimmer working," said Shandor. "I think it'll serve us best. I've also got everything aboard we should need. Is there anything you want from the laboratory before we leave?"

Tal blinked. "You mean we're ready to go?"

"That's right. I'm ready. If you are, climb in and we're on our way." He indicated the padded, comfortable-looking seat beside him.

Tal hesitated only a second. He had his dagger and his sword with him. There was nothing behind he needed or wanted. He slid into the skimmer, which tilted the least little bit, then readjusted itself to compensate for the load change. Shandor closed off the hatch, and they were ready to move out.

Before they left, Shandor had one more task to perform. He touched the control buttons on his belt and the force fields all popped back into existence, effectively sealing off all his storehouses and leaving Shalimar nothing but the ruin it seemed to be.

"Never know when I might need them again," he said. He touched a button set atop the right-hand side of the half wheel he used as a control and the little skimmer leaped forward in an almost silent burst of power. He turned the wheel and kicked the rudder pedal that controlled the rear air foils and the skimmer banked sharply to the left and headed straight into the Great Desert.

Tal, who had ridden in the shuttlecraft, fired a neuron gun, and used a personal deflector screen, was fascinated by the aircar.

"What keeps this thing up in the air?" he asked. "Why don't we fall?"

"There's a repellor tank fore and aft," explained Shandor. "A sort of antigravity device. Our engine is simplicity itself. Air is sucked in the front inlets, compressed, and forced out the rear jets under pressure. Rotors are set up in the air ducts to generate the electricity to operate the compressor, so the engine is a self-sustaining power plant. That means it'll run indefinitely. I figured it was our most dependable vehicle for pursuing Anode. It'll do two hundred and fifty kilometers per hour if I push it."

Tal nodded, as if he understood all this, then simply gave himself up to the pleasures of the ride.

Riding in the skimmer was nothing at all like flying in the jetboat. There, they had been high above the ground, frequently above the clouds, and everything had been small and distant and far away.

Here, though, they were less than a meter off the ground and the skimmer maintained that distance, riding up and down over the contours of the land, which meant that Tal was lower than he had been when on horseback. The landscape outside seemed somehow more peaceful and tranquil when viewed through the skimmer's canopy, with the environmental control system maintaining a pleasant twenty-eight degrees Celsius.

He noticed that Shandor handled the skimmer with casual skill. This did not surprise Tal. He could not imagine any situation the bronze man would not be able to handle with equal ease. One thing did puzzle him, though.

"How do you know where you're going?" he asked. "They've been gone for days and we're moving too fast for you to be tracking them."

"I programmed Anode's aura into the skimmer's computer banks. We should be able to follow him anywhere he goes. His aura has been ionized by the Infrastatic Stimulator. I have sensors that can trace that ionization. One such is plugged into our on-board computer. Wherever Anode goes, the skimmer will take us directly there."

The little aircar never hesitated as it slid smoothly across the Great Desert. Its almost silent engines kept up an even, steady thrust that moved it right along.

Tal amused himself by watching the landscape flow past the speeding aircar. He remembered the unpleasantness of the horseback trip out with the Kalathors. He smiled as he compared that with the luxurious comfort in which he now traveled.

When darkness settled over the Desert, leaving the rings as bands of snow across the ink-black sky, Shandor gave Tal some of the concentrated rations he had packed, but the skimmer never stopped. Tal discovered there were devices built in that provided the proper eliminatory relief, so there was no real reason to stop their journey.

Shandor appeared to need little, if any, sleep. He held the skimmer on a steady course, her twin-beam headlights boring a tunnel of brightness through the desert night.

Tal, after eating, leaned back in the padded seat and tried to compose himself for sleep. He did not know what lay ahead for him and Shandor, but with a barbarian's instincts he rested when and where he could.

He had let his eyes fall half closed, when a dark shape just to the right of the headlight beams suddenly arrested his attention. His blue eyes snapped open wide as he peered into the night.

"Shandor—" he began, but the bronze man said:

"I see it. There's more—ahead and to the right."

The skimmer slowed and turned slightly so that the lights fell upon a sight Tal wished he had never seen.

The shape he had glimpsed in the darkness had been the carcass of a dead horse. What lay in front of them, awful in the skimmer's headlights, was total carnage.

The Aryorians, some of the Kalathors, and most of the livestock had been slaughtered. Not just slaughtered, but butchered.

Shandor brought the skimmer to a halt and handed a glowrod to Tal. But he did not immediately open the bubble cover to the skimmer.

"What . . . could have happened here?" asked Tal, looking at the horribly mutilated corpse of Dr. Fel Palmerin, which lay immediately in front of the aircar.

"I can deduce," said Shandor grimly. "Anode has had a hand in this. But he is gone now. His aura is old and dissipating."

Both men emerged from the skimmer and walked together across the field of death.

There was evidence of a trememdous slaughter. Aryorians lay like butchered animals and Kalathors were dead there, too—many butchered like the offworlders.

Tal looked down at one Kalathor corpse. It was Rylleh, the Kalathor shaman. He who had said he would die here in the Desert. Near him lay the body of Adfor, the chief. His head had been split as if by a Kalathor battle axe.

But it was the Aryorians who had died most horribly. Many bodies showed evidence of cruel and inhuman tortures. Most were literally hacked to pieces.

Tal, who had seen blood and death before, was nevertheless sickened by it. So far as he could tell, in the shifting light of their glowrods, all the Aryorians had been killed. With a sense of growing panic, he found himself searching desperately for the corpse of Lanawe.

What he found, not far from the body of Dr. Palmerin, was Alun Akobar. And he still lived!

At first glance, Tål had thought him dead, like all the others, but as he turned the light from the glowrod away, he saw Alun's hand move, ever so slightly.

Instantly he was kneeling beside the bloody body of the offworlder. "Shandor!" he called once, then, more softly, to Alun, he said: "It is Tal Mikar. Can you hear me? Can you understand me?" The bronze man came up behind Tal just as Alun managed to open his eyes.

"Y—You...." His lips shaped the word, but no sound came out. His throat moved convulsively, then he managed to say it audibly: "You... came back... from the dead...."

"What happened here?" Tal demanded, his voice urgent. "Where's Lanawe? Is she alive?" He fought the urge to seize the Aryorian's body and shake him till he answered.

"Let me, Tal," said Shandor. The bronze man moved Tal aside with a gentle movement and knelt in his place. He lightly felt of the pulse in Alun Akobar's throat, then put one powerful hand against the man's forehead. "Alun," he said, and his voice had the soothing quality of softly breaking ocean surf. "Alun, I know it is hard for you, but you must tell us what happened here."

"Kal—athors...." The word was scarcely more than a whisper of sound. "... turned ... on us ... killed ... everyone ... everyone ... except...." A froth of blood appeared on his lips, his breathing became more labored. Shandor picked up his statement in a gentle, soft, almost hypnotic voice:

"Everyone except Anode. Is that not true? Anode and Lanawe Palmerin. Those two went away with the Kalathors, didn't they?"

Again Alun struggled desperately to speak. Blood bubbled up with each attempt.

"Y—Yes...." He managed to whisper. "Pri—soners ... both ... Anode ... and Lan—"

But Alun Akobar would never finish that sentence. In the middle of Lanawe Palmerin's name, he had died.

Shandor knelt by the body only a moment longer, then he stood up, towering well above Tal.

"So it begins," he murmured, and there was a strangely distant look in his flake gold eyes.

"The Kalathors have taken Lanawe and Anode!" Tal cried, his mind blazing with the memory of what the Kalathors did to their women, how they treated them. "We've got to go after them!"

"There is no danger," said Shandor, in a gentle, almost sad voice. "At least, none from those you call Kalathors."

"But you don't know them!" Tal protested, urgent action in his voice. "You don't know what they're like!"

"But I know Anode," the bronze man said, as he and Tal returned to the skimmer. Shandor took two devices from a sealed compartment. "He has been taken prisoner by no one. Whatever happened here—however it was instigated—Anode is the power behind it. Anode is the one responsible."

Shandor held a metallic rod in one hand and pointed it at the body of Dr. Fel Palmerin, which happened to be the nearest corpse. There was no sound, but after a few seconds the corpse began to blur eerily and then seemed to flow in upon itself and was gone. There was no trace of it left.

"What did you do?" asked Tal, in astonishment, his fears for Lanawe momentarily forgotten.

"I altered the vibratory patterns of the molecules. It seems kinder than leaving him for the desert scavengers." He handed a similar rod to Tal. "Point that end at the body and touch that button. Two of us can take care of this quicker."

Tal hesitantly pointed his first Infrastatic device and triggered it. The corpse of Alun Akobar melted away.

With his glowrod in one hand and the tube in the other, Tal moved across the field of slaughter, duplicating Shandor's efforts. The bronze man spoke first:

"The manner in which these people died, the violence and the torture, are Anode's trademark. His signature, you might say. Whatever the Kalathors did here was done under Anode's command. Then he and Lanawe Palmerin rode away with the killers."

"But Lanawe would never go willingly with someone who could do a thing like this," protested Tal. "She's just not capable of it."

"But Shara Vralon was capable of it . . . and more. In that incarnation, your Lanawe was fully as evil as Anode. Perhaps you're right and she has changed, but she *did* go with Anode.

The only question is: did she go willingly?"

"She did not go willingly," said Tal, definitely. But in his heart a voice cried out silently: *Please don't let it be willingly!*

TWENTY-THREE

The Kalathor encampment never had a chance.

These were the people of the Rope Clan, as Adfor's had been the Axe Clan. Now they were virtually nothing.

Anode and three riders sat their horses and looked at their helpless prisoners.

It seemed that the Kalathors of the Rope Clan simply stood grimly on the sand facing their handful of attackers. One might wonder why they made no effort to attack, and how so few—only two Kalathors sat with Anode and Lanawe—managed to subdue the fierce desert warriors.

The answer came simply.

Anode lifted what had once been a simple neuron gun and leveled it at Garth, the clan chief. There was no sound when he activated it, but in less than a second, Garth began to scream horribly. His screams became louder and more shrill and he leaped about, clutching his body in obvious agony though no mark appeared on his skin.

Then the screaming took on a different sound, a definite *gurgle* as Garth's body seemed to spread and shrink and fold in upon itself like a collapsing tent. The screams stopped when he was a head shorter and twice as wide as he had been. By then, blood was running from his mouth and nose and eyes. His head caved in like a deflated balloon and in a few more seconds he was nothing but a heap of crumpled, bloody clothing, burst skin, and spilled intestines. In the glob that had been Garth there was no trace of a bone. Bone molecules vibrate at a different intensity than molecules of flesh.

Anode was avidly enjoying himself. He was laughing hugely and his feral red eyes literally glowed. His skin was still bone-white, but there was a look of vital *aliveness* about him that could not be denied.

What had been a personal deflector screen lay across the saddlehorn in front of Anode. Both it and the neuron gun had been modified by him during the first few days of their journey away from Shalimar. Now they were crude but functional Infrastatics weapons. The neuron gun was now a simple alternator that could vary the vibratory rate of whatever it was aimed at over a short range. The deflector screen had been modified into a condenser which set up an Infrastatic force field about ten meters in diameter through which nothing could penetrate, not even air molecules. In a short period of time. the Kalathors sealed inside it would have exhausted their air supply.

In a way, Anode almost hoped they would refuse his offer; he especially enjoyed watching people die by suffocation.

"Hear me, men of the Rope Clan!" he shouted, knowing his voice could be heard, but faintly, inside the force field. "Your chief is dead. You saw the manner in which I killed him. I can kill you all like that—one by one—or I can simply wait and in a very short time you will be dead by suffocation. There are other ways, equally unpleasant ways, in which I could kill you. Your lives are completely in my hands. I can, if I so choose, let you live. Whether you live or die depends upon what you do and upon my whim of the moment.

"I am the White Death from the Desert! I have come to bring fire and death and suffering to all who oppose me—witness what I did to Garth! To those who follow me, to those who serve me, I bring looting and spoils, women, wealth, and power! I shall forge an army of terror! An army fit to ride with the White Death!

"I offer you of the Rope Clan a chance to fight in that army. I have heard that the Kalathors are the fiercest warriors on Earth. Yet I have captured you, alone! I have slain your chief, alone! I hold you helpless in my power, alone! You are as children to my will; yet I would make you *my* children! You have seen my power. Would you rather fight *with* me or *against* me?

"I have heard that the Kalathors love fighting above all else. Join the army of the White Death and I can promise you all the fighting you desire, with great spoils and looting at the end of it. Again I say: you saw my power! In a battle, think what it would mean to have power like that on your side!"

One of the Kalathors inside the force field stirred uneasily. "Garth was our clan chief," he said, but Anode cut him off:

"Garth is dead! And dead by *my* hand alone! By the laws of your own tribe that makes *me* your clan chief, does it not?"

The Rope Clan considered this. The fact that the air inside the force field was beginning to go bad may have had something to do with hastening their decision.

"You did kill Garth with your strange weapon," the first speaker acknowledged, and another cried:

"By law, you are our clan chief!" But the first speaker went on:

"But how can we follow you? We don't know what you are. You don't . . . you don't even look . . . human."

Anode laughed. A sound of pure evil.

"I am not human," he said. "I am the White Death from the Desert."

"But how do we know you would not kill us, too?"

"I can kill you at this moment. I can kill you as I killed Garth or I can kill you in any number of other ways. I can kill you later if I choose. I can kill you any time it pleases me or any time you displease me. The choice is yours. Die now, for a certainty, or die later, if I decide, or live, for so long as I choose. But whatever you choose, you will bend to the will of the White Death.

"As my servants, you will be protected from harm by others, have much fighting and much looting, and will be part of an army that will be feared wherever men walk and breathe and talk. The White Death will bring terror to all parts of the world."

The Kalathors inside the force field were beginning to gasp as their air supply became used up. Their suffering brought a glow of pure joy to Anode's face.

"We . . . accept!" one of them finally shouted. "We of the Rope Clan accept you as our clan chief!"

"But you are not of the Rope Clan! If I am your clan chief,

you are now of the White Death Clan!"

"Yes! Yes, the White Death Clan!"

Throughout all this, Lanawe Palmerin had sat hunched in her saddle, her head hanging, her black hair hiding her eyes.

She was aware of all that went on around her yet on another level she was not fully aware and it seemed as if she were witnessing some sort of dream, a nightmare, from which she must soon awaken.

She never moved as the survivors of what had once been the Rope Clan were inducted into the White Death Clan. Her burning eyes seemed fascinated by the sickening mess that had been the clan chief, Garth.

She remembered, below the level of the secondary thought processes, the scene of primeval horror when Anode and the Kalathors had wiped out the Aryorians. Anode had forced Lanawe to stay by his side while he personally inflicted gruesomely inhuman tortures on her dying father.

She remembered the scene but she never consciously thought of it, for to do so would be to go mad. But still she remembered even as she remembered Anode's promise to destroy those on the *X-97*.

"It will be so easy," he said. "I can modify your shuttlecraft communicator and a neuron gun to devise a simple Infrastatic Beamer that will follow the radio waves when the communicator is activated until the radio waves are picked up by the starship. Then the Beamer will activate a change in the molecular structure of the alloy from which the ship is formed. The ship will literally split in two as if cut by a knife. No one will survive." He laughed. "It will be delicious. Most delicious!"

Now, the camp of the White Death Clan was quiet. The sentries were posted and all, save Anode, Lanawe, and three slave girls, were asleep.

Anode and Lanawe sat alone in the chief's tent. Lanawe was pale and haggard, her eyes feverish and wild. Untouched food lay on golden platters before her and untouched wine filled silver cups. Her hands were held together in front of her, clasped so tightly the knuckles were white and the palms were bloody where her nails had dug. Her will was held by the power of Anode's feral red eyes as effectively as if she were chained to the floor.

Anode, across the low table from her, was enjoying himself hugely. He had one of the slave girls spreadeagled on the floor and was systematically touching various parts of her nude body with a white-hot metal rod. The girl did not scream because Anode had started the evening's pleasures by cutting out her tongue and forcing one of the other slave girls to eat it. These girls were forced to stand and watch, and Anode had promised them that each of them in turn would undergo the same torture as soon as the first girl died. He explained that he had wanted them to fully appreciate what they were going to endure by watching it inflicted upon the first girl. The last girl to die, who must first watch a hideous death inflicted upon the other two, would be the one whom Anode had forced to eat the dying girl's tongue. He promised her that she would eat the second girl's tongue, too.

The abject terror of the two waiting slave girls was so exquisitely delicious to Anode that he hoped to drag out the torture for the balance of the night. A death by pain and anguish was very satisfying to his hunger, but the fear engendered in the waiting victims was so intensely pleasurable to him that he wanted to savor it to the utmost.

He interrupted his enjoyment to turn his blood red eyes on Lanawe.

"What is it, my dear?" he asked, in a silken voice. "You don't seem to be enjoying your meal."

Lanawe stared back at him, her eyes wide, pupils dilated.

"You must eat," he insisted. "Unless, of course, you find the delicacies *I* enjoy more to your taste than the roast fowl and red wine."

"N—No—" gasped the girl, her face a mask of revulsion. "I can't stand it! It's . . . horrible!"

"Horrible?" Anode tossed back his dark hair and laughed, exposing his white teeth, the canines of which were unnaturally long and sharp. "But, my dear, I've explained to you that you are the reincarnation of Shara Vralon and of Keena. I myself have seen you administer tortures that would make what I am doing here seem pleasant to the victim. I've seen you, bloodied to your elbows, laughing like a fiend as some poor devil died in screaming agony. So I find it amusing when you call this little diversion horrible."

"I don't believe what you said!" But in her heart, she *did* believe it, for it was all so familiar to her. "I'm not . . . like . . . what you said."

"Perhaps you are not," Anode agreed. "But you have been. I don't think you've changed all that much. No one ever enjoyed inflicting pain so exquisitely as you did. I can't believe that you have suddenly changed."

Lanawe looked away from the scene of torment. That much of her will she could still control.

The memories of what she had been and what she had done were imprinted deep in the genetic structure of her makeup, but overlaying them were the memories of what she had done since Shara Vralon had fled from Earth to Aryor.

The good karma she had built up was strong, very strong. Lanawe did not understand all the ramifications, but she knew, somehow, deep inside, that while she had once been as Anode said, she was that way no longer. A change had been wrought in her soul, though she did not think of it in those terms. All she knew was that the scene across the table filled her with a shuddering sick horror.

Anode felt this horror and knew that it grew from Lanawe's knowledge of her own past evil. It was the psychic equivalent to a blush of shame and Anode found it to be delicious.

He laughed again. "Would you like to hear some details of what once brought you pleasure, my love?" He touched the writhing slave girl with the white-hot rod as he asked this.

"No!" cried Lanawe. "No! I don't want to know!" She turned her head away, but that was the extent to which she had freedom of action.

Anode laughed again. His appetite was whetted by the delicacies he was savoring on all sides.

"Let me tell you," he said, in a velvet voice. "I remember once, in Atlantis, when you took a slave girl, stripped her, bent her over a table and. . . ."

He was going to *enjoy* this night!

TWENTY-FOUR

Shandor eased the skimmer to a silent halt beside the ruined Kalathor village. It was the encampment of the Axe Clan, from which the expedition had set out for Shalimar.

"That's the second one," said the bronze man, in a grim voice. "Anode is welding together an army."

"The shuttlecraft that Lanawe flew should lie just beyond there," said Tal, pointing. "The rest of her people were with it."

Shandor delicately touched controls and the skimmer slid away in the direction Tal indicated. Neither of them expected to see the jetboat still there, but it was. What they *did* expect to see was there, however: the mutilated corpses of the balance of the Aryorian landing party.

"Why didn't he take the shuttlecraft?" Tal asked, as he and Shandor debarked from the skimmer. "If he really wants to get around, it could take him anywhere."

"True," agreed Shandor. "But it couldn't transport an army. We've seen where he's taken over at least two Kalathor clans. That's more people than this flyer could carry, and besides, Anode must be with his army if he would maintain control of them." The bronze man dilated the hatch in the side of the jetboat and stepped aboard. Tal took one of the tubes he had come to think of as Disposal Rods and began obliterating the rotting corpses. The stench of death still hung heavy in the air even when the last of the bodies had disappeared.

"I found another reason why he didn't take the flyer," said

Shandor, as he emerged, a black box in his hand dangling multicolored wires. "He's cannibalized her for parts to manufacture Infrastatic weapons. They'll be jerry-built at best, but they'll serve his purpose well enough."

Shandor looked at the black box. A partially disassembled neuron gun was wired into one side of it.

"This worries me especially," he said. "This is a crude Infrastatic Beamer. It was wired into the flyer's communicator." He looked up at the sky, spanned by the arching rings. "I'm afraid it's been used against the X-97. I'm afraid Anode has destroyed or disabled the starship."

He paused and surveyed the cleanup work Tal had done.

"Very good," he said, and Tal saw the unmistakable look of pain in the brooding flake-gold eyes. "Now let's do the same for any bodies at the Kalathor encampment and we'll be on our way. We've got to find Anode and stop him before more useless deaths occur."

When night came, their fourth since leaving Shalimar, the bronze man elected to stop and make camp. They were deep in the wooded hill country and it seemed to Tal as if he were going home.

It was cold that night, though there had been no snowfall yet, and the rings were pure silver across the diamond-pointed sky. Their breath frosted heavily in the air as they built up a pleasant campfire of aromatic pine.

"Why are we sitting half roasted and half frozen by a campfire when we could be snug and warm inside the skimmer?" asked Tal, sipping the mug of *glow* that Shandor had given him.

"Tonight I feel the need for an open fire," replied the bronze man, his usually vibrant voice muted and soft. "I need the sustenance that I told you I feed upon. I need to muse for a while on the question of inherent evil. I need the nourishment to my soul that is provided only through quiet contemplation of abstract philosophical truths. I need, in short, to strengthen myself for the coming battle."

"Let me ask you one question before you . . . begin," said Tal. "You said you found a weapon that might have been used against Lanawe's people, the ones who are still . . . up there." He gestured. "Do you think they're all dead?"

"I don't know, Tal," Shandor answered honestly. "But I fear they are. The Beamer was wired into the communicator. When the communicator was activated, and it had been, it beamed radio waves to a receiving device on the *X-97*. It also beamed the Infrastatic vibratory changes with the radio waves, perhaps instead of the radio waves. I say perhaps because I did not disassemble the device totally and analyze its capabilities. I recognized it for what it was and deduced the rest. I don't know precisely what Anode set it to do. It may have caused all electrical equipment to self-destruct, it may have deactivated their life support systems, it may have literally sliced the starship in two, it may have done nearly anything. But whatever it did, I'm certain the people who were left on the *X-97* are now dead."

Tal nodded, as if he understood. He did understand that Shandor thought all the Aryorians except Lanawe Palmerin were now dead. He did not understand all the reasons the bronze man gave for why he believed that. However, since he had met Lanawe deep in the equatorial ice belt, he had seen and experienced so many things he did not understand that understanding had ceased to be important to him. If a thing functioned, he accepted it and used it where necessary; if it did not function, he ignored it.

He ate a simple meal and prepared himself another cup of *glow*. He did not know what the ingredients were, but Shandor had shown him how to mix it. He put a measure of coarse brown powder in a cup, added a measure of grayish-white powder, half filled the cup with boiling water, added a measure of dark red liquid, filled it to the top with boiling water, and put in two measures of a thick golden liquid that Tal found, to his surprise, to be ordinary honey. That made a cup of *glow* and it was delicious, both refreshing and relaxing.

As he sipped it, he looked from under his eyebrows at the silent, brooding figure of Shandor. So quiet had he become that he might well have been molded from the bronze metal he so resembled.

Tal thought that he had never seen a more ruggedly handsome man, nor one with a more perfect physique. Shandor's body was so perfectly proportioned that one was unaware of his tremendous size unless there was something close at hand with which he could be compared.

For all Tal's life, Shandor had been the nearest thing to a god possessed by his people. Tal had by now become accustomed to being in Shandor's presence, though he had been very ill at ease at first; and he had to admit that were he to set out to design a god, Shandor would come very close to fitting his description.

Had Tal been more civilized, the shock of meeting his supreme being face to face might have been too much for him. But Tal was at heart a barbarian, with a barbarian's instincts, and to him the personal manifestation of a deity was startling and unexpected, but not something to be too concerned about. After all, gods are only human.

He had noticed that Shandor, too, had his human side. Although he had never seen the bronze man eat solid food, he had seen Shandor consume a great deal of *glow*. And in the close confines of the skimmer, he could not help but observe that Shandor eliminated the excess fluid the same way Tal did. He assumed that if Shandor ate, his other bodily functions would be the same, too.

Shandor had demonstrated pain over the suffering Anode was causing and had demonstrated a strong compassion for Anode himself, which was something Tal could not comprehend. So far as he could see, a sword thrust in the guts was what Anode needed.

He considered again what Shandor had told him about reincarnation. One part of his mind still rejected it, but another part, the deeper part, acknowledged the truth of what Shandor had said. The memories of Lan Regas—and of a thousand other lifetimes—lay buried in the recesses of Tal's brain and there were times when he could *almost* focus on them.

He shook his head and set his empty cup aside. He did not require the pondering of such abstract things for sustenance. In fact, instead of deriving nourishment from them, he found himself deriving a headache.

He curled himself up in one of the lightweight, yet incredibly warm, blankets that were packed in the skimmer and tried to relax himself into sleep. He looked away from

Shandor and let his gaze turn to the flickering images in the campfire.

He knew it was dangerous to look directly at a campfire; if an attack came from the darkness outside, one would be temporarily blind and therefore helpless, when one looked away from the fire. Yet, once again, Tal felt himself reassured by the nearby presence of the bronze man. Shandor radiated an aura of invincibility.

That was the last thought in his mind as Tal drifted off to sleep.

For a long time after Tal slept, Shandor did not move. His strangely hypnotic flake-gold eyes were hooded as his full mental faculties were turned inward.

Shandor withdrew himself completely from the dimensional plane that Tal Mikar knew as reality. He cleared his mind utterly of all thoughts, blanked out all sense perceptions, opened the way for the mind expanding *emptiness* of true meditation.

When the proper state of Awareness had been reached, Shandor one by one shut down the biorhythmic functionings of his autonomic nervous system. With the skill of an ancient *fakir*, he completely removed himself from contact with his body.

Then, when his consciousness floated free and unfettered on the cosmic winds of total awareness, he made the final necessary adjustment to his delta rhythm and loosed his essence upon the astral plane.

He projected.

It was a familiar experience for Shandor. He swept across the astral plane like a summer wind bending new wheat. He was rising, climbing, soaring upward to the highest levels of psychic awareness, reaching for the Akoshic records.

There was a sensation, like being buffeted by strong winds swirling from all sides, that Shandor knew was the essence of himself moving through the sea of essences that were, at this moment, sharing the astral plane with him. It was his soul touching other souls on an etheral level.

Then there was an awesome stillness, a silence, a feeling of almost palpable heaviness in the air. There were walls of marble around Shandor, with veined pillars half concealed by rich tapestries worked in intricate detail. The room was hoary with age, yet meticulously clean; empty as the sound of a closing door, yet somehow vibrant and alive; full of a hushed, silent stillness, yet thrumming with a sense of barely restrained power.

Shandor knew that all these feelings were subjective. They were his mental impressions of how something that housed the Akoshic records should look. Each soul that visited here came away with a different impression of what had been experienced. It was the content that was important here, not the framework.

To Shandor, it was as if he physically stood within the confines of this marbled room. He stood waiting and expectant. He had been here before.

These are the Akoshic records, the voice-that-was-not-a-voice said within his mind. *Know, O seeker of truth, that what is writ hereon is not foreordained. Everything that has happened is recorded here and everything that may happen is recorded here. All encounters and decisions have at least two possible alternatives. All alternatives are here, with their permutations, but the final decision is in the will of the individual soul and in the degree of karma that soul carries.*

All those who seek knowledge for the ultimate good of the Whole-which-is-greater-than-the-sum-of-the-parts are true followers of the Law of One. These souls are welcomed here and to them the Akoshic records stand open.

The voice-that-was-not-a-voice was silent.

Shandor let the spirit of agape love that permeated this high and holy place wash through him like a cleansing flood. In the afterglow of its purification, he thought of Tal Mikar-who-had-been-Lan Regas-who-had-been-Thon. He reached out for the record of that soul's progression through all its multitude of incarnations.

It was not a telepathic experience. The knowledge he sought was simply *there* waiting to be taken and examined. It was like an incredibly long rope, with either end lost in the shadows, and with a message or picture woven into every strand. He could examine the history of that soul's progression at any point he chose and one strand would display the overt deeds committed and physical acts performed; another strand would display the secret, hidden things the soul had sought to conceal; another strand would display the thoughts and desires and emotions the soul had experienced internally; another strand would display the secretmost, inner recesses of the soul's subconscious thought processes. All Shandor had to do was determine what he sought.

And what he sought were the future alternates for Tal Mikar.

He let the history of Tal's soul flow through his awareness till he came to the point where Tal lay sleeping by a campfire across from a motionless bronze giant.

From that point on the strands became tangled and branched off in many different directions. Many Ancients had thought the future could be foretold by studying the Akoshic records, but Shandor knew this was not true. The most essential factor in a soul's progression was the element of free will. If destiny were foreordained by the Akoshic records, the question of karma would be pointless. It was only through the exercise of free will that a soul could work out its karma and make progress toward the state of being a Master Teacher, such as he who had been the Christ or he who had been the Buddha.

Shandor examined the alternate futures that lay in store for Tal Mikar. There were many things he could do from this point forward and each of them had a different consequence and each consequence had a different resolution and each resolution had a different outcome and each outcome had a different consequence. The cycle went on.

Shandor let the alternate strands flow by swiftly. He was scanning only the ones that were interwoven with the black thread of Anode's presence. On these, there was also interwoven a golden-bronze thread that was Shandor himself.

Suddenly, as he scanned Tal's possible futures, he saw that the endlessly branching future alternates were narrowing inexplicably. It was as if Tal, in this incarnation, was to be the focal point of cosmic forces beyond his knowledge and beyond his control. If ever there was anything close to foreordaining, Shandor saw that it was here.

His interest quickening, he scanned ahead till, out of the mists of the future, he came to a change in the Akoshic records. The thread that was Tal Mikar had narrowed to a single strand and that one had become so intertwined with Shandor's own bronze-gold thread that the two seemed to coalesce and merge into one entity, yet one still enwrapped in the dark coils of Anode's life-force.

Shandor stopped scanning here. His soul was troubled. There was a darkness in his heart and he gave a psychic shudder, as if someone had walked on his grave.

There was something ahead here, something just a fraction beyond his knowledge right now, something that he should not know. Whatever was inscribed on this soul line in the Akoshic records was something that Shandor could not bring himself to learn.

He released Tal's soul line and turned away. Whatever lay ahead there, he would not face. The fear, he admitted to himself, was genuine. It was the fear that told him to turn away and not to ask the ultimate question nor to seek the final answer.

One word, one phrase, one expression, he did glimpse as he turned away. He had not wanted to see it, but it had been there, glowing evilly in the darkness ahead like the eyes of a lurking beast of prey, like the eyes of a demon from the pit, like the feral red eyes of Anode. It was the single word: UNDEATH.

It snowed during the night and Tal awoke to a world that was covered in white.

He had slept snugly within Shandor's miracle blanket and he emerged to blink groggily at the newly changed landscape all around him.

Shandor still sat unmoving, exactly as he had been when Tal fell asleep, but it seemed that not a single snowflake had touched him. His golden hair and bronze skin seemed to shed snowfall like water running off a duck's back.

But Tal could see that Shandor had moved sometime during the night. A pot of water for *glow* was at the edge of the fire, by the multicontainer in which the ingredients were kept. An empty thermal cup sat in the snow by Shandor's right knee. A second cup waited by the fire, obviously for Tal.

Shandor gave no sign that he saw Tal, as the black-haired

barbarian walked shiveringly to the edge of the clearing to relieve himself, then crossed to the fire to prepare a very welcome cup of *glow*.

He was taking his second or third sip of the steaming beverage, when the bronze man spoke for the first time:

"We must move very quickly," he said, his voice almost sad this snowy morning. "Anode's power is growing beyond measure. We must lose no more time."

While Tal consumed a meager breakfast and a second cup of *glow*, Shandor repacked the few items he had taken out of the skimmer. In a very few minutes they slipped into the little aircar and were on their way. The cabin interior was toasty warm.

"Are you still able to trace Anode's aura?" Tal asked, as the snowscape outside slid silently behind them.

"Yes, but it's getting weaker. He's moving fast." Shandor hesitated. "I . . . have this feeling, Tal. A crisis of major proportions is just ahead of us. I don't know what it is, or how to prevent it, but I know we have it to face." He banked the skimmer around a stand of trees, sending swirls of powdery snow away from the rear exhaust ports as he did. "That's why I feel we can't afford to lose anymore time in catching up to Anode. We must not let him gain more power!"

They reached the next Kalathor village by midafternoon. Before Shandor ever brought the skimmer to a halt, Tal could see the bloody evidence that Anode's army was growing. Horribly mutilated bodies lay frozen in grotesque postures.

The slaughter had occurred not too long before the snowfall, because the mounded humps of frozen corpses were not decayed at all. He and Shandor were probably less than a day behind Anode's army.

As always, Shandor insisted they take time to use the Disposal Rods on Anode's victims.

Tal, trudging from one grisly mound to another, was stopped dead by a ghastly moan from a pile of frozen corpses.

"Shandor! Here!" Quickly he raked the snow aside, moved two *things* that had once been human, and found a nearly dead Kalathor youth of perhaps ten winters.

The bronze man was beside him as Tal gently freed the

boy's body from the tangle of death around it.

"He obviously was among these others when he fell and Anode thought him dead," said Shandor. "Look at his legs—that's the work of an Infrastatic Alternator. The bones have been dissolved. But it was an axe blow that laid open his stomach."

Tal could see that the boy was dying. Only the warm blood and the soon-dissipated body heat of the dead men he had lain beneath had kept him from freezing and only the cold had kept him from dying immediately of his wounds. He had no chance.

Shandor gave him a sip from a vial he took from his multipocketed belt, and the boy's eyes flicked open for just a minute.

"Death—" he croaked, in a whisper. "The White Death . . . from the Desert . . . killed . . . everyone. . . ." His eyes rolled up in their sockets.

"How long ago?" asked Shandor, using the full power of his magnificient voice and hypnotic flake-gold eyes to hold the boy to life a moment longer. "How far behind them are we?"

"Death . . ." the boy gasped again. "The White Death . . . from the Desert . . . going into . . . the mountains . . . kill all Arcobanes . . . kill all . . . Thongors . . . kill all. . . ." His voice choked off.

"How long ago?" repeated Shandor. "How far ahead are they?"

"Death. . . ." the boy repeated. "The White Death. . . from the Desert. . . ." And he was dead.

"They're going after the Thongors!" cried Tal, on his feet in an instant. "They're going to slaughter the Arcobanes and then the Thongors! We've got to stop them!"

"And we will," said Shandor grimly. "This boy did not die in vain. He lived long enough to give us the information we need to beat Anode.

"We know he'll strike next at the Arcobane village. If we can reach there first, we can be ready for him. Do you know the quickest way to reach the Arcobane village from here?"

Tal considered. His blue eyes narrowed as he peered toward the not too far distant mountains. He thought of winding trails through the heavy growths of aspen and fir and mountain pine.

"I know a way," he said, at last. "But I'm not sure the skimmer can make it."

"We'll see," said Shandor. "Anode will have to take his army around and up by a fairly broad roadway. The skimmer is remarkably agile. Rough terrain is no handicap. It can go *almost* anywhere. Let's dispose of the rest of these bodies, then we'll make a run for the Arcobanes. This time it will be Anode who is in for a surprise."

It was also Tal who was in for a surprise. The little skimmer *was* remarkably agile. Shandor headed up the mountain trail in the direction Tal indicated and the little aircar proved as quick and graceful as a mountain goat.

The way was almost constantly up, but the skimmer never varied its slightly less than a meter altitude. Trees crowded so close they almost touched the sleek metal sides, but Shandor's sure, capable hands never hesitated in their manipulation of the controls. They slid between trees Tal would never have believed they could clear.

Occasional crevices or ravines proved no hazard at all. Shandor adjusted the controls, gave the rear exhaust jets an extra boost of power, and the skimmer hopped across very neatly.

"Can't do that if they're much over three meters wide," Shandor commented. "But we can handle anything smaller."

They stopped for the night when Tal assured the bronze man that they were slightly more than halfway to the Arcobane village. That night they stayed in the skimmer.

The next day, the going was rougher. Trees and boulders and rockslides barred their path. Shandor had to use an Infrastatic Alternator repeatedly to alter the vibratory patterns of these obstacles and to clear a way for the skimmer to get through. This slowed their progress somewhat, but not a great deal.

The little skimmer climbed on through the mountains, still never ceasing to amaze Tal with its agile mobility. Its Infrastatic generators hummed in protest at some of the demands Shandor made upon it, but the aircar met them all and by noon slid over into a high mountain meadow.

"It's open country from here," said Tal, indicating the direction across the waving grass. "The village is about five or six kilometers in *that* direction."

Shandor checked his scanners, then slapped the aircar into top speed.

"I read Anode's aura," he said, between clenched teeth. "He's very close and ahead of us!"

The skimmer streaked flat out across the meadow, whipping the grass to each side like the wake left by a rushing speedboat.

"Are we too late?" asked Tal.

"I don't know, yet," said Shandor. His bronzed features revealed no emotion, but his flake-gold eyes were grim.

The little aircar hurtled across the meadows, banking around occasional stands of trees, skimming over the small, rolling hummocks in the grassland, barreling across the flats like a runaway comet.

Tal clutched the bar on the instrument panel before him. The pace at which they were moving made him dizzy. He tried to see ahead to the Arcobane village, but it was not yet in sight.

He thought of Lanawe Palmerin and his fists clenched on the safety bar. He *knew* she had not gone willingly with Anode! He knew it, but in his heart he was afraid. He longed to see her and he dreaded seeing her and he did not know which he felt the strongest.

Then Shandor brought the skimmer to an abrupt, jerking halt. The clear plastic dome just cleared the crest of a small hillock and below them, less than two hundred meters away, was the Arcobane village.

And they were not *yet* too late.

The screaming Kalathors rode round and round the palisade walls. From within the fort an occasional defender would futilely cast his war spear at the fast moving riders. There were few, if any, hit.

To one side, away from the combat zone, Tal could see Anode. The leader of the White Death clan was dressed all in black which accented his alabaster hands and skull-white face. From that distance, Tal could not quite see the feral red eyes.

But he could see, seated upon a horse beside Anode, the slim, dark-haired figure in the Aryorian uniform. There were no chains, ropes, or fetters of any kind that Tal could see. Did that mean that she was there by choice?

Before Tal could speculate further on this, Shandor had shaken him out of his reverie.

"Come on, Tal! Give me a hand!" The bronze man was busily unloading devices from the storage compartment of the aircar. "We can still save them!"

Uncertain of precisely what Shandor expected of him, Tal slid out of the seat and began helping unload the oddly shaped devices that he could only assume were weapons of a sort.

The bronze man threw worried glances over the crest of the hill as his strong fingers hastily assembled various rods and filters and discs and cylinders into intricate combinations. All of it was baffling to Tal.

A tremendous "whoop" of victory caused Tal to look up in time to see Anode point his skeleton-thin arm at the barricaded gate of the Arcobane village. He had what appeared to be a neuron gun in his hand.

Even as Tal watched, the heavy timbers of the gate shimmered and dissolved away to nothingness; their vibratory patterns altered and their molecules scattered to the wind. The way was now open for the Kalathors to enter. Nothing could stop them.

Nothing—except the device Shandor leveled across the hillock and sighted on the beckoning gateway. He pressed a stud, made a minute adjustment to a calibrated dial, and a faint keening sounded from the weapon.

Three Kalathors rode full tilt into the gateway. There was a sudden vibration in the air around them, a coruscating burst of sparks, and the riders with their horses were flung aside as if they had been slapped back by a gigantic, invisible hand.

Across the gateway there was nothing visible; it yawned empty and inviting. Yet the Kalathors hesitated.

Anode made a fierce gesture and two more of the nomad warriors trotted their ponies forward. They did not ride madly forward, but rather came slowly and cautiously.

There was absolute and utter silence around the Arcobane

village as the two riders urged their mounts up to the gateway. There was nothing to stop their entry.

Yet stop they did, the horses rearing just as they came up to the gate. The warriors kicked them and slapped them with their quirts, but the ponies would go no farther.

Angered now, one of the warriors sprang to the ground, labrys in hand, ready to stalk into the village on foot.

Suddenly, arching into the open gateway, came a gleaming Arcobane war lance. It was well aimed. It should have struck the advancing Kalathor squarely in the chest.

Instead, the heavy spear deflected itself in midair, without touching anything visible, and fell to the ground.

The warrior stopped, startled, then reached out a hand tentatively. His hand seemed to be groping about in the air, touching nothing, yet it could not be moved forward.

"You set up some kind of deflector screen," said Tal, eagerly. "The Kalathors can't get through it."

"This is an Infrastatic Condensor," said the bronze man, patting the device he had used. "I created a force field with it that sealed the opening Anode made. I don't believe he can break it with his improvised weapons."

But Anode was trying. He beamed the modified neuron gun at a section of palisade to one side of the gate. The heavy timbers shimmered, then slowly dissolved.

Shandor made an adjustment to a calibrated gauge on his Condensor and seemed satisfied. Then he hastily completed the assembly of two other weapons.

By the time he was done with them, a pair of Kalathors had found that this new entrance was likewise closed to them.

The desert nomads were milling about uneasily. No longer were they galloping in great swirls around the Arcobane village. Now, by contrast, they circled and rode aimlessly in front of Anode.

By now, Anode was aware that something from outside the village was generating the interference. He turned his feral red eyes in all directions, seeking a possible cause, and a possible location for that cause.

Shandor, meanwhile, touched a button on one side of a disc roughly fifteen centimeters in diameter and three centimeters thick. This was one of the devices he had assembled.

There was no sound that Tal could hear, no change of any sort. And then, from away across the field, there was a faintly heard curse from Anode. He flung his modified neuron gun away with a convulsive jerking movement. Even from that far away, Tal could see it glowing cherry-red.

"I used my Infrastatic Controller to cause a backflash and overload," said Shandor, with one of his rare smiles. "It's time Anode knew who he was up against."

Slowly, deliberately, the man of bronze stood upright on the hillock. He had discarded his brown jacket and his cream colored tunic with brown piping was open down the front. His blond hair was riffled slightly by the breeze and his flake-gold eyes had a keen, faraway look to them.

Silhouetted against the scudding clouds and the arching double band of the rings, Shandor made the most heroic figure Tal had ever seen. At that moment, he looked like the god Tal had always thought him to be.

From far across the field of combat, Anode caught his eye. There was an almost palpable electric shock that split the air. For the first time in more millenia than Tal could imagine, the ancient adversaries faced each other again.

Slowly, deliberately, Shandor raised the Infrastatic Controller. Before he could utilize it, however, Anode wheeled his pony, Lanawe turning with him, and galloped madly, almost desperately, away.

Surprised and confused, the Kalathors milled a few moments longer, then they began to straggle out in pursuit of their leader. A few seemed inclined to want to charge the tall figure on the hillock, but most rode away after Anode. In a few moments they had all followed.

Shandor did not move till the last of the Kalathors had disappeared, then he turned to Tal and said: "Let's get these weapons broken down enough to get them back in the skimmer, then we'll go down to the village." He looked up and his strong white teeth gleamed. "This time I think we won one."

Ven Tamor and his warriors stood in the now opened gateway and watched the sleek little aircar come sliding up to them. War lances were leveled and swords were out and ready. The Arcobanes were looking for someone on whom to vent their spleen.

"I am Shandor," said the bronze man, through an outside speaker on the skimmer. "I saved you from the Kalathors. I need your help to defeat them and Anode."

"Step out!" cried Ven Tamor, striking the clear dome futilely with his heavy spear point. "Step out and face us!"

"I am Shandor! I have saved you this day."

And Lalon stepped forward. The Arcobane shaman peered intently at the occupants of the skimmer.

"Shandor is our god," he said, "but you I do not know. The black-haired warrior with you is a Thongor, a former slave, and a worker of great magic when last he visited our village. I cannot see such as he in the company of a god."

Before Shandor could reply, a burly Arcobane warrior brought his sword down shiveringly in the center of the clear plastic dome. The dome rang like a muted bell, but was not even scratched.

And then, with no advance warning, a hurled Kalathor spear transfixed old And Lalon and, with bloodcurdling screams, the desert nomads swept down upon them again.

The Arcobanes fled for the small protection of the walls, but several were cut down before they reached this meager shelter. A rain of spears and war axes rattled off the sides of the skimmer, but Shandor's aircar was unhurt.

Tal instinctively ducked when the first volley hit, but then he realized they were virtually impregnable. His fingers closed on the hilt of his sword, however, and his blue eyes gleamed with a battle lust.

Shandor hit the forward propulsive controls and leaned hard on the right airfoil to send the skimmer wheeling straight into the oncoming Kalathor horde.

The desert horsemen tried to wheel their mounts aside, but most were not quick enough. For a few seconds the aircar was quite literally buried in a heap of kicking horses and yelling, cursing riders. Then, like a duck shedding water, the sleek little skimmer slid out from under the mass and wheeled in a wide circle to get between the attackers and the village.

"Scatter them again, Tal!" Shandor cried, turning the controls over to Tal as he whipped around to retrieve the partially disassembled Infrastatics weaponry. "I'm going to get us some firepower!"

Before Tal realized what he was about to do, the bronze man had dilated one side of the skimmer and rolled free, the Controller dangling round his neck like an oversize medallion and the not quite assembled Condensor clutched in one fist.

Tal had handled the skimmer on more than one occasion, but his proficiency was nowhere near Shandor's. As it was, he zipped far to one side before he got the slender vehicle turned.

The Kalathors, those whose mounts were uninjured, now formed a whooping, squalling line and headed straight for the lone figure who stood between them and the Arcobanes.

Tal slammed the skimmer into full power and came barreling across virtually under the horses' hooves. The terrible pile-up was avoided this time, simply because the Kalathors were expecting it, but the charge was broken and Tal forced them to scatter and ride apart as he slashed in and out of their ranks like a sheep dog cutting sheep.

Again the nomad warriors cut and slashed and thrust at the darting aircar, but whatever material Shandor had used in its construction was quite impervious to their weapons.

Tal's plunge into the melee had provided Shandor with all the time he needed, however.

The Infrastatic Condensor flung its impenetrable force screen between him and the Kalathors and between the Arcobanes and the Kalathors. A desert warrior's spear glanced harmlessly off thin air less than a meter in front of him. Whipping up the Infrastatic Controller, Shandor made minor adjustments and the molecular vibration of certain areas of ground were altered, leaving the horsemen to plunge into pits that had not been there seconds before.

The Kalathors hauled back on their reins and wheeled their mounts for the distant hillside where the grim as death figure of Anode could be barely discerned with the slim figure of Lanawe Palmerin at his side.

Tal slid the little skimmer to a stop a few meters from Shandor and dilated the side. His legs felt a little shaky from nervous reaction as he emerged.

The Kalathors had taken with them all of their warriors

who had been injured, but left behind were two horses which had been lamed. Not wishing to see them suffer and, quite frankly, eager to vent some of his killing anger, Tal put them both to death with his sword. It was a quick and merciful death.

He turned to find that Shandor had deactivated their force screen. The bronze man joined him by the skimmer and they waited for the Arcobanes to reappear. They did not have long to wait.

Ven Tamor was the first to venture out. The grizzled old lance lord had taken a spear through the fleshy part of his upper thigh and he walked with a pronounced limp, but he walked alone and unaided.

"I am Shandor," said the bronze man. "And I have come to aid you against the White Death from the Desert."

Before he could say more a slim, brown-haired, gray-eyed girl took a tentative step forward.

"Tal?" she said, almost hesitantly. "Tal? It . . . is you?"

"Alytha?" Tal forgot everything else in the wonder of that moment. The Arcobanes, Ven Tamor, Shandor, the littered arena of battle, all faded away and his field of vision narrowed to the figure of the girl who was rushing toward him, her arms flung out and open. "Alytha!"

Then he was running, too, and they came together and clung together and held each other with a fierceness and a passion that all of time could not corrode. And the happiness of each of them, in that moment, was truly complete.

TWENTY-FIVE

To Tal, it was a memory in reverse. The skimmer left the Arcobane village behind in the cool stillness of early morning and slid almost soundlessly in the direction of the Thongor encampment.

Tal and Alytha sat close together inside the little aircar, the Infrastatic weapons Shandor had provided carefully stowed in back of them.

The wonder of their meeting was still fresh and vivid in Tal's mind. When Alytha had crossed the littered field of death to fling herself in Tal's arms, it had been almost too much for him, almost too wonderful for him to believe. He had kissed her and held her and kissed her again. And touched her gently, almost reverently, as if to assure himself that she was real and that she was there.

The Arcobanes had welcomed them into their somewhat battered village. Shandor had used the Infrastatic Condensor to seal the breached palisade and the Arcobanes had been in awe of his powers. That did much toward assuring them of his quasi godhood.

But Tal and Alytha were unconcerned about the Arcobanes' view of Shandor. They had eyes only for each other and to them, at that time, nothing else and no one else mattered.

Ven Tamor put a private hut at their disposal and they retired there almost at once to tell each other their various adventures since that long ago day when Tal was captured returning from the hunt.

Again and again, as they talked, they would reach out to touch each other, as if seeking physical reassurance that the other was really there.

Tal told her of his imprisonment by the Arcobanes, of Rendezvous, of his sale to the Farades, of Fen Melton, of the Ice Regions, of the attack by the Ice Warriors, of the coming of the Aryorians, of Lanawe Palmerin and her father, of the search they made for Alytha, of the quest for the Eternity Stone, of the finding of Shalimar, of Anode, of Alun Akobar's treachery, of Shandor, and of his subsequent part in routing the Kalathor hordes. He carefully refrained from mentioning the two times he had made love to Lanawe, but there was a look in Alytha's eye that made him believe she suspected more than he admitted.

Between kisses and hugs, Alytha told him *her* story, and Tal's blue eyes smoldered darkly when she spoke of her rape by the Arcobane warriors, but they shone with a grim satisfaction when she told how she had dealt with Vaj Kulan and Ren Sagvor and how she had become a lance warrior of Arcobane.

The next morning both emerged from the hut looking haggard and pale from lack of sleep, but with happy smiles on their faces and a glow about them that could not be mistaken.

Over the victory breakfast, and two cups of the *glow* that Tal enjoyed so much, Shandor laid out his plans for them.

"We've got to have the help of the Thongors," he said. "I'm sure Anode will make another strike here at the Arcobane village, but when he realizes it is hopeless, he is most likely to leave a token force here to hold us penned down, while the main body moves on to attack the Thongors. That's why I want the two of you to take the skimmer and get to Thongor as quickly as you possibly can. We've got to get a united front against Anode!"

And so, as soon as they had eaten, Tal and Alytha had packed the skimmer with the Infrastatic weaponry Shandor selected, and headed out for Thongor.

Alytha had been awed by Tal's easy familiarity with the aircar's controls. Tal was nowhere near as skillful as Shandor, but he had been an apt pupil and the little skimmer moved smoothly on its way.

Alytha was, in fact, somewhat awed by many things about Tal now. It had only been a few months since they had been separated, but Tal had a lean, hard maturity about him that he had not had before. He had gone into the crucible as a boy, but the tempering had made him a man.

And a man who consorted on easy terms with a god!

Alytha was reverent in the presence of Shandor, as were the Arcobanes, but Tal had been with him so long that his feelings had become quite relaxed. He no longer thought of the bronze man as a god, but he did feel that Shandor was more than a mere mortal.

On foot, it would have taken at least four days to hike to Thongor, but the skimmer covered the distance in slightly less than one day.

The shadows of the winter twilight were long and dark when Tal swept the skimmer down across the mountain meadow, past the remembered grove of ironwood trees, and across the tilled fields toward the palisade of his and Alytha's childhood home.

The sentries spotted them at once and the gate swung closed before they had covered half the open distance. When Tal eased the slim silver vehicle to a stop, the walls were bristling with war spears.

"Sar Lon!" Tal's voice was amplified through the outside speaker. "I am Tal Mikar, Outcast of your tribe, and with me I bring Alytha, daughter to Man Tavis. We must parlay. Come forth and talk!"

"Is this more of your Ancients' wizardry, Outcast?" answered the lance lord of Thongor. "Do you bring back the spirit of our daughter whom you stole from us originally?"

"I am no spirit, Sar Lon," Alytha said. "I am flesh and blood and I am reunited with my beloved. We bring you greetings from—Shandor himself!"

"What blasphemy is this?" cried Mor Haskin. "How dare you invoke the Name of Shandor in such a fashion." And he made the sign of the double helix.

"Remember the last time I was here?" Tal reminded them. "When I came in the skybird of the Ancients? Remember we sought Shalimar and the Accursed of Shandor, the Eternity

Stone?

"We found it! And, in the finding, learned the secret of why it is called Accursed. The Ancients who were with me have loosed an evil upon the land, an evil greater and more terrible than you can imagine, an evil, that in the end, brought them their destruction.

"The spirit of pure evil had been let loose upon our world and its loosing has caused the great god Shandor himself to awaken from the sleep of the ages to combat it. Anode, the evil one, cannot be defeated by anything mere mortals can do. Only Shandor can destroy him, and even he cannot do it alone. That is why I am here. I have come from Shandor himself to seek your aid in the war we must wage against the evil one."

By the time Tal had finished this diatribe, the gates to Thongor had been opened, cautiously, and Sar Lon, Mor Haskin, Man Tavis, and a handful of the more venturesome warriors had emerged to form a menacing ring around the skimmer.

"You have not come from Shandor!" the shaman disputed. "You are both Outcast and as such would be shunned from the presence of Shandor the Mighty."

Tal touched a button on the Controller and threw a Condensor shield around the periphery of the aircar. The Thongors were not aware of this, but under its protection, he opened the bubble dome so that he and Alytha could emerge to stand, hand in hand, facing their former tribesmen.

"Alytha," Man Tavis reached out to touch his daughter, to reassure himself that she was truly alive, but his hand met the cold, hard, unyielding, totally invisible force screen that Tal had created. He recoiled.

"What is it?" Sar Lon demanded, but Mor Haskin had already deduced the problem and its probable source.

"More wizardry of the Ancients?" he demanded, his fingers exploring the force screen.

"Wizardry of Shandor," Tal said. "As is this. Behold—" He gestured toward a sharp pinnacle of rock by the tilled fields. The rock was too large to be moved, so the fields had been planted around it, leaving it in the midst of the greenery.

Automatically, the Thongors looked where Tal pointed.

He touched another button on the Controller and the rock wavered, shimmered, then dissolved away into nothingness. There was sudden silence among the Thongors.

"The power to do this was given me by Shandor himself," Tal said quietly. "Had I so desired, I could have destroyed the walls of your village. With my own eyes I saw the walls of Arcobane erased by the evil one using a similar device."

"I, too, saw this," Alytha affirmed. "I was in Arcobane, an adopted lance warrior after I fled from the bloody embrace of Jad Thor. I was there when the walls shimmered and blew away like smoke. Kalathors from the Great Desert rode down upon us. We thought we were lost, that there was no hope, but Shandor—and Tal—saved us.

"They formed a shield, such as this"— her hand brushed the Infrastatic force field— "across the breached wall, then they came down in this strange craft and, by themselves, routed the Kalathors. And the Kalathors, as you know, are the fiercest warriors in the world!"

"This is all strange. . . ." murmured Mor Haskin. "These things have never happened before. What times are these in which we live?"

"These are new times, Mor Haskin," said Tal. "These are times such as Thongor has never seen before. The Ancients have come back to Earth. The Kalathors have left the Great Desert to attack Arcobane—and to plan their attack on Thongor!"

"On Thongor?" Sar Lon snapped to attention, his interest riveted. "What is this of an attack on Thongor?"

"The Kalathors plan such an attack," Tal answered, his blue eyes flashing. "Shandor and I have trailed them across the Great Desert. Village after village they have laid waste and ever does Anode's army grow. The White Death from the Desert, he calls himself, and he is that—and more! In the shattered remains of one sacked village, Shandor and I found a boy, more dead than alive, who told us what he had heard of Anode's battle plan.

"He told us that Anode planned to move against Arcobane next and then go on to Thongor. Shandor and I reached Arcobane barely in time to divert the attack and save the village. It was then that Alytha and I were reunited. But

277

Shandor has sent me to Thongor to warn you that we must band together if we would defeat this White Death from the Desert."

"Who is this 'Anode'?" asked Sar Lon. "How does he get the Kalathors to follow him? The desert nomads are fiercely independent."

"Shandor is all that is good, and I can attest that he is; but Anode is the essence of all that is evil. *He* is the 'Accursed of Shandor' whose tomb was the Eternity Stone and who was set free by the Ancients."

"The Ancients had much wizardry," said Mor Haskin, a speculative look in his old eyes. "But you say they could not defeat Anode?"

"Anode swept them down like sheaves of grain before a reaper's scythe. And the Kalathors who would not follow died the same way."

"If the wizardry of the Ancients could not withstand him, what chance have the swords and lances of the Thongors?" The shaman was obviously giving credence to Tal's story.

"The Thongors have *no* chance!" said Tal. "Unless . . . you have the power of Shandor on your side. I am here today, with Alytha, to ask you to join Shandor in his fight against Anode; to join Alytha and me, and the Arcobanes, in one great effort to drive this evil one back to the place from which the Ancients freed him.

"*Only* with Shandor's help can you stand against Anode. With my own eyes I saw Shandor defeat him at the Arcobane village. Every wizardry he conjured up, Shandor countered; and in the end, Anode fled the field of battle!

"With Shandor's help, you can stand against Anode and his horde from the Desert; alone, you will go down like autumn leaves before the first chill wind of winter. The choice is yours, Sar Lon. Make it wisely."

Three days later the troop of Thongor warriors emerged onto the plain outside the palisade of Arcobane.

Tal and Alytha rode in the skimmer, but Tal kept the little aircar to a pace the warriors could manage. It was most important that the troop stay together.

From as far away as they could see the Arcobane village, the war party could see the giant figure of Shandor and beside him, the smaller, less heroically proportioned figure of Ven Tamor.

The Arcobanes had rebuilt their palisade and made further improvements in their defenses. After all, the power cells in Shandor's Infrastatic weaponry were not inexhaustible. Tal could see no evidence of a second attack and wondered what Anode had been doing in the interim.

He also wondered about Lanawe Palmerin, but with Alytha beside him he tried not to think too much about her. The Thongors practiced a limited polygamy, but Tal knew that neither Alytha nor Lanawe would consider such an idea. Whatever had been with him and Lanawe was over and done with.

Yet Tal knew that Lanawe Palmerin would never be out of his life. She was part and parcel of him, as familiar as his own reflection (*as familiar as Shara Vralon to Lan Regas or Keena to Thon*), and there was no way he could expunge her from the recesses of his mind.

The nearer the lance warriors of the Thongors came to the palisade of Arcobane, the greater the tension became. These were hereditary enemies, this meeting would be the first peaceful meeting of these age-old foes in recorded history.

Tal heard the mutterings of the Thongors and saw the brawny fingers moving restlessly on the war lances. He knew something must be done to prevent an outbreak of hostility. He triggered the outside speakers on the skimmer:

"These are friends," he reminded them. "The bronze man is Shandor. It is he whom we have worshipped all these years. Both the Thongors and the Arcobanes give their pledge to Shandor. Remember now that we come together so he may lead us into battle against the greatest evil our world has ever known."

The bronze man heard this and came forward to greet them. His golden hair was riffled by a gentle breeze, his cream colored tunic with brown piping was open to reveal his muscular bronze chest, his corded arm muscles looked like wrapped steel cables with a thin sheen of bronze paint on them, and his flake-gold eyes sparkled and whirled as if stirred by tiny, internal whirlwinds.

"Greetings, Sar Lon of Thongor," he said, in his magnificently controlled voice. "I am Shandor and I bid you welcome. Ven Tamor of Arcobane, who was your enemy, is, on this eve of battle, your ally with me against a common foe—against man's oldest foe—against Evil itself! Thank you for giving us your added strength."

He raised his sword hand palm out in the ancient sign for peace, a sign ancient when even Atlantis was young.

Sar Lon hesitated only a second, then he made the same sign. For the moment, peace reigned.

With a sigh of relief, Tal dilated the hatch of the skimmer and he and Alytha piled out. Shandor greeted them warmly, his mighty bronze hand firm and hard as it clasped Tal's own.

"Welcome back, little brother," he said, and, though there was pleasure on his face, Tal sensed there was something wrong.

"Have you any word of Anode?" he asked, instinctively throwing one strong arm around Alytha as he spoke the name.

"We have," said Shandor, with a bitter nod. Ven Tamor and some of his warriors had joined them now and the Arcobanes and the Thongors eyed each other suspiciously.

"While you were gone, I sent out scouting parties," the bronze man continued. " They had no trouble picking up the trail of Anode and his Kalathor warriors. The trail heads due north, toward the polar jungle."

Tal failed to understand the significance of that, but before he could ask, Alytha spoke up: "Why is that so bad? He seems to have abandoned his plan of attacking Arcobane and then Thongor."

"Only temporarily," Shandor assured her. "You see, the polar jungle is where Anode's ancient fortress of Rynn is located. In it, he has Infrastatic weapons as powerful as anything I have in Shalimar." The bronze man looked toward the distant northland and his flake-gold eyes grew hard and cold. "At all costs, Anode must be kept from reaching Rynn! Once there, I'm not sure any power in the universe can stop him!"

TWENTY-SIX

The two armies came together at the very edge of the polar jungle.

Shandor had the Arcobanes ready to march by the time Tal and Alytha arrived with Sar Lon and his Thongors. The Thongors were allowed one night's rest, then at dawn they were on their way.

The pace was hard and steady. The kilometers reeled away beneath their marching feet and all the while the trail of Anode's Kalathor horde stretched away and away to the north.

Shandor and Tal, one or the other, used the skimmer to keep tabs on their fast moving enemy. The little aircar would eat up the distance, moving faster in a day than the following troops could in three, and report back on Anode's progress. Twice they were attacked by the tag end of the Kalathors, but there was never any real danger. However, it was obvious that Anode was now aware of being pursued.

One night at camp, on the sixth day of pursuit, Shandor, Tal, and Alytha sat by the council fire with Ven Tamor, Sar Lon, Man Tavis, and others.

"We should overtake Anode tomorrow," the bronze man said, as he sipped his cup of *glow*. "They have traveled fast, but we have traveled faster."

"We should rest for a day," suggested Sar Lon. "Our warriors are tired from many marchings. They have grown lean and weary from the length of the chase and the lack of sufficient food. We need at least a day to regain our fighting strength before we attack."

"We do not have a day," Shandor explained. "This night, Anode camps on the very border of the polar rain forest. Another day and he will be deep within it; so deep we can never rout him out. A day beyond that and he will be in Rynn, a place we must *not* allow him to reach!"

"What is so terrible about Rynn?" asked Man Tavis. "Will this Anode become invincible if he reaches there?"

"Something very like that," Shandor agreed. "The power of Infrastatic radiation has made a change in Anode's basic metabolism, as it has in mine, and left him something other than human. He now requires fear, hatred, and suffering to live upon. These emotions are food and drink to him. Without them, he will weaken and eventually die. With them, his strength, vitality, and cunning increase geometrically.

"But Rynn itself is to be feared. Anode had Infrastatic weaponry hidden there that is the equal of anything I have in Shalimar. Once he can reach it, his power will be virtually limitless. You know what damage he has already done with the cannibalized, jerry-built Infrastatic devices he made from parts of the offworlders' equipment. Think how much more terrible he would be with well-built, fully operational weapons. No, Anode must not reach Rynn. If he does, I am not sure he can be stopped."

Sar Lon considered this a moment. His rough-hewn features creased into a frown. "So we fight tomorrow," he said. "Tired as my warriors are, we press the attack. Then what—if we fail? What if we are unable to stop this Anode's army? What if they win?"

"Then," said Shandor softly, "pray that you die in battle, for any who fall into Anode's hands will curse their survival."

The bronze man's words hung heavy in the sultry evening air as the council broke up. Tal took a cup of *glow* and went to check the perimeter guards. Like the others, he was too nervous to sleep.

The last guard post he checked was the one farthest north. He stood talking with the warrior, a burly, bearded Thongor, for a few minutes, then he walked a distance beyond the guard point and stood alone in the shadows staring into the northland.

The tropical northern night was alive with brilliant stars and across the rolling veldt Tal could hear the cry of a hunting beast as it made a kill. The night was clear and still and beautiful, yet heavy with anticipation of the coming battle. Behind Tal, the campfires of Shandor's army dotted the veldt and there was the murmur of voices and an occasional sound of metal on metal as a sword or lance point was sharpened; but to Tal, all this was behind him and away from him, and he stood, for all practical purposes, alone there in the darkness.

And, alone there in the darkness, Tal let his mind return to Lanawe Palmerin. Where was she tonight? Was she alive? Was she well? Was she, perhaps, looking up at these same stars? Tal wondered.

He had seen her with Anode outside the Arcobane village and she had seemed unharmed. She had ridden away with Anode freely enough and there had been no chains upon her. Had she gone over to Anode's side? Could she willingly ally herself with the creature that killed her father and destroyed all her people?

Tal remembered Lanawe as he had known her in this lifetime, and he could not believe it of her. Even had she been as evil as Shandor insisted she was once, Tal knew that in this lifetime she had changed, had become a different person. Perhaps she was working off her karma.

How did he feel about Lanawe? Did he love her? Tal was at heart a barbarian and was not much given to romantic musings. He knew he loved Alytha beyond words, but did he love Lanawe, too? Could he love two girls at once?

If, as Shandor had told him, he and Lanawe were working off the karma incurred by Thon and Keena and later by Lan Regas and Shara Vralon, if this were true—where did Alytha fit into the scheme of reincarnation?

Was Alytha the reincarnation of someone Tal had known before, in some previous lifetime? Or was she someone new to him in this lifetime only? Was she old karma being worked out or a new beginning for the next step in his spiritual growth?

Tal did not know the answers to these questions and the comtemplating of them left him dizzy and confused. He was a simple man, a barbarian warrior, and such matters were not for him to worry over. He would do what he thought was right for him. More than that, no man could do.

With an angry shake of his head, Tal turned back toward the camp and found Alytha standing close behind him.

"You startled me," he said, almost accusingly. He realized she was downwind of him and thus he had not smelled her woman scent as she approached. "You move quietly in the night."

"You think deep thoughts, my love," she replied simply. "I sensed your heart was troubled and I came to you." She put her arms gently around Tal's broad chest. "The night is short, and with the dawnlight we may die. Let me love away your fears." She kissed him lightly, gently, on the lips.

"They are not fears," said Tal, drawing her close against him. "At least, not fears like fears of death. It is just—everything is *different*. What I mean—things change. I don't understand anymore." He kissed her forehead and cradled her in his arms.

"Shandor tells me he is not a god; then he tells me things only a god could know. Things that happened long and long ago in a place called Atlantis. He tells me that Lanawe Palmerin and I have lived before, have known each other before. There is between us what he calls karma—a sort of blood debt—and in this lifetime we must settle it.

"I do not understand these things, Alytha. I do not believe them, and yet in a way I do. I do not believe Shandor is a god; yet I knew he is more than a man. All this"—he gestured—"confuses me. I don't understand things anymore. I feel like everything is getting away from me."

"It is a new time," Alytha agreed, her body pressed hard against Tal's. "New things are happening. But you, my love, are part and parcel of it all. You are the rope that binds all our fates into one bundle. I sense in you a destiny greater than you know."

Tal kissed her again, more thoroughly this time.

"I love you, Alytha," he said. "I love you beyond my words to say."

With nothing else said, as if of one mind, they knelt there in the darkness of the grassy veldt and Tal made a bed of his tunic and jerkin and Alytha's robe. And there, beneath the arching silver rings that looped the midnight sky, they loved each other with a gentleness and a sweetness that was beyond their previous imaginings. Each touched within the other the deepest wellsprings of human need their hearts contained. It was a night that would remain precious to them both for so long as they lived—for it was a night that would never come again.

The attack was at dawn.

Shandor scouted the enemy camp from the skimmer and directed troops to the attack. Sar Lon and the Thongors swung out to the right, Ven Tamor and the Arcobanes circled left, while Tal, Alytha, Shandor, and a mixed Thongor-Arcobane division charged straight in over the veldt.

The beginnings of the polar rain forest that housed Anode's fortress of Rynn were a gray-green smear on the horizon as the attackers moved into position.

Shandor began by throwing an Infrastatic shield around the Kalathors' horses. The battle would go better for the attackers if the desert warriors remained afoot.

Evidently Anode had rigged warning devices that were triggered by Infrastatic weaponry. Shandor had barely set the shield when a great shout went up from the just rising Kalathor camp and the warriors came boiling out to meet the attackers.

The two armies closed rapidly. Tal was at home in this environment; this was what he was born to do!

His long sword naked in his right hand, a keen bladed dagger in his left, the blue-eyed warrior sprang at his foes. At his side, screaming a bloody battle cry, came Alytha, her own sword out and ready.

Shandor, from somewhere to Tal's left, lanced a blast of Infrastatic power into the surging Kalathors—only to see its effects annulled by a counterblast from the spectral figure of Anode in the center of the camp. Shandor made an adjustment to his weapon; then Tal lost sight of him.

A stocky Kalathor sprang at Tal and Tal ran him through. Then two more faced him and Tal had to fight for his life. Alytha slashed one's sword arm off at the elbow, then disemboweled him while Tal disposed of the other.

The battle was fierce and fast. Closing, engaging, killing, whirling to the next enemy. It was constant movement: leap, thrust, hack, turn, stab, lunge, thrust, parry, riposte. There was the clang of steel on steel, the meat cleaver sound of muscle-driven blades "chunking" through flesh and bone. The screams of the wounded and dying, and the hoarse, raw-throated yells of the attacking warriors, were on all sides.

Tal took a sword through the large muscle under his arm, not deep, but painful, and had an equally painful slash across his thigh. He had a half dozen other cuts and scratches, but none was serious. His strong sword arm and his catlike agility saved him time and again.

As the battle swirled about like a noisy, multicolored eddy, Tal caught occasional glimpses of Shandor and Anode. The bronze man did not physically take part in the battle. He circled the periphery of the fighting and used his Infrastatic weapons to aid the attackers. Anode circled—always opposite Shandor—and did likewise. The two old enemies never came together.

Tal saw Alytha's sword wrenched from her hand as a corpse fell on its blade. Temporarily defenseless, she faced a burly nomad warrior with a blood-spattered labrys. He raised the twin-bladed battle axe and Tal hacked his arm off smoothly at the shoulder.

The man reeled away, blood pumping from his stump, and Tal tossed his own sword to Alytha, retrieving the labrys in one swoop and bringing it up in a blinding slash that opened a Kalathor from crotch to throat.

Although they were outnumbered, the Kalathors were holding their ground; they were the fiercest warriors on Earth. The Thongors and the Arcobanes were near exhaustion. The battle was so evenly matched, Tal realized, that it would be Shandor and Anode who finally determined the outcome.

Screaming like a berserker, Tal laid about him with the double-headed battle axe. The terrible weapon opened a temporary gap around him and Alytha. With the girl covering his back, Tal waded back into the battle, his tireless arm hewing down the enemy with the gore-covered axe.

The Kalathors gave ground before Tal and his madly whirling axe. No one could stand before his onslaught and few tried. He was determined to end this thing today. He was determined that Anode and his Kalathor horde would be destroyed. He split skulls and hacked off arms and crushed chests and ripped open bellies and never slowed his advance, literally wading in streams of blood. It was a battle for singers to make songs about!

Suddenly, Tal realized that again there was a cleared area around him. He stopped, leaned for a moment on his axe handle, and sucked in great gulps of air. He realized he was parched with thirst and near to collapse. He wheeled around to get some perspective on the battle.

There, not ten meters away, stood the tall, deadly pale figure of Anode. His bone-white face had a sardonic smile as he looked at Tal and Alytha. He was clad in black from throat to wrist to foot. His white hands held a strange black box set with buttons and dials and switches. Behind Anode, looking terrified and disheveled and haunted, was Lanawe Palmerin.

For one frozen instant the four figures faced each other, then, with a piercing scream, Alytha launched herself at Anode, her sword point thrusting for his heart.

He touched a control on the black box.

Alytha flung the sword away, flung her arms and legs wide and spreadeagled herself in midair—and *hung there!*

Her body arched backward till Tal could see her face, upside down, contorted in pain and fear. She gave one throat-tearing scream of unendurable agony, then her body was flung a dozen meters away, cartwheeling in the air, and fell—her arms and legs flopping like a broken toy—almost at Tal's feet.

"Kill me, too, you devil!" roared Tal, and he leaped at Anode, the labrys up and ready to strike.

Suddenly, the world went into extreme slow motion. Tal knew he was running, yet it seemed that he lifted one foot very slowly, leaned his body slightly forward, stretched out the leg very slowly, placed his foot carefully on the ground, then very slowly lifted the other foot. He saw blood drops, flung from the axe blade, turn and twist slowly, slowly, slowly as they drifted lightly away to one side.

"You will not die this day," said Anode, and his hollow voice sounded ordinary to Tal's ears, though he suddenly realized all sounds of the battle had faded away. "Death is not for you. For you—is the *undeath!*"

Tal saw Anode's ghostly face grinning wickedly, there was an intense point of pure white light that swelled to fill his entire universe, and then there was nothing.

Tal was aware of gentle hands touching his face. He moaned and tried to move, but he was restrained. A warm liquid touched his lips and he tasted *glow*. Sounds of movement and a murmur of voices were in the darkness around him.

"Where. . . ." he began tentatively. "Where am I? What happened?"

"You are safe." It was the voice of Shandor. "The battle is over—for today."

Tal tried to move, but felt restraining hands. Was he injured then in some way? At that thought, he remembered Alytha and how Anode had blasted her with his strange weapon. His body convulsed with the effort to rise.

"Alytha! Where is Alytha? Is she all right?"

There was a strong yet gentle hand resting lightly on his brow, but Shandor made no answer. The background voices died away to silence. That silence gave Tal his answer.

"Alytha is . . . dead." He did not make it a question.

"Yes, my son." It was the voice of Man Tavis. "Alytha is dead. Truly dead. We have brought back her body and . . . buried it." The voice broke.

"I want to see it!" said Tal. "I want to see her body!" Then he realized something else. "Why is it so dark? Where are we? Why can't I see anything?"

"Take it easy, Tal." That was Shandor's voice. "You're safe now."

"Why can't I see?" Violently he wrenched one hand loose and brought it to his face. There was nothing over his eyes. Groping blindly in the darkness, his hand felt a wavering warmth, a campfire. A campfire close to him. Then he understood.

"You're blind, Tal," said Shandor gently. "There's nothing I can do. You are permanently blind."

TWENTY-SEVEN

Tal took the news surprisingly well. He did not eat for the first day, taking only an occasional cup of *glow*, but his spirit did not break as Shandor had feared.

The bronze man had his most important Infrastatic devices with him, yet they could not work miracles. Nothing could restore an optic nerve that had been removed Infrastatically more completely than could have been done by laser surgery. Shandor knew, before Tal awakened, that his friend would never see again.

But there *was* hope. The bronze man broke the idea to Tal the evening of the first day.

"I've been thinking of something, Tal," he said, carefully, watching the young man's face to gauge the effect of his words. "I have an idea you may be interested in hearing."

"There are only three things I'm interested in hearing," growled Tal, clenching his jaw as he spoke. "That my sight can be saved, that Alytha is alive, and that Anode is dead." His voice cracked with bitterness at the end.

"It has to do with your sight," Shandor said. "I can't exactly restore it, but I do have an idea."

"What?" Tal was suddenly interested. He turned his blind face toward Shandor and the hope was painful for the bronze man to see.

"It's . . . an idea. It might not work." He hesitated. "But then it might." He moved closer to Tal. He signaled the others to move away so he could speak privately with Tal. He filled them each a cup of *glow*.

"Tal, what does the word *telepathy* mean to you?"

"Well—" A quizzical shrug. "I'm not sure. Something about knowing what other people are thinking. A shaman can do it—sometimes."

"That's a good enough answer. Telepathy is the ability to read another person's mind. Everyone had this ability to some small extent. I have a machine that *may* be able to stimulate this latent ability you have, may be able to help you develop it yourself. It you can, if you are able to reach into another person's mind—mine, for example—you may be able to pick up the images received on his optic nerve and be able to 'see' through his eyes. I think it's worth a try."

Tal considered this.

"I agree," he said. "Anything is worth a try. And if this works, I'll have a chance to kill Anode."

Tal was afraid to let himself hope too strongly. He had been fighting despair all day alone there in the dark, and he did not know if he could survive having hope offered and then shattered. Instead, he let his hate for Anode carry him through. He would not desire this to work so he could see; he would desire it to work so he could kill Anode.

"I'm ready," he said grimly. "What do I have to do?"

"Rest easy for a moment." Shandor's voice was calm and gentle, reassurance in the midst of the fear and uncertainty. "I'll set up the Ultronic Projector." Tal felt the coolness of metal lightly touching his temples. A hand slipped something round and cold under his beaded headband on either side of his head. "We're ready now," said Shandor.

There was a moment when Tal felt nothing, then he became aware of a dizzy swimming sensation in his head. He felt *things* that he did not recognize. Strange emotions pulled at him: tension, fear, anger, curiosity, grief. For the first time he was aware that emotions had color: grief was pale blue, curiosity lemon yellow, anger dull red, fear lime green, tension steel gray.

He tried to sort out the emotions, but they were too much for him. Despair and depression, rage and determination, pain and heartbreak. Tal could not keep them all under control.

"It is working."

"What was that?" His voice sounded unnaturally loud.

"Don't speak. It isn't necessary."

"What—? Who?"

"Don't speak, Tal. I can hear your thoughts. Can you hear mine?"

"Shandor?"

"Yes. The Ultronic Projector is working. We've established a telepathic link."

"It's . . . hard . . . to hold onto your . . . thoughts. . . ."

There was an abrupt cessation of the emotional input Tal had been fighting.

"That's enough for the moment," said Shandor. "We've established that it can be done. How do you feel, Tal?"

"Tired. . . ." He seemed unutterably weary. "The hard part was all the *feelings*, all the emotions. I could *feel* what everybody else in camp was feeling. It was almost too much."

"Emotions are the easiest things to read. Children especially can sense them. You were overwhelmed by them, but you hung on enough to pick up my thoughts. It's a start. Tomorrow we'll do better."

The dreams came to Tal for the first time that night.

In the dream he was making his way along a narrow eyebrow trail against a sheer cliff face. He hugged the stone close against his chest and inched his way forward by sliding his feet along the incredibly narrow ledge.

Suddenly, behind him, he heard a sound. He knew that he could not turn his head to look behind him without dislodging himself from his precarious perch. Then he heard Alytha's voice:

"Tal! Tal, save me! Save me, Tal! Help me!"

He sat bolt upright in his sleeping furs, his hands groping blindly before him, Shandor's strong arm around his shoulders.

"It was a dream, Tal," the bronze man said. "It was only a dream."

Tal tried to sleep again, but when he did, it was only to return to hear Alytha's voice calling for help, but to find that he could not reach her. Her voice kept tearing at his mind. He heard it, over and over again: "Save me, Tal! Help me!"

He was haggard and wan the next day when Shandor

resumed the experiment.

"This time try to bypass the emotional input," the bronze man said, as he helped Tal to a quiet place at the edge of camp. "Concentrate on my mind. I'll think thoughts directly *to* you and you do your best to block out all but my 'voice.'"

"What is the camp doing?" Tal asked. "I mean . . . it's been three days since the battle. Are we making any move to pursue Anode?"

"It has been more than three days," Shandor told him. "Nearer to a week. And, yes, we're doing what we can. We have Anode and the Kalathors surrounded. We didn't win the battle, but we stopped their advance into the polar rain forest. It's a standoff right now. We can't close in on them and they can't get away. While we're poking at each other trying to find a weak spot, I'm trying to help you regain a measure of sight."

"But why? I mean . . . why me? Why are you doing this for me?"

"First, because I care about you, Tal. You're a good friend, and you've been my friend in lifetimes before. Second, I'd try to help anyone if I could—the more we can relieve our fellow human's pain, the less karma we have to carry. And third, because I sense something in you, Tal, that is of prime importance to stopping Anode. I don't know what it is nor how I know it, but I sense that somehow you are the fulcrum by which this whole time and place can be changed. You are the focal point of powers I do not pretend to understand, let alone control. So, for whatever purpose you must serve, I will do what I can to aid you."

The test went easier this day. Tal still felt the inrushing groundswell of emotions battering at him and the ragged tag ends of random thoughts, but he picked up Shandor's specific thought images very quickly. In a very short time the degree of telepathic communication was superb, but he could never tap into the optical images Shandor set up for him.

They took a rest and Tal sipped a cup of *glow* while Shandor left to confer with Sar Lon and Ven Tamor. Suddenly, amid the general level of camp noises, Tal became aware of someone moving close by where he sat. He listened to the footsteps and knew they were too heavy to be other than a man's. He heard the coarse garments brush together and knew it was not Shandor. He smelled the woodsmoke scent and the unwashed body odor underlying the pine scent of the high country soaked into the clothing and deduced his visitor was a Thongor. He heard a familiar hoarse breathing and was almost certain of the identity.

"Hello, Man Tavis," he said. "It is kind of you to visit."

"I came to see how you were feeling," said Alytha's father.

"I am well," said Tal, then he hesitated. he felt a rush of emotions from Man Tavis: nervousness, guilt, grief, accusation. It caught him by surprise. Had Shandor left his device on? "Is . . . is Shandor anywhere around?" he asked and, at Man Tavis' negative answer, he added: "Is one of his machines close at hand? Perhaps activated?"

"No. He took his device with him when he left. There is no one here but you and me." Tal caught a sudden, wavering, blurred image: *dark hair; strong, fine-boned face; beaded headband; the once blue eyes now gray and glazed over!* "And I thought . . . Tal, are you all right?"

Tal tried to answer, but he could not speak. The image he saw opened and closed its mouth several times, but said nothing. He saw his mouth widen into a grin and all the face but the dead eyes lighted up like a candleflame.

"What is it, Tal?" There was genuine fear in Man Tavis' voice. "Tal, is something wrong?"

"No," the sharply handsome features that Tal was watching said, "but call Shandor, please."

He looked out over the camp as Man Tavis turned his head. He saw, for the first time, how Shandor's siege camp was set up.

"Don't go!" he called, as he watched the rows of tents approaching as Man Tavis walked away from him. "Stay with me—but call for Shandor."

He looked around the landscape and Man Tavis' eyes focused on him again. He stood up and saw himself walking toward the startled warrior. He raised his arm and saw it extending itself. The sensation was like looking at a reflection of himself in a perfectly mirrored sheet of water.

He heard Man Tavis shout, but only dimly. Mostly he was reveling in the sheer delight of "seeing" again, even if only through another person's eyes.

The bronze man came on the run—and half the camp with him, it seemed—and to Tal the best thing was that he could "see" him as he approached.

"It works!" he yelled to Shandor. "I can see! Your idea works!"

Quickly he sketched out what had happened. While he talked, he watched himself through Man Tavis' eyes. His face was animated, he used his hands expressively; only the grayish eyes were dead.

"Try 'seeing' through someone else's eyes," suggested Shandor, and Tal watched himself frown as he made the effort. Suddenly he was looking through Ven Tamor's eyes and could see a visibly shaken Man Tavis standing to one side.

With increasing ease, Tal found he could switch from mind to mind and telepathically pick up the optical images each brain was receiving. He was acutely aware that some of the warriors had eyesight far superior to others.

The one mind from which Tal was unable to receive optical images was Shandor's. Tal could pick up his thoughts easily and clearly, but try as he would, he could not "see" through the bronze man's flake-gold eyes.

"It's no use," he said, at last. "Your eyes won't work for me."

"It must be an effect of the Infrastatic Stimulator on the optic nerve," said Shandor. "But it doesn't matter. There are enough others whose eyes will let you see. Come on, let's walk around the camp!"

Tal found walking to be awkward at first. It was difficult to determine how far to step and how to balance when he had nothing to judge by except outside input. The sensation was as if the optical images were what *he* was seeing rather than images *of* him. He tended to walk in response to what the other person saw. He constantly had to fight to avoid this. He had to remind himself that what he saw was not what *he* saw, but that what he saw was *him*.

It was difficult, but Tal managed it. In an hour, he was handling himself almost as well as a sighted person would have done. It was an exhilarating experience.

That night he ate a hearty meal, helped by "seeing" what he ate. It was a wonderful feeling to sit by the campfire, sipping a cup of *glow*, and watching the shadow play of the firelight across his own face. Tal had never before realized what a truly wonderful thing sight was. And this was a miracle for which he could *really* give thanks to Shandor.

He rolled up in his sleeping furs in a happy frame of mind. Anode had done his worst and, with Shandor's help, he had beaten him! Tal felt he could do anything.

He slept. In his dream, he walked through a shadowy, darkened forest. Ahead of him, he saw Alytha. He ran to her and called her name, but she fled from him. He ran after her, still calling her, still trying to reach her; but no matter how hard he ran, he could not seem to gain on her. He made one desperate lunge and awoke, trembling and covered with sweat.

He cast about with his mind, but all he encountered were sleeping minds except for the guards. Briefly, he looked through the eyes of each of them, but there was nothing to see except darkness.

Tal lay back and tried to compose himself for sleep. He tried to will his body to relax, to loosen up, but it was too tense and jittery. He lay there in his own private darkness and felt the warmth of the campfire friendly on his face.

Then he was aware of a sound. Faint at first, it became not louder but closer. It was a shuffling, scuffing sound, as if a person walked without lifting their feet.

Tal projected his mind, but picked up no optical images. He quested outward with gentle telepathic fingers, but received no thought patterns or emotional color. The thing that approached with slow, shuffling steps might be dead for all Tal's telepathy could discover.

Fear began to build as he heard the thing's slow, steady, inexorable approach. He could hear the sound as of naked legs brushing very lightly together as the thing walked. There was the smell of newly turned earth and a damp smell of moldy garments. There was no sound of breathing. The shuffling steps stopped and Tal knew that the thing was just across the campfire from him.

He reached out with an almost panic-stricken burst of

telepathy, but picked up no image, no thoughts, no emotions. *Deadness.*

"*Tal....*" The voice was faint, weak but recognizable. It sounded again, softer than a breath: "*Tal....*"

"Alytha?" Tal knew he was awake, but dreaming. He spoke the name softly at first, as soft as the voice inside his head. "Alytha?"

"*Tal, are you there? Can you hear me?*"

"I hear you, Alytha," said Tal, tears running from his sightless eyes. "I hear you. I hear you!" His shout roused the camp.

The first pair of eyes opened to see Tal, his face beaming with joy and wet with tears of laughter, kneeling across the campfire from—

"Shandor protect us!" Man Tavis cried, leaping away from the campfire. He did not touch any of his weapons. Instead, he made the sign of the double helix.

Across the campfire from Tal, standing gray and grim, was the corpse of Alytha with clots of gravedirt still clinging to it!

Others around the camp awoke and looked toward the scene of the disturbance, but none dared approach. Tal did not move from his kneeling position, yet his blood froze in his veins as he "saw" the apparition that stood across from him—silent and ghastly and dead.

"Don't move!" Shandor's mighty voice stilled everyone. The bronze man had been meditating and the shouts had called him back from the astral plane. He alone sensed the import of what was happening here.

"*Tal!*" It was Alytha's voice. There was no mistaking it. "*Tal, I need you! Help me, Tal!*"

Through his borrowed vision Tal could see that the corpse did not speak. It simply stood there, still and mute and dead. The voice he heard was in his mind, speaking to him alone.

"Alytha...." And then he realized the futility of speaking to a dead body.

"Tal!" Shandor's voice was a whiplash. "It's Anode. He's doing this."

"*Tal, help me....*"

"Anode had used an Infrastatic Controller to move Alytha's body, Tal. And he's kept it preserved. Used a

Stimulator. See. The body shows no signs of decay and Alytha's been dead for days." The bronze man came closer. There was *something* here, but he could not put a name to it.

"Tal, I need you! I'm dying! Help me, Tal. . . ."

"Alytha's here," said Tal. "I can hear her in my mind."

"Alytha—" Shandor said the name and stopped. His flake-gold eyes suddenly narrowed and sparkled as understanding came to him. "Can you . . . contact Alytha?"

"I don't know. I haven't. . . ." Tal swallowed, then tried to clear his mind, to make it more receptive to thought images. Carefully he blanked out the emotional input from the watching warriors.

" Alytha? Alytha, do you hear me?"

"I hear you, Tal! I hear you!"

"Where are you, Alytha? I hear you, but they tell me you are . . . dead."

"I am dead, Tal—to your world and your time. I'm near, very near, but, oh, so far away!"

"You're in an alternate universe, aren't you?" Shandor's thought images were like his voice, mellow, powerful, confident, and reassuring.

"I'm not sure." There was hesitation in her voice. *"I can . . . sense your presence there . . . out there . . . but it's so different here. Everything is gray . . . foglike . . . and shapes are blurred."* A pause. *"And it's cold. Shandor, but it's cold!"*

"Tal, Anode has done something to Alytha worse than death. He had stolen her life essence—her ego, her soul, if you please—and imprisoned it in one of the alternate universes with which we cohabitate, separated only by our vibratory patterns. In our universe, her body is dead, because her life essence has left it."

Tal's mind was stunned, dazzled, questing.

"I don't understand. . . ."

"Nor do I," Alytha added.

"Then I will try to explain. No, better still, open your minds, both of you, I will give you the concept in totality, as a gestalt. Then you will understand."

Tal let his mental barriers down and felt a warm inrushing of images. He saw and grasped and understood concepts *instantaneously* that Shandor would have needed days to explain verbally.

He saw and understood that all matter is made up of infinitesimal particles that are held in the illusion of solidarity by their fixed rate of vibration. Air atoms vibrate at a different rate and in a different rhythm from atoms of flesh or atoms of wood. He saw and understood that Infrastatics was a means of artificially modifying the vibratory rate or the vibratory rhythm or the vibratory pattern of any atoms, say, causing atoms of wood to vibrate in rhythm with atoms of air, resulting in wooden palisades blowing away like puffballs of smoke.

He saw and understood the concept of light wave vibrations and sound wave vibrations and even the various vibrations of the human brain as it functioned, one of which was telepathy, all of which could be stimulated and magnified and focused by Infrastatic interaction.

He saw and understood how radio waves and video projection could exist all around and throughout a society without ever impinging on that society's consciousness unless a proper receptor were utilized, a receptor that was tuned to the properties of that unique vibratory pattern: a receptor such as a radio crystal or a television antenna.

He saw and understood how other dimensional universes could exist all around and throughout what he knew as the *real* universe and yet be totally unknown to his universe unless a proper receptor were utilized, a receptor which was tuned to the properties of that unique vibratory pattern: a receptor such as an Infrastatic Projector.

He saw and understood how Anode could separate the life essence that was the *essential* Alytha and isolate it in one of the multitude of variable infinities coexisting with his own. He saw and understood this and something more as well. . . .

"She's dying, Shandor! Her life force is being cancelled out by the negative universe where Anode has left her!"

"I see. It is clever on Anode's part. He plans to lure me into the negative universe to rescue Alytha."

"Help me, Tal. . . ." pleaded Alytha. *"Please help me. . . ."*

"We've got to save her, Shandor! Whatever it takes, we've got to save her!"

"She will die soon, I can see that. The negative universe is inimical to life as we know it. It absorbs the essence of her life-force. It she is not rescued soon it will be too late."

"What can we do? How can you save her?"

"I have an Infrastatic Projector. I could beam myself into the negative universe and beam Alytha out, if it were that simple. But Anode has set a trap for me. I don't know what it is, but he did this to Alytha and then let her contact us so I would know she was dying and had no chance unless I went after her. I don't know what he plans, but I know it is a trap."

"We can't just let her die!"

"I don't plan to let her die. I'm going to risk whatever Anode has planned. . . ."

"Wait, Shandor! Let me go! Let me go into the negative universe and get Alytha!

There was amoment's pause as Shandor considered Tal's suggestion. Tal released the bronze man's mind for an instant and tuned in the optical images from Sar Lon's mind.

He saw himself still kneeling across the campfire from Alytha's body. He saw Shandor standing to one side. It seemed as if all the camp were gathered about them. For the first time he became aware of the turmoil among the warriors.

Silently, he withdrew himself and turned his mind back toward Shandor.

"We haven't much time, Shandor. You have to project me into the negative universe! We've got to save Alytha!"

"All right, Tal. I don't like doing this, but we've got to try to save Alytha. Here's how we'll do it. . . ."

Tal listened as Shandor mentally outlined the steps they would follow, then, with something of an effort, he brought himself back to the excited babble of the completely awakened camp.

"I'll get the things we'll need," said the bronze man, turning away from the group. "Tal, get two men to help you handle Alytha's body. We'll go outside the camp. We'll have to be alone!" This last he called back over his shoulder.

"Right," Tal agreed. He mentally tuned in on Man Tavis' optical nerve images so he could "see" what was happening.

"Help me wtih Alytha's body," he said, watching himself

gesturing at Man Tavis and two other warriors. "Shandor and I have got to get her outside the camp. It's a trick on Anode's part and we've got to beat him!"

By the time Tal and the other warriors had maneuvered Alytha's cadaver outside the periphery of the camp, Shandor had joined them with the necessary Infrastatic weaponry.

"You must leave us now," the bronze man told them. "What Tal and I propose to do requires total concentration."

Before the warriors left, Tal used the eyes of one of them to familiarize himself with the controls of the Infrastatic Projector Shandor had brought with him. Once the warriors had departed, Tal was left totally blind since he could not pick up optic images from Shandor.

The bronze man positioned Tal beside the upright corpse of Alytha. Tal held the Infrastatic Projector tightly against his chest. He knew that one small device was the only chance Alytha had to live.

"Do you understand what you have to do, Tal?" There was a note of worry in the bronze man's powerful voice.

"Yes. Please hurry. I can sense Alytha getting weaker."

"All right, Tal. I'm activating the Controller now."

"I'm ready."

"Hurry, Tal," came Alytha's plea. "Please, hurry. . . ."

Tal felt a tingle that ran all over his body like the sensation of goose bumps. There was a moment of shifting as if something inside him had turned over sickeningly. He felt mildly nauseated. There was an instant of unsteadiness as if he stood on the deck of a ship at sea. And then it was cold! It was colder than Tal had ever known—colder even than the Ice Regions—and Tal felt a strange weakness, as if he were sick with a fever.

"Tal! Tal, you're here!" He heard Alytha's voice, not mentally, but vocally, and he reached out with his mind to try and receive her optic images.

"Alytha?" He said it tentatively, then the first wavering image came into focus.

He saw a tall, dark figure with a face almost as dark as Fen Melton's under a shock of snow-white hair. The figure opened its lips, which seemed oddly transparent and bloodless, and the teeth were black squares against the pale whiteness of the open mouth.

"Tal? Is it you?" A black arm reached out to touch the apparition and Tal felt fingers against his chest.

"Alytha . . . what . . . ?" Then she was in his arms and for a moment there was nothing else at all.

"Tal! Are you there? Did you get through? Did you reach Alytha?" There was urgency in Shandor's mental communication.

"Yes. Yes, I'm here."

"Good. We have no time to waste. Use the Projector. Get Alytha's life essence back into her body!"

"Right. I'm activating it now."

"Not just yet!" said the voice behind him.

"Who . . . ?" Tal saw himself turn at the sound of the voice. Alytha turned her head, too, and through her eyes he saw the figure that faced them.

"Anode!" The fear in Alytha's voice was genuine.

"Yes, pet. And now I have you both!"

Anode was tall and looked bulky in his flowing white robes. His face was black as midnight, black as death, and his eyes were lambent green flames. His hair was snow white and the arm extended toward Tal ended in a hand that looked like an ebony claw.

For a minute Tal was puzzled. He remembered Anode with a bone-white face, black robes, and feral red eyes. Why were the colors now reversed? What had happened?

Then he realized that this was a reverse-image universe. He had "seen" his own black hair as white and Alytha's pale arm as dark. He took a deep breath and said, with more courage than he actually felt:

"I've come for Alytha. You can't stop me. I have an Infrastatic Projector. . . ."

"You fool!" Anode said, with a mocking laugh. "Do you think any weapon can stand against me?"

Then Tal, through Alytha's eyes, saw the black-faced figure in the flowing white robes leap savagely upon the muscular figure with its back to her—the figure that was himself!

Tal felt steel-like fingers close upon his throat and he was thrown heavily to the ground. He lost the thread of Alytha's optic images in the sudden violence and he was blind!

Blind, he lashed out desperately and his fingers closed on an arm, an arm too hard and muscular to be Alytha's.

Anode struck him brutally in the face, hard, smashing blows with all the supernormal strength of his shoulder and arm behind each swing. Tal held onto the one arm he had seized and yanked. Anode fell on him and Tal twisted so that they both rolled sideways.

He knew that if he ever let Anode break free he would be helpless in his blindness, so he pulled his head down between his shoulders as far as he could, tucked his chin into his chest, and tried to wrestle his attacker closer. Anode kept hitting him with his free hand, but Tal dragged him nearer and nearer by the one arm he held.

He kicked out with both legs, made contact with Anode's whippet-thin body and scissored his legs around his opponent's waist. He twisted sideways as they rolled about and suddenly, with a lunging movement, he had Anode on the ground on his back and Tal was sitting astride him, his legs locked on Anode's waist.

For the briefest second he picked up an optical image from Alytha and he could see himself there, precariously atop the green-eyed, white-haired, black-faced horror that twisted and lurched beneath him. That one second of "sight" gave him the perspective he needed and his strong hands closed on Anode's throat. Slowly, carefully, gleefully, he squeezed tight on Anode's windpipe. He could feel the muscles bulging in his arms and shoulders and he knew sweat had popped out on his face from the violence of his exertions. A few seconds more and Anode would be dead!

Then a sunburst of pain exploded inside his skull. He felt all the nerve endings to his left arm erupt in white-hot agony, then go dead. He lost the use of his right arm the same way.

He could not breath! Desperate, Tal fell away from Anode. Something was happening inside his head. . . .

"You fool!" The sneer was plain in Anode's mental voice. *"My physical attack was a diversion. I'm taking over the master controls of your brain!"*

"Not yet you're not. . . ." Tal pulled all his efforts into the mental duel that now waged.

He felt a Presence in his head. He was aware of pressure along the center of his skull. He knew a moment of unreasoning panic.

Then he stretched out a mental block.

He could not describe the sensations he felt, but he knew Anode was there, inside his mind, reaching out with telepathic fingers to snuff out the spark of his life.

He felt his heart flutter wildly. His pulse became erratic. His lungs no longer responded. Anode was effectively killing him!

Tal fought. He used the telepathic skills Shandor had been trying to teach him and ran tentacles of self along the neural paths in his brain. He sensed Anode triggering the synapses of certain neuropsychic programs and he mentally seized the thought images as he had physically seized Anode's body.

Anode mentally deactivated Tal's autonomic reflexes and Tal mentally reactivated them, but he could not gain ground. Anode was a past master of this form of attack and Tal was overmatched.

Once he threw a neural barrier across Anode's attempted blockage of his aorta. He kept his heart pumping, but Anode caused his lungs to cease taking in oxygen.

Tal shot a telepathic probe to free his lungs, and Anode triggered synaptic circuitry to cause him to flood his own system with adrenalin.

Before Tal could react to that, Anode clamped down on his heart and shut off his lungs simultaneously. Confused and dazed, Tal felt his brain weakening, his life-force slipping away. Anode had him!

TWENTY-EIGHT

For what seemed an eternity, Tal hung there—his life essence draining away into the inimical stuff of the reverse-image universe, his bodily functions faltering under Anode's attack—and then he sensed another presence there with him in the darkness of his mind.

"Tal?" Alytha asked softly. *"Can I help?"*

"Yes!" Tal managed to say. *"Fight him . . . my heart. . . ."*

"You can't do it," Anode gloated. *"I have you beaten."*

"Not just yet. . . ." Tal gasped.

Suddenly Anode's grip on his heart relaxed and Tal felt blood pumping through his veins again. He lunged a telepathic thrust against the restraining bonds and, after a moment's silent struggle, he broke through and his lungs gratefully sucked in great gulps of air.

"We can beat him, Alytha! Help me hold him off!"

"I'll . . . try."

With Alytha's mental strength added to his own, Tal felt he was a match for Anode. He blocked each neural probe the attacker tried and sent out mental attacks of his own, drawing additional power from Alytha's mind and will. Step-by-step, he forced Anode into retreat.

Suddenly Anode was gone.

As abruptly as he had felt the pressure come, he felt it withdraw. He knew Anode was no longer in his mind.

And just as abruptly he was blind. Totally blind.

"Alytha. . . ?" He sent a mental probe questing outward, but there was no response. Alytha was not there. Anode was

not there. He was alone.

"Alytha!" Tal lurched to his feet. Blind, he staggered vainly in a circle, waving his arms before him. "Alytha!"

But there was no one there. Both Anode and Alytha had vanished. Tal was alone, and blind, in a universe that was slowly draining his life force from him.

Panic hit him. His blindness became the focal point of the fear. *If he could only see. . . !* But blind, he had no chance.

He forced himself to stop. By sheer will power he forced his unreasoning fears back into proportion. All his life Tal had been a physical person who solved his problems by strength alone. But this battle was a battle of his will power, a battle of his mind with his mind.

And Tal won the battle. He forced down his panic and, while not making the fear go away, reduced it to a level he could deal with effectively.

"Alytha?" he called. "Alytha? Are you there?" Then he tried a mental call: *"Alytha? Where are you?"*

"She is gone." It was as soft as the whisper of the wind.

"Anode!"

"She is gone, Tal Mikar. You are alone, utterly alone. It was only a trap, and it worked perfectly!"

"Shandor will save me! You can't. . . ."

"Good-bye, Tal Mikar."

Tal sensed that Anode had withdrawn. Somehow, in the deepest fibers of his being, Tal sensed his absolute and total aloneness.

He turned in a blind circle, his hands thrust out before him. He was caught, caught in as neat a trap as had ever been laid. He had played right into Anode's hands. He realized now that Anode's physical attack on him was out of character for Anode. But it was perfectly in character for Tal Mikar. Anode had known he would respond immediately to a physical threat, and Tal had not disappointed him.

He cursed himself for his own stupidity. Why hadn't he immediately used the Infrastatic Projector to beam Alytha to safety? Why hadn't he done that and then followed her? Why had he let Anode trick him in such a clumsy, childish way?

Tal knew the answers even as he asked the questions. He was a barbarian. For him, physical violence had been the answer to virtually every problem he had ever encountered. Anode had reasoned this out and, by presenting a threat in terms Tal understood, he diverted Tal's attention from the real plan.

But what was the real plan?

Tal considered that. Anode had gone to some little effort to lure him into this reverse-image universe and then to strand him there. Why would he do that? If he had lured Shandor there, Tal could understand it, but what would Anode gain by trapping Tal there?

Shandor was still free to lead the Arcobanes and the Thongors. Alytha had apparently been restored to her body. So what purpose did it serve to lure Tal here and trap him outside his body?

And then the answer hit him.

At first he could not believe it. It was too preposterous to be true, yet it made perfect sense. And if Tal were right, then Alytha—and Shandor—were in terrible danger!

Tal knelt down, clasped his arms around his knees, bowed his head. He concentrated every mental faculty he had into one massive push to reach through and contact his own space-time continuum.

It was blank. He stretched groping fingers of thought outward and it was like dragging a stick through deep mud. He pushed them with every fiber of mental power he could muster, but the interface was too thick. He realized Anode must have amplified Alytha's thought waves to allow them to reach through.

Sweat was running down his face and he felt weak from the effort involved, but Tal kept at it. He *had* to break through! It was the only chance for Alytha and Shandor. Maybe the only chance for the world.

Even as he struggled, he felt the alien essence of this strange universe draining away his life-force, damping his life energy, slowly, but most surely, killing him.

Tal fought the effects of the reverse-image universe. He fought the thick muddiness of the interface. Most of all, he fought the rising fear and panic inside his own head.

He pushed his mental images out with all the strength of his mind behind them, but he sensed it was futile. It actually seemed that the harder he struggled, the denser the interface grew. It seemed as if the universe in which he was a prisoner was working against him. It seemed as if creation itself were in opposition to him.

At that moment the answer occurred to him. This was a reverse-image universe. White was black and black was white. Everything seemed to work exactly reversed to his own universe.

Tal relaxed, let his mind go blank. He stopped trying to force his thought patterns through the interface. Instead, he let his mind become a receptor, an empty vessel waiting to be filled.

"I can't believe you defeated Anode." It was Shandor's mind he was tapping.

"Alytha made it possible. It was her strength added to mine that made the difference." Who was that?

"Don't be silly, Tal." That was Alytha, and Tal knew, with a horrible certainty, to whom she was speaking. *"I helped, but you were the one who actually drove him back."*

And Tal knew that he was too late. He had figured out Anode's plan, but not quickly enough. Anode had already taken the first step!

Tal opened his mind as completely as he could and totally relaxed. That way he picked up the first weak, wavering optical images from Alytha's eyes.

He saw Shandor. The bronze man was walking across a dark plain toward the distant lights of the camp. Beside him, just ahead of Alytha, walked—*Tal Mikar!*

Tal shuddered as he saw "himself" walking through the ringlight. He shuddered because he knew it was Anode inside his body. Anode had trapped Tal inside a negative universe so he could have a means of getting behind Shandor's lines, of penetrating his guard, of reaching his unprotected back.

Even as Tal watched through Alytha's eyes, he saw the body of Tal Mikar gasp, stagger, stumble, clutch its chest, and fall prone on the ground.

"Tal! What is it?" Alytha bent over him and, through her eyes Tal saw his own pain-racked face getting closer.

"Tal? Are you all right?" Shandor bent over the body, his strong, bronze hands turning it expertly. *"Tal! Can you hear*

me?"

Then, faster than Alytha's brain could register, but slow enough for Tal to see since he scanned each optical image independently, Tal Mikar's body jackknifed erect, flinging Shandor effortlessly aside. In that same abrupt gesture, Anode, in Tal's body, ripped the Infrastatic Projector from the bronze man's grasp.

Shandor was on his feet instantly, but Anode, in Tal's body, was quicker. He snapped a switch and the bronze man stopped short—his golden body encased in a transparent, yet lightly glowing cube of statis.

Through Alytha's eyes, Tal watched as Anode made minute adjustments to the stolen weapon. The statis field enclosing Shandor glowed more warmly, but was otherwise unchanged.

"*I don't understand. . . .*" Anode seemed genuinely puzzled that nothing more happened.

"*It's simple, really.*" Shandor's voice betrayed none of the emotions he must have been feeling. "*My ring is an Infrastatic Vibrajector. It can't break your statis field, but it can keep it from collapsing on me.*"

"*Then you will live on to watch my ultimate victory.*" Anode made further adjustments to the Projector; then, satisfied with the results, he broke off a controlling switch and hurled it away. "*There,*" he said. "*The statis field is now mind-keyed to your brain wave pattern. No power on Earth will allow you to cross it. Your Vibrajector may prevent its crushing you, but I have insured that you will never escape it! You have lost, Shandor, and I have won! After eons—I have won!*"

Through Alytha's eyes, opened wide in horror, Tal saw his body turn and approach. The grayish-blue eyes were still and dead and lifeless, but the handsome, boyish features were twisted in such a look of utter malignancy that Tal himself almost recoiled.

"*Come, pet. We have much to do this night.*"

"*You . . . you're not Tal.*" It had all happened too fast for Alytha to comprehend.

"*I am Anode! And this night, after time longer than you can imagine, I have defeated my enemy! Shandor is no longer a threat to me! I am free and he—he is the one entombed alive!"*

"I'll find a way!" Shandor's voice faded behind them as Anode, in Tal's body, seized Alytha's arm and bustled her away. *"I don't know how, Anode, but I'll find a way...."*

Tal, through Alytha's eyes, watched as the terrified girl was led farther and farther away from the camp. Then, when Alytha was stumbling dazed with fatigue, Anode, in Tal's body, dragged her into a grove of trees.

There, securely encased in a statis field, was Anode's body. Tal watched as his body activated the Infrastatic weapon that removed the statis field. There was a moment's pause, then Anode's body stood up, the bone-white features smiled, and Tal knew his own body had been abandoned.

"It is good to be home." The spectral figure walked around Tal's cadaver. *"And this . . . shell. It served a good purpose, but it is no longer needed."* He made an adjustment on his Infrastatic Disperser.

"What are you going to do?" Alytha was terrified.

"I no longer need this body of your mate's, and leaving it here intact is too much of a temptation." He leveled the Disperser at Tal's body.

To his horror, Tal, through Alytha's eyes, watched his own body dissolve into wisps of smoke and blow away on the night wind. It was gone, destroyed down to the last atom! Now he was indeed a prisoner, a doomed prisoner. He had no body to come back to!

TWENTY-NINE

The Fortress of Rynn, Anode's hideaway in the polar jungle, was in a slightly better state of preservation than Shandor's city of Shalimar had been.

Lanawe Palmerin was held captive in one of the chambers of a tower whose top pierced the green rain forest canopy. Outside the unbarred windows there was a waving sea of lush greens, alive with the tropical jungle sounds. Inside, there were only the barren stone walls and a rude sleeping pallet.

Lanawe's once-tailored black uniform was now in rags. Her body bore numerous bruises and welts. Her once-lustrous black hair was uncombed and her blue eyes looked huge and haunted in her pale, drawn face.

But worse than the physical suffering she had borne, was the suffering of her spirit. While not actually tortured, Lanawe had been forced to endure every humiliation to which a woman can be subjected. Anode had forced her to do things, and to submit to things, that left her skin crawling with disgust and made her sick with self-loathing. He had carefully explained to her that these emotions were quite literally the foodstuff he must have in order to survive, but this did not lessen her mental anguish an iota.

Worst of all, when she let herself think of it, was the knowledge of the person she had been before and the things she had done before. She knew she was the reincarnation of Shara Vralon and, before her, of countless others back to Keena of Atlantis.

As Keena, and later as Shara Vralon, Lanawe knew she had

been directly responsible for causing the deaths of hundreds, perhaps thousands of innocent people. And not just their deaths, but their slow, horrible, lingering deaths. Lanawe knew she had done this and she knew she had delighted in it, rejoiced in it, reveled in it! It was the knowledge of this unspeakable guilt she carried that weighed most heavily on her soul.

Anode had been gone for several days, leaving Lanawe a great deal of time in which to think. What she had been thinking was not pleasant.

Thoughts of karma and the debts for which her soul had to pay were uppermost in her mind. Anode had assured her that she would suffer in direct proportion to the suffering she had caused in her previous incarnations. He had told her that regardless of what it took, the scales would be balanced.

Lanawe wept often at the knowledge of what she had been before. Anode had told her, in precise details, just what sort of person she had been and the pleasures she had derived from torture, maiming, and death. In her present incarnation this knowledge sickened her, disgusted her, and she wept often from the terrors of her previous lives.

She had contemplated suicide on more than one occasion, but Anode, anticipating this move, had explained that suicide was one of the greatest karmic debts a soul could incur. Her only hope was to somehow work off some of the karma by unmitigated good deeds.

But Anode had seen to it that there were no good deeds for her to do. Instead, there was a constant, steady stream of humiliations, debasements, perversions, and psychological tortures which she must either submit to or perform. Anode had even forced her to murder innocent captives, by proving that he would torture them to death slowly if she did not kill them quickly and mercifully. She did, but the fact that it was still murder put unbearable guilt feelings on her conscience.

Lanawe would have prayed, but she had no god. Instead, she would kneel, clasp her hands, and, through her tears, whisper, again and again: "I'm sorry! I'm sorry! Oh, I'm so sorry!" And that, though she did not know it, was a prayer in its own right.

The windows and the door to her prison were unbarred,

but Anode had sealed them Infrastatically so securely that nothing larger than a molecule of air could enter. He had left her enough food and water for three days, then told her, just as he left, that he might be planning to leave her there to starve. He was laughing when he disappeared down the stairs.

Lanawe was in her first day without food when Anode returned, and with him was Alytha.

"Hello, pet," he said, as he dragged the terrified, nearly naked girl into Lanawe's chambers. "I hope you didn't miss me." His feral red eyes were alive with unholy glee as he looked at his two prisoners. "I've brought you company."

At first Lanawe did not answer. She looked from Anode to the girl, wondering what new form of torture this could be, wondering what perverted acts Anode would force them to perform.

"This is Alytha." Anode's voice was a sibilant sound that reminded Lanawe of the jungle snakes that coiled outside her windows in the night. "You remember Alytha, the mate for whom Tal Mikar was searching." Anode laughed and in his laughter there was only pain and suffering and death.

At the name of Tal Mikar, Alytha's body had jerked as if Anode had struck her a blow. Lanawe looked at her and a flicker of the Lanawe Palmerin of old came back into her blue eyes. So this was Alytha, the girl Tal loved!

"I will leave you girls alone," said Anode, with another of his ghastly laughs. "I'm sure you have a lot to talk about. And think about this: I may decide to let you starve till one kills and eats the other. Think about that." Still laughing, he left them alone in the chamber.

Alytha sank down on the floor and covered her face in her hands. She wept as if her heart were breaking.

Lanawe took a step toward her, then stopped. What if this were some new diabolical trick of Anode's? What if he had found a new way to torment her?

"Alytha?" She said the name tentatively. "Are . . . you really Alytha?"

The weeping girl looked up at her with swimming eyes and the pain in her face could not have been faked.

"How did Anode get you?" Lanawe asked. "When . . .

when Tal was with me . . . with us . . . we were . . . were looking for you. . . ."

Alytha mumbled something Lanawe could not hear.

"What . . . what did you say?" she asked.

"Tal is dead."

"Dead? But . . . how?"

"Anode. There was a battle. I was captured. Tal rescued me. He was . . . he was . . . blind. Anode killed him. Turned his body into smoke. It . . . just blew away." Alytha bowed her head again and Lanawe instinctively put her arms around the girl's trembling shoulders.

Alytha scrubbed her eyes smartly with the backs of her hands and looked up at Lanawe.

"Anode has won," she said. "He killed Tal and Shandor is his prisoner. Without Shandor and Tal, the Arcobanes and the Thongors will fall easy prey to the Kalathor warriors." She dropped her head. "It is over. It is over and Anode has won."

"He has not won yet," Lanawe said fiercely. "I don't know how, but we'll get out of here! Somehow . . . if it's at all possible, I'll help you escape. Somehow . . . somehow we'll defeat Anode!"

"I only wish Tal were alive. . . ."

"I know," said Lanawe, hugging Alytha tightly. "I know. But, in some strange way, I almost feel as if Tal were here with us. And I know if he were, he'd want us to fight Anode as long as we can!"

"Yes," said Alytha, and the look she gave the doorway through which Anode had passed was frightening to contemplate. "And fight him we will!"

Tal heard all this through the telepathic link he had established with Alytha's mind. He heard it, but he could not respond to it.

Try as he would, Tal could not break through the dimensional interface and communicate with Alytha. He could scan her optical images, monitor her audial reception, but he could not let her know he was there.

When he had watched, through her eyes, as his body was destroyed down to its final atoms, Tal had plunged to the ultimate depths of despair. His entrapment was now permanent and his death was assured. Even if he could figure out how to escape from the reverse-image universe in which Anode had so cleverly imprisoned him, he had no body in which he could return. His life essence would be dissipated if he returned and slowly dampened out if he remained. It was the end for Tal.

And yet, the barbarian's instinct for survival was strong in him. Tal was too much the primitive to remain in the doldrums for long, and too much the barbarian to surrender meekly without a battle, however hopeless.

He did not know what he would do or what he could do. He only knew that he would do something.

And so he had maintained his tenuous mental link with Alytha. He did not know what he was hoping for, but he did know that it was better than doing nothing.

He watched, through her eyes, as Anode led her deeper and deeper into the polar rain forest. At last they reached the ancient fortress of Rynn.

The lush tropical jungle had overgrown all the buildings, save for a few whose tops reached up into the matted canopy overhead, and had thus protected them from the ravages of time and the elements that had so taken their toll of Shalimar.

Anode, like Shandor, had Infrastatic shielding over the key installations of his stronghold and, at a touch to his Controller, they opened to reveal a still vital and functioning fortress.

Alytha had been literally dragged up a flight of winding stone steps after they had reached the top level the force-lift could reach. Inside a vaulted chamber, Tal had been startled to find Lanawe Palmerin a prisoner.

In a way, it had been a relief to see her there. In his heart, Tal had been tormented by the question of whether or not Lanawe had gone willingly with Anode. Her imprisonment here, and her ragged, disheveled state, attested to the fact that she was not here by choice.

Tal was a silent observer to the exchange between the two girls and he was a likewise silent observer as they talked together and made obviously futile plans for the balance of the afternoon.

It was bitterly cold in Tal's reverse-image universe and he felt the terrible weakness, like the aftermath of a fever, as his life essence was slowly but steadily dampened down.

Through Alytha's eyes Tal watched the sudden tropical twilight sweep over the polar jungle. Through a break in the foliage outside the window they watched (and Tal watched with them) as the rings turned rosy pink from the setting sun, then milk-white across a star-speckled sky.

Anode did not reappear and so, hungry and thirsty, the girls lay down to sleep.

Both were tired and sleep came quickly. Alytha's optical images no longer came in, but Tal could pick up the surface reflections of her dreams. In fact, the dreams came in with a sharper imagery than did Alytha's waking thoughts.

At first, this realization meant nothing to Tal, but then an idea began to grow in his mind. It was a faint, nebulous, uncertain idea in the beginning, but to Tal any action was preferable to no action, so he decided to try it.

First, he sent little tendrils of thought-probes out among the motor control areas of her brain. He scanned for and recognized the neural synthesizers that controlled her autonomic reflex system. He sorted through the nerve endings that supported her life and marked off the ones that affected her ego state individually.

Slowly, with infinite care and patience, he closed down certain neural circuits and shunted others through different nerve ends and blocked off certain mnemonic areas, till he had the ego identity that was essentially Alytha secreted in a restricted area below the level of the secondary thought processes.

This left her brain open and empty of a motivating identity.

Tal accomplished this not through any knowledge he had of how the brain worked, but by telepathically scanning the internal circuitry and *feeling* what each neural connection did or was supposed to do.

Now, with equal care and patience, like a man boarding a very small, very unsteady boat that might flip out from under him at any moment, Tal filled up the vacated neural synapses with the essence of *himself*.

There remained, at last, only the merest thread linking him back to the reverse-image universe. The problem of breaking that thread was all that remained to him.

Somehow, he had known from the beginning what the answer would be. The reverse-image universe was a perfect mirror image of his own world. Everything worked exactly backwards.

The image of Tal that Shandor had projected into the reverse-image universe was exactly as Tal had been at the moment of projection, except reversed. His dagger, for example, was on his left hip instead of his right. In this strange, fog-shrouded universe there was no up or down. Gravity, as a force, did not exist. Everything was simply *here*.

Tal knew what he had to do and he did not hesitate. He forced enough of *himself* out of Alytha's mind to enable his projected "body" to move. He withdrew his dagger, placed it carefully over his heart, then, with one abrupt gesture, thrust it into his own chest up to the hilt.

There was a sudden sharp pain, a moment of vertigo, and Tal opened his eyes to stare up at a vaulted stone ceiling. He lifted one slim brown arm and looked at it in the ringlight. He had come back—into Alytha's body!

THIRTY

At first the sensation was too overwhelming for him to react. Tal was so excited about the fact that he could see again, actually *see* again, that for a moment he forgot everything else.

He sat upright on the pallet and simply luxuriated in being able to look around the ringlit room and actually *see* things. It was a feeling he had thought never to experience again. He knew that no matter how long he lived, the wonder of sight was a thing he would never again take for granted.

After a few moments, when the marvel of being able to see began to pall, Tal became aware of other, odder sensations.

He was in a woman's body—and to all intents and purposes the body was him—yet Tal was a man and he discovered, for the first time, that the biorhythms of a woman are different from those of a man.

The internal body rhythms were alien to him. He sensed, without knowing how, that his body—Alytha's body—was a few days away from her menstrual cycle. The tuning emotions and inner pressures that made her a woman now affected Tal, and he was bewildered.

To Alytha, the sensations her body registered would have merely meant the impending onset of her period. To Tal, who had no feminine experience to draw on, they were strange, unsettling, and somewhat frightening.

He reacted to Alytha's body exactly as if it were his own, so the difference in biorhythms was a pronounced difference for him.

He mentally explored this body in which he found himself. He had known Alytha intimately and so there was no mystery in the physical attributes of it, yet it was a different sensation when he had to realize that this body was now *him*—or, more accurately, that *he* was now *her*.

The realization that he had a female slit between his legs instead of his dangling maleness unsettled him greatly at first, but he adjusted to it by the simple expedient of putting it out of his mind. He had other, more pressing matters to consider. Foremost among them was Anode.

Tal rose to his feet. He felt a bit awkward at first—Alytha's body was lighter, slimmer, and smaller than his own had been. There were many more differences in men and women than he had supposed.

He looked down at Lanawe's sleeping form. His first thought was to wake her and tell her what he had done; then he realized that even if he could convince her of the truth, it would accomplish nothing. No, the important thing was getting out of here. Getting out of here and going after Anode.

Tal made a circuit of their cell. Then a second and a third. It was on the third circuit that he saw their chance.

In one upper corner, fully three meters above the floor, the ringlight poured in through a jagged rent in the stone wall. A rain forest tree limb reached almost to the opening. *If* Anode had not seen it, *if* there were no Infrastatic shield, *if* Alytha's body could climb up to it—there was a *chance* they *might* escape.

Quickly, eagerly, he touched Lanawe's shoulder. The girl opened her eyes and stared at Alytha-Tal in bewilderment.

"What is it?" she asked, obviously frightened. "What's wrong?"

"Nothing," said Tal. The sound of Alytha's voice startled him and he automatically cleared his throat. "I think I see a way out."

"W—Where?" Lanawe looked where she/he indicated.

"That hole. If I can climb to it, maybe we can get out."

"There's no way to reach it. Besides, Anode has Infrastatically sealed this chamber."

"Maybe." Tal cleared his throat again. "And maybe Anode only sealed the door and windows. Anyway, it's worth a try."

He walked to the wall, measuring it with the practiced eye of a Thongor mountain warrior. "I'll need your help," he said. "Let me stand on your shoulders."

He showed Lanawe how to stand with her back braced against the wall and how to make a stirrup of her hands to cup Alytha's bare foot. It took two tries, but at last Tal was perched precariously atop the girl's shoulders.

He stretched to the full length of his borrowed body, but Alytha's arms were too short to reach the opening. However, they did reach a thin cornice above the window. Tal gripped this and slowly, deliberately he lifted Alytha's weight off Lanawe's shoulders. The offworlder, weakened by her ordeal, slumped down gratefully as Alytha's body dangled free, held only by the weakening grip of muscles Tal had overestimated.

He put Alytha's foot against the stone casement and got enough purchase to lever his female body high enough to get his elbows onto the cornice. It was only about eight centimeters wide, but Tal managed to bend and twist and get one knee onto it.

This put the crack within easy reach. A moment more and his head and shoulders were outside. Anode had overlooked the opening!

"Come on!" He called down to Lanawe. "We can get out. We've got to escape before Anode comes back!"

"I . . . I can't!" Lanawe cried, her eyes flooding with hot tears. "I can't climb up there. I can't reach you!"

"Wait a minute!" said Tal. Awkwardly, since he was half in and half out the small opening, he stripped off the deerskin tunic that Alytha had on, untied the leather loincloth, then fastened the two garments together to let down as a rope to Lanawe. It was not long enough.

"It's not any good!" Lanawe insisted. "I can't make it!"

"Yes, you can! Now listen—walk back to the pallet, run this way, jump up onto the windowsill, and jump from there and grab the rope I made. You can do it!" But what Tal wondered was whether Alytha's muscles could hold Lanawe's weight.

He squirmed around in the opening, bracing Alytha's naked body as firmly as he could. "All right!" he called. "I'm ready!"

Lanawe missed on the first try. She caught the garment rope on the second attempt and Alytha's arms and rib cage were scraped on the stone as Tal held her sudden weight, but Lanawe's hands slipped and she fell back to the floor.

"Try again!" Tal called down, then he cleared his throat.

The third try sent sharp pains through Tal's already raw scrapes, but Lanawe held on. Tal braced Alytha's body as best he could and Lanawe climbed high enough to rest her elbows on the cornice that had aided Tal.

"Come on," gasped Tal, Alytha's muscles trembling from the strain. "Stand up on the cornice and hold to the bottom of the opening!"

Lanawe pulled herself upright and balanced there, breathing heavily in the humid tropical night.

Tal rested a minute, then took time to rearrange Alytha's few garments back into place. He felt more ill at ease with his naked *female* body than with his *male* body nude. He felt somehow more exposed.

He twisted around until most of him was outside the wall. He tried not to think of how many meters it was to the ground, to the tangled jungle floor far below. Instead, he concentrated on the heavy tree limb about a meter and a half from where he crouched. The ringlight made it uncertain at best, but Tal knew there was no other way.

He took a deep breath and leaped.

Again he misjudged Alytha's muscles. Knowing that her arm muscles were weaker than his, he allowed for a similar weakness in leg muscles. In consequence, he almost overshot the limb and barely managed to catch himself on it.

"Are you all right?" Lanawe called, fearfully, her voice muffled by the thick stone wall.

"Yes," answered Tal, once he got situated on the limb. "Climb on up through the hole."

In a moment Lanawe's head emerged and the larger girl had to wriggle fiercely to worm her way out.

Tal scrambled back along the limb, then transferred to another, slightly lower. He reached up and braced the limb that Lanawe would have to reach.

"Jump for the limb!" he called. "Hurry! It's our only chance!"

Lanawe hesitated a moment longer, then leaped wildly for the branch. She crashed into it and wrapped her arms and legs around it desperately. For a long time she simply clung there, recovering her composure.

At last, Tal had to urge her on.

"Come on," he said, reaching up to pat her shoulder. "We've got to go."

The tree was a huge old jungle giant and Tal had no difficulty in making his way along the limb and down to the trunk. Alytha's lighter bodyweight and slim agility helped immensely. Lanawe made it, too, but with less ease.

The tree trunk was thickly crusted with twisting llianas and Tal went down them like a ladder. In a matter of minutes he and Lanawe were on the ground, ankle deep in thick loam on the floor of the rain forest.

"Now what?" asked Lanawe. She was rapidly gaining complete confidence in her companion's ability to do anything.

"We've got to reach Shandor. I remember where Anode and—" Tal cleared his throat. "I remember where Anode left him prisoner."

"What are we going to do? Anode can't be stopped. He can't be defeated." Lanawe was still under the spell of Anode's power.

"I don't know what we're going to do. I only know we've got to free Shandor somehow. He's our last hope."

Tal set off through the ruined city of Rynn. He was impressed at how much better preserved it was than Shalimar had been, yet most of it was tumbled into ruins. The time lapse since the Second Infrastatic War was staggering.

Tal had no idea where Anode was nor if any of his Kalathor warriors were inside Rynn, so he and Lanawe kept to the deepest shadows as they made their way out of Anode's ancient stronghold. The ringlight penetrated only dimly through the rain forest canopy and the darkness made their travel doubly difficult, but time was too important to waste. They had to reach Shandor as soon as possible.

They soon left the confines of Rynn behind and were almost running through the polar jungle. To Tal's other worries was added the uncertainty of how long Alytha's consciousness could survive shut away where he had it. He would not permit himself to think of what must happen to *him* when Alytha was restored to her body.

Near dawn, they paused briefly to rest and eat some of the luscious tropical fruits growing around them. Lanawe, who had not eaten for two days, would have gorged herself had not Alytha/Tal prevented it.

"We've got to go on," she/he said, after about thirty minutes. "Anode must know by now that we're gone, and it's about six or eight kilometers to where Shandor is a prisoner."

They emerged from the rain forest onto the tree-dotted veldt with the sun turning the rings to a rosy pink band across the hot blue sky.

They paused briefly to scan the veldt for any sign of Anode or the Kalathors or of Shandor's warriors, but the waving grassy plain was empty and still between the clumps of trees.

Lanawe and Alytha/Tal made their way from copse to copse. That way they minimized the amount of time they were exposed in the open. Still, by jog-trotting, they made good time.

It was nearly two hours past dawn when they reached the copse where Tal's body had been dematerialized by Anode's Disperser.

Alytha/Tal stopped there and looked about, hoping there was something to give him hope, something to make him think his body might be restored. But there was nothing. His body was gone. It could not be brought back.

"Why have we stopped?" asked Lanawe. Tal hesitated for a long moment before he answered:

"No reason. No reason at all."

Tal set off again and this time desperation pushed him to the limits of Alytha's strength. He had to reach Shandor! *He had to!*

Lanawe had difficulty holding the pace, but she tried. In less than an hour she was reeling drunkenly and staggering toward exhaustion. Alytha's body was in not much better condition, but Tal forced it to move ahead.

They saw Shandor's prison before they saw him.

The statis field glowed warmly, even in the sunlight. Tal saw it through the trees as they entered the copse.

"There. . . ." he gasped. "There . . . it is!"

Lanawe sank down to the ground when they reached the cube that encased the bronze man. Alytha/Tal leaned against the rough bark of a tree and simply stared with red, burning eyes at the prisoner.

"So you escaped." The bronze man's voice was muffled, but still audible.

"Yes." Tal did not feel that it was necessary at this time to explain all that had happened. "This is Lanawe Palmerin." The other girl looked up at the sound of her name.

"I see," said Shandor. "Tal has told me a lot about you."

"I've got to get you out of there!" said Alytha/Tal. "I don't know how, but I'll do it!"

Shandor shook his head.

"You can't," he said. "The Vibrajector in my ring is barely enough to hold the statis field. There's no way you can break it."

"You have a Disperser," said Alytha/Tal. "That should vary the molecular vibration pattern enough to free you."

"It won't work," Shandor assured him. "Anode has mind-keyed this statis field to my brain wave patterns. No matter what devices you bring, it is ultimately *my mind* that activates the field. It cannot be broken so long as my mind is alive and functioning."

"You mean you'd have to *die* to escape?"

"Something like that, pet."

The voice was Anode's and it brought Alytha/Tal whirling about into a snarling half crouch and sent Lanawe stumbling to her feet.

"Did you really think you had escaped me?" Anode's feral red eyes burned with an unholy gleam in his bone-white face as he stepped up to the two girls.

"I watched your rather ridiculous escape and followed your broadly marked trail through the jungle. I could have scooped you up at any moment I chose."

"Then why didn't you?" screamed Lanawe. " Why didn't you, you devil?" Her voice broke and she began to sob.

"Why didn't I? And miss this wonderful moment—this *savory* moment—when you realize how foolish your hopes were? When you realize that it's all been for nothing?"

323

Anode's voice was satin and velvet over ice cold steel.

"You were playing with us," said Alytha/Tal, clearing her/his throat. "Like a cat plays with a mouse."

"Exactly," agreed Anode. "And for much the same reason. To kill you is good, but simple death is like raw, uncooked, unseasoned food to me. It will keep me alive, but I crave the rich, subtle flavorings of torture and the exquisite taste of desperate hopes allowed to soar before being abruptly crushed." He laughed, and in the laughter was only pain. "*That* is the most delicious meal of all. The look on your faces when you saw me—the fear and the horror that clutched at your hearts—oh, that was a *delicious* meal!" And Anode laughed once more.

"It won't work," said Alytha/Tal, with much more conviction than he felt. "You can't keep us prisoner. And somehow, someway, we'll free Shandor!"

Anode laughed again and there was even a note of genuine amusement in it.

"Shandor will never be free again," he said. "And as for keeping you a prisoner. . . ." He raised his hands and the black robe fell back to reveal a Disperser exactly like the one he had used on Shandor. "I think you will regret those words, my dear." He touched a button on the Disperser.

Instantly, Tal felt a constriction around Alytha's body like the pressure of water against him when he swam. There was a glow in the air around him. He held out his hands, Alytha's hands, and they encountered an invisible, immovable shield or bubble which completely encased the female body he inhabited. The realization of what it was hit him with sick suddenness.

"Yes, it is a statis field." Anode gloated as he saw the knowing fear grow in Alytha/Tal's face. "You have no Vibrajector to hold it, so your body will be slowly crushed millimeter by millimeter. I shall enjoy watching it." He laughed again.

With horror, Tal felt the pressure slowly mounting, growing stronger and stronger against him. He looked at Shandor, but the bronze man could only watch with helplessness. He looked at Lanawe and the girl seemed crushed and pathetic. He looked at Anode and the feral red eyes blazed in the pale, gaunt face.

There was no help and no hope. Alytha's body would be crushed—and when she died, Tal Mikar would die, too! Anode had finally won.

THIRTY-ONE

Tal felt a great wave of helplessness sweep over him. So it was over and Anode had won. It had all been for nothing.

He did not know when the idea came to him, but suddenly it was there. It was a chance, a slim chance, but better than no chance at all.

"Shandor?" Tal sent the single word out in a telepathic whisper.

"Tal? Where are you, Tal?" The bronze man became instantly alert. He did not know how Tal was reaching him, but he was obviously concerned lest Anode intercept the message.

"I'm here—in Alytha's body." Tal saw the look of sudden shock on Shandor's face and he opened his mind in one great flood so that the bronze man could see it and accept it as a gestalt. *"I have an idea, but I don't know if it will work."*

"What is it? We can try anything."

"Could your Vibrajector break the statis field if it weren't mind-keyed to your brain waves?"

"Y—Yes. Yes, I think it could, but how—?"

"Can you withdraw your mind like you do when you meditate? Can you pull back out of your head?"

"You mean astral projection? Yes, but that's on another astral plane. That won't get me out of the statis field."

"Do it. I'm going to try to make a telepathic transfer from Alytha's body to yours, but your consciousness has got to be reduced below the level of wakefulness or it won't work." Tal looked at Anode and wondered if the creature had really

tuned out his telepathic sensitivity, or if he was again playing a diabolical game with them.

"You just meditate," Tal went on, feeling the pressure against Alytha's body increasing each second. *"I'll make the transfer—if I can—and then, since your mind will be effectively shut off, I can use the Vibrajector to break the statis field!"*

"Very good!" said Shandor. *"And there's just a chance it will work. Here I go—"*

Tal waited a few seconds, although each second brought the statis field tighter and tighter against Alytha's body. The pressure was becoming painful.

Then Tal brought all his mental faculties to bear and tried to pull everything that was *himself* into one compact ball. He put every ounce of effort at his command into the thrust. He reached out with fingers of insubstantial mental tension and groped for the shell that was Shandor's brain.

And he found it!

Tal held it in one shaky, unstable minute ripped loose from the fabric of time and then, like quicksilver on a slanted board, he *poured* himself across the space and into the body of Shandor.

The transition was dizzying. Tal experienced acute vertigo and would have fallen had the statis field not kept him upright. And then he found why he had not been able to pick up Shandor's optic images.

The Infrastatic Stimulator had somehow altered the bronze man's optic nerves. His flake-gold eyes saw much, much more than Tal had ever dreamed. He saw the wavering heat images from the living bodies around him. He saw the spectrum of colors from ultraviolet to infrared. He saw the pulsating life aura that surrounds all sentient entities. The visual input was staggering. Tal saw things he had never before imagined.

It took him several seconds to absorb the strange and dazzling images and to get used to seeing the world as Shandor saw it. He looked through the warm glow of the statis field (vibrantly scintillating with infinitely tiny impulse patterns) at the back of Anode's head (his aura a twisty, murky dark mist), at the dispirited, defeated Lanawe Palmerin (her aura a tremulous yellow fading to lavander), and at the glowing cube (alive with coruscating energy) which encased the apparently fainted form of Alytha (her aura a delicate pale blue).

Then Tal activated Shandor's Vibrajector to full power. As he felt its forces internally attacking the Infrastatic shield around him, he could see the interleaving energy grid constrict even tighter around Alytha. Her flesh was being compressed. She had only seconds to live!

Tal decided to risk everything on one desperate ploy.

"Lanawe!" The word was a mental whiplash that jerked the girl to her feet and brought Anode wheeling around. All that saved Tal was the omnidirectional nature of telepathic communication. *"Attack him! Seize the Disperser!"*

"So you want to match skills with me again, eh?" Anode could not locate Tal's position. *"You really are a fool."*

"Lanawe! If you love me, if you have ever loved me, attack now!"

Anode laughed. *"You don't think she. . . ."* But the rest was lost as Lanawe Palmerin, her aura blazing red as Anode's eyes, leaped full upon him and ripped the Infrastatic Disperser from his hands.

Tal realized that in another few seconds the Vibrajector would have done its work and he would be free—but in another few seconds Alytha would be dead. At this moment, everything depended on Lanawe.

Anode sprang with more than human swiftness and grappled with the wild-eyed girl.

"Give me the Disperser!" he snarled, and the weapon was tugged and twisted between them for what seemed an eternity.

The dancing energy pattern in front of Tal wavered and dispersed. He had freed Shandor's body!

"Anode!" And the monster whirled, his red eyes hot with fury.

"How did you—?" A sudden, high-pitched whine from the Disperser caused him to leap to one side. "What are you doing, girl? That's an overload!"

"I don't care!" screamed Lanawe, her aura fanning out a deep royal blue shading to purple. "I'm going to pay for my evil but that girl will live! I'll die to see that she does!"

The Infrastatic Disperser suddenly glowed with a pinkish light, a light that swelled to envelope the girl holding it. The pinkish light paled out to a pure whiteness that flamed into blinding brilliance and then died away, leaving no trace of the weapon, or of Lanawe, or of a good two meters of dirt where she had been standing. Nothing was there now save an empty crater.

The sound of Alytha's body falling brought Tal and Anode around. The statis field was gone. Alytha was saved. Lanawe Palmerin had paid her karmic debt. She had willingly given her life that someone else might live.

"So it comes to just the two of us," said Anode, his red eyes burning in his bone-white face, his aura a smoky cloud. "As before, as always, the two of us."

"Not quite," said Tal, in Shandor's rich, deep voice. "You see, I'm not Shandor. I've merely taken over his body. I am Tal Mikar: he whom you knew as Lan Regas and as Thon. Shandor cannot kill you, Anode—but I can!"

"Can you?" laughed Anode, advancing to meet his enemy. "Can you indeed?"

The two giants closed and Tal found a strength in Anode's wiry body he had not dreamed possible. Shandor's body was muscled with cords of plastic steel, but Anode, bone thin and frail looking, was easily his match.

Tal closed Shandor's corded bronze fingers around the monster's neck, and Anode swept his hands away as if they were the hands of a child. Tal struck him with the full strength of Shandor's mighty arm and shoulder, but the blow scarcely slowed his attack. In response, Anode swept his arm around in a slashing arc that sent Tal reeling backward.

From the corner of Shandor's flake-gold eyes, Tal saw Alytha struggling to her feet. The fall had awakened her as if from a deep sleep. Her aura was pale blue shading to violet.

But he had no time to look at Alytha. He had to deal with Anode. He seized the man's billowing black robes and lifted him overhead, but Anode kicked him in the face and they both fell, with Anode on top. Anode's bony fingers closed on Tal's windpipe and it took all the bronze man's strength to break their grip.

Anode seized the front of Shandor's tunic and heaved the bigger man effortlessly to his feet and threw him away, almost casually. Staggered, Tal went sprawling and barely rolled clear of the tremendous kick Anode launched at his groin.

Alytha was on her feet now, Tal saw, as he circled Anode. The thought of what this monster had tried to do to her—and of what he had done to Lanawe Palmerin—sent a renewed burst of hatred through him and galvanized his muscles into a sudden attack.

He sprang upon Anode, and it was as if a child wrestled an adult. Anode's feral red eyes sparkled and his aura was a billowing smokelike cloud as he effortlessly turned Tal's attack aside and sent the bronze man's body hurtling backward. To Tal, it seemed as though Anode's physical strength had actually multiplied since the fight started.

And then he knew.

Anode's strength *had* increased. Hatred was one of the emotions that Anode fed on. The hatred Tal felt for him gave him renewed strength and vigor.

If Tal did not control his hatred for Anode, the creature would grow stronger and stronger. He could not be defeated by any conventional means. How, then, could Tal win?

"You're not so cocky now, are you?" Anode sprang with animal suddenness and, seizing Shandor's tunic, whirled the bronze man's body overhead and flung it savagely to the ground.

Stunned, his wind gone, Tal grasped in the chaos of his mind for the key that would destroy Anode without increasing his power. He had to *not hate*. He had to. . . .

Then Anode whirled him aloft again and smashed him brutally, violently to earth.

Only half conscious, Tal tried to focus his wavering thoughts, but Anode leaped astride his prone body and wrapped his clawlike fingers around the bronzed throat. His red eyes flamed as he squeezed slowly, slowly, slowly. . . .

Tal brought his thoughts around to Lanawe Palmerin. A great wave of pity and compassion for the suffering she had gone through welled up in him. Lanawe, and so many others like her, had suffered so much and died so needlessly that Tal felt an overwhelming desire to do something to give purpose and meaning to her death. As he felt this, and felt in his heart the pain Lanawe and Alytha must have felt, the compassion within him became like a physical presence—*and he felt Anode's fingers weaken!*

"You will die!" shrieked the monster, fighting the sudden weakness in his hands. "You will die and the girl Alytha will be my slave! I'll force her to do things you can't even imagine!"

Tal felt his hatred for Anode surge back and with it Anode's grip on his neck tightened! His windpipe was being crushed.

"It is over, Thon!" gloated his enemy. "It is over, Lan Regas! It is over, Tal Mikar!" Anode cackled like a maniac. "And most of all, Shandor, for *you,* it is over!" Anode laughed again and in his laughter was no humor and no pleasure and no sanity.

Tal looked up at Anode with blurring eyes and saw that the nearness of his final victory had pushed him over the edge. Anode no longer even bore the semblance of humanity about him.

And Tal remembered, in a sudden flash of psychic recall, what Anode had been like when he had first known him in ancient Atlantis. Anode had been tall and strong, darkly handsome, and with the finest mind, aside from Shandor's, that Tal had ever known.

He looked at Anode now, even as the blood pounded in his ears and his sight grew blurry and dark, and what he saw was a pitiful sight. With the sudden rush of pity Anode's grip weakened!

Tal looked at Anode and saw the waste and loss his life had been. He thought of the unspeakable centuries that Anode had lain cold and alone in an alien universe, the only subject in his own personal hell. He realized what Anode had suffered by causing others to suffer, and, with a start, he found that he was genuinely grieving for the needless pain *everyone* had had to bear. What were those words Shandor had quoted?

> *The pain we lay upon the soul*
> *Of our brother's heart fills us.*

*The grief he bears, we, too, must bear
And the death he dies kills us.*

"Stop it!" screamed Anode. "Stop it! You're dying and I've won!"

But his voice sounded weak and somehow pitiful to Tal. He saw the desperation as his opponent tried to hang on to the initiative, the initiative that had already slipped beyond his hope of recovery.

"No!" screamed Anode. "No! I've won! Do you hear me? I've won!" His aura was dissipating in ragged tatters like a cloud of smoke in a freshening wind. "No! I've won! I've won!" There was terror in his voice.

Tal realized, with a sudden burst of insight, the unutterable loneliness that Anode must have suffered. He imagined, with a great rush of pity, how terribly alone Anode had been. He suddenly saw Anode, who fell weakly away from him, not as a ravening monster, but as a poor, lost, lonely creature who could only live on the pain of others. A person who could never know the sound of happy laughter, who could never know the sweetness of a loved one's gentle touch, who could never know the warmth of loving and being loved, who could never know how precious life could really be.

"No," whispered Anode, writhing on the ground as if in agony. "No, don't. Please, don't. . . ." His aura was floating out to the winds, growing thinner and whiter as it dissipated. "Please . . . don't. . . ."

Tal saw the infinite capacity for good that had once existed in the person of Anode, before he had let himself sink into a bog of fleshly lusts. He saw the potential for greatness that had somehow become warped and twisted. He saw that it was all such a waste, such a foolish, useless, tragic, empty waste!

A tear welled up in Shandor's flake-gold eyes as Tal came to realize what a miserable, pathetic creature Anode really was. The tear welled up and trickled slowly across the lean, bronzed cheek.

And a drop of blood, in perfect unison with the tear, ran across Anode's cheek.

Anode screamed!

Instinctively, Tal reached out his hands, Shandor's hands,

and touched his ancient enemy. The compassion was open on his face.

"I'm sorry," he said, kneeling over the strangely shrunken figure in the black robe. And then he said the words of power, the words more potent than any other the human tongue can shape: "Let me help you."

Anode gave one strangled gasp and his head fell back. The feral red eyes glazed over. At the moment of true death, such a look of infinite sweetness and gentle goodness came over his countenance that Tal could not believe it was the same person he had known as Anode.

Then, before Tal's startled eyes, a remarkable transformation took place. The skin of the head stretched tighter and tighter as if the flesh beneath it were melting away. The lips drew back into a snarl, but the snarl was a rictus of death. The eyes sank into the head, leaving only gaping black skull holes. The nose shriveled and peeled away, exposing the white bone beneath. The hair turned loose and fell out. The gums withdrew and disappeared. The teeth dropped into the grinning skull mouth. The bones of the skull itself calcified and split and crumbled into dust. The skeleton beneath the robe collapsed. Anode was gone.

"Shandor?" Alytha came forward slowly. "What . . . what did you do?"

"I am not Shandor. I am Tal Mikar." Quickly and concisely he explained to the girl what had happened. He told her everything—from the destruction of his own body to the "borrowing" of hers to the psychic transfer with Shandor.

"But where is Shandor now?" asked Alytha. "And what will become of you when he comes back to his body?"

"I don't exactly know where he is," said Tal, choosing to ignore the second question. "But I'll see if I can contact him."

"Shandor!" He sent out the telepathic call, wondering how long his own consciousness would last after the bronze man responded. *"Shandor, where are you?"*

"What is it, Tal? Can't you reach him?"

"I don't know. Wait." *"Shandor! Shandor, can you hear me?"*

"I . . . hear you. . . ." The voice was a whisper of a whisper in his mind.

"Shandor? What. . . ."

"I'm dying, Tal." The voice was deathly weak. "I . . . won't . . . last much . . . longer." There was a pause as if the strain of talking drained his strength.

"Tal, what is it?" Alytha had not forgotten how to use her telepathic powers.

"I don't know. Shandor says he's . . . dying."

"What's wrong, Shandor? What's happening?"

"It is over. It must be so." Shandor's mental voice hesitated. *"There is no dividing line between good and evil. The two are so inextricably intertwined that absolute evil cannot be destroyed without destroying a measure of good as well. You see, they are both part of the Whole—part of the Law of One. And each death, even the death of one such as Anode, diminishes the Whole by just that much.*

"Tal, in Shalimar, in the laboratory where you found me, under that same Infrastatic Stimulator is your body. I cloned it when I first found you so badly wounded by Alun Akobar. Remember? It has been Infrastatically modulated to full growth. It is there—alive and healthy. Take the skimmer. Go to Shalimar. Go quickly. Make the psychic transfer to your cloned body. You will be Tal Mikar again. And my . . . body can die . . . even as my soul is dying."

"I . . . don't understand," said Tal. "I did not mean to harm you. I only meant to stop Anode."

"You have learned many lessons in your reincarnations, Tal, but one last lesson you must learn for your soul to reach its next growth level: evil cannot be stopped or destroyed. Evil can only be converted into something that is not evil.

"Even love, such love as you used against Anode, will not safely destroy evil. Evil must change itself into something good, and the change must come from within. You can persuade evil to change, you can convert it by example, but you cannot force it to change. If you do—you lose more than the evil you destroy."

"Please, Shandor." There was pain in Alytha's mental voice. "Please, don't die!"

"What is happening here is one of the essential natural laws I told Tal about. It is . . . right." The mental voice grew weaker and fainter. *"Go quickly, Tal, Alytha. Go . . . to*

Shalimar. Tal's . . . body . . . is there. He will be . . . himself . . . once again." The voice was less than a whisper. *"Goodbye . . . and remember me . . . when I am gone. Whenever you think of war—that is far, far from me. Whenever you think of love—I am that, all of that, only that."* There was a pause. *"It is . . . for death . . . that life is made. . . ."*

There was only silence.

"Tal, is he?" Alytha's voice trembled.

"I . . . think he is."

Tal stood up. He stretched out his hand, golden-bronze and corded, and touched Alytha's shoulder.

"It is over," he said softly. "At last—after all the ages of man—it is over."

"And us . . ." said Alytha. "What will become of us?"

"Us?," echoed Tal. "We are the first of a new generation. A new people for a new time. We are the Children of the Law of One. Our sons and daughters shall grow up learning the truth of what Shandor taught. It will be a new law for our new people.

"Come, Alytha. We will go to the skimmer and then to Shalimar and then—home."

And together they walked across the veldt under the rings like bands of silver across the arching blue sky.

A SUDDEN MADNESS

By Ralph Hayes
PRICE: $2.25 T51693
CATEGORY: Novel

BETRAYAL, MURDER, AND LOVE!

A story that could happen anywhere. Three black men were shot dead in their own yard by cops on a burglary call. The police department erupted with a coverup scandal, and the town was ripped by violence!